From the Kiwi Kingdom series

THE ISLANDS

BY

ROSEMARY THOMAS

Titles previously published which are included in this Book

Kohana's Quest – First Printing March 2018, by the Author

Koa's Kingdom – First Printing August 2019, by the Author

Other Titles by Rosemary Thomas

Under the Blowholes Spray

The Kiwi Kingdom is also on Facebook.

Information about the publishing of titles by the Author can be found on this page. Organisations that care for Kiwi and other animals in the real Kiwi Kingdom are also promoted on this page.

Acknowledgements

Information about places, the species, distribution and the lives of Kiwi and other animals integrated into the story was obtained from the following sources:

http://en.wikipedia.org/wiki/Kiwi

http://www.nzhuntinginfo.com/game/tahr

http://www.nzhuntinginfo.com/game/chamois

http://www.wildaboutnz.co.nz/index/weasels

http://www.gorgeouscreatures.co.nz/NZ+Possum+Fur/Possum +History.html

Marshall Cavendish Animal world: Hedgehogs and Tenrecs 1993

The Incredible Kiwi, a Wild South Book by Neville Peat

Road Atlas of New Zealand, Paul Hamlyn., 1975

Hema Maps, New Zealand handy Atlas, Rob Boegheim, 2010

The stories within this book and all the characters in them are pure fiction. Any similarities to events or people are a coincidence.

Kohana's Quest

Koa's Kingdom

Odelia's Challenge

KOHANA'S

QUEST

CHAPTER ONE

KEONA'S RETURN

Keely the Roa Kiwi wondered where her mate Kaori was, as she adjusted the grass in their burrow on Conical Hill overlooking Lake Kaniere. Their children Kian and Kana were already asleep in their tunnels as the early morning sunlight touched the lake hills. As Keely heard Kaori's footsteps near the burrow, she also detected many other footsteps following him! Wondering who Kaori had brought home with him, Keely darted to the opening to be confronted by a familiar figure!

"What are you doing here?" Keely gasped with amazement, as her Mother, Keona stood before her; Keona's mate Keio's twinkling eyes also beamed back at her. A number of adult Kiwis were gathering around Kaori, a few had their children with them. Keely slipped out of the burrow to hug both her mother and Keio. She looked around with a smile at the faces, recognising some from her visit to Okarito years ago when accompanying her brother Kupe on his southern quest.

"You have brought the whole community with you!" Keely's words were a statement. Her mind whirled as she wondered how they were going to accommodate everyone.

"Don't worry Keely." Kaori broke in. "I have been keeping all the old burrows in good condition." He turned to the crowd gathered around him. "I have shelter for all of you, though it will be a little cramped to what you are used to. The Rowi who used the old burrows here...."

"Had very modest requirements!" Keka the leader finished Kaori's sentence for him. "Kedar's burrow is the same. We are just grateful you have some shelter for us. We will be moving on to our new home when we have had a good rest." Looking down at the lake, Keka added, "Nice place you have here."

"I know you will all be tired," Keely addressed the crowd, "but do you want some supper before you go to your shelter?" There were many smiles, but shaking of heads to her query.

"Thanks for the offer, Keely," Keka replied, "but we have had a good feed on our way. All we need now is some rest."

"I insist then, that we all have a feed together when we get up this evening!" Keely was firm.

She was answered by a chorus of "We will be here" from the crowd, as Kaori started to lead them off to their burrows. The noise of the Okarito Kiwis arrival brought Keely's sister Keilana and Ketara, Keely's daughter out of their burrows.

"Mum! Nan! Were their cries as they rushed to be reunited with Keona.

Once inside Kaori and Keely's burrow, the babble of voices brought Kian and his sister Kana out of their tunnels, to be introduced to their grandparents and new uncle Keon and aunty Kailah. At first they were shy with these strangers, but Keio's twinkling eyes and quiet gentle manner soon drew Kian and Kana to Keio's side, where they plied him with lots of questions about their life at Okarito and their journey to the lake. When it came time to return to bed, there was no dissent when Kian and Kana were told to share a tunnel with their new uncle Keon and aunty Kailah.

While Keona was approaching Lake Kaniere through the bushland she felt a mounting sense of both pleasure at revisiting familiar places and pain at revisiting the place where Keanu was taken from her. Keio sensed the emotion within Keona and stopped to give her a cuddle

"We don't have to go to the lake if it is too painful for you" Keio reassured Keona. He remembered how stricken she was when they first met and knew the turmoil she was in. "We can always go back and go around the back of Tuhua to reach the Arahura valley."

Keona gave Keio a grateful smile. "I want to see the lake again, but can we travel along the western side instead?" Keio looked at Keka who nodded. They intended to visit Ollie Owl, but Keona didn't have to be there for the visit.

The travellers were grateful it was still dark when they reached the track that led to Sunny Bight for it was on open farm land and were relieved when they reached the safety of bushland at Conical Hill. Keka and Keio were thinking of climbing up the slopes to dig some temporary shelters when they spotted a familiar figure leaning over the water at the lake's edge and he was talking to an eel!

"Kaori! Is that you?" Keio called softly. This was lucky. They had thought he was still in Arthurs Pass.

Kaori turned around to see the crowd with a delighted grin. "I will be with you in a minute." He called back.

Ernie Eel was the leader of the lake eels now and made regular visits to Kaori to check all was well with him and his family. "It seems you have some visitors, Kaori," Ernie eyed them with both interest and delight. "I would like to meet them properly later."

"I will make sure of it." Kaori replied before turning to meet the new arrivals.

"This is an unexpected pleasure!" Kaori greeted Keio, Keona and Keka with a grin. "Are you here for a visit or are you staying?" he asked with both interest and concern. He could see Keka and Keio had brought the whole community with them – it meant something drastic had happened to bring everyone up here.

"We are at the lake for a visit," Keka smiled back, "but we are on our way to our new home up the Arahura valley. Some of the Arthurs Pass Kiwis live there now and have invited us to join them. Our home has become too noisy for sleeping, now that humans use machines to fly others to the glacier. There is rarely any peace!"

Keka then added with a sigh, "You may have noticed how few of our young ones we have with us. They are all that is left of last year's breeding season!"

Kaori looked at the young chicks in shocked silence and waited for Keka to continue.

"Both the eggs and young chicks are regularly preyed upon by animals who insist on taking them" Keka said with anguish. We have tried to make friends with them and change their behaviour, but they aren't interested." Keka added with sorrow.

"What about Kedar's community?" Kaori asked, "Will they be coming too?"

"They are having problems as well," Keka acknowledged "but Kedar insists they are staying put."

"I can assure you Keka; that noisy flying machines rarely fly in this area and you and your families are safe here." Kaori reassured him. "You can stay as long as you like. Come along, for I have some places for you to stay."

Keka gave Kaori a grateful smile. "You heard him." Keka addressed his community. "For once we don't have to dig our shelter for sleeping." This news brought many smiles to their weary faces as they prepared to follow him up the hill.

In the lake Ernie was racing across to Hans Bay to spread the news of Keona's return. No-one had expected to see her again after her loss of Keanu when Kanai had tried to take over the community. Other eels in the lake that saw Ernie's swift passage knew something was up, and followed him. By the time he had reached Daisy duck and her family at the water's edge, Ernie had a large group on his tail. Daisy saw their approach with some anxiety. Ernie didn't bring a contingent with him unless something drastic was happening.

"Ernie!" Daisy quacked with alarm. "What has happened?"

Ernie gave her a large grin "Guess who is back?"

"Ernie, stop talking in riddles!" Daisy's voice was still sharp. "Who is it?"

"It's Keona!" Ernie spoke in triumph, to gasps of amazement from both Daisy and the eels. I was talking to Kaori when Keona and a large group arrived. It looks like she has brought the whole community with her!"

"I will tell Ollie Owl!" With that, Daisy rose to fly into the forest, taking her family with her.

Ollie glided swiftly and silently over the grassland. He was about to grasp his prize when a voice woke him! "Ollie! Ollie! Wake up!" with a sigh, Ollie opened his eyes to see an excited Daisy Duck standing before him on the tree branch. He hoped to return to his dream world later.

"What is the matter Daisy?" Ollie asked, wondering what was so urgent to disrupt his sleep time. All the animals knew not to disturb his sleep unless it was urgent.

"Keona is back, and she has her community with her!"

A vision Ollie didn't want to revisit immediately came to him! - The lifeless body of Keanu Kiwi, Keona's mate, lying outside the old school cave and beside him, Owen Owl his father who was badly injured after trying to protect Keanu from Kanai Kiwi who had tried to destroy the school and take over the community.

"Where are they?" Ollie was concerned. He had received reports of trouble in the south and knew something drastic had happened for the whole community to be here. He had a quick look at the sky – it was dangerous to be flying in the open at this time of day.

"They are with Kaori in Sunny Bight," Daisy replied with some sadness.

They both knew Keona was not yet ready (if ever) to return to the place where she had lost her mate.

"We will have to give them a welcome." Ollie was decisive. "If Keona can't come to us, we will go to her. Tell everyone, (and Kaori) we will have a meeting at the picnic area this evening." Ollie commanded Daisy. With a smile Daisy rushed off to do his bidding. News of Keona's return spread through the bush like wildfire. It was decided that the night animals would take the boat over, while the day animals started on their trek.

Urgent quacking at the opening of Kaori's burrow woke him from his doze.

He exchanged amused glances with Keely, for they both knew plans were being made! "Come in Daisy. What's up?"

As Daisy waddled in, a figure appeared from behind them. It was Keona. She had recognised Daisy's voice.

"Keona!" "Daisy!" They cried with delight to see each other and had a cuddle.

"How you have grown!" Keona exclaimed.

"Yes, I have children now too." Daisy smiled back at her. "You will see them this evening." Turning to Kaori, Daisy added "Ollie is inviting everyone to a meeting at the picnic area this evening."

"We will be there." Kaori promised her.

Satisfied, Daisy made her way outside. She checked the sky, for a Harrier was now living nearby and extra care had to be taken when moving around during the day. Keeping under the canopy, Daisy made her way back to Hans Bay to collect her family. Back on Conical Hill, families in surrounding burrows had woken and watched with both interest and delight to see a duck visit Kaori's burrow. "What's happening?" Keka called out from his burrow after Daisy had left.

"There's nothing serious." Kaori called back. "Ollie Owl is putting on a welcome for you all at the picnic area this evening"

"I'm looking forward to it." Keka replied, before quiet was restored to the hill.

Ollie had trouble sleeping after Daisy's visit. He had word from Kona the Haast Tokoeka Kiwis leader, also Kedar the leader of the Southern Brown Kiwis at Okarito and Kanoa the Roa leader at Paparoa; that the numbers of their young chicks had plummeted. Attacks had occurred on eggs and young chicks from hostile possums, stoats and weasels, but humans with dogs had come last season and taken most of the remaining eggs away from Kona and Kedar's community as well. The dogs had mussels on, but could smell where their burrows were! The humans' taking of Kiwi eggs was a new strange development. What were the humans doing with the Kiwi eggs? He needed to find out, but how?

CHAPTER TWO

REUNIONS

That evening, everyone was up early to feed and prepare for the coming meeting. The day animals had already gathered in the forest at the picnic area, chattering as they waited for everyone to arrive. There was movement in the water too as Ernie brought his community of eels close to the water's edge.

After a feast of worms which Keona, her daughters and granddaughter's had gathered, Kaori and Keely lead the Okarito community to the picnic area. Glimpses of the late evening sun on Mount Tuhua made Keona smile. She realised how much she had missed this place during her long absence, but knew from talking to Keely and Keilana that the home bushland she had left was no longer the same, now that humans had moved in and built homes in the area. She did not voice it, but something was drawing her to visit the family burrow, if she could find it.

In Hans Bay there was feverish activity at the boat's hiding spot. Mossy branches were lifted and the boat examined. Ollie Owl, Percy Possum and Sam stoat were happy with its condition and many paws, including the hedgehogs and weasels were used to manoeuvre the boat into the water. Once everyone was on board, the journey to Sunny Bight began. Although excited, everyone spoke in whispers in case any humans living at Sunny Bight were outdoors.

"It's like old times." Sam Stoat murmured to Percy Possum and Harry Hedgehog.

They both smiled their agreement. "Are you thinking of building another raft Sam?" Harry asked, remembering the fate of the last one they made, which sunk in the storm.

"It's a thought." Sam half seriously considered it. "I would love to visit the Island again and see the burrow we sheltered in. We would be better off taking the boat though."

"Maybe we could have a look on the way home?" Harry suggested. He had been bitterly disappointed on missing out on the first trip. He had no intention of missing out this time!

The friends looked at each other with a grin "We have a plan." Sam announced with satisfaction, a little louder than he intended.

"What are we planning?" Ollie Owl enquired with a gleam in his eyes. It didn't matter that these three were now responsible adults; they still had the adventurous spirit of their youth!

"Um," Percy Possum hesitated, and then took a deep breath to make an announcement.

"We are making a detour on the way home." Ollie raised his eyebrows and waited. "We are going to visit the Island." Percy finished. The gasps and grins of delight at this news from everyone left Ollie only one option.

"That's settled then."

Ollie had visited the Island several times since Kupe Kiwi had been laid to rest in the Eel's sanctuary; but had felt Kupe's presence when he visited, and knew his spirit was on the Island. Ollie wondered whether Kupe would make his presence felt during their visit.

Soft twilight remained when they arrived at Sunny Bight. The boat was skilfully hidden among some flax at the stream which meandered into the lake next to the picnic area. As they walked into the clearing, the day animals also emerged from the forest, along with Kaori and Keely who led Keona and the Okarito community out to meet them. Ollie led the way to Keona and Keio and Keka. "Welcome Everyone" Ollie beamed to the crowd. "Welcome Home Keona; and welcome back Keka and Keio!" I hope we can look forward to more of these occasions in the future." Before he could say any more, Keona was mobbed with old friends waiting to hug and talk to her. With a grin, Ollie stepped back and found a spot to talk to Keka and Keio. While chatting about the community's trip, Ollie noticed how few young chicks were present.

"I see you have been having similar problems to Kedar's community, with keeping your young chicks." Ollie observed to Keka.

"Yes." Keka sighed. "It is one of the reasons we left. We are heading to the Arahura valley. Some of the Arthur's Pass Kiwis are living there. They tell us it is very quiet there, with plenty of food. They have invited us to join them."

Ollie managed to hide his disappointment that the community weren't staying at the lake; but understood that the upper Arahura would suit their needs better than the lake.

"That's not far away for you to visit us again." Ollie offered brightly.

"Or for you to visit us too." Keka beamed back. "Our new home will work well for us. We are much closer to both the Arthurs Pass and Three Sisters communities now. It's a shame Kedar won't move his community, Keka added in sorrow.

"Yes," Ollie agreed. "I'm worried about Kedar and Kona's communities, now that humans have started taking their eggs as well." Keka and Keio looked at Ollie with shocked looks.

"You didn't know?" when they shook their heads, he added "It seems you got out just in time." In the silence Ollie pondered. "I want to know what the humans are doing with Kiwi eggs, but am not sure how to find out!"

"Someone would need to follow them," Keio offered, "but humans have vehicles that are too fast for any bird to keep up with."

Protea Pigeon and her friends were sitting nearby heard the conversation and looked at each other.

"We have friends all over this Island. I'm sure if we can get word to everyone to watch what humans are doing near Kiwi sites, we should get some answers."

Keka wandered over to the water's edge where Keona was talking to an Eel and introduced them.

"Keka meet Ernie. He is the leader of the Eels now." Keka nodded and smiled.

"Are Keanu and Kupe still being kept safe?" he asked.

"They are." Ernie reassured him. "No one will ever disturb them again!" Ernie added firmly.

"Aren't they at the school?" Keona was puzzled. "Where are they?"

"Humans disturbed their grave at the school." Ernie advised her gently. "Both Keanu and Kupe were moved to our sanctuary at the bottom of the lake."

"I owe you my gratitude." Keona responded. She felt anxiety lifting from her. The dread of visiting their grave to find it disturbed or missing was now gone. She wondered when or how she would get to make a visit back home when Ollie came for a chat. He saw her gazing at Hans Bay and asked the question that everyone wanted to know.

"You aren't interested in a visit to your old home?"

"It is still there?"

"It is" Ollie smiled

"I would love to." Keona smiled back, and so it was arranged; that when the community was ready to move on, they would make a visit to Hans Bay to see the new school and Keona could see her old home.

The meeting went on into the early hours of the morning. Early morning light had yet to touch the lake hills when the boat set off for Hans Bay.

9

"We want to be at the Island before the humans get up." Ollie advised the boat passengers. "We will spend the day there and head for shore tonight."

Although the rowers were now tired, they crossed the lake in record time, finding a small beach facing away from the Hans Bay shore to land and pull the boat up out of sight of anyone sailing on the lake.

On the Island Ferns both familiar and new were to be explored along with fungi, plants and moss climbing the trunks of trees, which formed a large green canopy overhead. Sam Stoat and Percy Possum led Harry Hedgehog and their families on a meander through the forest, feeding as they went.

As they walked, Harry Hedgehog was in wonder at the beauty of this place, and thought wistfully to himself, "*Oh Kupe! If only you were here now to share this with us!* "

"*But I am here, Harry.*" Kupe's voice seemed to be just behind him. Startled, Harry looked behind him.

Only Helena and their children were there. She gave him a smile, which Harry answered and asked her "Are you okay?" When Helena nodded her agreement, Harry turned back to find Kupe's spirit walking beside him. No-one else seemed to be able to see him.

"*It's wonderful to see you again.*" Harry spoke to Kupe in his thoughts.

"*Yes,*" Kupe replied. "*What brings you all to the Island? Ollie has been over a few times, but has never tried to talk to me. I was beginning to think I would never get any visitors to talk to.*"

"*We will have to change that!*" Harry vowed in a determined tone, to which Kupe laughed. "*Kupe, did you know your mother was home?*" When Kupe shook his head, Harry continued. "*We have just been over to Sunny Bight to welcome her. Keona and Keio have brought their whole community with them and are staying with Kaori.*"

"*Did they say how long they are here for?*" Kupe asked a worried look on his face. He knew something drastic had happened for them to shift the whole community.

"*I didn't get to ask why or how long they are here, but I saw Ollie having a long talk with Keio and Keka. I will try to find out for you what is happening.*" Kupe smiled his gratitude.

Just then, Percy stopped and stared up at the trunk of a tree which soared way above all the others.

"Is this it?" Harry Hedgehog asked Percy.

He was referring to the tree where Kupe and his friends sheltered from the storm.

"I think so." Percy smiled and led them around the base of the tree till he came to a dip, filled with ferns. He pulled the ferns aside and there was an opening, leading to a big space under the trunk. Percy plunged inside, re-emerging soon after with a grin.

"It's just how we left it! Come on in!"

Everyone scurried in (including Kupe), though behind them was Ollie and his family too.

As soon as Ollie was settled, he looked around, for he could feel Kupe's presence in here!

Percy turned to everyone with a smile. "Well, it seems the only one missing is Danny." At that, a loud quack was heard outside! – It was Danny.

"Come in Danny." Percy invited him in. Danny squeezed himself in between Percy and Sam Stoat.

"Shame Kupe couldn't be here." Danny spoke up. There were murmurs of agreement to this. Harry stole a look at Kupe, who grinned and nodded to him, so he spoke up.

"Actually Kupe is here!" Harry announced to everyone's amazement. "I have been having a lovely talk to him on the way here."

"How?" was Ollie's question.

"By talking to him in my thoughts" Harry advised him.

At that, all the animals took on a thoughtful look as they talked to Kupe in their thoughts. Slowly, Kupe's shape appeared in the room.

"It's lovely to see you all again." Kupe grinned.

Kupe was introduced to all the new arrivals; Hakea, Hovea and Hoanie Hedgehogs, and also Slinky and Shimmy Stoat. Harry then steered the conversation to Keona's arrival.

"Ollie, do you know whether the community are here to stay or are they visiting?"

"The community is at the lake for a visit." Ollie advised Kupe. He knew Harry had asked the question for Kupe's benefit. They are on their way to their new home in the Arahura valley. Some of the Arthur's Pass Kiwis are living there now and invited them to live with them." Ollie didn't elaborate any more on why the community was here. He would talk to Kupe later.

The sun was well up and the birds were busy in the trees when everyone agreed, it was time for a rest. As the cave grew quiet, Kupe said farewell to his friends, who he knew would be back soon, now they knew he was here.

Keona pushed aside a branch of the Salt and Pepper Bush. She smiled to see the familiar opening of the family burrow. Orchid Owl and her daughter Odessa kept watch as Keio, Keon and Kailah waited outside for Keona as she plunged into the darkness of the tunnels. As they waited, Keio looked around. Over head the trees formed a canopy; a little stream ran between the trees towards the lake, masses of ferns covered the forest floor. In the distance he could see a fence and a light from a human's home shone into the forest. Keio knew it was a matter of time before humans built here too.

Keona wondered how the burrow would feel after being left for so long, but the burrow seemed to welcome her. After exploring all the passages, Keona sat down in the sleeping area she had shared with Keanu.

"Oh Keanu! I wonder how our life would have been if you had lived!" Keona thought to herself.

"I wonder too!" Keanu said, as his spirit appeared next to Keona, giving her a sad smile.

"We have another daughter. Her name is Keilana. She also has a family now and is living over in Sunny Bight with Keely and her family." Keona smiled back at him.

"I will have to pay them a visit" Keanu mused, before adding *"You are looking well."* He could see Keona was expecting again.

"Of course she is!" Kupe's voice interrupted as his spirit appeared in front of them. He then added with a grin, *"When is my new sister due?"*

"She will be here in a few weeks." Keona informed them.

She shook her head with amazement at Kupe's perception. *"We should have time to get settled in our new home before she comes."*

"Are there any others?" Keanu wanted to know. He was feeling aggrieved that this new family member wasn't his.

"Yes," Keona replied with a happy smile. *"You have a brother, Keon and another sister, Kailah."* Keona informed Kupe.

"I would like to meet them some day." Kupe requested.

"I will see what I can arrange, next time we are at the lake." Keona promised.

"Keio is still looking after you well?" Kupe enquired.

"He is." Keona replied with a radiant look on her face. *"I couldn't be happier."*

"We can't ask for any more than that, can we Dad?"

In the lengthy silence Keona added *"I'm sorry our life together was cut short."*

"I'm sorry too." Keanu agreed, adding. *"I'm glad you've found happiness again."*

Keona nodded her thanks. They both realised that this was the goodbye they had been deprived of earlier.

"Have a good life." Keanu managed to smile.

"I will." Keona smiled back as his spirit began to fade then disappeared. *"I will see you again Mum."* Kupe promised with a grin.

"Please look after him." Keona pleaded with Kupe. She knew Keanu needed his support

"I will, don't worry." Kupe reassured Keona before he too disappeared from view.

Keona didn't know how long she sat there, with her memories, but she was stirred from her revere by footsteps and Orchid and Keio's voices calling her.

"I'm here!" Keona called as she stood up, to find Orchid and Keio approaching, with Odessa, Keon and Kailah following close behind, with concerned looks on their faces.

"I'm okay," Keona reassured them. "I've just been saying goodbye."

"Kupe has been here?" Keio asked. He knew that Kupe's spirit was still at the lake.

"Yes," Keona replied, and Keanu as well."

Keio sensed Keona was feeling emotional after the encounter and came to give her a hug.

"Are you ready to join the others yet, or do you want some more time?" Keio asked.

"We will need to move soon." Orchid said with a worried look around. "It will be daylight shortly. We will need to be at the school cave before humans and their animals start moving around."

"I'm ready." Keona replied with a happy smile, but I want to show you something first." Leading the way to the small tunnel that Keoni and made so long ago. The marks that Keoni had made seemed to be almost as fresh as the day that he had made them. A light moss cover now protected them. She looked at the stunned faces of Keio and their children with a smile and gave them a hug. "It had that effect on us as well when we first saw it too."

With that, she led her family out of the burrow to begin the climb of Mount Tahua to the new school cave where the community were settling in for a rest. They would begin the final journey that evening.

At the school cave, there was another surprise waiting with Keka. It was Kane from Arthurs Pass. He gave her a big grin as Keona recognised him.

"News came that you were on your way, so I've come to take you to your new home.

CHAPTER THREE

THE GUARDIANS

The soft twilight before dawn was emerging at Lake Kaniere as Odessa landed at her sleeping spot among the branches of the Totara tree. Her other family members were already at their spots nearby. Odessa had a quick preen before she too closed her eyes to visit her dream world.

Normally she enjoyed the fun of chasing mice and other creatures in places she could only imagine. They always got away, but she had the knowledge they would be back for another chase in her next visit. This morning, however she was being visited by a vision that both puzzled and troubled her.

A young Roa Kiwi was sneaking into a cave she didn't recognise. She did recognise the Kiwi though – Her mother, Orchid had told her about seeing Kalea's chick which had Kalea's fair colour and Kupe's brown eyes! From a dark corner of the cave Kohana dragged out a book. Odessa recognised the book too – It was the Kiwi Kingdom Book! They had one at the school cave on Mount Tuhua. Everyone knew it was a very special book that could only be read if it called you to read it! She had been told how her grandfather Owen had made Kupe Kiwi leader after he had wanted to read it. Kohana kept looking around furtively as she read. She could feel someone was watching her, but didn't know how or where they were. When finished, Kohana put the book back before sneaking outside; being careful that no-one saw her come or go.

Did this mean Kohana was the next Kiwi Kingdom leader? If so, why was Kohana looking at the book in secret? How and where did she get the Kiwi Kingdom book? Was there another copy of it? Odessa would try to find out at school tonight.

Odessa was seeing Kohana again. She was in a school cave with other animals, that were reading books. An adult female Kiwi was taking the class. Kohana was looking at a map – it was of the Buller region.

Why was Kohana studying the Buller region? Everyone knew it was outside the Kiwi Kingdom and that Kiwis there were hostile to the Kiwi Kingdom! Odessa gave a loud gasp as she suddenly knew the reason for the vision. Kohana was planning to visit the hostile area and Odessa was to be there to protect her on her journey!

"Odessa! Are you alright?" Orchid's voice woke her from her dream.

Odessa opened her eyes to see her mother looking at her with concern. Her father Oswin and two sisters, Ophira and Owena were also peering to see what was happening.

"It's alright Mum," Odessa reassured her with a smile. "It was only a dream. Sorry to disturb you."

"Try to dream of something nice then." Orchid advised her.

Odessa closed her eyes and pretended to sleep, but when she thought everyone was settled again, opened her eyes to think about what she had seen. Odessa knew she would have to study much harder than she normally would. She would have to look at the maps too, to plot a safe passage where they would be going. Odessa would also have to find out where friendly owl communities were. She knew she couldn't do this on her own.

Orchid saw Odessa was still awake and in deep thought. Something serious was happening to her daughter and she meant to find out what was troubling her!

At school that night, Odessa casually asked Ollie if the Kiwi Kingdom book was the only one.

"Why, do you want to read it?" Ollie was immediately alert.

"No," Odessa smiled back at him. "I was just wondering if anything happened to this book, would the Kiwi Kingdom be lost forever?"

Ollie thought for a moment. "No, it wouldn't. Kalea took the original with her when she fled to Three Sisters Mountain community."

"That's good to know." Odessa replied then moved to the shelves to pick a picture book that Emily had made of South Africa.

"Is there any particular reason for seeing that book?" Ollie asked her. He was still alert.

"No, I like seeing things from other places, and I know I will never get to visit there." was Odessa's reasonable reply. Odessa waited till Ollie was distracted by other pupils, to return to the library to get out the map book.

Orlando Owl from Mahinapua saw her studying the map and wondered where she was going. Animals didn't study maps unless they were planning a long journey! Orlando admired Odessa from the first day he had seen her in class. It was too soon to talk about the future, but he wanted her for his mate one day.

When it came time for Ollie to teach the male Owls about the other Owl leaders and their communities, the female owls usually escaped to start their night feeds, for their future was in raising their young. Tonight, however Odessa stayed behind to look at the book on South Africa. Orlando realised Odessa wasn't really reading the book. She was listening to Ollie's lecture, but why?

When the school session had finished, Oswin Owl had a chat with Ollie, how his girls were going at school.

"They are doing well." Ollie reassured Oswin. "Odessa surprised me this evening with her interest in the Kiwi Kingdom Book." Ollie nodded at Oswin's startled look.

"No, she didn't want to look at the book; but she did want to know what would happen if something happened to it. I was able to reassure Odessa that there is another copy if something did happen to ours." She also seemed to be very interested in Emily's book on South Africa this evening."

"That is strange." Oswin said slowly. "Odessa didn't sleep well at all today. We will have to keep a close eye on her."

"We certainly shall!" Ollie agreed.

As Odessa flew through the trees she heard movement behind her. Settling on a branch, she looked around to find Orlando coming to land next to her.

"You aren't heading home?" Odessa asked.

"I wanted to talk to you first, about your trip."

"I didn't realise anyone had noticed." Odessa replied anxiously and then more quietly, "We need somewhere more private to talk. Follow me. We will go to the old school cave."

Through the forest they weaved silently, before landing at the base of the cliff, now covered in vines and ferns.

Odessa pushed aside some ferns to enter the dark space behind it. Orlando swiftly followed her.

"Are you sure it is safe in here?" Orlando asked anxiously.

"If we stay near the entrance, we will be fine should anything happen. Also we will be able to see or hear if anyone comes near."

"I saw you looking at the map of the Buller area. Why are you going there? I also noticed you were listening to our lesson on Owl leaders and communities. What is happening with you Odessa?"

Odessa gave a little sigh, then told Orlando about the visions she had had, and the knowledge that she was to be Kohana's protector on her journey.

"Will you be coming back?" Orlando couldn't help asking, realising that his hopes and dreams might be leaving when she left.

"I don't know." Her reply was equally anxious. Then with a maturity she didn't realise she possessed Odessa asked the question that neither of them had been expecting so soon.

"Do you want me to come back?"

"Yes."

"If I can't come back, I will send for you."

"In the meantime, I will help you with all the information I can give you." Orlando offered.

"Thank you." The relief on Odessa's face was obvious. "I won't have to pretend to read books during your lessons anymore!"

They both chuckled at that before returning to more normal matters.

"Have you had a feed yet?" Odessa asked as she was feeling hungry herself.

"No. Shall we?" Orlando asked, letting Odessa go first. She had a good look around to ensure all was quiet before slipping out into the night; followed closely behind by Orlando. Their coming and going had been seen though, by the Fantails who had a nest in a neighbouring tree, and was the subject of much talk the next day.

When Orlando returned to Mahinapua much later than he normally did, his grandfather Oscar was waiting. Oscar didn't fly as far as he used to now, but he liked to keep an eye on what the younger ones were doing.

"Were you kept in at school?" Oscar asked. He could see that Orlando wasn't his usual self.

"No, nothing like that" Orlando managed to smile. He turned to look at Mount Graham which hid Lake Kaniere and gave a big sigh. "I need time to think. It looks like I will have to grow up sooner than I thought I would."

In the following silence, Oscar turned to give Olivia his mate who was in the next tree, a meaningful glance. She immediately flew off to find Orlando's parents. She returned with Odin and Ocena, who crowded around him.

"What's up son?" Odin liked to get to the point when there was a discussion to be had. "There is so much to tell." Orlando began. "You had better make yourselves comfortable!" Oscar couldn't help smiling at this remark.

"You heard him!" Oscar piped up and immediately looked around for a more comfortable branch than the one he was on. Everyone else took Oscar's cue and made them-selves more comfortable too.

"I've been talking to Odessa, Orchid's daughter." Orlando began. She has had a vision of Kohana Kiwi at Three Sisters Mountain. Kohana was reading the Kiwi Kingdom book, which means she is to be the next Kiwi Kingdom leader. She was reading it in secret. Odessa also saw her reading a map of the Buller area, where Kiwis are hostile to kiwis from the Kiwi Kingdom. Odessa knows that Kohana is planning to go to the Buller area and that she is to go with Kohana to protect her.

"How is this to affect you?" Odin asked.

"I intend to have Odessa for my mate, when the time is right." Orlando was to the point. "Odessa now knows that, and if she is unable to return, will send for me. But..." and here Orlando hesitated. After a small silence, he made his plea. "But, I want and need to go with her!" I know Odessa won't be able to protect Kohana by herself. She hasn't the knowledge of our communities who can or will help us when needed or to avoid those who won't. Besides," Orlando continued, "If Kohana makes her life in the North; it may be some time before we return – if we return."

"Does anyone else at Lake Kaniere know about this?" Oscar asked in the silence while Odin and Ocena were digesting this news.

"No, I don't think so." Orlando replied. "Odessa asked Ollie if there were any other copies of the Kiwi Kingdom Book. He confirmed that there was one that Kalea took to Three Sisters Mountain. Odessa also pretended to read a book so she could listen in on our lesson on leaders and communities. When school finished, I had my talk with her."

"Did anyone see or hear your talk?" Oscar wanted to know.

"No. She took me to the old school cave." It was very quiet there and we didn't see anyone else around."

"Well," Oscar addressed Odin and Ocena, "Do you agree to Orlando taking on the role of protector too?"

Odin looked at Orlando's determined face.

"Orlando will go anyway, so it might as well be with our blessing." At this Orlando gave his parents a big smile.

"Thanks Mum and Dad"

"I will go with you, when you go for lessons tomorrow." Oscar advised Orlando.

"We are coming too." Ocena piped up. She knew that once the situation became known, plans would be made that might prevent Orlando from returning to Mahinapua to see them again.

"Yes," Odin agreed. "Ollie will want to head to Three Sisters as soon as he can. He will be taking you and Odessa with him."

"Have you eaten yet tonight? Ocena asked. She looked at Orlando's tall lean frame. He would be as big as Oscar one day.

"I have, thanks Mum."

Oscar also looked at Orlando's lean frame.

"Then, you need to eat much more!" Oscar commented. "If you want to travel and protect anyone, you will need to double what you are eating; so go and find some more to eat and make sure it is substantial! Come back in a few hours and we will see what you need to know about other communities."

With Oscar's orders ringing in his ears, Orlando flew off into the forest. He managed to catch a weasel – Kiwi Kingdom rules didn't apply here! Feeling suitably full Orlando sat on a tree near the lake. He felt both elated and sad at the same time. His life was about to change but he was going to miss his life here and the wisdom his grandfather gave him. He made a mental note to check on the map for suitable spots for a future home in Buller, hopefully near a nice lake like this one.

When Odessa settled on her perch for her sleep the next morning, Orchid noticed she seemed calmer and even had a little smile on her face. When Odessa found herself watching Kohana read the Kiwi Kingdom Book again, she watched her with interest, trying to work out how old Kohana was – how close was she to being independent and mature enough to sneak off to make her own life. Odessa had no doubt that is what Kohana intended. Odessa also realised Kohana had some learning to do for her role as leader. If she was to attempt to take the Kiwi Kingdom to the North, she would have no influence if she had not been initiated into the role. Odessa then wondered how Kohana would react to having a guardian accompanying her on her travels. Would Kohana welcome her presence, or consider her a nuisance, to be ignored? This quest was going to be very interesting indeed. When Kohana studied her map, Odessa took particular notice to see if Kohana had a route in mind – tracing paths or particular areas. Odessa saw Kohana was trying to commit places to memory. She didn't have a plan yet! Odessa was happy then, to slip into a deep dreamless sleep.

Orlando, on the other hand, had a great deal of trouble getting off to sleep. Facts from Oscar's lecture on communities were racing through his head. The elation of being accepted by Odessa as his future mate was revisited; as was the adventure of travel to Three Sisters Mountain. The prospect of an unknown future when Kohana was ready for her journey was also mulled over. And to top it all off, that Weasel was giving him indigestion!

Storm clouds were gathering on the coast when Orlando, his parents and Oscar flew into the school cave. Orlando didn't care though; he was looking forward to seeing Odessa again and giving her his news.

Odessa's eyes widened when she saw Oscar and Orlando's parents arrive with him at class. Orlando came straight over to her with a big smile to announce.

"There is to be a change of plan. I'm coming with you."

The students were set their usual work, but little was actually done as they realised something important was going on with Orlando and Odessa.

Ollie sent his son Oriel to fetch Odina his mate and Oswin and Orchid. By the time they arrived, the rumblings of thunder could be heard near Conical Hill. Ollie dismissed school for the night. Students were better with their parents when storms were around.

The three families gathered around in the comfort of the library as the storm raged overhead to hear the news that at Three Sisters Mountain, the Kiwi Kingdom had a new leader that needed guidance and that two family members were to accompany her to her and their future in the north.

"When will you be going?" Orchid asked. She was having trouble accepting the fact that Odessa would soon be leaving; not knowing if or when she would see her again. Her only comfort was that she still had Ophira and Owena.

"We leave as soon as the weather is clear, probably tomorrow evening."

Ollie didn't mention it, but he had word from Kanoa in the Paparoa range that his community was suffering from large losses to their young chicks too, but near his community burrows humans were putting strange boxes that looked like traps! *What animals were the humans trying to catch?* Ollie wondered. He just hoped the traps weren't for Kiwis.

CHAPTER FOUR

THE NEW LEADER

Both Odessa and Orlando were feeling emotional when it was time to leave the lake. They had been woken early to feed before the first part of their journey. Goodbyes had been said, with promises to return when they could. With a final smile to their families, Odessa and Orlando rose to follow Ollie into the sky. Ollie's mate Odina and their children Oriel and Odele followed behind them.

The night was clear and full of stars, with no hint of the wild night before. Orlando noticed Ollie was using slow deep strokes of his wings, Orlando guessed he was conserving energy, so copied him and found it was much easier to fly and keep up. Soon everyone was using the same rhythm. Ollie headed for the coast where the sea breeze gave welcome lift. Following Ollie, they rose higher, till he spread his wings out extra wide and began to glide. Both Orlando and Odessa were exhilarated by this experience. They had never tried gliding before. Ollie took a look back to see how everyone was keeping up and continued on.

The twinkling of lights moving around off the coast had Orlando puzzled.

"What are those lights? Orlando asked Ollie.

"They are humans in fishing boats." Ollie answered. Many creatures live in the sea. Humans eat some of them."

The combination of slow wing beats and gliding took them up the coast and over the bright lights of Greymouth and Cobden to the Rapahoe Range; where Ollie landed in a tall tree, which had plenty of foliage to hide amongst.

As everyone crowded around, Ollie gave a big beam of delight.

"Well done!" Ollie congratulated both Orlando and Odessa and his own children Oriel and Odele. "I didn't expect to get this far tonight. All going well, we will reach Three Sisters Mountain tomorrow night. It is time for a feed now, before daylight comes. We will shelter here until the sun has set tomorrow."

Ollie and Odina took Oriel and Odele for their feed while Orlando and Odessa teamed up to find theirs. Odessa found some insects and Orlando found a mouse which they shared.

They were about to return to their shelter tree when a Morepork Owl came through the trees to land on the branch next to them.

"Who are you and what are you doing here" he demanded.

"This is your territory?" Orlando asked. The owl nodded.

"I am Orlando and this is Odessa." Orlando introduced them to him. We are visiting with another owl and his family. He is Ollie from Lake Kaniere. We will be moving on up the coast to Three Sisters Mountain tomorrow."

"The owl was thoughtful. "I have heard of Ollie."

As Orlando was talking, Odessa saw movement below them. It was a stoat! Without thinking, Odessa launched herself off the branch to grab the stoat, which wriggled and tried to bite her before Orlando swiftly joined her to end its struggles.

"Would you like to join us?" Orlando offered to share their meal.

With a gleam in his eye, the owl immediately joined in. When Orlando and Odessa were full, they moved back to let the owl continue his feed. He looked up with suspicion, but they gave him a reassuring smile.

"We are finished. You can have the rest."

"Thank you," Said the grateful owl. "I have a family to feed." He called his mate who had been watching with interest from a distance. Between them, the pair was able to take their prize back to their hungry family. Before he left the Owl gave them an invitation.

"If you are ever back this way, do call in to visit us. We are Ozzy and Orena."

"Thank you, we will." Orlando promised.

On their return, Ollie enquired if they had enough to eat. He had some mice sitting nearby.

"Those mice can keep till tonight." Orlando advised him. "We have had some insects, a mouse and part of a stoat that we have shared with one of the locals who took the rest for his family."

"It is always good to keep in with the locals." Ollie approved.

When Odessa visited her dream world that morning, she found Kohana was no longer reading books, but looking determinedly out towards the north! She just hoped they reached her before she started her journey. Odessa opened her eyes and gave a sigh.

"What's up?" Orlando asked with concern as he moved closer to her.

"Kohana is no longer reading books for her journey and she is looking north with a very determined look on her face! I just hope we get there before she leaves."

Odessa was feeling tired as Three Sister's Mountain came into view. She knew the others were feeling the same. There had been a stronger breeze for this part of the journey, which had tried to force them inland. Ollie landed by the school cave, followed swiftly by Orlando and Odessa. Odina and the children weren't far away. He could see that Kalasia Kiwi was taking a class. Activity in the room stopped as Ollie strode in, followed by Orlando and Odessa. He had a quick glance around the room. Kohana wasn't there.

"Hello Ollie! This is a surprise." Kalasia welcomed him. She had noticed him scan the room. "Are you looking for someone?"

"Hello Kalasia, We are." Ollie replied. "Do you know where Kohana is? Also, where do you keep the Kiwi Kingdom book?"

At this point Odina and the children entered the cave to join Orlando and Odessa.

"She has been reading it?" Kalasia asked, but didn't wait for an answer. I see your family is in need of some food and rest. We will deal with that first." Kalasia then addressed the class.

"We have some visitors who have come from Lake Kaniere. We will finish early tonight, but class will start at the usual time tomorrow."

Most of the students left the cave, except several young owls which were Oriel and Odele's age. They crowded around them, asking lots of questions, before one flew off into the night, to fetch their parents, who brought some food with them.

Odessa spoke to Kalasia with urgency. "Kalasia, I have had visions of Kohana reading the Kiwi Kingdom Book in secret. She also has been looking at a map of the Buller area."

Kalasia looked alarmed at this news. "I know she is determined to go there! Please! We need to talk to her before she starts her journey."

News of their arrival had spread around the community like wildfire. Kalasia's mate and leader of the community, Kapali now arrived with Kalea and Koro.

"Have any of you seen Kohana tonight or know where she is?" Kalasia asked urgently. "She has plans to go to the Buller area, and..." she paused, "she has been reading the Kiwi Kingdom book." Kalea gasped at this news. Kohana had been moody and distant in recent months, and now it seems she was leaving without saying goodbye!

"I think she is already heading north." Kapali said thoughtfully.

"Where is a map?" Odessa asked. "Can you show us where and when you last saw her?"

"It was a few hours ago." Kapali said as he looked at the map. "She was heading down the other side of the mountain. I asked her where she was going and she said she was having a look at the river." Kapali pointed to the thin blue line with his claw. "The Ohikanui."

Odessa looked at Orlando and Ollie. They both nodded.

"Odessa and Orlando are here to be Kohana's protector. I will go with them now to find her. We will try to persuade her to return to be initiated in her role. If she refuses, then Odessa and Orlando will continue with her on her journey untill they are sure she is safe and settled in her new life." He then turned to Odina and his children. "I will see you soon. Have a good rest now."

The other parents offer to help search for Kohana was accepted gratefully. The more eyes that was available to find her, the better. As Ollie, Orlando and Odessa rose to fly over Three Sister Mountain, the local owls were answering the call to help.

Kohana was making her way steadily towards the river, occasionally stopping for a worm she happened to feel underfoot. She was feeling elated that her plan to start her new life was working. She had a plan to bring the Kiwi Kingdom to the north, but that would come later. Kohana felt some guilt that she hadn't said goodbye, but knew that if she had, she would have been prevented from going. Kohana also felt some annoyance that Kapali knew of her plan to visit the river.

By the time they realised she wasn't returning she would be well on her way to the Buller. Overhead an owl was gliding silently. Seeing the movement below, it landed on a nearby tree and watched her progress, before putting out his call. Kohana ignored the call. The local owls frequently made calls to each other.

A little later, Kohana was not able to ignore the three owls flying towards her. She recognised one of them. It was Ollie Owl, the guardian of the Kiwi Kingdom from Kaniere! She knew immediately, that her plans were in jeopardy! They landed in front of her. Shortly afterwards, they were also surrounded by owls who had helped in the search.

"Hello Kohana," Ollie greeted her. "We need to talk to you."

"If you want me to return to Three Sisters Mountain, I won't go. There is no need for me to go back."

"There is the small matter of your role as the next leader of the Kiwi Kingdom; that we have to sort out before you leave."

He saw her eyes widen at his words. "Yes, Kohana, we know you have been reading the Kiwi Kingdom Book, which means you are now the next leader of the Kiwi Kingdom; but, you will have no authority either inside or outside of the kingdom untill you have been initiated into the role."

"I'm not going back!" Kohana insisted. "Can you do it here?"

"I can."

"Kohana Kiwi, you have been chosen as leader of the Kiwi Kingdom. Are you ready for this role?"

"I am."

"Do you, Kohana, promise to uphold the laws of the Kiwi Kingdom?"

"I do."

Do you, Kohana, promise to serve and protect all the animals of the Kiwi Kingdom?"

"I do."

"Do you, Kohana, promise to promote a kingdom where all animals live in harmony with each other?"

"I do."

"By the power invested in me, Ollie Owl, Kohana Kiwi, you are now leader of the Kiwi Kingdom." Ollie then added, "The leader usually carries an amulet, which is the mantle of leadership at all times; but as you are about to travel to an area where you will be in danger, the amulet will remain in the Kiwi Kingdom book until or if you return."

"What makes you think I may not return?" Kohana was defiant.

"Kehi the northern leader promised to look after your mother Kalea if anything happened to Kupe, but gave orders for her to be eliminated if she went there. It was only luck that one of the local Kiwis heard of the plan and persuaded her to go to Three Sisters Mountain instead. Kohana, you are going to need protection." He could see she was going to protest. "I introduce Orlando and Odessa who will accompany you on your journey untill you are settled and happy in your new life. That is not negotiable!"

Kohana gave Orlando and Odessa a glare before stomping off on her journey. Being shadowed; was not part of her plan!

"Try to look after Kohana, and just as importantly, look after yourselves." Ollie said with a sympathetic smile.

"We will." Orlando promised, before turning to fly after her, but they were stopped by the local owls. "You have already had a long journey. Rest and feed first. We will follow her till you are ready. We will also tell our northern communities you are coming."

"Thank you." Orlando expressed their gratitude. They were still tired (and hungry) after their journey and welcomed some respite before they started what was going to be a difficult quest.

"I had a feeling this was going to be an interesting journey, and judging by Kohana's attitude to us, it is going to be." Odessa said in conversation as they searched for some food.

Yes," Orlando agreed. "We will have to watch we don't put ourselves in danger while watching her."

"Or, that she doesn't do it to us as well." Odessa added.

"At some point Kohana may put herself in danger." Orlando voiced the scenario they both hoped wouldn't happen, but knew it probably would.

"We will have to decide whether we intervene or not."

"I agree." Odessa's response was quiet but firm. "We can only advise Kohana if we see she is heading for trouble; but if she won't listen, we will have to let fate take care of itself."

After their feed of some moths and mice they sat for a short while, listening to the sounds of the night. Owls could be heard calling in the distance. Kiwis could be heard too, on the mountain.

"We should make a move soon." Odessa was regretful that this pleasant break had to end. "We need to catch up with Kohana before day breaks and she goes for a rest."

The red light before dawn was forming on the horizon, as they emerged from the forest canopy to sit on a treetop to get their bearings. An owl who had stayed nearby for them called out. An answering call came some distance away.

"Kohana is over there." the owl advised them. "Good luck."

"Thank you for all of your help." Orlando thanked them before they set off.

Orlando made a quiet call when they came near the area they were directed to. An equally quiet call came back from a Totara tree where a female owl was waiting for them.

"You will be pleased to know Kohana has made a burrow here." She informed them, pointing to the hollow at the base of the tree. "You should be able to rest now till she rises this evening."

"Thank you." Odessa replied. "We will."

Orlando found a spot under the canopy where they were hidden from any raptors out and about during the day but had a view of the entrance to Kohana's burrow.

Odessa was happy in her dream world, soaring in the sky, when a vision of Kohana sneaking out of her burrow came to her! Immediately, she opened her eyes and shifted on their perch to see Kohana furtively looking around outside her burrow. It was broad daylight too. Odessa's movement also woke Orlando, who wasn't at all pleased to see Kohana up to mischief already!

"Kohana!" Orlando barked at her. "You are putting yourself in danger! Get back in your burrow at once!"

"What if I don't?" Kohana sneered back at him.

"If something bad happens to you, it will be your problem, not ours!" Orlando's anger was plain.

"I agree!" was Odessa's emphatic reply, before they both turned their heads away and closed their eyes.

"Why not?" Kohana was insistent. "You are supposed to be looking after me."

"You are an adult, Kohana." Odessa reminded her. "Adults do not put themselves in danger without a good reason. If you expect us to chase after you in the day time when it is dangerous to be out, you will be putting us in danger as well. Have you forgotten your Kiwi Kingdom pledge to serve and protect already?"

This question was met by silence and Kohana's return to her burrow.

At Three Sisters Mountain, Ollie checked where they were keeping the Kiwi Kingdom book. He now understood how Kohana could read it in secret, for it was stashed in a dark area of the cave where anyone could hide.

"It is best to keep it in sight on the library shelves." Ollie advised Kalasia. "That way, if anyone is interested in it, you will know straight away and be able to let me know."

28

At Lake Kaniere, Orchid had received some interesting news from Protea Pigeon's friends at Franz Joseph. They had seen a building in the township with a statue of a large Kiwi outside. Out the back there were some fenced areas where they had heard the sounds of young kiwi chicks calling to each other. Is this where the humans had taken the eggs? And if so, what were they going to do with the chicks?

CHAPTER FIVE

JOURNEY TO THE NORTH

The first evening of their journey brought pouring rain. Odessa and Orlando saw Kohana briefly leave her burrow to search for a feed near the tree, and then withdrew again.

"She obviously isn't in a hurry to move on in this weather." Orlando observed.

"We need to feed as well." Odessa replied. "It is probably best if we take turns. If she moves on while I'm away, just keep her in sight and I will call if I find you gone on my return."

As Odessa flew out from the tree, Kohana called out to her.

"Where are you going?"

Odessa turned around and flew down to the entrance of Kohana's burrow. Even though she was being soaked, she gave Kohana a smile.

"Like you, we need to feed too. Our food isn't quite as handy as yours. Orlando may go out for his feed when I return."

With that, Odessa turned to fly into the forest where animals were scurrying everywhere to avoid the rain. After feeding well herself, she returned with two mice for Orlando, who eyed them with gratitude.

"There is no point in both of us getting wet." Odessa said as she shook herself dry.

Several hours later the weather cleared and stars could be seen in the sky. Kohana came out of her burrow to feed before coming to the base of the tree to look up at them.

"I will be moving on soon. Can we talk before we move on?"

Orlando and Odessa looked at each other. They both had noticed the "we". Was Kohana beginning to accept them?

"Of course." Orlando replied as they flew down to join her. On reaching the floor, Orlando had a good look around. He felt vulnerable to be down here for any length of time. Turning his attention to Kohana, Orlando noticed she had a different, calmer air about her now.

"I want to thank you." Kohana began. "You are the first animals to treat me as an adult. I am grateful for that. I appreciate that you have been sent to protect me; but is it really necessary to shadow me? I was hoping for some independence on this journey."

"It was our plan to keep you in sight, while you are travelling, without actually hovering over you." Odessa began.

Kohana gave a happy sigh at this. "That is a relief!"

"We would only come to intervene," Odessa continued, "if we saw there was any danger or if you called for us."

"That's fine." Kohana gave a smile. "I might enjoy this journey after all."

"We appreciate," Orlando began, "that you want some independence, which we will give you as much as we can; but remember, you are a leader. Most leaders in the animal world (and even among humans) have some protection with them, because they never know when their safety will be threatened." Orlando noticed that since they had started their talk, some owls had come to watch and listen. He just hoped that they were friendly.

Kohana was silent as she digested this, then gave a little sigh as she acquiesced to the reality that she would never be completely alone again.

"You are right, of course." Kohana admitted.

"I have something else for you to think about too." Orlando added.

"Is it another unpalatable truth?" Kohana asked. Orlando nodded.

"You have to consider that in the Kiwi world, Leaders are usually male. Those that are outside the Kiwi Kingdom get to be leader by fighting for their position. Are you able to fight?" Orlando paused to let Kohana consider this, "Or, can you defend yourself? If you can't, then you need to learn."

"I've never had the need to defend myself till now." Kohana was thoughtful "You have certainly given me plenty to think about. Now, it's time to move on."

With that, Kohana turned and at a leisurely pace, made her way towards the river, which could be heard in the distance.

Orlando and Odessa gave her a few minutes before preparing to follow. In that time an owl came to a low branch to talk to them.

"Is that Kohana from Three Sisters Community?" He asked.

"She is." Orlando confirmed. "You are doing very well with her. Just call if you need any help. There is always someone around. Our territory extends to the Buller River. Good luck."

"Thank you, we appreciate it." Orlando thanked him.

On reaching the Ohikanui River, Kohana was waiting for them.

"This will be our home till we reach the Buller." She said, before moving on.

Both Orlando and Odessa looked around them. On both sides of the river, the land was clothed in thick forest. The river was sitting in a long narrow valley. The valley walls quickly rose in steep slopes to hills and mountains. From reading the map, they knew there was no easy way out for Kohana untill they reached the Buller, so they could relax untill they came near the Buller River junction. Both Orlando and Odessa went searching for food as Kohana made her way along the valley floor. Her pale fur made her easy to spot again.

Their journey along the river valley settled into a routine where Kohana would call them to have a chat before setting off on her path. She also made sure they knew where she was sleeping before settling into her temporary burrow.

At times when it was raining, Kohana would stay put untill the rain passed through. After all, there was no rush to finish this journey. A feeling of safety and security seemed to accompany them as they travelled.

This lasted untill one night when they heard Kohana give a yelp and a scuffle in her direction! Immediately, they flew in, to find Kohana battling a large possum, which was almost as big as she was. It took the three of them to dispatch this creature, whose long claws had also left their mark.

"Are you alright?" Odessa asked, noticing that Kohana was shaking and blood was running down her front.

"I will be, when I get over the shock!" Kohana shook some more.

"Come and have a dip in the river." Odessa ordered her. "We need to see what injuries you have."

Kohana gasped as she plunged into the water, but began to enjoy it too much. When she could feel the cold through her feathers, she knew it was time to get out.

Odessa had a look at Kohana's front. There were some wounds, but they looked clean and had stopped bleeding.

"If you can keep your front clean untill your wounds heal, you will be fine." Odessa advised her. "You will need something clean to line your burrow in the morning too."

"Do we just leave the Possum?" Kohana asked, feeling a little sorry for it.

"No. It's good food for us." Orlando replied. "When we have had enough, I will call the local owls to have the rest."

"I will go and have a feed too, but I will stay in sight." Kohana advised them.

When Orlando and Odessa were ready to share their meal, Orlando sat on a nearby tree and called out as loud as he could. His call echoed down the valley. It didn't take long for a couple of owls to come to join him.

"Do you need some help?" They asked concerned.

"No." Orlando smiled. "I have a feed for you. A possum made the mistake of attacking Kohana Kiwi. We have finished what we need. You can have the rest."

On seeing the meal that had been left for them, the owls were amazed.

"There is enough here for all of us!"

It wasn't long before there was a large gathering of owls, both large and small to share this unexpected treat.

"Thank you." came the chorus in their direction as Orlando, Odessa and Kohana quietly moved on. Regularly, Orlando would take a flight high over the valley, to see what lay ahead. One night he could see an opening ahead and knew they were near to the Buller River. It was time to plan the next part of their journey. The next evening when it came time for their chat with Kohana, Orlando asked the question that had been on both his and Odessa's mind.

"Kohana, I have seen that we will reach the Buller River soon. What plan do you have for when we cross the Buller River?"

Kohana looked anxious, when she heard this news.

"I know there is a bridge, a long way up the Buller River, but I haven't seen anywhere near this river, where I can cross safely."

"Can you swim?" Odessa asked. Kohana shook her head.

"Then, before you go much further, you need to learn." Odessa informed her. "I will stay with you while Orlando will see if there is a place on this side that has shallow water for you to practice in."

Orlando launched himself from a branch overhanging the water to make a slow but thorough search of the river, turning around at the last stretch where it met the Buller River. He was able to report back that not far away was a suitable spot to practice.

While they were waiting for Orlando to return, Odessa asked the question that had been on their minds.

"Have you a plan for when you get across the Buller River? You will be in hostile territory then."

"When I left home, it was my plan to just arrive and introduce myself to the first Kiwi I met, but I now know I will be going straight into danger. I will have to cross in the daytime when Kiwis are sleeping, so I have time to travel some distance into the territory before I meet anyone. For my identity, I will just say I am Kohana. If there are questions about my family, I will say that my father died before I was born (which is true) and that I brought myself up as my mother went off with another male as soon as I was able to look after myself."

"The promotion of the Kiwi Kingdom will have to come much later, if it is practical to do so. If I find it is too dangerous to stay there, then I will withdraw." Kohana paused before asking; "Do you think I my plan will work?"

"It just might." Odessa replied. "It's good you have an escape plan if things don't work out."

"I have to try." Kohana's tone was determined.

What Kohana didn't mention, was her determination to confront Kehi! – Why he promised her mother, Kalea a safe place to go, then give orders for her to be eliminated when she came!

CHAPTER SIX

KEHI'S TRIALS

When Kehi returned from the Kiwi Kingdom, to be met and have questions asked before he had crossed the Buller River; he knew that the power he had enjoyed before his visit was now being challenged. It was only a matter of time before he had to fight for his position, his life, and more importantly, his family.

With heavy hearts, Kehi and Kiyo sent Koro to make sure that Kalea didn't cross the Buller River, for they knew they probably wouldn't see him ever again. It would be too dangerous for him to come back, but at least they had the comfort of knowing that Koro was safe. It didn't take long for Koro's absence to be noticed and one evening, Kainan the Kiwi who was Kura's mate and now also had plans to challenge Kehi, approached him.

"We haven't seen Koro around. Is he sick?"

"No," Kehi replied calmly. "He's left."

"Where has he gone?" Kainan was alarmed he hadn't been told by his informants.

"He's gone to the Kiwi Kingdom."

"Why is he going there?" Kainan was angry Koro had escaped without anyone knowing.

"He is interested to see what it is like."

"When is he coming back?" Kainan wanted to make sure they were ready for Koro's return

"He isn't!" Kehi's tone hardened; along with the glare he now gave Kainan. Kainan also noticed that Kehi's claw was clenched, ready to strike.

Kainan backed off a little, for he wasn't ready to challenge Kehi just yet.

"Who will succeed you?" Kainan wanted to know.

"We will have more chicks of course." was Kehi's response.

Kainan nodded, before he turned away. Kehi watched Kainan's receding back with disquiet. He was now regretting that he had let Kura and Kalani her son live after Kakate had brought her and Kalani back to Kehi's territory. It seemed that not only had Kalani succeeded in killing Kupe, the best Kiwi leader on the Island, but Kura had influenced Kainan with her ambitions. He had a feeling that his mate Kiyo was now a target. How could he protect her and his chicks when the breeding season came? Kehi was grateful to see his old friend Khai sidle up to him.

"You have trouble there." Khai murmured to him. "You will have to watch your back!"

"I know." Kehi murmured back. "I'm worried about Kiyo. I'm sure she is a target now too. I'm just glad that Koro is safe from them."

"He is?" Khai asked. There had been rumours that Koro was already dead.

"I made sure of it." Kehi was able to smile.

"I'm sure they will try to eliminate Kiyo soon. Breeding season is nearly here."

"Have you any family you can send her to for the season and have them look after your chick?"

"I hate the idea of being a stranger to my child, but it may be the only way. I will have to talk to Kiyo about it."

"Take care not to talk too loudly in your burrow!" was Khai's final warning before he shuffled off. It was too dangerous to talk for too long.

A week later Kiyo said a silent, but tearful farewell. The sun was well up before she ducked out of their burrow. Khai was waiting to take her to safety. Travelling in the day time was the only way to ensure she would get out of this territory alive. Kiyo's family lived in the far north where she and their chick would be safe from any attempts to harm them.

When Kainan attempted to approach Kehi regarding Kiyo's disappearance, Kehi was ready for him.

"Kiyo is fine." Kehi told him. "It is none of your business where she is or what she is doing. She will return when she is ready." The conversation then took a turn that Kainan wasn't expecting. "How is Kura?"

"She's fine. Why do you ask?" Kainan was nervous of the steely look Kehi was giving him.

"Good! If you, Kura and your family want to remain in my territory, make her behave herself! Remind her, that Kakate's fate will happen to you, and I won't spare her or your children next time!" With that threat ringing in Kainan's ears, Kehi stalked off. He knew that many ears, both friends and foe were listening to his ultimatum.

A little later Khai came to visit Kehi. He was looking worried.

"Some friends aren't happy at your ultimatum to Kainan." Khai began.

"Your threat to Kainan they can understand, but to eliminate his female and children, they can't accept."

Kehi gave Khai a sad smile.

"They are threatening to go over to Kainan's side?"

Khai nodded miserably to Kehi's question.

"You can tell them, that it is Kura that is the biggest threat. I feel sorry for Kainan who has become the latest pawn in her plans for power and territory. Ask them", Kehi added, "to remember that Kakate and Kura were thrown out of this territory after threatening my family. That Kakate killed Kapali's father to take over at Three Sisters Mountain and either killed or forced Kiwi off their territory on half of the mountain; before Kupe Kiwi removed him from power and forced them back here to live under our rules." Kehi paused to let Khai absorb what he said before continuing.

"How is she the threat?"

"Kura encouraged her son Kalani's resentment of Kupe for sending them back here. He went to The Kiwi Kingdom and killed Kupe. Now we are back to where we started, with Kura and Kainan threatening me and my family again for power and territory. Friends should consider that Kainan and Kura are much more intolerant than I am; that they too will be at risk when I am gone. The only way that my family and this community will be safe, is for Kura and all that carry her blood are gone."

Life settled to an uneasy and lonely normality for Kehi untill he was woken some months later to Kiyo snuggling up to him.

"What took you so long?" he murmured.

"Kerewa." Kiyo murmured back with a smile. With that, they both welcomed sleep.

Kiyo was feeding one evening, when she was confronted by Kura.

"So your back, Is there no chick?" Kura enquired, with a searching look at Kiyo's body.

"Not this year." Kiyo calmly replied.

They were interrupted by loud rustling as Kehi burst out from nearby bushes.

"Kura!" Kehi shouted at her. "Didn't you listen to the warning I gave Kainan?" Kura had the sense to step back from Kehi's fury.

"What are you talking about?" Kura pretended ignorance.

"I have warned him, and now I am warning you, that if you don't behave, that Kainan, you, AND your children will end with the same fate as Kakate! Don't come near Kiyo or any of our family again!"

"You wouldn't!" Kura tried to bluster.

"I will! Now go!"

Silently, Kura turned and left, but as she did so, the look she gave Kiyo left both Kehi and Kiyo in no doubt that she was in danger. Back in their burrow, Kehi comforted Kiyo with a cuddle.

"Do you want to go back to your family to live?" Kehi offered her an escape from their life of danger. She shook her head.

"It won't do any good. They will be able to concentrate on getting rid of you then. There is no guarantee that they won't come after me afterwards."

Kehi knew that Kiyo was right. He just had to make sure she was never alone. Kehi was not happy that his enemies were only a few scratches away from breaking into his burrow whenever they chose. He had considered moving to a burrow that was among friends, but knew that this move would only put them in danger. Instead they made sure that their conversations were neither interesting nor valuable.

Over the next couple of years, another son Koa, and a daughter Kiana were added to Kehi and Kiyo's family in the north.

The uneasy peace that had settled on the community continued untill one wet night, when Kehi and Kiyo went out to feed together. Heavy rain beat down and strong wind howled through the trees; drowning any noise or calls, and ruffling all the ferns vigorously.

"I hope the weather is better for your trip in the morning." Kehi said in Kiyo's ear. She smiled and nodded. Breeding season would soon be here. She wanted to be away well before it began.

As Kehi stopped to retrieve a worm under his feet, Kiyo indicated she was going to the old log beyond the patch of high ferns. She waded into the ferns as he was swallowing the worm. Kehi immediately followed her. He came to the log, but there was no sign of her! Trying not to panic, he looked around the ferns before climbing onto the log and looked beyond. Nothing! Kehi's intuition told him that Kiyo and his unborn child were already beyond him. In grief and anger, Kehi sat motionless on the log, ignoring the wet and cold untill some hours later a friend saw him and fetched Khai.

Khai took one look at Kehi and knew that the worst had happened! Kiyo had been taken!

"Come Kehi, it's time to go home."

I'm not going back there!"

"No. You are coming to mine. We will make you a new one."

"But you will be in danger then."

"As you pointed out, we are all in danger anyway. Come!" Khai commanded him.

"If anything happens to me you are in charge."

"It already has! I think joint leadership by both you and me is best until you get over it."

Kehi didn't object. He was succumbing to the shock of losing Kiyo and hours of exposure to the wind and cold. Kehi half slid and half fell off the log, onto the ferns. As he struggled to get up, he realised he was surrounded by a crowd of shocked but sympathetic faces. Those faces formed a bodyguard that were to stay with him from now on. They were on instruction not to let Kehi out of their sight for any reason. Any move against him was to be met by lethal force! Spies were also sent out to track Kura and Kainan's movements.

The sun was up and well past Kura's bedtime. This morning she was near the Buller River, feeling both elated and worried. Kura hadn't expected to wait so long for the opportunity to progress her plans for power; but now, the elimination of Kiyo had gone to plan. By the time Kehi had scaled the log, her lifeless body was hidden out of sight. While Kehi was grieving, they had plenty of time to drag Kiyo away to a place where no-one should ever find her. She looked over to the depression in the ground with a smile. It was an old mine shaft, the bottom of it was full of water, with a passage to a cavern in the river. Kiyo should have been swept well away downstream by now, if eels hadn't already taken her.

Kura was also now worried. Their plan to also eliminate Kehi had to be delayed now. They hadn't expect him sit for so long that he needed help to get down from the log, or that his supporters would come to take him away. He no longer lived in the burrow where her supporters could break in and attack. An attempt by one of her supporters to get near Kehi had resulted in disaster! His body had been dumped at the entrance of her burrow.

As Kura turned to leave, movement in the tree above the river made her stop. It was a pair of owls and they were looking intently at the river. Had Kiyo's body appeared? She went to have a look, but footsteps from the riverbank made Kura stop. She slipped to hide by a tree. As she did so, she saw all of the males in the community including Kainan, Kehi and Khai coming towards her.

"Why have they all come here?" Kura's anxiety was increasing.

Kura didn't know that she had been under surveillance till now. When she went to the river and the mine shaft, word was sent back to Khai and Kehi, who immediately set off with all their supporters.

The sound of running feet also brought out Kainan and his supporters who followed them. Everyone knew there was to be a confrontation. On reaching the river, they could see Kura by the mine shaft and she was moving to hide behind a tree; but they stopped when they saw a wet kiwi emerging from the river bank. It was a pale grey female. Both Kura and Kehi saw her eyes and knew immediately who she was!

CHAPTER SEVEN

THE OLD MINE SHAFT

In the tree, Orlando and Odessa were alarmed! Kohana's plan to quietly enter Kehi's territory had failed. A large number of kiwis were in the forest, and they were coming towards her!

Odessa was especially alarmed to see a large female who was closer than all the others and she was looking at Kohana with evil intent! Kohana couldn't help herself, she gave an alarm call. This woke all the local owls, who came to see who needed help. At Odessa's call, Kohana immediately stopped.

"What is it Odessa?" Kohana spoke as quietly as she could. "Is someone there?" Kohana noticed a number of owls come to land in the trees surrounding the mine shaft. Kehi and the community also saw the owls arrive. Kehi was the only one who knew what it meant, and gave a big smile, which surprised Khai.

"The Kiwis know you are here." Odessa informed Kohana. "You are surrounded! Do you want to go back?"

"Thank you for the warning, but no. One crossing is enough for today!"

During the past few weeks Kohana had swimming training while she healed from the Possum attack. Her training had been successful, for Kohana had swum well when crossing the river; but she had found it tiring to swim across the strong current. She knew she wouldn't make it all the way back again.

"We have to protect our new arrival, if we can." Kehi said to Khai as he saw the way Kura was looking at Kohana. "If Kura sends her down the mine shaft, I will go in after her and help her get out. You know what you have to do." Khai nodded.

"What are we going to do?" Odessa said to Orlando. "There are too many of them to protect her from them all."

"Just remember, not to get hurt yourself!" Orlando reminded her.

At this point, Oren the local Morepork leader came to sit with them.

"Is this Kohana?" he asked. Orlando nodded. "She has quite a welcoming crowd. I hope it is friendly."

"It isn't!" Orlando's voice was bleak.

Oren gave a call which told the owls to be on alert and ready to move.

Kohana could now feel the many eyes on her. Giving herself a little shake, Kohana Squared her shoulders and held her head high as she slowly but deliberately walked forward, scanning the bush around her as she walked. Kohana saw the depression ahead and went to skirt it. Kehi hoped she would walk on the opposite side to Kura, so they would have a chance to reach her before Kura did; But Kohana turned towards her and found herself face to face with Kura.

Odessa launched and swooped down at Kura as Kura moved towards Kohana. Kura ducked but tried to strike Odessa as she passed. Luckily Kura missed and Odessa returned to the Branch with Orlando and Oren.

While this was happening, Kehi started to move forward. Khai and his followers formed a ring to stop Kainan and his supporters from following him.

"Please let me through!" Kainan pleaded with Khai. "I might be able to reason with Kura."

"It didn't work before." Khai replied grimly. "You are staying here."

"What are you doing here?" Kura hissed at Kohana.

"You know who I am?" Kohana stayed calm.

"You look just like your father! I will never forget or forgive Kupe for sending my Kakate to his death."

"Your Kakate took other Kiwi's lives in your quest for power and territory. It is time to stop." Kohana replied firmly. "Where is Kehi?" Kohana called out, in a loud voice. "The leader of the Kiwi Kingdom is here to see him."

Before Kehi could reply, Kura's fury got the better of her.

"No you won't!" Kura cried as she rushed forward to strike at Kohana's neck. Kohana ducked and struck back herself. Her slash of Kura's throat left both of them surprised. Before Kura collapsed, she gave Kohana an almighty shove. Kohana found herself stumbling backwards down into a very deep dark hole. As she fell, Kohana could see water at the bottom.

I'm in for another swim was Kohana's thought before she hit the water with a big splash.

Above ground, pandemonium broke out. There was a fierce battle after Kainan and his supporters saw Kura collapse. They then realised their cause (and their lives) were at risk.

Oren, Orlando and Odessa flew down to the edge of the mine shaft to look.

They could see that Kohana had surfaced and was being swept out of sight into a passage. Kehi came running up.

"Look out!" he yelled. "I have to go in to help her."

"There is a way out?" Orlando asked

"Yes, but it is difficult." Kehi replied as he leapt into the shaft.

Kohana tread water as she was swept along in the tunnel. The total blackness that lay ahead, made her afraid. *"What if there wasn't a way out and she was trapped in here to drown?"* Then she heard a big splash behind her and the sounds of someone swimming. Kohana moved to the side of the channel and dug her claws into the tunnel. She knew she needed to conserve some energy for whatever lay ahead.

"Who's there?" Kohana called out.

Kehi was grateful that Kohana had called out. He now knew which tunnel she was in.

"It's Kehi." He called out. "I'm here to help you get out. You won't make it on your own."

"You've been in here before?"

"Yes, when I was younger." Kehi replied as he caught up with her.

"I know you are Kupe and Kalea's daughter. What is your name?"

"I'm Kohana."

"Well Kohana, at the end of this passage we will seem to hit a wall, but underwater there is a short passage to a cavern where we will be able to escape to the river. In the short passage you will have to hold your breath untill you get through to the other side." Kehi paused. "Do you think you can hold your breath for that long?"

"I haven't had much practice, but I can only try."

"Good. Now while we are in the passage, the water may force your body against the roof and make it difficult to get through. If that happens, turn your body over and walk along the roof till you get through."

Kohana nodded as she took her claws out of the wall. She felt much better now that she had help and some idea of what lay ahead. The darkness that enveloped them didn't seem so threatening now. All too soon, they came to the wall that Kehi had told her about. Kohana could feel the current trying to pull her under. Taking the biggest breath that she could, Kohana then used her claws to move her body down under the wall and into the passage.

Kohana tried to swim through, but found her back forced against the roof. She remembered Kehi's instruction and turned her body over to try walking. It helped when Kehi gave her a little push to get started. At the end of the passage she could see dim light and knew she was nearly there, which was just as well as her lungs felt they were going to burst. Once free of the passage, Kohana clawed her way to the surface where she gasped for air. Kehi came up with her and gave her a big grin. He hadn't been sure he would make it through there either.

Kohana tread water while she looked for somewhere to hang on. She was in need of a rest before they journeyed any further. Kehi read her mind, for he needed one too.

"Let's come over here and have a rest for a little while." Kehi indicated an area at the side of the cavern which was shallow and had some rocks to sit on. "We have another swim before we can get back."

As they came closer to the water's edge, Kohana spotted a dark feathered shape floating in the water. It was obviously a Kiwi. She looked at Kehi.

"Have you lost anyone in your community recently?"

Kehi followed her gaze to the shape and his face crumpled. It was Kiyo!

"I can see it is someone you know. Who is it?"

"My mate Kiyo and our unborn chick disappeared, a couple of nights ago. I knew she had been taken, but I didn't know where." Kehi went up to Kiyo and took her to the edge to cuddle her. He knew it wouldn't help Kiyo now, but it gave him comfort to hold her one last time.

Kohana sat quietly on a rock while Kehi said goodbye to Kiyo.

"Shall we try to take Kiyo with us, so we can give her a proper resting place?" Kohana asked when she saw Kehi was ready to move on.

"I would like that." Kehi agreed as he took some interest in her. *This young and available female was the leader of the kingdom he had wanted to join, had already shown courage tenacity and compassion in the short time she had been here. Yes, she would make an excellent mate.*

"What are you thinking?" Kohana asked, after seeing the quizzical look Kehi was giving her as they prepared to take Kiyo with them.

"I'm in need of a mate now." Kehi said. Given that we are both leaders, we would make a good match. What do you think?"

44

"I might be a good mate for you, but I'm not sure you are a good mate for me."

Kehi was taken aback, he wasn't used to being refused, but the troubled look on Kohana's face told him she had an issue that needed to be addressed if he wanted a relationship with her.

"What is it that makes you doubt me?" Kehi asked. "Is it my age?"

Kohana gave a little shake of her head.

"It's a matter of trust." Kohana answered, looking at him with accusing eyes. "You promised my mother, Kalea a safe place to go, then gave orders for her to be eliminated when she came."

"I'm sorry." Kehi was stunned. *How did she know that? Who was listening and watching my arrival?* "When I returned from my trip to see your father, I had every intention of giving her a safe place to be and also intended to join the Kiwi Kingdom. But, when I reached the other side of the river, Kainan and his supporters were waiting for me. I knew immediately that if I didn't say the things they wanted to hear, that my family and I would be killed there and then. It is the reason, that Kiyo and I sent Koro to make sure Kalea didn't cross the river. It was hard, as we knew we might never see him again, but at least we knew he was safe."

Kohana could see the anguish in Kehi's face and softened her attitude to him.

"I forgive you." Kohana said simply. "Did you have any other children?"

"We have three. Two boys, Kerewa and Koa, and a girl, Kiana. They are hidden in the north."

"They are hidden?" Kohana was shocked.

Kehi nodded sadly. "I haven't met them yet. I had to send Kiyo away before every breeding season, otherwise both she and the children would have been killed; and of course, I would have been next. My community and I are in your debt for finally freeing us from Kura's ambitions." Kehi said with admiration in his eyes.

"I'm feeling guilty about that." Kohana confessed.

"You mean your kingdom policy of not to kill?" Kohana nodded.

"Well, we finally have the chance to change things here, don't we?"

"We do." Kohana agreed.

45

With their future agreed upon, Kehi and Kohana moved Kiyo towards the cavern entrance, holding her with one claw and swimming with their other claw. Pushing through the ferns that hung down into the water, the bright sunshine hurt their eyes as they allowed the current take them downstream, steering as close to the shore as they could. A bank of gravel lay ahead. Kohana gave a quiet call, in case Orlando and Odessa were nearby.

Once Kehi had vanished out of sight into the tunnels of the old mine, Oren, Orlando and Odessa flew back to the safety of the tree branches.

"Hopefully this is the last we will see of scenes like this." Orlando commented to Odessa and Oren as they watched the fierce battle below.

"How?" Oren was puzzled. "These Kiwis have been behaving like this, ever since they have been in this area."

"If Kohana survives her second swim for this morning, then big change will come. She is the new leader of the Kiwi Kingdom."

"She is? This means that our area will be in the Kiwi Kingdom! I must tell everyone the good news!"

While Oren flew to tell his community of the coming kingdom, Orlando and Odessa turned and flew to trees overlooking the river. They wanted to be nearby if Kohana needed help when she came out. Orlando knew Kohana was already tired after her first swim, and now she was being tested with another.

Orlando and Odessa were dozing at their perch, where some of the local owls had joined them; when a soft call made Odessa instantly alert. Kohana was out and she was calling them! Odessa opened her eyes and moved to peer down into the water, alerting Orlando as well. They could see both Kohana and Kehi in the water and they were hanging onto a Kiwi body. By now all the owls were awake.

"We are here." Odessa answered her. "Who have you got with you?"

"It is Kiyo. We are bringing her to the gravel bank so we can take her to a proper resting place."

Odessa looked at Orlando. "We will need a mat to carry her on. There is some flax near the gravel. All we need is a sharp stone." Orlando nodded as they flew down to the gravel, ignoring any danger that may be in the sky. The owls joined them, some keeping a sharp eye on the sky for any Hawks or Harriers than might be around, others watching out for Kohana and Kehi who could be seen approaching the gravel bank.

"Can we help?" Oren owl asked. "What are you looking for?"

"We are looking for a sharp stone so we can cut some flax."

"What are you doing with the flax?" Oren was fascinated.

"We are going to make a mat and rope so Kehi's mate can be moved easier on land. Ah! Here's one!"

Orlando picked out a small stone that had a sharp side on it with his beak and flew over to the flax where Odessa was already pulling at a flax leaf that would be suitable. Oren looked on as Orlando quickly separated the leaf from the bush by rubbing the sharp stone against the leaf. More leaves followed untill Kohana was sure they had enough leaves.

With the arrival of Kehi and Kohana with Kiyo, the owls went to the water's edge. Kehi and Kohana tried to pull her out with their bills, but she was too heavy. The owls used their beaks to get Kiyo out of the water, but they too could not move her any further.

"Have a rest with Kiyo." Orlando advised Kehi and Kohana. He could see she was now exhausted. "We have some flax that we will make into a mat and ropes."

Kohana give him a grateful smile.

Orlando and Odessa led the owls to the flax where they showed them how to hold and split the flax into both wide and narrow lengths, before plaiting it into a mat and some ropes.

"How did you learn this?" Oren wanted to know. No animal he knew had these skills.

"There was a book in our school library where we learnt it." Orlando looked at Oren's puzzled face with a smile.

"When the Kiwi Kingdom comes, we will start a school for all animals that want to attend and we will teach you how to read books where you will learn skills like this."

The owls dragged the mat and rope over to Kehi and Kohana who had recovered well from their journey in the mine shaft. The mat was placed next to Kiyo where she was rolled onto it and the ropes attached. Between Kehi, Kohana and the owls, Kiyo was pulled over the gravel to the bank, where they needed to make some stops during their climb up the hill.

At the top, they saw Khai and Kehi's supporters were standing around and looking into the mine shaft. Kehi gave a quiet call and they came rushing over to help with the ropes.

"You can have a rest now." Kohana thanked Oren and his owls. "Thank you for all your help."

Oren sent his owls for their sleep, but none were inclined to leave. They went to sit in the surrounding trees, but had no intention of sleeping while interesting things were still going on.

Kehi noticed there was no sign of Kura, Kainan or their supporters.

"Where are they?" Kehi asked Khai.

"They won't be giving anyone any more trouble." was Khai's response. He looked at Kiyo on the mat. "You have a place in mind for her?"

Kehi looked perplexed. He hadn't thought about where he wanted Kiyo to be. Kohana saw his worry and made a suggestion.

"Do you have a special place where you and Kiyo liked to be, or even a place where Kiyo liked to be?"

Kehi gave Kohana's suggestion a little thought then gave a little smile.

"I know just the place. It isn't too far."

Under a giant Pohutukawa tree which had a nice view of the river, they dug a deep hole before wrapping Kiyo up in the mat with the rope and lowered her into it. Once the ground was covered again, Kohana shredded some of the ferns that had been removed and scattered them over the disturbed soil.

"What are you doing?" Kehi asked with some puzzlement.

"I am helping the ferns to grow again."

"We have just learnt something else here, today." Was Oren's comment to his followers, sitting in the tree. It wasn't until much later, when the Kiwis finally departed to their burrows that the Owls also retired to their sleeping spots.

CHAPTER EIGHT

NEW BEGINNINGS IN THE BULLER

Kehi knew that both Kohana and his supporters were ready for their sleep after such a tiring morning, but he knew he had to take advantage of the power that he had regained, and establish both his and Kohana's authority on this area. As Kehi's supporters were about to leave for their burrows, he made an announcement.

"I know everyone is ready for sleep, but it is urgent that we have a meeting of everyone, including our partners, and most important of all, any supporters of Kura and Kainan that didn't come this morning. There was a small silence, before there were nods of agreement. Khai answered for them all.

"You are right, of course. We will make sure that everyone is there."

Kehi took Kohana to a small valley where the community had any meetings. The forest formed a canopy overhead that gave protection from any flying predators that might be about. Orlando, Odessa and the local owls came too, and settled themselves in the surrounding tree branches.

In a short while a large number of Kiwis came to sit on the slopes, wondering who this young female was with Kehi. Her swim in the river had made her pale grey fur look almost white, making Kohana's appearance more striking than it usually was.

The absence of Kura and her supporters told them that change had come. Kohana felt sorry for a bunch of cowering females and their children who, after being forced into the area huddled together in fear. She knew they were the mates of those who had supported Kura.

I will put a stop to this violence and fear! Was Kohana's thought, as she saw them cringe. Her determined look was interpreted by some that they had another Kura amongst them!

"Thank you all for coming." Kehi began. I introduce to you Kohana, who is the leader of the Kiwi Kingdom. She has done me the honour of agreeing to be my mate." There were gasps at this news. "Kohana has come to bring the Kiwi Kingdom to our area. It is the last area on this Island to become part of her Kingdom."

For those who aren't aware, Kura and her supporters have been sent to their ancestors. We have found Kiyo and she is now at rest in one of her favourite places. Before we decide on the future of these families who supported Kura, Kohana will tell you what the Kiwi Kingdom will mean to your lives."

Kohana looked around to give everyone a smile.

"First of all," Kohana announced, "there is to be no more killing!" there was steel in her voice as she said it, which made everyone sit up and take notice.

Kehi and Khai will still be your community leaders as they are now. I have the welfare of all the other Kiwi communities throughout this island to consider as well as yours which will keep me busy. In all the other Kiwi Kingdom communities, other animals are involved, as they will be here. During my journey to your community I was protected by Orlando and Odessa." Kohana turned to them in the tree. "Will you both please join us?" The crowd gasped as a pair of morepork owls came to land next to Kohana. Kohana gave Odessa a gentle touch with her claw and gave her a fond smile. "Odessa's family at Lake Kaniere are the guardians of our kingdom. I say "our" because you all are now part of it. When we are away or the Kingdom leader dies, our guardians run the kingdom and keep the rules untill a new leader is chosen."

"Speaking of rules, there are a few, which may take a little of adjusting to."

There were murmurings and raised eyebrows at this advice.

"The first is, *Respect and help all animals regardless of who or what they are.*"

"The Second is, *"You may not injure or kill any animal you meet in the kingdom."*"

"The Third is, *"Establish a school for your Kiwis and other animals to learn to live in harmony together."*"

"If any Kiwis would like to help with teaching at the school, please let me know. I will get Orlando and Odessa to help set up the school. Parents are encouraged to attend with their children to see how it operates and what is taught there.

The Kiwi Kingdom will make this area a safe area for everyone who live here and for others to visit or even join us to live, including Kehi's family. You all know of Koro who had to be sent to The Kiwi Kingdom for his own safety. Kehi and Kiyo also have three other children, Kerewa, Koa and Kiana who had to be hidden till now."

Kohana then turned her attention to the families of Kura's supporters. They had already heard that there was to be no more killings and the sympathetic look she gave them, made them realise they no longer had to fear that they would be sent to their ancestors.

"I am sorry you no longer have your partners," she looked at the children "or your fathers, but they chose to go with Kura and Kainan. It is not for me to decide whether you remain with this community, but if you do, we will expect you to live in peace and abide by the Kiwi Kingdom rules. If you are sent away, you will have to establish a new community on your own over in the Alps to the east of us."

Kohana then turned to Kehi with a smile, "I will leave you to make your decision." before moving to stand aside with Orlando and Odessa.

Thank you both," Kohana said quietly, "for everything you have done for me. I know I would never have made it here, without you. You don't have to protect me as closely now as you did, for I have Kehi to protect me now.

"If you wish, you can join your friends back in the trees. I will see you sometime tonight."

"We will just check where your burrow is, before we sleep ourselves." Orlando replied, before he led Odessa back into the branches of the tree where Oren and his mate were waiting for them.

As the meeting continued, one of the Kiwis stood up with a question.

"What if we don't want the Kiwi Kingdom here?"

"Those who don't want to live in the Kiwi Kingdom will be sent to the Alps to the East." Kehi replied firmly. "The only reason the Kiwi Kingdom has not been introduced here before now, is that Kura and Kainan made it clear that I and my family would be killed if I did."

Kehi then turned to the females awaiting their fate.

"If you are allowed to stay, are you prepared to live in peace with us and live by the Kiwi Kingdom rules?"

They all nodded vigorously, for none of them relished the prospect of being sent to a strange place. With no males around for protection and the production of more children, their community wouldn't be viable for long.

"What if they don't live by the Kingdom rules?" asked someone else.

"If anyone, whether it is any of these females and their children, or anyone else, doesn't live by the rules," Kehi replied, they will be expelled."

"Is it so hard to respect and help all animals, or not to injure or kill any animals?" Kehi asked in exasperation. "That is the main thing being asked of you all."

"What if some animal attacks us?" was also asked.

"Then, of course you do what is necessary to defend yourself."

He allowed a silence for a minute or so for everyone to consider this.

"We will have a vote." Kehi announced. "Those who insist these females leave, please stand up."

Everyone stayed seated.

"Who prefers to live outside of the Kiwi Kingdom?"

Everyone stayed seated.

"Good! We will have another meeting when the school is established, to let you know where and when it is held. Are there any more questions?" Everyone remained silent.

"It is time to go home."

With that Kehi turned to Kohana and led everyone out of the valley and to their burrows. Kohana noticed that there were plenty of other burrows nearby when Kehi showed her the entrance to her new home.

"Kiyo must have enjoyed having close neighbours." Kohana remarked as she entered the burrow, which looked similar to her parent's one.

"Kiyo hasn't been here." Kehi replied. "I moved here after she disappeared. It wasn't safe for me to stay in that burrow. I was surrounded by enemies. You don't know what a relief it is to have them gone."

"This is a new beginning for you too, then?" Kohana asked, as she plumped up the dry grass for them to sleep on, before settling herself down on it with a happy sigh. Kehi came and snuggled down next to Kohana. He noticed that she had a completely different smell to Kiyo, which was a relief. Kehi didn't want to be reminded of what he had lost.

"Yes," Kehi replied. It is a new beginning for me too."

At Kanoa's community in the Paparoa Range, humans had come to check the boxes that had been left near their burrows. Members of the community had heard loud noises after some animals had been caught. Kanoa risked a peek as the human opened a box grabbed the stoat and stuffed it into a sealed bag. The human then put some food into the trap before leaving to check other boxes. Kanoa was happy to see the Stoat be taken away, for it had been responsible for the death of many of their chicks. Other Kiwis reported that Possums, Weasels and stoats had been taken away from other boxes. As none of them ever returned; Kanoa realised humans were here to help them. He must get word to Ollie!

CHAPTER NINE

THE NEW SCHOOL

Orlando asked Oren if he knew of any caves near the kiwi burrows.

"What would you want them for?" Oren asked. "There aren't any perching spots in them."

"No." Orlando agreed, "But they do make a good place to set up a school."

"I will show you after we have fed this evening."

Even though it was shorter than usual, Orlando and Odessa had their best sleep since their adventure had begun. When they awoke, the moon was lighting the night sky and all the other owls in the community had already set off to find their first feed. Kiwi calls could be heard in the distance. Relishing their free time together, Orlando and Odessa set off to explore the forest, feeding as they went. In a valley, Odessa spotted some familiar twinkling lights and called Orlando.

"Look what I've found!"

Orlando followed Odessa towards the lights and the shape of a cave entrance was revealed. Landing on the floor, Orlando and Odessa wandered inside marvelling at all the glow worms inside. Odessa couldn't help herself, and she called out to them

"Hello Glow worms! We are Orlando and Odessa. We have glow worms like you in our community at home."

Most of the glow worms put their lights out at the noise Odessa made, except one, who answered her.

"Hello Orlando and Odessa. I am Giana. What brings you here?"

"We are looking for a place like this to use for a school." Odessa explained. "We would be teaching other animals such as Kiwis to read and learn about the world we all live in."

"Can we join in?" Giana asked.

"Yes, of course!" Odessa agreed.

The other glow worms gradually put their lights back on. They realised that change was coming to their cave. More noise and light would be part of it, but to learn about the outside world would be worth it. Orlando and Odessa walked further into the cave, noticing it was a big space, which was dry and had many rocks for sitting on. They agreed this would be an ideal place. They just had to let Oren and Kohana know.

As they said their goodbyes to Giana and the glow worms, a shadow came over the entrance. It was Oren. He came to land next to them.

"You have found the cave." Oren smiled at them. "What do you think of it?"

"We think it will be ideal." Odessa replied. "We have already spoken to Giana about it, and they are agreeable to us using it."

"Who is Giana?" Oren wanted to know.

"Giana is the leader of the glow worms." Odessa explained. "It is their home, after all. It is only right that we get their acceptance. They will be joining in the classes too."

"Giana," Odessa introduced her to Oren. "This is Oren, the local leader of our Owls. They will be joining in the classes too."

"Hello Oren." Giana spoke to him." "How many leaders do you have?"

"We have many leaders for our communities on this Island." Oren advised her.

"What is this Island?" Giana asked. For the glow worms had no knowledge of what lay outside their cave."

"That is something you will learn in the classes." Odessa advised her.

"We will look forward to it." Giana said as she farewelled them.

"We just have to tell Kohana that we have found a place for her school." Orlando advised Oren.

"That's good." Oren replied. "I heard her calling you and was told you were here."

As Oren led Orlando and Odessa through the forest, he couldn't help thinking how much the lives of his group had changed in the short time that Orlando and Odessa had been here. Learning new skills and interacting with other animals is something that owls in their area had never done before. Seeing Kohana's familiar pale shape below, as she moved through the forest, Orlando and Odessa landed on the floor in front of her. Oren stayed on a nearby branch. He still didn't feel comfortable being down on the ground.

"Hello Orlando and Odessa," Kohana smiled. "Have you settled in well?"

"Yes, we have." Orlando reassured her. "We have also found your school cave!" as Kohana brightened at this news, "Guess what we found in there?"

Kohana shook her head, wondering what it may be.

"There is a colony of glow worms! Just like the Kaniere cave. Their leader, Giana is happy to have a school there."

"We will have to contact Ollie and get some books sent up here, unless we can get some from Westport?" Odessa asked Kohana.

"I'm not sure we can get books from Ollie now that the deer have moved from Kaniere." Orlando countered. "Westport may be our best way of getting them." He turned to Oren. "Oren, are there any large animals such as deer or chamois living in this forest?"

"What do they look like?" Oren wanted to know.

"Deer are tall animals that walk or run on four long legs, have a large brown body, with a long neck and have pointy ears. The males have antlers that look like tree branches on the top of their heads." Orlando explained. "Chamois are smaller with a dark body, a white neck and face, with a dark stripe on their face, and have two antlers on their head that point behind them."

Oren thought for a minute, before answering.

"I think we have some deer here, but I don't think I have seen any of the Chamois."

"Good." Orlando was relieved to hear this news. "We need to make friends with them."

At Oren's astonished look, Orlando explained. "Deer were part of the Kiwi Kingdom at Kaniere, and they used to give our Kiwis a ride when they had a long journey, or help us carry something that was too heavy. We will need the deer to carry any books that we find at Westport for the school."

Kohana's eyes were shining. "I think we have a plan. If we can make friends with the deer; then go looking for the books we need."

"We also need to think of what lessons we can give before we have our books," Odessa reminded them. "Just in case it takes some time to get them. The community may lose interest in the idea if we take a long time to get organised."

"You are right of course!" Kohana exclaimed. Ideas for lessons were put forward between them, untill Kohana was satisfied that they had the basics to start the school.

As they were talking, Kehi arrived after wondered what Kohana was up to.

"We are organising the school." Kohana explained happily.

"So soon?" Kehi was amazed.

"We have found a suitable cave to hold it in." Orlando informed Kehi. "Would you like to see it?"

"Of course we would." Kehi replied, seeing Kohana's bright eyes at the prospect of her new scheme.

As Orlando and Odessa led Kehi and Kohana through the forest to the cave, Oren flew back to the cave to tell Giana that they were getting some Kiwi visitors to see the place where the school was being held. Other kiwis that saw the little procession came to see what was happening. Once word got around, a large crowd gathered at the cave.

As they walked to the cave, Odessa managed to get a moment alone with Kohana.

"Are you settling in well too?" Odessa asked.

"Kehi is very kind. We are getting on well together."

At the cave they found Oren and the glow worms were having a discussion about the subjects that were being taught.

"We are sorry to disturb you again so soon," Odessa apologised to Giana. "but our Kiwi community are keen to see where we are having the school."

"We are happy to have visitors." Giana replied. "Please bring them in."

Orlando introduced Kehi and Kohana to the Glow worms.

"This is Kehi, the leader of the local kiwi community and his mate, Kohana who is the leader of the Kiwi Kingdom, which now is in nearly all kiwi communities on this Island."

"Kohana, does this mean you rule the whole Island?" Giana was astonished. Glow worms had leaders for their communities, but not one that ruled all of their communities.

"It does." Kohana replied with a smile.

"Can we talk about your role some more, later?" Giana asked

"Of course. I will look forward to it." Kohana replied, before turning to the crowd.

"Please come in everyone and have a good look around. If you have any comments, questions or suggestions, feel free to say what is on your mind."

Much later after fielding many questions on what would be taught and how they would teach the subjects, most of the Kiwi community left, though a few that were interested in helping at the school stayed behind to learn what they could do.

Before they all parted later in the night, Orlando promised to look for some flat stones to write on and look for some chalky stones to write with. Oren promised to keep a look out for the deer he had seen and Odessa was to look for any small fallen logs or bungies to use as shelving and also arrange for some more flax to be cut and brought to the cave. It was to be made into mats for the cave floor and bags for carrying the books.

Before they went to sleep in the morning, Odessa spoke to Oren.

"Is it possible to get word to the Owls at Three Sisters Mountain community that Kohana has arrived safely; she is now the mate of Kehi the leader and that the Kiwi Kingdom has now been introduced to the Buller?"

"I will see to it." Oren said with a smile.

A couple of nights later Kalasia Kiwi was taking her class at Three Sisters Mountain Community when Odion, the leader of the local owls flew in with Odessa's news.

"We need to let Kapali Kalea and Koro know." Kalasia told him. "Can you find them for me? Also can word be sent on to Ollie at Lake Kaniere? He will need to know as well."

When Odion owl left, the lesson was abandoned as the children peppered Kalasia with questions about the news.

"Could she show them where the Buller was again?"

"Would the Kingdom be ruled from the Buller now?"

"Would they be able to visit or live in the Buller now too?"

"Would Kalea and Koro and their family be going to the Buller now?"

"Would they be getting a visit from Kohana and Kehi?

As Kalasia was trying to answer some of these questions, Odion owl returned with Kapali, Koro and Kalea.

"What is the news of Kohana?" Kapali asked with a worried look. They had all expected the worst when she had disappeared without telling them of her intentions.

"You won't believe it, but she has arrived safely. Also," Here Kalasia hesitated because of the impact it would have on Koro. She looked at him with sympathy in her eyes, "Kohana is now Kehi's mate; and the Kiwi Kingdom has been introduced to the Buller."

Everyone was silent for a minute as they considered the implications of this news.

Kalea was the first to speak as she gave Koro a cuddle.

"This can only mean that your mother is gone. You will want to find out what happened?"

"I will, but we will have to make sure it is safe there now. I will never forget the fear that Mum and Dad lived with while I was there."

Koro looked at Kalea with concern, wondering how she felt, with her daughter now with a male (his father) who was much older than her – the opposite of their own relationship. Kalea read his thoughts and smiled.

"Our relationship isn't exactly "Traditional", but we are happy together. My only concern is that they both are happy in their relationship too."

"If the Kiwi Kingdom has been introduced," Kapali was thoughtful, "It should be safe to come from or go there now. Someone from here needs to go there to find out how safe the area is. I will send one of our owls up there and talk to Orlando and Odessa."

Kalea then offered a suggestion.

"Perhaps if we send a message to Kohana, giving our congratulations and ask if she wants or needs anything? We may get an idea of how she really is."

Kapali turned to Odion.

"Can you go up to the Buller and speak to Orlando and Odessa and find out what has happened there and get a message to Kohana?"

"I will." Odion agreed, before flying into the night. Before he left for the Buller, he farewelled his mate Oana, who had three Owlettes to care for on her own while he was away.

"I will be back as soon as I can." Odion promised her. "Hopefully I will only be away for a few nights. I have asked the others to help you feed our chicks while I'm gone."

Oana gave him a grateful smile as she fed the three hungry mouths in the nest.

As Odion flew north, news of his coming was already being sent ahead of him.

"That didn't take long." Oren commented to Orlando as they prepared to sleep in the morning. At Orlando's enquiring look, he explained. "Odion the leader from Three Sisters Mountain is on his way."

CHAPTER TEN

THE NEW ARRIVALS

The night was dark when Kohana and Kehi awoke and moved out of their burrow for a feed. She looked up at the starry sky with wonder. It had been a month since she had arrived and so much had happened in that time, including the new life that she could feel forming inside.

Kohana thought of her arrival here where she had to confront and defeat Kura; resulting in her being pushed into the old mine shaft. Being rescued by Kehi and becoming his mate. The community change to Kiwi Kingdom rules and the opening of the school which had also been successful.

A visit by Odion owl from the Three Sisters Mountain had resulted in a promise to send them some books from their library. The arrival of the books would take pressure off the need to find them locally. Charmaine and Charlotte the chamois had volunteered to bring them to the Buller. Kohana didn't know that Charmaine and Charlotte were bringing some visitors with them.

The making of new friends among the animals here also made Kohana smile. The native wekas, pigeons, tuis, bellbirds, fantails and silvereyes were all now sleeping, but the deer family standing quietly among the trees as she passed, always had one pair of ears or eyes alert for changes around them.

Kohana remembered how cautious the deer were to joining the Kiwi Kingdom, for at first they could see no benefit to having contact with other animals. However when Kohana advised them that if any of the animals saw humans with guns in the forest; they would come and warn them so they could run away. The deer then agreed to be part of the community.

"Hello Syd and Daphne" Kohana called softly.

"Hello Kohana." Daphne replied. "Is all well in the community?" Daphne's enquiring tone alerted Kohana that there could be a problem.

"I think so." Kohana replied. "What is concerning you Daphne?"

"We have seen a group of three kiwis that we haven't seen before sneaking around and hiding behind trees. One was an adult. The other two were younger."

"Where did you see them Daphne?"

"We saw them in the next valley." Daphne turned her head towards where she saw them last.

"Thank you Daphne."

Kehi had seen Kohana stop to chat with the deer, so he went on ahead of her, expecting to see Kohana when she had finished. It was a little while before he realised that Kohana wasn't coming and decided to have a chat with the deer to see what had delayed her.

Kohana steadily made her way through the forest, stopping occasionally to feed, her senses heightened for any movements or noises around her. She drew comfort from the fact that Orlando and Odessa were in the treetops above shadowing her. They had obviously seen or heard her conversation with the deer and decided to come along. Near the next valley a giant Totara tree stood. As Kohana came closer she stopped. She could sense that the kiwis were here.

Near Lake Jewell in the far north Kamora kiwi was feeling anxious. Had she done the wrong thing in sending the children to see why Kiyo had not come this breeding season? She had intended sending only Kerewa, but Koa had insisted on going to protect him and Kiana refused to stay on her own. Kamora was hoping that she hadn't sent them into trouble. Kamora had given them strict instructions that they had to be extra careful and to come back if they could not find Kiyo.

Kerewa knew they weren't far from their mother's community now, for they could hear the big river that their mother had told them about. Up to now they hadn't seen any kiwis in this area, but the sound of footsteps had sent them hiding behind the Totara tree. They noticed a pair of Morepork owls come to sit in the branches and look at them.

There was a small silence then they heard a loud clear female voice call to them.

"Who is there? Please come out!"

There was silence as Kerewa, Koa and Kiana looked at each other in fear, not knowing what to do. It was obvious that they had been discovered.

"I am Kohana, the leader of the Kiwi Kingdom. You are safe here." The female voice called to them again.

The Kiwi Kingdom! Kiana's face showed her amazement. Before Kerewa or Koa could stop her, Kiana swiftly stepped out from behind the tree to face the pale grey female who stood before her.

"We are looking for our mother Kiyo. Can you take us to her?" Kiana asked.

"You must be Kiana." Kohana said. "Welcome home. Are Kerewa and Koa with you?"

Kiana turned to the tree as Kerewa and Koa came out.

"How do you know our names?" Kerewa asked with a worried frown. Their existence was supposed to be secret here.

"Your father told me." Kohana said simply. Just then, they could hear a male call in the distance. Kohana answered him. To the children's amazement, she then looked up at the owls to instruct them.

"Orlando, Odessa, will you please show Kehi where we are? Tell him that his children are here."

At that the owls flew off into the forest.

"Have you had a feed yet?" Kohana asked them.

"Not yet," Kerewa admitted. "We were more concerned at finding our mother. We know she couldn't be far away from here." As he spoke about his mother, Kerewa noticed that Kohana's eyes had a sad look, and knew immediately that something had happened to her.

"Your father has much to tell you when he comes. Perhaps it would be good to eat something while you are waiting for him?"

The sympathy in Kohana's eyes confirmed to Kerewa that their journey to see their mother had been in vain. As Koa and Kiana set off together to feed in the immediate area Kerewa stayed by Kohana.

"You aren't hungry?" Kohana asked quietly

"No. I will feed later." Kerewa looked at Kohana. "She's gone, isn't she?"

"Yes." There was a little pause. "Your father will take you to where she is resting so you can say goodbye to her."

"Do you know, did you see, what happened?" Kerewa asked as he felt anger rising in himself.

"I didn't arrive untill after it happened, but your father's friend Khai told me about it. All I can say is that the kiwis that did it have been sent to their ancestors. This area has joined the rest of the Island and is part of the Kiwi Kingdom now. Do you know about the Kiwi Kingdom in your area?"

"We have been brought up on it." Kerewa managed to smile. He then looked at Kohana with interest. "You say you are the Kiwi Kingdom leader; do you know about the first leader Keoni?"

It was Kohana's turn to smile.

"I should do. He is my great grandfather!"

"You will have to come up to our area soon." Kerewa answered with a big grin. "There is someone there you should meet."

Just then the sound of running footsteps and Orlando and Odessa's landing in the nearby tree heralded Kehi's arrival.

Koa and Kiana came back to stand by Kerewa as Kehi came up to them.

"At last!" Kehi said as he gave Kiana, then Koa and Kerewa a big hug. "I'm sorry your mother isn't here too."

"When will we see her?" Kiana asked anxiously. Kehi drew her to him to give her the news they hoped they wouldn't hear.

"Your mother is with our ancestors now. That is why she didn't come up this year."

Kohana saw Koa's face crumble and went to cuddle him and Kerewa. Much later after the new arrivals had been to say goodbye to their mother, they were taken to the school cave where a class was being held. A mix of both adults and children of Kiwis, Owls, Possums, Stoats and Bats were present.

"Do you have a school in your area?" Kohana asked Kerewa. Kerewa shook his head.

"Are any of you interested in joining in?" Kohana asked.

"I do!" Kiana and Koa said together.

"I would like to, but I need to get back to tell Mum's family what happened." Kerewa explained. I know they will be worried. Would you like to come with me?" Kerewa offered to Kohana.

"I would like to come, but it would have to be after the breeding season." Kohana replied, looking at Kehi. "I am Kehi's mate now, and your new brother or sister's egg will be laid soon. Perhaps when they are hatched and big enough to travel I can bring them up then?"

Kerewa didn't show it, but he was annoyed his father had beaten him to being Kohana's mate.

"Out of interest," Kerewa asked Kehi casually, "Are there any available females here that might like to live in the north?"

Kehi gave a little smile before he replied, as he knew that there were both eyes and ears watching and listening.

"I know there are some; in fact I'm sure that someone will want to come back with you."

63

"You will want to know about sleeping arrangements." Kehi advised them. "There is plenty of room in our burrow for all of you, but the burrow I shared with your mother is available if you want, and it would be your burrow if and when you stay."

"Come and look at our burrow, anyway." Kohana added. "You will need to know where we are if you decide to stay in the other burrow."

Their walk to the burrows took much longer than expected as everyone who saw them came over to say hello, including some of the females who had recently lost their mates. The fact that an available male had arrived, immediately sparked much interest.

After checking Kehi and Kohana's burrow, which Kehi had already lined with ferns, ready for the new arrival, they set off for his old burrow. As they went, Khai came running up.

"Kehi, Kohana! You have got some more visitors! They have brought some large animals with them!"

"The animals will be Chamois that have brought some books for our school library from Three Sisters Mountain." Kohana explained to the children as they all followed Khai through the forest.

As they came to the chamois standing near the river bank, their backs laden with saddle bags full of books, Kohana spotted some familiar faces.

"Mum! Koro! Kapali! Ollie!" Kohana cried as she rushed to give them a hug, except Ollie who hopped up to a branch near Orlando and Odessa, only to be mobbed by the local owls who had also been keeping an eye on Kehi"s family since they had arrived.

"Thank you so much Charlotte and Charmaine," Kohana went over to give them a hug too. "for bringing these books up here for us. You must be ready for a rest now."

"We will do soon." Charmaine replied. "Is your school nearby so we can deliver these books?"

"It is about 10 minutes' walk from here." Kohana informed them. "Can you make it that far?"

"Lead the way." Charmaine said.

Before they set out, Koro and Kalea were introduced to Kerewa, Koa and Kiana. Seeing it would be sleep time soon, Kapali and Kohana took the chamois to the school cave while Kehi took Koro Kalea and the children to the burrow he had shared with Kiyo.

"Are you enjoying your life up here?" Kapali asked as they led the chamois through the forest.

"I am." Kohana confirmed. "We have been very busy with establishing the school and also we will be adding to the family this season. I am glad Ollie is here, as I wanted to find out how our other communities are managing."

"How are you managing this community?" Kapali wanted to know. He didn't mention it, but the Kohana that greeted them today was completely different to the one that left Three Sisters Mountain.

"I'm not." Kohana's reply was firm. "Kehi was the local leader when I came and after the Kiwi Kingdom rules were established, I made it clear that Kehi was still in charge as I would be busy with issues from all the other communities we have."

"That is very wise." Kapali approved. "Ollie was wondering whether you were ready to hear about Kiwi Kingdom issues."

"I am." Kohana confirmed. "How is the community at Three Sisters?"

"Not much has changed since you left, except that a certain book is now on plain view in the library."

Kohana gave a little smile. "On Ollie's instruction no doubt."

"Yes," Kapali confirmed. "There is to be no more sneaked reading of it."

In the school cave, the chamois were glad to sit down while the heavy loads they had been carrying were removed and willing claws moved their precious cargo to the shelves which had been built for them. Giana and the Glow worms watched with much interest as the new additions to the school were brought in. They were also intrigued with these new creatures that they hadn't seen before, which Kohana introduced to them.

"Giana, please meet Charlotte and Charmaine Chamois. They are part of the community at Three Sisters Mountain. They also help at the school there."

"Welcome to the Buller." Giana said to Charlotte and Charmaine. "Thank you for bringing the books to us. We are looking forward to seeing them."

"You have a nice home in this cave." Charlotte replied. "You don't find it is too noisy with the school here?"

"Yes, it is noisy, but we have learnt so much already, we don't mind."

After they had said their goodbyes, Charlotte asked Kohana whether there were any Chamois near here.

"No. But there is a deer family here which is part of our community. Do you want to meet them?"

"Yes, we would like to hear what it is like to live here." Charlotte replied. "We will be returning to Three Sisters Tomorrow though."

"So soon?" Kohana asked.

"Yes," Charlotte replied. "It will be our breeding season soon. We promised our mates that we would be back for it."

"I understand." Kohana replied. "We are in the middle of our breeding season here too."

As Kehi came to the entrance of his old burrow he hesitated, this was the first time he had been back since Kiyo disappeared.

Koro pushed inside, followed by Kalea, Kerewa Koa and Kiana. Koro grinned with delight. As he explored, it was the same place he had left. Kehi reluctantly sidled in. Kerewa knew immediately why Kehi didn't want to be in here. He could feel the different atmosphere from the comfortable place he now lived in.

"This is completely different to the burrow you have now." Kerewa commented to Kehi. "What was it like to live here?"

"It was terrible." Kehi admitted. "We were surrounded by enemies. Many of the walls here are very thin, so our neighbours could hear almost everything we said." Kehi took Kerewa to a far wall to scratch it. As Kehi scratched, a hole began to form. "We never knew whether we would wake up from our sleep. It is the reason I sent Kiyo away every breeding season. I hated not knowing you, but I knew that neither Kiyo nor any of you would have survived."

Wordlessly, Kerewa gave his father a big hug.

"It is all over now. If you don't mind though, I would prefer to share your burrow. I don't feel comfortable in here either."

It was then arranged. Koro and Kalea stayed at the old family burrow while Kapali, Kerewa Koa and Kiana stayed with Kohana and Kehi.

When Charlotte and Charmaine left the Buller the next evening Kapali went with them, for he had duties to get back to at Three Sisters Mountain. He had spoken to Ollie and reassured him that Kohana had matured since she had come here and was ready for her role as the kingdom leader.

Syd and Daphne came to farewell the chamois. The deer had been fascinated by their tales of meeting Kupe Kiwi and their involvement with the Kiwi Kingdom by teaching at the Three Sisters Mountain School and giving the kiwis rides between the communities. There was a happy meeting too when Koro and Kalea rose to find Kehi Kohana and the children waiting to take them for a feed together. Kehi and all his children caught up on what they had been doing with their lives and their plans for the future, while Kalea and Kohana were able to put behind them the fraught relationship that they had when she had left home.

"How long are you able to stay?" Kohana asked as there were many questions she wanted to ask, especially when it came to bearing and raising children.

"We will head back after you have delivered your egg." Kalea advised her. "I remember how anxious I felt when I delivered Kamaka, but I had so much support from your Aunt Keely it wasn't as difficult as I thought it would be."

A week later Kerewa left for home. He had a partner with him as Kehi had predicted, though it wasn't one of the new widows. Her name was Katana. Kohana had promised to bring Koa and Kiana with her when his new brother or sister was big enough to travel.

One moonless night Kohana knew it was time to deliver her egg. Kehi immediately fetched Kalea who came to sit with her.

"We will be with Khai." Kehi said as he went outside where Koro was waiting for him.

After they left, some of the local females who already had borne chicks came in to keep them company and offer encouragement. After much effort, a large white egg lay on the fern bed waiting for it. Kohana was tired after her struggle to produce the egg and snuggled down for a sleep. She was also starving hungry too, but that would have to wait till Kehi came to relieve her from keeping the latest member of the family warm.

CHAPTER ELEVEN

OLLIE'S VISIT

When Ollie Owl received word that Kohana had successfully reached the Buller, introduced Kiwi Kingdom rules and was Kehi's mate, he could hardly believe his ears; especially when he thought of the petulant and completely inexperienced kiwi that he had given to the care of Orlando and Odessa. Also, what had happened to make the Buller a safe place for Kohana to introduce the Kiwi Kingdom? He had to go and see for himself, just what sort of leader she had become and whether she was ready yet for the role she was destined for.

On this mission, Ollie chose to visit Three Sisters Mountain first, to see what information they had on the situation in the Buller. He was surprised to find that books were being sorted and saddlebags being made for the chamois to carry them. Kalasia Kiwi and Charmaine Chamois were supervising the activities when Ollie arrived.

"Hello Ollie." Kalasia gave him a beaming smile. "I take it you are on your way to the Buller?"

"I am." Ollie confirmed.

"Kohana has requested we send some books for the Buller School that she has started. As you can see, we are sorting them for her. Kapali, Koro and Kalea are accompanying the Chamois up there. Would you like to join them, or is your journey more urgent?"

"That's a good idea." Ollie agreed. "I came to see if you had any information on how safe it is to travel there."

"I believe it is." Kalasia replied. "Odion made a trip up there as soon as we received word from the Buller Owls. He has much to tell you."

"You can be very proud of Orlando and Odessa." Odion greeted Ollie, when Ollie found him. "They not only cared for Kohana on her journey, but helped her to become a brave, courageous and effective leader."

"How?" Ollie was intrigued.

"They treated her as an adult." Odion replied. "No-one had done that before, and she both appreciated and responded to that. They were able to negotiate with her how much independence she had, though also reminding her that as a leader she needed protection."

"She was able to accept that?" Ollie asked amazed.

"They told her that most animals and even human leaders have someone to protect them, because they never know when danger will come. On the journey up to the Buller, they had to come to Kohana's aid when a large possum attacked her."

"Was she badly hurt?" Ollie was alarmed at this news

"No. She did have some injuries. They got Kohana to bathe in the river, and made sure they were healed before moving on to the Buller. The main thing that saved her was that Orlando and Odessa had already advised her that she had to be able to defend herself."

"She has never had to ever think about that." Ollie commented, thinking of how protected Kohana had been in her previous life.

"Exactly!" Odion emphasised. "They advised her that in places outside the Kiwi Kingdom, leaders are usually male and have to fight for their position. Orlando also put it to Kohana that if she could neither fight nor defend herself, she had to learn. Orlando and Odessa were feeding when they heard a scuffle and found Kohana already battling the Possum. She did need their help to defeat it though. They also helped her to learn to swim so she could cross the large river to reach the Buller area. It came in handy when Kohana got there and Kura pushed her into an old mine shaft that was full of water!"

"What?" Ollie could hardly believe his ears!

"Yes!" The gleam in Odion's eyes told Ollie that an incredible tale was about to be told. "Kohana had a plan to arrive when everyone was asleep, but it turned out that all of the community males were there, including Kehi. Kura had killed Kehi's mate a couple of nights before and they were about to confront Kura when Kohana turned up. Kohana had to defend herself against Kura and won, but ended up in the mine shaft. Kehi went in after her and they came out together with the body of Kehi's mate. By then she had agreed to be his mate! While they were in the mine shaft Orlando and Odessa saw an awful battle where all Kura's supporters were killed. It was the last killing there, because after they buried Kehi's mate they went on to have a meeting of the whole community where Kohana was introduced and the Kiwi Kingdom rules were brought in."

"They did it willingly?" Ollie found it difficult to believe.

"It was made clear that anyone who wouldn't live by the new rules would have to leave and live in the Alps. They took a vote on it and everyone agreed."

"They accept Kohana as their leader?" Ollie couldn't help being doubtful.

"She has insisted that Kehi is still their community leader."

"I'm going to find this visit very interesting." Ollie said finally. "She certainly hasn't wasted any time since she has been there, getting a school established already. I'm wondering what else I will find when we get there."

"Hopefully a Kingdom leader ready for her duties." Odion replied, knowing the problems that Ollie had been coping with in the kingdom.

When it came time to cross the Buller River, they crossed at the bridge, bringing back memories for Koro. The last time he crossed it, he had to sneak over. Koro then led the way to the community. It felt strange, being able to walk and talk freely, without worrying about who could see and hear what you were doing and saying. When they came near the community, Koro spotted Khai foraging among the trees.

"Khai! Is that you?" Koro called.

"It is. Who are you?"

At first Khai didn't recognise Koro who was now more mature than the boyish Kiwi that had disappeared from the community. A female Kiwi who looked very similar to Kohana stood with this Kiwi. Khai was also amazed at the large animals that were quietly standing behind him, with laden bags on their backs. An Owl was with them too.

"It's Koro. Where is Dad?"

"I will go and get him." Khai replied with a grin. Their arrival would cause quite a stir in the community.

As Kehi and Kohana were reunited with Koro and Kalea, Ollie spotted Orlando and Odessa in the tree above and flew to join them, only to be mobbed by the local community of Owls.

"Welcome to the Buller Ollie." Oren grinned as Ollie was surrounded by Owls wanting to hear of his life at the lake.

"I run the school at Lake Kaniere; also my role as the guardian of the Kingdom has been to keep the kingdom rules while we have been waiting for a new leader to come." Ollie told them. "I have helped local leaders with any issues they couldn't deal with too. I am here to see if Kohana is ready to take over that role now that she is leader of the kingdom."

"Orlando and Odessa," Ollie turned to them. "The Kingdom owes you our thanks and gratitude. We had no idea you would be so successful. You not only protected Kohana on her journey, but taught her some wisdom of how to be a leader. You are now free to live your lives as you choose."

"Thank you Ollie" Odessa replied, "But I think we may still be needed in the future."

"You've been having more visions?" Ollie frowned.

"No," Odessa smiled. "Kohana is having Kehi's chick soon. She has promised to take her chick up to the north when she accompanies Kehi's children back home. If Kehi stays here, and we think he will, they will need protection."

"You think he will want to stay to protect his position?"

"Yes." Orlando confirmed. "Look what happened last time he left to visit the Kingdom. Some of the mates of those who opposed him are still living in the community."

"Hmm, I think you may be right." Ollie sighed.

"We also have to consider," Odessa added. "That Kohana may want to tour all the other communities as Kupe did when he became leader. Her kingdom is established, but she may want to see for herself how they are managing. If she does, Kohana will need us to protect her on that journey too."

"You are right of course." Ollie agreed. "Just make sure your role as her guardian doesn't come before your own needs."

"We have plenty of time yet before we need to settle and start our own family." Odessa said lightly, ignoring the yearning she was beginning to feel for Orlando.

When Orlando moved in next to her, Odessa couldn't help giving a little tremble. Hoping Orlando hadn't noticed it, she relaxed completely against his body. Something she hadn't done before.

"When do you think that will be?" Ollie asked with interest.

"We may be ready next breeding season."

"If things change you will need some help to keep Kohana protected."

"Members of our community are willing to help." Oren chipped in.

Before Kapali and the chamois departed the next evening, he had a chat with Ollie.

"You don't have to worry about whether Kohana is ready for her role." Kapali reassured him. "She has matured since she left home and she has arranged everything here so she can concentrate on her Kingdom duties."

"She will be going north with the children once their chick is hatched though." Ollie voiced his concern.

"Yes" Kapali agreed, "Apart from ensuring the children return home safely, she is using her visit for a fact-finding tour of whether the area is open to being part of the Kingdom. Kerewa told Kohana that they were brought up on the Kiwi Kingdom, but they don't have a school there."

"It looks like some more books will be needed." Ollie said with a smile.

"We have plenty more books we can send. The only restriction is the amount that the chamois can carry." Kapali reassured him.

Later that night Ollie went in search of Kohana. He found her feeding near Kehi.

"It is time for you to take on your leadership role. I have much to tell you."

"I'm ready." Kohana replied, leading Ollie to the Meeting area. Kehi followed too, but kept at a distance. He had already arranged with Kohana to keep guard while she had her talk to Ollie.

"Do you know all the communities in the kingdom and their species?" Ollie asked Kohana. She had to think for a minute before she answered.

"I know that southern brown Kiwis called Tokoeka live in the Fiordland area. Their leader is Kona. We have some Southern Brown Rowi in Okarito, near the lagoon. Their leader is Kedar. We also have our species which is Roa, inland at Okarito. Their leader is Keka." We have a Roa community at Arthurs pass. Their leader is Kane. Kanoa is the Roa leader in the Paparoa range. Kapali is our Roa leader at Three Sisters Mountain community. Kehi is the Roa leader here at Buller, Koha is the Roa leader of the North Buller community and Kaine is the leader of the Tasman community."

"Very good." Ollie was impressed. He noted she already knew the leaders of the northern kiwis that they hadn't had contact with yet. "There are changes to the locations of a couple of our communities. Did you know that the Arthurs Pass community has expanded into the valleys south of Arthurs Pass?" Kohana shook her head. "Also Keka and our Roa community from Okarito have now joined the Arthurs Pass Kiwis in the Arahura valley." Ollie could see Kohana's shock at this news.

"What happened to make the whole community move?"

"Keka and the community visited me on the way to their new home." Ollie informed her. "He told me that humans' flying machines to the glacier were too noisy for them to sleep, but the main reason is that the animals there are taking kiwi eggs or killing kiwi chicks before they were big enough to defend themselves. Keka did say they have tried to make friends with the animals and change their behaviour, but the animals aren't interested.

"How many chicks have Keka's community got left?"

"Only five were left last season, so they moved before they have any for this season."

"What about Kedar's community? How many other communities are having this problem?" Kohana asked realising a major threat to the Kingdom was happening.

"The problem is widespread." Ollie said with sorrow. "Kona's community in Fiordland and Kedar's community are losing most of their chicks, along with Kanoa's community in the Paparoa Range. A worrying new development is that humans are also taking some eggs from Kona and Kedar's community. Apparently there is a place at Franz Joseph Township where the humans are bringing Kiwi chicks up. We don't know what they are going to doing with them yet."

"How long have the humans been taking the eggs?"

"They started doing it last season. It is impossible to hide from them. The Humans have dogs that can smell where burrows are and show the humans where they are."

"If humans are only taking eggs from Kona and Kedar's community, what is happening in Kanoa's area?"

"I have some good news recently from him." Ollie was able to smile. "The humans have put animal traps by their burrows and are taking away the animals that are preying on the eggs and chicks."

"That's wonderful news!" Kohana's eyes were shining. She looked thoughtful for a moment before continuing. "That's what they are doing with Kona and Kedar's chicks!"

"What are they doing?"

"They are looking after them for Kona and Kedar's community. The chicks will be a year old soon, won't they?"

"Yes." Ollie was puzzled.

"Kiwis are usually a year old before they can completely defend themselves." Kohana replied. "I believe that both Kona and Kedar can look forward to some new members of their communities soon when their chicks are big enough to look after themselves."

"You think so?" Ollie was doubtful.

"Yes," Kohana replied happily. "Kiwis are protected now. I will have to send word to both Kona and Kedar to expect some new members of their families soon, and not to be too upset when humans take their eggs. The humans are making sure that some of the chicks survive."

"How will you do that?" Ollie asked, wondering how organised she was with sending of messages.

"Our pigeons are well connected though out the Island. I will send word tomorrow to the pigeons at Franz Joseph to let us both know when the chicks are being moved and also to Kona and Kedar."

"Thank you." Ollie said. "I was concerned how you would manage things from here, but I see you will be fine."

"Is there anything else I should know or be doing?" Kohana asked. She had a feeling that Ollie was holding something back.

"Have you any plans to do a tour of the Kingdom communities?" Ollie asked. It is always easier to deal with communities when you have been to them or spoken to their leaders."

Kohana thought for a moment before replying.

"You have been leader of the Kingdom for quite a while. How long did it take for the communities to accept your leadership?"

"I have only been the Guardian. It isn't the same." Ollie flustered. This young leader was far too smart and knowing he realised.

"You under-value yourself and your role, Ollie!" Kohana admonished him. "Are you afraid they won't accept me?"

"Well, yes." Ollie admitted.

"I will consider a tour at some stage, but I am not going to rush off straight away." Kohana advised Ollie. "Imposing my will or views on communities is not how I will lead."

"How are you going to lead?" Ollie wanted to know.

"Our communities are already established and managing themselves." Kohana reminded Ollie. If the local leaders want my advice or want me to visit, I will be happy to do so. Please convey this to them if them ask."

"I will." Ollie promised with a wry smile. "I will head back tomorrow evening." He had already been fielding questions from all the communities, wanting to know what their new leader was like and when they were getting a visit. The only thing for it was to pay them all a visit himself. Unconsciously he gave a little sigh.

"What is it Ollie?" Kohana was already alert to Ollie's dilemma. "What is the problem?"

"You don't miss a thing!" Ollie exclaimed. "The communities are already asking what you are like and when they are getting a visit! I was just thinking that I would have to visit them all in your absence."

Kohana realised she would not be able to delay her visit to the Kingdom communities.

"I will do the tour." Kohana conceded, but it will have to wait untill our chick is hatched and the children returned to the north first. I will also have to fit in with Kehi and this community's needs too."

"You will take the chick with you?"

"No. It is better for it to stay here with Kehi."

"You aren't taking any Kiwi support with you?"

"My Owl community will be my protection. They served me well on my journey here. I am not expecting any problems they can't help me with on my next journey."

Before Ollie left the Buller the next evening, he came to say goodbye to Kohana and Kehi.

"You have done very well Kohana. I will look forward to seeing you on your trip south and Kehi; make sure she looks after herself."

"I will." Kehi promised.

As they watched Ollie fly into the darkness, they both knew that big change would come for both of them.

CHAPTER TWELVE

MEETING WITH KURI

Predawn light was creeping over the forest and birds were starting to stir in the trees as the time came to head north. Kotare stood at his father Kehi's feet as Kohana prepared to leave. Koa and Kiana stood with Kohana as Syd the stag and his hind Daphne strolled into view. Syd and Daphne had agreed to take them north. Also waiting in the tree branches were Orlando and Odessa. They had an arrangement with Oren for the local owl community to watch Kehi and Kotare while she was away. Koro and Kalea had already left for Three Sisters Mountain after meeting the newest member of the family.

After Koa and Kiana had mounted Daphne, Kohana, Orlando and Odessa mounted Syd; watched by the whole community. As Syd and Daphne moved off into the forest Kohana looked back at Kehi one last time. While Kohana was away he had a big decision to make. Kehi had to choose whether to stay here with Kotare for the duration of her tour of the kingdom or for the family to go with her; putting Khai in charge while he was away. They both knew that if Kehi went with Kohana, that Kehi may not regain the leadership when he returned.

Kohana revelled in the new freedom this journey to the north gave her. She soon accustomed to being rocked to sleep as the deer journeyed through the day. When they rested at night, Orlando and Odessa would fly off to search for their feed while Kohana Koa and Kiana would scour the forest floor for theirs. As they came close to home, Koa gave a soft call. There was no response. Koa turned to Kohana with a frown.

"Something is up." Koa couldn't help the alarm in his voice.

"Do you think it because we are on the deer?" Kohana asked.

"It could be, but Kamora or Kerewa should be about."

"Call for them again; only this time, do it loudly!"

"KAMORA, KEREWA." Koa yelled at the top of his lungs. "WHERE ARE YOU?"

Orlando spied rustling approaching amongst the ferns at the deer's feet.

"We have company coming from this side!" Orlando warned.

"Show yourselves!" Kohana commanded "Or you will be trampled by these animals!"

"Syd, Daphne, feel free to kick or stomp if you feel threatened." Kohana told them firmly

At this last instruction, the rustling stopped and slowly the kiwis stood up. Kohana could see they were surrounded on all sides. She was thankful, that they were in a position of safety for now.

"Is Koha here?" Kohana asked calmly.

"Who wants him?"

A voice next to Syd answered. Kohana looked down into the eyes of a male who was giving her a calculating look, and knew it was him.

"I am Kohana, Kehi's mate." Kohana informed him. "I am here to return Koa and Kiana to their family."

"Why isn't Kehi here?"

"He stayed behind to ensure his leadership stays safe and to supervise our newborn son."

"What happened to Kiyo?"

"She was killed along with their unborn chick. The kiwis that killed her have been punished."

"You can leave Koa and Kiana here."

"I am not leaving untill I have spoken to Kamora and Kerewa."

"What do you want with them?" Koha's voice was still hostile.

"I want to make sure it is safe for me to leave Koa and Kiana with your community."

"Will you take my word for it, that they will be safe?"

"No."

Kohana's firm but confident tone and unwavering stare back, told Koha that this was no ordinary female and wondered where Kehi had found her. Koha made the mistake of moving closer to Syd and found a large hoof being kicked in his direction. Kohana Orlando and Odessa had to hang on tight as Syd roared and turned his head to sweep around him with his antlers, making Koha and all the kiwis scramble out of the way.

"Can't you control that animal?" Koha yelled in both fear and anger

"I am." Kohana replied. "I did give them permission to act if they felt they were threatened." Kohana then gave Syd a stroke with her claw to reassure him.

"Where are Kamora and Kerewa?" Kohana asked again. "Also, where is Katana? I need to know she is safe here too."

"Why did you bring these animals here?" Koha demanded to know, ignoring her question. "Why have you got owls with you too?" Koha had not seen such a large male owl before.

"They are part of our kingdom." Kohana replied. "Have you heard of the Kiwi Kingdom?"

"Who hasn't?" Koha replied. "Are you saying that the kingdom is active?"

"Yes." Kohana confirmed. "Your area and the Tasman are the only areas that are not part of it. The deer agreed to give us a ride here and the owls are here for my protection."

Koha gave Orlando and Odessa a quick look and found himself on the receiving end of a calculating stare himself.

"Can't you make them leave?"

"They will leave when I do."

"Koa, where is Kamora's burrow? Can you show me where it is?" Kohana asked, deciding to ignore Koha, seeing he wasn't co-operating with her.

"It isn't far," Koa told her. "It is on the slope of this hill." He urged Daphne to start the climb of the steep slope in front of them. Syd turned to follow her, but before he did, gave a kick out with both of his hind legs and did another sweep of his horns. Before Kohana entered the slopes she looked back. Koha and the community were following them. A little way up the hill, they could see two kiwis standing at the base of a tree.

"Move away; or you will be trampled!" Koa called out. Seeing Koa and Kiana sitting on a deer hind and a stag following behind, the kiwis quickly ran to get out of the way. As they came close, Kohana could see the entrance to the burrow, half hidden by ferns.

"Kamora, Kerewa, its Koa. Are you there?" He called as he came up to the entrance. Koa heard a muffled call back. "We are here!"

"They are here!" Koa told Kohana as Syd joined Daphne and sat down to let the kiwis off their backs.

"Syd, Daphne, stand in front of this entrance and make sure no kiwis come near from this side. Orlando, Odessa will you take a position either side of this tree to make sure no kiwis come in from the side or above."

Kohana gave them her orders before following Koa and Kiana inside the burrow.

78

From his position lower on the slope, Koha could hear and see Kohana's instructions being carried out and knew there was nothing he could do to stop the meeting.

"We had better make ourselves comfortable." Koha told his followers. "They will come when they are ready."

As he waited, Koha had to hide his disappointment that Kehi had not come. Koha wanted revenge for the loss of his daughter Kiyo. He would not have given her to Kehi if he had known that her life would be taken. When Kiyo had come home for the laying and incubation of her eggs, she had said she had come for the support of her mother and that because Kehi was away a lot, it would be nice for them stay and get to know their grandparents. It was only when Kiyo failed to come home and Kerewa came back from his visit, that they learnt the truth. That all the time, both she and the children were in danger. Koha became more convinced that Kohana was more than just Kehi's mate. *Who and what is she? Did she have a hand in his daughter's death in order to become his mate? Just what is she here for?"* This though made Koha realise that his grandchildren and mate might be in danger! He cursed himself for not being stronger in standing up to the animals, He aimed to find out!

"Stay here." Koha ordered his followers as he stood up and started to stride up the hill.

Inside the burrow, there was a joyous reunion between Kamora and Kerewa, and Koa and Kiana. Kohana was relieved to see Katana beaming at Kerewa's side and that they all looked well. Beyond them Kohana could see another female kiwi and wondered who she was. The female kiwi was looking at her with a big smile as though she knew who she was.

Once their greetings had been done with, they sat down. Kohana was then introduced to Kamora and the mystery female, whose name was Kuri. Just then, there was a shout from Syd.

"Kohana, Koha is here. He is insisting that he comes in. He says he has to make sure his family is safe"

"Koha is your grandfather?" Kohana asked Kerewa with wide eyes. Kerewa nodded.

"Send him in Syd, but make sure he is alone."

As Koha entered the burrow, he could see that everyone was sitting down, and relaxed. He could also see Kuri. *"What was she doing here?"*

"As you can see, Kohana," Koha began. "Kamora Kerewa and Katana are well. It is obvious to me that you aren't just Kehi's mate. Just who are you and what are you doing here?"

"I am here because Kerewa invited me." Kohana began, with a little smile. "He told me that there was someone here that I should meet. As I told you, I am Kohana. I am also the leader of the Kiwi Kingdom. What makes you think your family are in danger from me?"

"I knew you were a leader of some sort!" Koha exclaimed. "It occurred to me that you might have disposed of Kiyo in order to be Kehi's mate and be here to dispose of our grandchildren."

"As you can see, everyone here is unharmed and very comfortable. Kiyo was already dead when I arrived at the Buller to see Kehi. I was lucky not to be killed myself and have Kehi to thank for rescuing me from a flooded mineshaft that I was pushed into."

"Who killed Kiyo?" Koha wanted to know. "I want revenge!"

"I understand your grief and anger Koha, but all of those who were involved in Kiyo's death have been eliminated. They will not hurt anyone ever again."

"What about their mates and children? Weren't they sent to the ancestors too?"

"No." Kohana answered firmly. "I had already made it clear that there was to be no more killing. A vote was taken by the community whether to expel them to the Alps on their own or allow them to stay if they lived in peace with the community and lived by Kingdom rules. They are still with the community."

"You will regret it." Koha warned.

"Time will tell." Kohana stayed calm.

"Why is Kuri here?" Koha wanted to know. "I take it Kerewa; you wanted her to meet Kohana?"

"Do you remember Kohana," Kerewa began. "When you told me that you were Keoni's great granddaughter?" Kohana nodded. "Well Kuri's great grandmother hatched Keoni's egg and looked after him till he could look after himself. She will tell you all about it."

Just then Syd shouted out.

"Kohana! The Kiwis are advancing. What do you want us to do?"

"I will send them home." Koha said as he got up and went outside.

"Just a minute," Kohana also said as she got up and went outside too.

"Everything is fine in here." they heard Koha announce. "You can all go home."

Kohana waited till the kiwis started to disperse then thanked the deer and owls for staying on guard. "You can rest now. I will see you tomorrow."

When Kohana returned to Kamora's burrow, the family were waiting for her.

"When my great grandmother passed down the story of the Kiwi Kingdom," Kuri began, "We had no idea that his legacy still lived on and is still active today. It is wonderful to meet the current leader who is also Keoni's great-granddaughter. Kamoku the leader at Lake Kaniere community and his mate Kailee had a large family that had been spread through communities on this Island.

Keoni was their last child. Sadly, Kailee died after she delivered his egg. My grandmother Kuri lived next to Kailee and went over to see how she was, to find Kamoku running away from the burrow. When Kuri found Kailee's body with the still warm egg, she decided to take it home and look after it. Kuri's partner Kale wasn't very happy to look after someone else's child at first, but as they didn't have any children of their own; he agreed. Of course, before long they were expecting one of their own. Keoni had a sister Kaimi that also lived at Lake Kaniere, so they got her to help with hatching Keoni's egg. Even then, Keoni was lucky to survive as his egg was thicker than normal and Kaimi had to break the egg with a rock to help Keoni get out. Keoni lived in the family burrow and he made it his own.

When he was very young, Keoni was already making friends with other animals and protecting them. The community saw this and made him their leader. He made friends with Southern Brown Kiwis that also lived at the lake and they joined the kingdom he created there too. It all ended when humans came to Lake Kaniere to live and the Kingdom scattered to different parts of the island. Keoni's mate was Kaimani, Kuri and Kale's daughter, which means our families are connected."

"One last thing, I want to ask you," Kuri said. "Do you get visions?"

"What sort of visions?" Kohana wanted to know.

"They were of the future." Kuri replied. "Keoni could see the future."

Kohana now knew that some of the dreams that drove her to come to the Buller had been visions, but she did not mention it.

"I can now fill you in what happened to the Kingdom." Kohana told Kuri. Before Keoni left Lake Kaniere, he left behind a book for the next leader. He also made his friend Orion the Owl the guardian of the kingdom.

Odessa who is with me on this trip is from the current generation of guardians. My grandparents used to live in Punakaiki and moved to Lake Kaniere where my father Kupe was born and became the next leader. He went on a quest to find all the communities that were part of the original kingdom. Some were still living under Kingdom rules; other communities had to be rescued from those who had wanted the area for themselves. Both my family and yours have suffered from this."

"What do you mean?" Koha was puzzled.

"I am talking about Kura and Kakate her first mate. They were banished from Kehi's territory for causing trouble. At Three Sisters Mountain community they either killed or forced kiwis in the community off their territory to take over half the mountain. Dad forced them back to Kehi's territory to live under his rules.

Kehi eliminated Kakate but let Kura and their son Kalani live in his community. (Koha was shaking his head at this) Kalani went to Lake Kaniere to kill dad. Dad knew he was coming and sent mum away. She ended up at Three Sisters Mountain where she is happy with Kehi's son Koro. Kura became the mate of Kainan and they then started causing trouble again for Kehi. They succeeded in killing Kiyo and would have killed Kehi if they could."

"Both Kura and Kainan are gone?" Koha asked.

"Yes."

"What about their children?"

"They are gone too."

Koha was silent for a moment before looking at Kohana.

"You want to bring the Kiwi Kingdom here?"

"It would be nice if your area joined, but your community would have to agree to it."

"What are we agreeing to?"

Kohana detailed the three rules of the Kiwi Kingdom.

"Kehi and his community have agreed to this?"

"Yes."

"What if our kiwis are attacked?" (Koha was thinking of stoats and Possums that came regularly to prey on their eggs and young)

"Then you may act to protect them."

"What if someone won't live by the rules?"

"They are to be expelled from your territory."

"I will ask them." Koha promised.

At Okarito the sun was high in the sky, but Kedar was being woken.

"Dad, wake up!" Kahill called as he raced into his father's burrow. "Kohana was right, they are here! Humans have just left three kiwis in the old burrows."

Quickly, Kedar followed Kahill through the forest. It was time to welcome the newest members of their community home. Kahill showed Kedar where the three kiwis had been placed.

"Hello," Kedar called quietly at the entrance of the first burrow. "I'm Kedar the leader here. What is your name?"

"I'm Kilian." came a muffled reply. "Why am I here?"

"Your mother and father live here." Kedar told him. "Your egg was taken by humans to hatch and look after you untill you were big enough to look after yourself. Welcome home. It is sleep time now, but we will come and show you the best feeding spots when you wake up."

"Good." Kilian replied. "Do you know where my friends are?"

"Yes," Kedar replied. "I am just going to talk to them too."

Behind them a little crowd had gathered. News had travelled fast of the new arrivals.

"Can I come?" Kilian asked.

"You can." Kedar agreed.

Kilian blinked as he emerged again into the bright sunlight. He was feeling really confused. The humans had come just after he had settled for his sleep and put him in a dark box. He heard two of his friends being put in boxes too. They wondered where they had been taken to.

Kedar turned to the crowd as Kilian emerged.

"Kilian has come home."

At that there was a cry from a pair that recognised him as their own.

As they came forward, Kilian could see that he had the same markings as the male and knew he was his father. His mother and father came to give him a cuddle before they followed Kedar and Kahill to the next two burrows that were near each other.

"Hello," Kilian called out. "We are home."

"Is that you Kilian?"

"Yes. Come out. Our families are here to meet us."

Carefully his friends came out of their burrows to be surrounded by a number of strangers, who soon became friends and family.

"Do you want to stay here, or come and sleep with your families?" Kedar asked. "You can have these burrows when you are ready to have your own families."

All three elected to go and see and sleep in their family burrows for the rest of their sleep time.

In the Haast, Kona and his community were also welcoming some of their kiwis' that had been returned to them. For the first time in years, Kona felt some hope for the future.

The evening had come and Koha had called a meeting of the community.

"I introduce to you Kohana. She is the leader of the Kiwi Kingdom."

There was a loud murmuring at this news.

"I know this is news to many of you who thought the Kiwi Kingdom ended with Keoni. Kohana's father Kupe revived the kingdom. Kohana is here to see if you are interested in joining her kingdom. There are a few rules that communities in the kingdom live by.

"To respect and help all animals regardless of who or what they are."

"You may not injure or kill any animal you meet in the kingdom."

"Establish a school for your kiwis and other animals to learn to live in harmony together."

We are allowed to defend ourselves if we are attacked. If we agree to join the kingdom and someone doesn't live by the rules, they will be expelled. Have you any questions?"

"What is a school? And where and how do we run it?"

"A school is a place where you learn many things that you aren't taught at home." Kohana replied. "I will help the Owls that have come with me to set up the classes, but we will want some kiwis or animals from here to take over the teaching of lessons when we leave. Are there any caves near your community where classes can be held? Caves are used elsewhere in the kingdom for protection from the weather and any predators that might be around."

"What about Kehi's community? They are worse at fighting and killing than us."

"They have already joined the kingdom."

"We will have a vote on joining the kingdom" Koha told the crowd. "Those who want to join, please stand up."

A small number, including Koha's and Kuri's families stood up, but the majority stayed seated.

"I can see that the majority of your community are not ready for the changes needed." Kohana responded. "I have no wish to split your community, so you can continue on as you are. If you change your minds later, then we will revisit." With a smile to everyone present, Kohana moved to leave both the meeting and the area.

"Where are you going?" Koha asked. He knew Kohana would leave the area as quickly as possible. "I want to talk to you before you leave."

"I am just going to collect the deer and owls and prepare to go." Kohana informed him.

Kohana knew Orlando and Odessa were in a nearby tree and went over to them.

"Orlando, can you please find Syd and Daphne? It is time to go home."

"They aren't far away." Orlando told her. "I will go and fetch them."

Kohana didn't know it, but the community was already being split.

"Given that most of you have voted against me, it is best that someone else will lead you. I am going to join the Kiwi Kingdom." Koha told the crowd. "So, you now need to vote for a new leader. Those who want to come to the Kingdom, please follow me." With that, Koha turned to follow Kohana along with those who voted to join the kingdom.

There was a long silence after Koha and his followers left to join Kohana.

Koha and Kuri's families had been in the area for as long as Kiwis lived here and under their rule the area had been kept stable. In the coming weeks those who attempted to mould the community to their way of leadership, started an exodus of many more to both the south and to the north.

As the deer came to Kohana and Odessa, there was a small crowd with her.

"There are too many of us to catch a ride back with you." Kohana told Syd and Daphne. "You go ahead and tell Kehi that I am bringing some Kingdom supporters with me. Orlando and Odessa will protect us from here."

Little did Kohana know that in coming nights she would wish the deer were still there to give her a lift home.

CHAPTER THIRTEEN

THE RESCUE

Oren was worried as he went looking for Kehi. It would soon be daylight. His mate Opal had been keeping an eye on Kotare Kiwi while he played in the forest with some of the older children. She had stopped to feed on a mouse before continuing her surveillance. It took her a short time to realise that Kotare was no longer with them as they returned to the burrows. She noticed that none of the children had raised the alarm that Kotare was no longer with them. *Perhaps Kotare had already slipped back home on his own?*

"Kehi, are you there?" Oren called as he flew over the forest. Then he spotted him, talking to Syd and Daphne. Kotare wasn't with him either. He noticed Kohana wasn't there; neither was Orlando or Odessa. *Had they stayed in the north?"*

"I'm here." Kehi called back. "Is everything alright?"

"We are checking when you last saw Kotare." Oren began. "Opal was keeping an eye on him while he was playing with the other children. She noticed he didn't come back with them." Kehi failed to hide the look of alarm that came over his face at this news.

"Which children are they?" Kehi asked. "What burrows did they go back to?"

"Opal is keeping watch near the burrows. I will take you to there."

Oren led the way, with Kehi following as fast as he could. Word was soon sent to Khai who joined him along with other kiwis who saw Kehi running.

"Kotare's missing." Were the only words Kehi could say.

Kehi had barely digested the news that Kohana was walking back with some members of Koha's community, when Oren came with the news that Kotare was missing. Kehi was immediately filled with dread, remembering the night that Kiyo went missing. One second she was with him, the next she was gone forever. How would Kohana react if Kotare had been taken as well while she was away? Was foul play at work here too?

Would he have to send families away, and would it be enough to ensure his family's safety? He already knew the answer to the last question. Kehi was just glad Kohana wasn't here while he dealt with this latest crisis.

Opal gave a soft call as she saw Oren leading Kehi and the community towards her and landed on the floor before them. When Opal indicated the burrows where the kiwi children had returned to, Kehi and Khai looked at each other with grim faces. These were children who had been allowed to stay after Kiyo had been slain.

As Kohana and the new members of her community trekked south, she started to feel anxious. When she went to sleep in the morning she could see Kotare. He was in a deep hole and it looked like a cave behind him. Kotare was looking up and calling!

Kohana was relieved to see Kotare was alive, but for how long? How did he get in there? Unable to sleep, Kohana got up and went outside, looking up into the tree above her burrow, knowing Orlando and Odessa were there.

"Odessa." Kohana tried to whisper as she called to the owls. The worried look on Kohana's face had both Odessa and Orlando come down immediately to land at her side.

"I've seen Kotare." Kohana began. He is trapped down a deep hole. It looks like he is in a cave. I saw him looking up and calling. I don't know how long..." Her voice trailed off as worry became too much.

"I will go and find Oren." Orlando decided. "He may know of caves that are formed like that. We will get all owls in the area to start looking for him in caves they know about."

With that Orlando launched himself into the air, being careful to stay under the canopy. Owls that he passed knew something important was happening – owls don't fly in the day unless the matter is urgent. They followed him to his next rest stop. Flying under the canopy was much harder and more effort than in open skies.

"Do you need help?" Orlando was asked as he got his breath back.

Orlando nodded. "I need to get word to Oren, where to search for Kotare Kiwi." Kotare is the son of Kohana, the leader of the Kiwi Kingdom."

"I have heard of her. Where is Kotare?"

"He is in a deep hole that has a cave. He will need help to get out. That is if he is still alive when he is found."

"How old is he?"

"Only a few months."

"We will come to help search, but we will also send word ahead." At that the owl put out a loud call, which was answered from the distance.

As Kohana turned to go back to her burrow, Koha called out to her from his family's burrow.

"We know you may not sleep, but come and rest with us. You shouldn't have to cope with that alone."

Kohana was too overwrought to try to be strong and independent. She slipped into the small space and snuggled in between Kamora and Kiana. At first Kohana gazed out to the morning light wondering and worrying what happened, but eventually tiredness took over and she drifted into a dreamless sleep.

At the burrows, the entrances were surrounded before Khai called out.

"Bring out your children. We want to talk to them."

Reactions to his call varied from fear to sullen compliance when it was realised that there was no escape.

"Who was playing with Kotare?" Khai asked. This was met with silence, until Opal pointed out those she had seen with him.

"What happened and where is he?" Again this was met with silence.

"Did you kill him?" Kehi couldn't help himself.

"No." Came a timid reply. "He just disappeared! We don't know where his went."

"What were you doing when you noticed he wasn't with you?"

"We were racing through the forest. When we stopped, Kotare wasn't with us. We went back the way we went in, but we couldn't find him."

"Why didn't you tell someone when you got back?"

"We were scared."

Kehi gave a big sigh.

"You must remember you are in the Kiwi Kingdom now. That means helping when something like this happens. You did not help by keeping quiet about it." Kehi turned to the crowd around the burrows. "The sun is nearly up, so it is too late to go looking for Kotare now. We will collect the children first thing this evening and go looking for him then." Kehi then spoke to the children. "You can help us this evening by showing us where you went in the forest. Go to bed now and get a good sleep."

"We aren't being punished?"

"No. You haven't done anything to be punished for. Kotare is lost

somewhere. We just have to find him. We need your help so we know where to start looking."

Kotare was having the time of his life, running through the forest with some of the older children in a race. Tall ferns were all around as he ran through them, trying to keep up with the taller kiwis. Kotare was unable to stop when a hole appeared in front of him, and he found himself tumbling down into a deep dark space. Kotare felt his head hit a rock as he fell and everything went black.

Kotare woke and wondered what the bright light was high above him, and then he remembered that he had fallen in here! Kotare started calling for help, but no-one answered. He realised that no-one would answer for some time as it was daytime and they would all be asleep. Kotare looked around him. In the dim light he could see he was in a big space. It was a cave like the school cave he was in earlier that night. Then Kotare saw some shapes in the corner. He got up and had a look. They were the bones of animals that had fallen in here before him. *At least I'm not alone in here.* Kotare thought. *It's a shame they can't talk to me.*

Kotare heard some dripping in the cave and knew that there was water there, and maybe some worms in the damp ground. To Kotare's joy, some gentle probing soon produced a couple of worms. He could feel that there were more worms under the ground, but he would leave them untill later; seeing that he might be here for some time. Kotare went back to the bottom of the hole where he had fallen in. Some soft ferns were growing there. Making him-self comfortable, Kotare went to sleep; not knowing the panic and worry his disappearance was causing.

It was early afternoon when Oren was woken by owl calls coming from the north. Oren answered them to then hear the message that Orlando was coming with help to search for Kotare. He was in a cave at the bottom of a deep hole. *How did Orlando know that?* Oren wondered. Opal and the other owls in the community had woken when Oren answered the calls and heard the news. Oren soon had a number of owls crowd around him.

"We are going to need a basket for Kotare to sit in and some rope to pull him up with." Opal advised Oren. We have baskets in the school cave. We just have to make some rope. Should we also get Syd and Daphne to help pull Kotare out? I will go down to the river and see if I can find the sharp stone that was used when we made the last rope."

With that Opal flew off to the gravel bed on the river bank, members of the community following in her wake. When Opal and her helpers returned with flax leaves in their beaks and claws, Oren had been to see Syd and Daphne. They had agreed to help and had brought the basket back to Oren's tree. Orlando and his group of helpers were also sitting next to Oren. Unfortunately, Oren had not heard of the cave at the bottom of a deep hole.

"You have organised the rope already!" Orlando exclaimed with a smile.

"What is a rope?" One of the northern owls asked.

"You will see when we find Kotare and start making it. We will need it to help get him out of the hole."

Oren then intervened. "Well done everyone, but now it is time for a rest, for we have a busy night tonight."

"How did you know where Kotare was?" Opal asked Orlando.

"Kohana saw him calling. She also saw he was in a cave that was at the bottom of a deep hole."

"Has anyone told Kehi the latest news yet?" Opal asked.

"Not yet." Oren admitted.

"I will let him know." Opal said as she launched from their tree. Keeping under the canopy, Opal soon found his burrow. The day birds, singing and fluttering in the tree branches quickly stopped and searched for cover to see an owl amongst Them! They were relieved to find she wasn't interested in them but flew straight down to a kiwi burrow.

"Kehi! Are you there?" Opal called at the entrance to his burrow.

"Who is it?" Kehi's sleepy voice answered.

"It is Opal. I have some urgent news for you."

"What is it Opal?" Kehi asked as he came into view.

"Orlando is back with some owls from the north to help with the search. He has told us that Kotare is in a cave that is at the bottom of a deep hole. I have some flax leaves cut so we can make some rope to help him get out when we find him."

"How does he know this?" Kehi asked.

"Kohana saw where Kotare was and he was calling out."

"Thanks Opal. I will call when we are ready to make the search."

A much relieved Kehi went back to bed. The fact that Kotare was able to call out, and the owls in the community were already organising a rope to pull Kotare out, helped Kehi get some much needed sleep. Footsteps and murmurings outside Kehi's burrow woke him in the early evening light. Kehi put his head out to find all the children who had played with Kotare and their mothers were standing outside waiting for him.

"Have you had anything to eat?" Kehi asked, before thanking them for coming. It was a relief that he didn't have go to collect them.

"Not yet," one of the mothers admitted. "Finding Kotare is more important."

"Have a search around here, while we are waiting for everyone to come." Kehi advised them with a smile. "I will call you when we are ready to go."

A short while later Khai and other community members came up as Kehi searched for a feed himself.

"The children and their mothers are missing!" Khai said with alarm.

"They have already come to help." Kehi informed him. "They aren't far away. I sent them for a feed while they were waiting."

"Children, it's time to go!" Kehi called in his loudest voice.

The sound of voices and footsteps heralded the return of the children and their mothers. Kehi's call also woke any owls who weren't already awake.

"It sounds like the Kiwis are ready to go." Oren commented to Opal and Orlando. "Opal, ask Syd and Daphne to come. We will get them to carry the basket and flax leaves." He then spoke to all the owls that had chosen to sleep with them during the day. Go with Opal and the deer. If you happen to hear Kotare calling, go to the nearest tree and give us a call." With that Oren and Orlando flew to meet Kehi and his community.

"Hello Kehi." Oren called as the Kiwis came into view. "Opal and all the other owls here are meeting with Syd and Daphne who are bringing a basket and flax for the rope. They have gone to the tree where she last saw the children. We can start searching from there."

"Thanks Oren." Kehi replied. "It's nice to see you back Orlando. Children, it's time to show us where you went on your race. Mothers, stay right next to them. We know Kotare is down a deep hole. We don't want anyone else falling in there too."

As the kiwis moved steadily through the forest, Kotare was waking up.

At first he wondered where he was, and then he remembered and looked up at the fading light above him. Kotare gave a couple of calls and realised they sounded quiet even to him. No-one would hear him! At the top of his voice, Kotare bellowed "HELP! HELP!" At first there was no answer, so he called again.

Opal had taken the owls to the tree where she last saw Kotare. The deer were waiting at the base of the tree. She was about to point the owls in the direction that Kotare was running, when one said. "I think I can hear him calling "Help!"

The owl flew in the direction he heard the call, other owls going with him. Kotare's second call was heard right in front of them, but all they could see was tall ferns. The owls sat in the trees surrounding the ferns and called back to Opal.

"We can hear Kotare calling here, but we can't see him."

Kotare heard owls calling nearby, so he called again.

"HELP ME! It's Kotare! I need help!"

"Kotare, we can hear you!" The Owl called back to him. "Help is coming."

When Kehi and the community came to Opal's tree, she had good news for them.

"The owls can hear Kotare calling. They have surrounded the area where they can hear him. Just walk in the direction where you can hear their calls. Syd and Daphne will follow."

Opal then told the owls to call out their location for the Kiwis. Orlando lead the Kiwis to the chorus of owl calls till they finally came to an area of thick tall ferns. Owls sat in all the surrounding trees. Kehi looked grimly at the area and could see why the children couldn't find Kotare.

"Kotare!" Kehi called out as loud as he could. "Can you hear me?"

"Dad, I can hear you! I am here!" Kotare's voice came from in the middle of the ferns.

"Children you have done your job. Can you wait by the tree with your mothers?"

"Isn't there anything we can do?" One of the mothers asked.

"You can help make the rope when we find the hole he is in."

Kehi and Khai formed a line with all the adults and very slowly walked into the ferns.

"STOP!" called two of the Kiwis as a hole appeared in front of them. Everyone came to look, but all they could see was darkness.

"Are you there Kotare?" Kehi called.

"I can see you!" Kotare called back.

"We are going to send down a basket with some rope to get you out. We may be a little while as we have to make the rope." Kehi told him.

"Can I have a feed while I'm waiting?" Kotare asked him.

"You have food down there?"

"Yes. I've already had some worms. I know there are more here."

"Don't go too far away then." Kehi ordered him. "I will call when we are ready to send down the basket to you."

As Kotare went in search of a feed, the kiwis and owls went to work, stripping and weaving the flax into rope.

"I don't think we have enough flax." Opal said with worry, looking at the length being made.

"Let us try it first, before you go off for more." Oren advised her.

When the rope was ready, they attached it to the basket at one end and around Syd the Stag's body at the other end.

"Kotare, are you there?" Kehi shouted down the hole. Darkness had settled around them now that night was here.

"I'm here dad." Kotare called back.

"We are sending down the basket now. Let us know if it doesn't reach you."

Kehi and Khai sat near the hole and pushed the basket over the edge. It quickly disappeared into the darkness as the rope uncoiled behind it. When the rope attached to Syd was pulled tight – he had moved near the edge now; Kehi called down to Kotare.

"Can you see the basket Kotare or hear if it is near you?"

Kotare could hear the basket as it slide down the side of the hole. It stopped just above his head. Luckily there was a slope. He just might be able to climb up and get into it.

"It is just above me." Kotare called back. "I will see if I can climb in."

Before he attempted to climb in the basket, Kotare turned to the animal bones in the cave.

"Goodbye, I'm sorry you can't come with me."

He was surprised to hear a voice behind him.

"Our bodies can't come with you, but we can." Kotare was amazed to see the spirits of all the animals that had been trapped in the cave. "We've been waiting for someone to come and help us get out so we can join our ancestors."

Kotare gave them a big smile before turning to climb up to the basket. As Kotare put a leg out to grip the basket; it swung out, leaving him to fall back on the floor. The animal spirits then crowded around the basket, to hold it in place for Kotare.

"Try it again." They encouraged him.

The second attempt was a struggle, but Kotare made it, dropping into the basket with a thump, which was felt by Syd. The spirits quickly piled into the basket with him.

"I think he is in." Syd informed Kehi and Khai.

"Are you ready?" Kehi called down to Kotare.

"I'm ready." Kotare called back.

"Syd, you can start pulling." Khai informed him.

Syd turned and steadily walked away. When the basket reached the top, it flipped onto its side. Kotare and the spirits came tumbling out. *"Goodbye"* Kotare called to the spirits in his thoughts as he watched them glide up into the trees. *"Goodbye and thank you."* They called back.

"Are you alright?" Kehi asked Kotare as he scrambled away from the still moving basket

"I'm fine Dad." Kotare reassured him as Kehi came to give him a cuddle.

"Syd, you can stop now." Khai called to him.

Kohana was feeding in the forest as they steadily made their way south. Suddenly she had a vision of Kehi cuddling Kotare and knew he was safe. She couldn't help the beam that came across her face.

"Kohana?" Odessa asked, seeing the expression on her face.

"Kotare has been rescued." was Kohana's happy reply.

95

CHAPTER FOURTEEN

DECIDING FOR THE FUTURE

Kehi was troubled as he searched his area for a feed. The night was young, but he knew that Kohana would return anytime now; bringing Koha and some of his community with him. How would they settle into his community and just as importantly, how would Koha adjust to living under another leader? He had planned to go with Kohana on her quest, leaving Khai in charge while he was away. Kehi had been prepared to concede leadership to Khai and his family, for they had proved their loyalty to him since Kiyo was taken from him, but he wasn't prepared to leave if a power struggle between Koha and Khai emerged to split the community. Kehi hoped Khai wouldn't have to look over his shoulder as he did when Kakate and Kura were in the community. He realised that he would need the help of the community to prepare for the new arrivals. It was time to call a meeting. Having made his decision, Kehi made a loud call. Everyone who heard him came running.

"What's wrong Kehi?" they asked.

"Nothing is wrong, but we need to have a meeting. Can you ask everyone to come to the meeting place?"

A short while later everyone assembled on the valley slopes, wondering what Kehi wanted to discuss. Their last meeting had brought the Kiwi Kingdom to their community. What change was coming now?

"Thank you all for coming." Kehi began. "Kohana will be returning soon. She is bringing some members of the Northern Buller community with her to join us. They include Koha the leader and his family. We need to prepare for their arrival by making some burrows for them."

There was a small silence while this news was digested. Khai also was wondering how Kehi felt about another leader coming and settling into their community. Kehi had confided his intention to leave Khai in charge while Kohana was on her quest. He knew that Kohana would be travelling alone now.

"How many can we expect?" Khai asked "And where are we to make the burrows?"

"There are several families that I know of coming" Kehi advised him.

"I feel we need community agreement where they are placed, given that we may get more members come to us in the future. Whether you want them to be separate to us or mixed in with us. It is for you to choose."

After some discussion, it was decided that some burrows would be mixed in and others to be separate. Once their locations were decided, everyone went off to begin digging the burrows. It wouldn't matter if they were small. The new arrivals could make them how they wanted when they came. It was important that a home had been made to welcome them into.

Kotare came to help Kehi dig a burrow. He was surprised at how many worms appeared as they dug. Once he was full, he wanted to know what to do with others he dug up.

"Just put them in the bushes." Kehi advised him. "They will be a feed for someone later."

The first light of day was on the horizon when the last burrow was finished and everyone was ready to retreat to their own burrows.

"Thank you everyone and have a good rest." Kehi advised them. As he spoke, two familiar figures swooped to land in the tree above him. It was Orlando and Odessa.

"Are they here?" Kehi asked Orlando

"They are." Orlando confirmed. "Kohana asked us to find you."

Kehi turned to the crowd. "Who's coming to welcome them?" With that he led the community to meet the latest members of their community and welcome back home Kohana, Katana and Kerewa, Koa and Kiana.

"Welcome to your new home Koha; Welcome everyone. We have your burrows ready for you." Kehi spoke his welcome as the new arrivals led by Kohana appeared. Koha looked at the young kiwi at Kehi's feet with a twinkle in his eyes.

"I see young Kotare has recovered well from his little adventure. He caused a little concern for a while there."

"Just a little." Kehi replied with equal understatement.

"Mum!" Kotare called as he spotted her and flung himself at her for a cuddle.

Kehi and Kohana exchanged smiles above him. There was plenty of time to catch up later. Koha introduced the members of his and the other families who had come, before they were shown to the burrows that had been prepared for them.

"Thank you, we hadn't expected this." Koha said as he chose a burrow which happened to be next to Khai's.

"I'm Kehi's next in command." Khai told Koha. If you want or need anything, I'm just next door." Khai told him with a grin showing Koha his burrow.

"And I'm just over here." Kehi added with a smile, showing Koha his burrow.

"You have moved?" Koha asked remembering the other burrow he shared with Kiyo.

"Yes." Kehi replied, the smile leaving his face. "That burrow was among enemies. I couldn't go back to it after Kiyo died. I will take you to see where she lies later."

"When everyone is in their burrows, I will get you to take us."

When Kehi returned, Kamora came with them. Kehi led them to the young patch of ferns that was growing under the Pohutukawa. Both Koha and Kamora looked around them and at the river flowing below.

"Thank you for choosing such a lovely spot" Kamora smiled.

"You can thank Kohana." Kehi replied. When she spotted Kiyo floating in a cave connected to the mine shaft, I was able to say my goodbye to Kiyo there. It was Kohana's suggestion to bring her back to rest in a place that Kiyo loved."

Kamora Nodded. "I would like to be nearby when it's my time to join Kiyo."

"We both would like to be here." Koha joined in. "Is there a plan for us this evening?"

"I will show you the best feeding areas and show you our school and meeting areas. After that your time is your own."

As they were leaving, Kerewa Koa and Kiana came. "We just came to let Mum know we are back." Kerewa explained. Kamora gave them a cuddle before leaving them.

"We will see you this evening." Koha called back to them.

Kotare was asleep in his tunnel when Kehi rejoined Kohana in their burrow.

"I've missed you." Kehi murmured as they cuddled together.

"Have you made your decision yet?" Kohana asked, referring to her coming quest.

"I had intended to come with you, leaving Khai in charge, but with Koha here, I'm not sure that I can. I don't want Khai to be worrying about a challenge to his authority while I'm away."

"We could invite Koha and Kamora to come with us to see where the kingdom began and meet other kingdom leaders; also Kerewa will be here." Kohana reminded him. "I take it you will hand your leadership to him eventually? Perhaps it would be good for him to be in joint leadership with Khai while you are away. There is Koa too, though he isn't quite ready for adult responsibilities yet."

"You are right, that I need to consider the future of my leadership." Kehi acknowledged thoughtfully. I hadn't expected any of the children to be here, but now that they are; I will have to find out whether Kerewa or Koa are interested in taking it on. If they are, then a joint leadership with Khai would be a good introduction for them. If they aren't, then I can entrust the leadership to Khai as I had planned."

When Kehi and Kohana came out of their burrow that evening, Koha and Kamora were waiting for them.

"I hope you slept well?" Kohana asked Kamora as they showed them the feeding spots.

"We did." Kamora replied. "It won't take long to make it like home again. I expect it won't be long before you head south?"

"We want everything settled here first. Actually, we were going to ask if you and Koha would like to come with us." Kohana saw the surprise on Kamora's face.

"You would have a chance to see the place where Keoni grew up and Koha would get to meet other communities and their leaders in the kingdom. From what Ollie Owl the Kingdom Guardian told me, every community is very different."

"You have just given us a great deal to think about."

Kamora stole a look at Koha who was grinning and could obviously hear the conversation. "What about the children? Will they be coming?"

"Kotare will be coming of course, If Kerewa Koa and Kiana want to come; they will be welcome. We haven't found out their preference yet."

"Who will be leader while Kehi is away?"

"Kehi has appointed Khai as leader while he is away. If the children choose to stay and have experience as leader, then they will co-lead with Khai.

"Will it work?" Kamora was amazed.

"It has worked before when Kehi was grieving for Kiyo."

By now, they had reached the school. Kamora and Koha were delighted to see Kerewa, Koa and Kiana already there with kiwis from his community and other animals to receive their lesson. Kamora was also fascinated to see some of the students looking at pictures in a book and practicing weaving flax as they looked.

"What is that they are looking at?" Koha asked

"It is a book." Kohana told him. "Humans make them and we have learnt to use them too. Those students are learning how to weave mats to sit on and baskets to hold things"

"Are all schools like this?" Koha asked quietly, seeing the change that it brought to animals lives.

"They are." Kohana replied proudly. She saw Koha's sad look and had to ask. "What is wrong?"

"I'm just sorry my community didn't have the courage to try this new path. I'm glad I came though. When time permits, I will join in too."

Kehi was about to lead them to the meeting area when Orlando came to land on the tree branch in front of them.

"Hello Orlando what is happening?" Kohana asked.

"Have you seen Syd and Daphne?" Orlando asked with a worried look.

"Not yet, why?"

"Hunters are coming with guns! Odessa is keeping watch."

Kohana ran into the cave. "Everyone, go to the back and keep very quiet untill we tell you it is safe." Kohana then advised Giana and the glow worms to turn their lights out. She then went back to Orlando. "If you find them before we do, send them to cross the river to the Ohikanui valley."

At that, Orlando flew into the air, calling out to Syd and Daphne.

"Is that the stag that brought Kohana to my area?" Koha asked, as Kehi and Kohana increased speed as they began to run through the forest and called out to Syd and Daphne too. "Surely they can look after themselves?" Koha remembered Syd's aggression towards him on Kohana's arrival to his area.

"Not against hunter's bullets they can't!" Kohana replied. Just then there was a loud bang that echoed through the forest. Kohana looked at Koha.

"I just hope we aren't too late!"

Kohana led the way to the spot where Syd and Daphne liked to rest, but they were gone.

Syd and Daphne were dozing when they heard Orlando calling them. He sounded urgent.

"We are here!" Syd called out to him.

"Quick!" Orlando called from the top of the tree. "Run to the river and swim over to the Ohikanui valley. Hunters are coming."

As Syd and Daphne turned to leave, gunfire rang through the forest. They needed no second bidding and fled for their lives. Orlando flying with them to make sure they stayed safe. It was only when they were safely across the river and out of sight; that Orlando returned to report that Syd and Daphne were out of harm's way.

"Shouldn't we be hiding?" Koha was worried now.

"We are protected so humans aren't allowed to hunt us now, but it would be best if we take shelter in case any bullets come our way." Kohana looked at Orlando "If the pigeons haven't already fled, tell them to leave the area till morning."

As Orlando winged his way to do her bidding, quickly and quietly Kehi led them back to their burrows, where everyone else was sheltering too. In the distance, they could hear the hunters coming. A family of terrified possums were about to scramble up a nearby tree.

"No," Kohana called out to them. "They will find you there. Come with me." She then led them into her burrow. "Hide in the tunnel at the back." Kohana ordered them, while she led Kehi and Kotare to the side tunnel, out of sight of the entrance.

Soon heavy footsteps came their way, pausing now and then. To Kohana and Kehi's horror the fern at the entrance was pulled back and a bright light was shone into their burrow before the footsteps moved on again. *"Why were they searching Kiwi tunnels? Surly the hunters weren't after Kiwi too!"* Kehi and Kohana waited untill the frogs had restarted their night chorus before tentatively emerging from their burrow. All was quiet in their area. The occasional shot could still be heard in the far distance towards the township.

"It is safe to come out now." Kehi called out loudly. At his words, all the other kiwis came out of their burrows too, along with a very grateful family of possums.

"I will go to the cave and check that they are all safe." Kohana advised Kehi. "I will call if I need you."

At the cave Kohana was greeted with both darkness and silence.

"It's Kohana. Is everyone in here still safe?"

Slowly the glow worms put their lights back on. Kohana went to the back of the cave to find a much larger crowd than the one she had left.

"The hunters have gone back to the town now. We will restart class tomorrow, so you can all go home now." A relieved crowd including Kerewa Koa and Kiana followed Kohana outside.

"I need to talk to you about the future." Kohana told them as everyone else dispersed to their homes. She then led them to the meeting area.

"Very soon Kehi and I will be leaving for a visit of the other communities. Koha and Kamora may come with us. We need to know whether any of you are interested in taking on the role of local leader when Kehi is ready to step down. If you are, then we will get you to co-lead with Khai while we are away to get experience in the role."

There was a small silence at this news.

"Kehi hasn't a preference for who will follow him?" Koa asked, looking at his older brother.

"There isn't any point in having a preference, if the role is not wanted." Kohana pointed out. "Kerewa, do you want the leadership role?"

"If you had asked that while we lived in the north, I would have jumped at it, but since coming here, I can see it is much more complicated than I thought it would be." Kerewa gave a big sigh. "The leadership is for someone else to take. I just want a nice quiet life with Katana."

"Have you spoken to Katana about it?" Kiana asked.

"I have." Kerewa smiled back at her. "She is happy that being a leader isn't part of our future.

"Koa, Are you interested in the role?" Kohana asked.

"I'm interested." Koa began.

"So am I." Kiana cut in.

"But I would like to go on your visit with you to meet all the other leaders."

"So would I." Kiana finished for them.

"I suppose you want me to fill in for you while you are away?" Kerewa asked Koa and Kiana.

"Would you?" Koa asked with a hopeful look on his face.

"What is the alternative?" Kerewa asked Kohana.

Khai would be taking over the leadership."

"It would end for our family?"

"Yes."

"I will do it."

"Thank you!" Both Koa and Kiana spoke as they gave him a cuddle.

Kohana left them to give Kehi their news.

The next evening Khai was waiting for Kehi as he emerged from his burrow.

"Can we talk?" Khai asked.

"Of course," Kehi replied with a smile, as they moved away from the burrows. "I was coming to see you later anyway."

"I expect you will be staying when Kohana leaves on her tour?"

"No," Kehi paused. "Kohana and I have had a talk about both Koha and the children's arrival and the future of my leadership. Koha and Kamora are coming with us on the tour. Although Koa and Kiana are interested in future leadership, they also want to come on the tour too. Kerewa has agreed to co-lead with you while we are away. Are you agreeable to that?"

"Can I ask something?" Khai asked.

"Of course, what is it?"

"I want my son Kailan to co-lead with us. Our family needs to think of the future too."

"That sounds like a plan." Kehi agreed with a smile.

It was agreed that any issues would be dealt with together.

CHAPTER FIFTEEN

GOING HOME

Life seemed quiet in the Buller community after the departure of Kehi and his family. Syd the Stag and Daphne were giving them a ride to the Kiwi Kingdom. On their return, they were intending to live in the Ohikanui valley, away from any hunters. They were grateful for the warning to escape from the recent visitors who had caused havoc for the whole community. They knew that the hunters would return sooner or later and had no intention of being near them again.

Oren was already missing Orlando and Odessa who were also heading south, with a stop to see Odion and Oana at Three Sisters Mountain. Kohana had told them it was time for them to start their own lives. She had a good family support around her now and Oren's community were available if she needed any help. After some discussion, they decided to return to Lake Kaniere and Lake Mahinapua to see their families and find a suitable nesting tree with a lake view! Before they left, Orlando invited Oren to visit them at the lake, an invitation he intended to keep.

The quietness in the Buller didn't last for long. Kerewa was quietly feeding with Katana nearby, when Oren came looking for him.

"Kerewa, there are some kiwis coming from the north. I think there are about six of them."

"Can you get Khai and Kailan to come and then show us where they are?"

As Oren left to find Khai and Kailan, Kerewa's mind was already thinking of how to deal with the new arrivals. He guessed that they were fleeing from the new order in the north, but would the new arrivals be suitable to become part of the community? They would have to be firm on the observance of Kingdom rules.

"I'm here!" Kerewa called as the sound of running footsteps heralded the arrival of Khai and Kailan.

"Do you know who they are?" Khai asked, with a grim look on his face.

"No, but I have a feeling that they are fleeing from the new order that Koha left behind. I feel we should be welcoming, but firm that Kingdom rules be obeyed. "

"We will get an agreement from them that they will obey the rules before they are allowed to stay. If not, then we will escort them out of our territory towards the Alps. Do you agree?"

"I agree." Kailan said happily.

After a little thought, Khai nodded his agreement too. "I presume we will be getting some more joining us soon."

"I expect so." Kerewa replied. "We should start as we mean to carry on, whether Kehi and Koha are here or not!"

Khai couldn't hide a grin at Kerewa's words and wondered how Kehi would react if he could hear them!

"Lead us to them, please Oren." Khai said, feeling a little more cheerful that the young ones were happy to take control of the situation.

In the Ohikanui River Valley, Syd and Daphne were having a rest while the family were searching for food nearby. Kohana was enjoying her visit to now familiar places, where she learnt to swim, and where she had her fight with the possum. She also recognised the calls of the local owl community in the distance and wondered if they would come to visit them. Kohana didn't know it, but they had already been spotted and that their progress was already being relayed to Odion at Three Sisters Mountain.

Orlando and Odessa were feeling elated at being completely free and at last they were going home. They had already visited Odion and Oana, who were surprised that they were no longer acting as Kohana's guardian.

"Kohana has good family support around her now. You will meet them when they get here." Odessa informed them. "Oren and his community are available to help if she needs them too."

Their excitement mounted as the Lake Hills came into view. Lake Kaniere lay dark and quiet as they crossed to Hans Bay. For once there were no lights from any of the homes that lay near its shore. As they came to Mount Tuhua Odessa gave a call. Her mother Orchid answered, telling them to come to the school. Both Orlando and Odessa were unprepared for the sight that awaited them as they flew in to the cave. The whole community was there, both night and day animals as well. Orlando's family was among them too, crowded around a mat where Ollie lay. They could see wounds to Ollie's body that could not be healed. The crowd let Orlando and Odessa through to stand next to Ollie's mat.

"What happened?" Orlando asked to no-one in particular.

"The Harrier got him." After seeing Orlando's vengeful face, they added. "The Owls have dealt with it."

Odessa leant down to speak to Ollie.

"Ollie, it is Odessa and Orlando. We have come home."

Ollie opened his eyes and gave them a little smile. He mouthed the words "Welcome Home." Before he closed them and gave a little sigh as he allowed his spirit to leave and be free in the spirit world, that till now he could only visit in his dreams.

In the Ohikanui Valley, Kohana stopped her feed and went to the water's edge, where her tears mingled with the flowing water of the stream. Kotare seeing her distress came up to cling to her legs. Kamora had been feeding with them, took one look and called for Kehi as she came to try to comfort her.

"What is it?" Kehi asked with concern as he wrapped them in his body. There hadn't been anything to indicate any problems till now.

"Ollie has been killed." Kohana managed to say.

One of the local owls had been sitting quietly in the nearby tree watching the visitors as they moved along the valley. The mention of Ollie's name perked up his ears. Every owl on the Island knew who Ollie was.

"What did you say?" The owl called down to Kohana.

"A Harrier badly wounded Ollie and now he has died." Kohana informed him. Can you get word to Oren and Odion? His son Oriel will be the next Kingdom guardian." The Owl flew off to do her bidding.

"Did you want to go straight to the Lake?" Kehi asked, in case Kohana wanted to go there first.

"No. He will already be buried before I can reach there. I will say my goodbye while we are there."

In the Buller, Oren led Khai Kerewa Katana and Kailan to the valley where the Kiwis had been seen and landed in a tree overlooking the track that led to their area. In the distance Kerewa could see Kiwis he recognised from his old community.

"I know them." Kerewa remarked to Khai and Kailan, before calling out to the new arrivals.

"Hello and welcome. What brings you down here?"

Their tired grim faces told their tale of woe before they spoke.

"We are hoping you will take us in. Where's Koha?"

"Is it that bad up there?" Their grim nods confirmed the horror they had left behind.

"Kehi and Koha are having a well-earned break at present.   Kerewa informed them before introducing Khai and Kailan. "Khai Kailan and I are in charge here now. We feel sorry for what you have been through, but before we can take you in, we need you to agree to the Kiwi Kingdom rules. Can you remember what they are?"

"Um, Not to kill." Said one Kiwi.

"To respect and help all animals." Said another.

"Have a school to meet and get on with other animals." Said someone else.

"Do you all agree to these rules?" asked Khai, looking at them individually.

"Yes." They all chorused and nodded their heads.

"Out of interest, what if we hadn't agreed?" asked one.

"We would have escorted you out of our territory to the Alps." Kailan said with a gleam in his eye as he pointed to the distant mountain range.

"That will happen if you break the rules." Kerewa added firmly.

"Come along," Khai told the new arrivals. "We have feeding grounds to show you, along with the school and our meeting area for anything the community needs to discuss, not to mention organising your burrows before morning comes."

Syd and Daphne sat down for Kehi and his family to get off. They had reached the base of Three Sister's Mountain. Kapali and Kalasia were waiting for them, along with Odion and Oana.

"Thank you for bringing us and have a good rest." Kohana said before making the climb up the mountain. We will see you when we are ready to move south."

"Thank you for telling us about Ollie." Odion said after greeting them. "Oren and I went down to his farewell along with all the other leaders."

 "How are Ollie's family coping?" Kohana wanted to know.

"They are coping." Odion replied. "Oriel has lots of support, with Oswin Oscar and Orlando there to help with any decisions he isn't sure of."

"Oscar is there now?" Kohana was surprised.

"Yes. Oscar doesn't fly far these days, but he was determined to make it to the farewell. He has decided to spend his time at Kaniere now."

As Kapali and Kalasia led them up the mountain, Kohana asked if they had any concerns with their community. Kohana didn't think anything of it, but both Koa and Kiana stayed close by as they had their conversation.

"What would we be concerned about up here?" Kapali asked. "We haven't had any Kakates around here recently and our community hasn't complained about anything for a long time."

"What about the survival of your young?" Kohana asked. "Nearly everywhere else the communities need human help to maintain their numbers because their young are taken and eaten while still in their egg or killed while they are too small to defend themselves. Did you know that Keka's community near Okarito had to move because they lost most of their young to animals who insisted on eating them?"

Kapali was silent for a moment as he considered Kohana's words.

"It's happening here too!" Kapali admitted sadly. "We didn't know there was anything that could be done about it. How are the humans helping?"

"At Kanoa's community, humans are putting down traps to catch the animals that prey on their young. They are having a lot of success there too."

"I haven't been down to Kanoa's community." Kapali was thoughtful. "I think it's time I paid him a visit."

At the school cave the community had gathered to welcome them. Kohana was reunited with Kalea and Koro. Kamaka and his family were waiting for them too. Everyone who remembered the young Kohana was amazed at her transformation to the self-assured caring adult that she had become. Kotare quickly found some new friends to play and explore this new place with. Koa checked out the library, seeing what books they had there. Koha and Kamora joined him. They all stopped at The Kiwi Kingdom Book. Kalea and Kiana saw them gathered around it and came over.

"I see you have found The Kiwi Kingdom Book." Kalea said with a smile as she very gently ran her claw over the claw sign on the cover. "You should see the real one."

"Kohana has promised to take us to Lake Kaniere on this trip." Kamora replied. "I'm wishing we had brought Kuri with us now, though I'm not sure she would have climbed this mountain."

"Who is Kuri?" Kalea wanted to know.

"Kuri is the great granddaughter of the female who rescued Keoni's egg."

Kalea looked at Kamora with a stunned look.

"I think we should try to arrange a visit for Kuri, to the place where Keoni came from." Kalea began. "Do you think she would cope with riding on a chamois?"

"I think she would love it." Kamora replied, with shining eyes. I would love to come too."

"You can count me in too." Kiana added.

"We will make it a ladies trip then." Kalea concluded with a smile.

"Are we allowed to look at the book?" Koa asked, knowing it was special.

"I'm sorry, but no, unless you intend to be the next leader of the Kiwi Kingdom?" Kalea asked with a smile.

"Kohana has read it?" Koa asked.

"She has. It is part of the new leader's preparation for their role."

Koa was tempted to say, that if anything happened to Kohana, he would be back to read it. But he remained silent and forced himself to move on and look at other books.

On the island Odessa examined the tree hollow with delight and gave Orlando a big smile.

"It will be perfect." She declared, looking out across the water towards Hans Bay and Mount Tahua.   The thick canopy of forest on the Island sheltered them from the weather coming in from the Tasman Sea. Her mother Orchid had been disappointed that they hadn't settled near them on Tahua, but understood their need to find their own place.

CHAPTER SIXTEEN

THE MESSAGE

When it was time for Kehi's family to visit Kanoa at the Paparoa community, Kapali was with them. Everyone loved the wild beauty of the coast as they moved south. Seeing and smelling the sea spray as the waves rolled in to the shore along the wide windswept bays. At Punakaiki, Kanoa and Koana were waiting for them.

"Have you seen the rocks yet?" Kanoa asked with a grin. The sound of waves crashing could be heard in the background.

"I have," Kohana replied with a beam, "Though I was only little when Mum brought me and I had lots of fun getting very wet!"

With that small warning, the unsuspecting family were led on a sealed path through thick bushland that formed a tunnel overhead. As they came closer to the crashing waves, the ground shook under their feet.

"What is that?" Koha called in alarm. He had been in earthquakes, but this was much stronger than any quakes he had felt.

"That is the waves crashing into the rocks." Kohana replied with a smile. "It is quite safe here. Humans have been coming here for many years to enjoy this."

As they came out into the open, the family were amazed to see the strange rock formations all around them. Thin grey slabs of rock stacked on top of each other in many shapes and sizes. Fascinated, they followed the winding trail till they felt a big thump and heard a loud whoosh as water shot up through a blow hole. Suddenly they were ducking as a large spray of water rained all over them. Kotare squealed then laughed, running around soaking wet. When the next wave came he stood and lifted his head up to feel the spray of water flow over him; while everyone else had retreated to a safe distance.

"He is really enjoying it." Kehi murmured to Kohana.

"Yes," Kohana agreed. "I was the same at his age. The joy of it will stay with him when he grows up." Kohana became silent as she allowed the special atmosphere of this place flow over her. She was drawn to a rock platform overlooking the sea.

"I want to show you something." Kohana said as she invited Kehi to follow her. Kehi carefully picked his way through the rocks as she led him to the platform. "This is where both Keoni and Kupe pledged to their partners." Kohana whispered as they stood together and looked out over the ocean. They smiled as they felt Kotare come and cling to their legs. Suddenly she had a vision of a grown Kotare standing here with a female.

"It's where Kotare will come for his pledge too."

"You can see it?" Kehi asked. Kohana nodded.

"What will I be doing Mum?" Kotare asked, after hearing his name mentioned.

"You will come back one day."

"I hope it's soon." Kotare declared. "This has been fun."

As Kanoa led them up into the range where his community lived, Kapali asked how their young chicks from this season were going.

"It's the best season we have had." Kanoa was relieved to say. "It would be very different if we didn't have the traps."

"I'm looking forward to seeing them and how they work." Kapali replied. "We could do with some of them in our community."

"Is it bad up your way too?" Kanoa asked with sympathy.

"We have only a few chicks left." Kapali said with sorrow. "Up to now, I thought there wasn't anything we could do about it, but Kohana mentioned that you were getting help from humans, and that their traps are working well. Out of interest, what are those things on your legs? Kapali asked.

"They are bands that the humans put on us." Kanoa replied and stopped to look at everyone else's legs. "They don't come to your communities do they?"

"The only humans we've had near us are hunters!" Kehi replied in disgust.

"We don't have hunters here." Kanoa reassured them.

"What are the bands on your legs for? Koha wanted to know.

"They tell the humans who we are." Kanoa explained. Sometimes they come to catch us and put us in a bag to weigh us before they let us go again. We were scared when they first came with their dog to do their checks, but we are used to it now." He looked at Koana fondly. "Koana still likes to give them a scratch if she can manage it, when they catch her."

"Someone has to show them who is in charge here!" Koana replied with spirit.

Kanoa's happy grin showed everyone he was happy she was in charge.

As they came to the community burrows, Kapali realised he had an even bigger problem. – How was he to get help from humans for his community, if they didn't know they needed help?

After everyone was settled in their burrows, Kanoa took Kapali outside again to look at the traps the humans had set, showing him where the animals went inside. Kapali could smell something rotten inside. He could also smell a stoat smell on the side!

"Is a stoat in there?" Kapali wanted to know.

"No, the rotten smell is the bait, and the stoat smell is where the humans rub the stoat on the trap to attract others." Kanoa informed him.

Kapali looked all around the trap; there was wire on most sides, with nowhere to leave a message. He climbed on top, which was covered in board. *"Good!"* Kapali thought. *"I will be able to leave them a message here!"* Kapali jumped off and started to search the ground.

"What are you looking for?" Kanoa was puzzled.

"I am looking for a rock or stick." Kapali explained. "I want to leave the humans a message that we need help."

Kanoa joined him in his search, till finally they found a sharp rock. Kapali put the rock in his bill and climbed up on top of the trap. He tried to write his message, but it didn't show very well. *"What if the humans missed it? My mission would have been in vain."* Kapali knew it worked in dirt, but would the humans see it there?

"We need some dirt!" Kapali exclaimed.

"What do you want the dirt for?" Kanoa realised he was being educated.

"If we smear the dirt on here, the humans will be able to see my message!"

Kanoa quickly dug down through the leaf litter and moss to the dirt and flicked some up to Kapali who quickly smeared some over the message he had written. It worked! He could see the message now.

"You can stop now." Kapali told Kanoa as the dirt was starting to cover him too and gave himself a shake to remove most of the dirt.

"How does it look?" Kanoa wanted to know

"Come and see." Kapali invited him with a grin.

Kanoa climbed back up on top and was amazed at what he saw.

HELP

3 SISTERS ^

"What does it say?" Kanoa wanted to know. He had seen the books humans had made when he visited Lake Kaniere with Kupe, but he didn't remember how to read the language.

"It says "Help. Want traps for Three Sisters Mountain." How long will it be before the humans come back to check the traps? Kapali asked as he looked at the cloudy sky. "I hope rain doesn't wash my message away before they come."

"What if we cover it with more dirt and leaves?" Kanoa suggested. "The humans seem to know when there is an animal in the traps and come then."

"That's a good idea." Kapali agreed as he looked around. "They must have a way of seeing that we don't know about."

Kanoa and Kapali worked quickly to cover the words etched into the wooden top before they retreated to Kanoa's burrow; for daylight would be here soon, and with it, stoats weasels and all the other day animals.

Doug from DOC sat down at his computer to check the footage from the cameras in the Paparoa range, before they reset for the next twenty four hours. He smiled as he recognised Kanoa and Koana as they passed the camera. Doug was about to grab his cup of coffee when he stopped. Behind Kanoa and Koana were a large family that he didn't recognise. He could see they didn't have bands on, so where had they come from, and why were they here?

Doug was even more intrigued when Kanoa brought a male from the group to look at one of the traps. Doug noticed the male had a stone hanging around his neck. Who had put it there? The local Kiwis didn't usually bother with the traps now. This Kiwi was certainly checking it out well, even getting up on top! Doug was stunned at what he saw next. This Kiwi had a stone in his bill then started using it as a tool to make marks in the wooden top before covering it with dirt. When this kiwi wiped the dirt away Doug could see there were words! Kanoa looked at the words too, before they covered the top with more dirt and leaves. Doug had seen enough! He had to get up there to see what that message was and give these new arrivals a check and band them.

"Cheryl!" Doug called, "Where's Malcolm? We have some work to do at Punakaiki."

"Do you need all of us?" Cheryl wanted to know.

"Yes, we need all of us."

Sleep was rudely interrupted for Kehi and his family that morning. A dog with a muzzle came to their burrow and a human hand well protected with a glove came and pulled out Kehi and Koha who were lying close to the entrance. Kohana knew they would be next as Kamora Kiana and Kotare came to crowd around her in fear. Despite their protests, and attempts to claw the humans hanging onto them they were measured and weighed before bands were put on.

"Oh!" Kohana said with a grim smile. "This must be what Kanoa means by a check! We might as well get it done so they go away and leave us in peace." At that Kohana walked confidently forward towards the gloved hand and much to the holder's surprise, jumped onto the glove to be pulled out into the harsh sunlight.

"Mum!" cried Kotare at seeing both his father and mother taken away.

"It's alright." Kohana reassured him. "Come out and join us."

As Kotare accompanied by Kamora and Kiana came to the burrow entrance, a smaller gloved hand came to gently pick him up for his checks too.

Once Kehi and Koha were done, they were put into a box where Kapali was already waiting for them. He had been separated from Kanoa and Koana who were watching the scene from their burrow with big grins on their faces. Kapali had panicked when he was lifted upside down with his legs to be put in the bag for weighing, for his amulet had slipped off his head.

Kapali tried to catch it with his bill, but missed and struggled in vain to free his legs to retrieve it.

When the bag was opened, Kapali could see the human had his amulet over his arm. After picking him up, and laying Kapali in his arm – Kapali noticed this human still had a good grip of his feet! The human lifted up his amulet and had a good look at the river washed stone.

"It's pounamu." Doug declared before slipping it back over Kapali's head again. "I wonder who and what you are in your world? Cheryl, did you bring any trackers?"

"They are in the blue bag next to the box."

Kapali found a much larger ring being attached to his leg.

Cheryl noticed the large pale female was much calmer than the others, but very observant of everything that was going on. Something told her this female was special too.

"We will put a tracker on her too." Cheryl said as she passed one to Malcolm to put on Kohana.

Everyone was relieved to be returned to their burrows, with Kehi's family ready to settle down for their sleep again. Kapali however, remained anxious whether the humans had seen his message and loitered by the burrow entrance while the humans packed up and carefully followed them. He was happy to see them stop at the trap where he had left the message and clear off the dirt and leaves.

"Is this for real?" Malcolm asked.

"See that Kiwi that has followed us?" Doug pointed at Kapali as he tried to hide behind the tree, "He wrote it! – It's all on tape." Doug came half way back and knelt down closer to the ground. When Kapali put his head around to see what was happening, Doug was looking at him.

"We are coming to help you." Doug said quietly before turning to leave.

"What happened?" Kanoa asked when Kapali returned

"They found the message and they are coming to help."

CHAPTER SEVENTEEN

THE ULTIMATUM

In the Buller, Kerewa Khai and Kailan were happy their new arrivals were settling in well, even though more were trickling down as conditions deteriorated in the north. The calm atmosphere ended one evening when Oren alerted Khai to another group coming from the north, though this group were coming from a different direction. As Kerewa and Kailan rushed to join Khai, he developed a feeling that trouble was coming with this group. Khai decided to put out a call to the whole community. The more community members available to support them the better!

As everyone, including Kerewa and Kailan gathered around him. Khai gave them the news that he thought that this group of arrivals were bringing trouble, and he needed all of them to support him. With their agreement to help, Khai then led the community to meet the coming threat.

Kaine the Kiwi leader from the Tasman was angry. For many years peace had reigned in the vast forested area in the north when Koha had been the leader. With no warning members of Koha's community had started arriving and causing havoc in Kaine's territory, with their inability to adjust to a new way of living. He paid a visit to Koha's territory to find chaos! Half the community was now missing and those that remained were too busy quarrelling and fighting to take any notice of anything Kaine said.

All he could discover from one sad and disillusioned Kiwi was that Koha had abandoned them to join Kehi's community. The Kiwi didn't know where to go to escape the madness that now reigned here.

A grim Kaine was now on a mission to find out why Koha had abandoned his community and wanted answers on how to manage the situation, not to mention the malcontents now causing trouble in his area.

As Kaine's group came closer to Kehi's area, they noticed owls gathering in the trees around them and shadowing them as they walked. In the distance they could see a group of Kiwis waiting for them. In fact, it looked like the whole community had turned out to meet them, though Kaine couldn't see either Koha or Kehi. As Kaine's group came closer, Kerewa recognised him.

"It is Kaine, the leader of the Tasman community." Kerewa informed Khai.

"The Kiwis back home are probably causing him trouble."

When Kaine's group came close enough to speak, He stopped to shout out his demand.

"Where is Koha? Bring him to me NOW! The anger in Kaine's voice was plain.

Kerewa, Khai and Kailan stepped forward together.

"Hello Kaine," Kerewa began. "I am Kerewa, Koha's son, and this is Khai and his son Kailan. We are in charge here while both Koha and Kehi are away. I take it you want to talk about the community in the north. Will you please come with us to our meeting area to have a talk?"

Kaine knew he had no choice, but to obey, so he nodded his agreement to follow them while the remainder of the community fell in behind his group. At the meeting area Kerewa Khai and Kailan chose to sit at the bottom of the valley, with Kaine and his supporters across from them, the community sent to sit on the slopes around them. Kaine noticed the owls had come to watch proceedings here as well.

"Why are the owls here?" Kaine wanted to know.

"They are part of our community now." Khai informed him with a smile.

"What sort of community have you got, that Koha abandoned his?" Kaine's anger still flowed.

"Dad didn't abandon his community." Kerewa spoke in Koha's defence. "There was a vote of the whole community, whether to become part of the Kiwi Kingdom, which went against him."

"They made him leave?" Kaine asked with concern.

"No," Kerewa replied with care. "The vote made his position there no longer viable."

"Why didn't he send word to tell me what had happened?"

"There wasn't time." Kerewa explained. "There was another vote of those who supported dad and we all left the area straight away to come here."

"Why didn't you come to us? We would have taken you in." Kaine was puzzled.

"They already had a home waiting for them here." Khai said kindly. "Koha wanted to be part of the Kiwi Kingdom. Did you know the current leader Kohana is now Kehi's mate?"

"What happened to Kiyo?" Kaine was astonished at this news.

"Sadly, Mum was killed." Kerewa began.

"That has all been sorted." Khai interrupted in a tone that left Kaine in no doubt of the outcome.

"So, you've had a few issues here as well." Kaine commented thoughtfully.

"You could say that." Khai admitted, "but it is all under control here now."

"Well it isn't under control up north and they are coming and causing havoc in our area too!" Kaine was still upset. "Something needs to be done about it! When are Koha and Kehi coming back?"

"I think we can expect them will be away for some time." Khai informed him. "They are accompanying Kohana on a tour of the entire Kiwi Kingdom, which will take them down to the bottom of this Island in Fiordland. Any problems will have to be sorted between us."

"You mentioned that Kiwis from the north are causing trouble in your area." Kailan pointed out. "When any new arrivals come here, we give them an ultimatum to abide by the rules of our area, or we won't allow them to stay. Perhaps you can enforce that rule too? Also, we make it plain, that if they don't obey our rules, they will be expelled from our territory and the Kiwi Kingdom, which only leaves the Alps for them to live in."

"An ultimatum; I like that." Kaine finally smiled. He knew what to do when he returned to the North Buller! "Out of interest, how far up does Kehi's territory go these days?"

"We can take you to our school where we keep maps of this Island and show you." Kerewa offered, "but if you have any plans to take over the area that is now uncontrolled, then we need to renegotiate where boundaries will be."

"That's fair." Kaine agreed, realising that he had been outmanoeuvred.

A walk to the school was carried out; again with Khai Kerewa and Kailan leading Kaine and his supporters and the community following them, this time to ensure justice was done. Kaine and his supporters had never seen a book before, so Kerewa had to explain what they were seeing on the map.

"This is the ocean that surrounds our Island." Kerewa pointed to the blue areas on the map. "That is your area in the Tasman. This Kehi's area and we are here, and there is the uncontrolled area." Kerewa pointed to the areas on the map. "Do you agree to your boundary being here?" Kerewa pointed to the half way point between the Tasman and Buller."

"Your father's territory will be in mine now." Kaine pointed out.

"It isn't my father's territory anymore."

"Are you going to come with me and sort out those Kiwis that are still fighting?" Kaine asked Kerewa.

"No." Kerewa declined. "I'm sure you will sort those in your territory. The others on our side should soon stop fighting when they find there is no territory for them to fight over now. If not, we will sort them when they come here."

"You don't care about your community!" Kaine tried to make Kerewa feel guilty.

"I refuse to feel guilty when that community rejected us!" Kerewa countered coolly, he wasn't going to let Kaine see the anger he was feeling. "Their predicament is of their own making. It was their choice to continue living by old ideas that don't work anymore."

"And your Kingdom does? Kaine asked in a disbelieving tone.

"It certainly does." Khai smiled. "The remainder of this Island has chosen to live by Kingdom rule. You should try it!"

Stone-faced, Kaine abruptly rose; his supporters rose with him.

"You are leaving so soon?" Kailan asked.

"We have work to get back to." And with that Kaine stormed out of the cave to head north.

There was a small silence after Kaine and his supporters left. Khai and Kailan looked at Kerewa to see he was deep in thought. They knew he was already planning something to counter Kaine's ambitions.

"Can someone check no-one from Kaine's group is watching or listening what we do?"

Oren called to his owls in the surrounding trees.

"One of them is hiding behind a tree." Oren informed Kerewa.

"Eliminate him!" Kerewa ordered Khai and Kailan.

"Are you sure?" Khai asked, "what about Kingdom rules?"

"They are suspended till we deal with Kaine." Kerewa informed him. "I know Kaine was intending to kill me if I had gone with them. After killing the remainder of dad's community, they would have been back to take over here!" Khai and Kailan went out to do Kerewa's bidding. The community watched silently, wondering what Kerewa would do next.

"Do you want us to keep watch on Kaine and his supporters?" Oren asked.

"I want you to keep well away from them if you can, and warn other owls in the north to do the same." Kerewa informed him. "We need to concentrate on helping as many of dad's community as we can. Send word to the north that all Kiwis from Koha's old area are in mortal danger. They are to move south, but to avoid Kaine and his supporters. Those that are already in Kaine's territory are to be warned to move south if they can, or move to the east out of his territory."

Oren quickly flew to do Kerewa's bidding. Within hours, Kiwis in Koha's old area were being approached and given the grim news of the coming danger. By morning, Kiwis in Kaine's territory knew as well. Once local Kiwis were sleeping an exodus began.

When Khai and Kailan came back, Kerewa asked if the Kiwi was gone.

"He saw us coming and fled for his life!" Kailan informed Kerewa.

"I also yelled at him to never come back and to make sure they stay their side of their territory, or else!" Khai added.

"Good!" Kerewa was satisfied.

When the Kiwi caught up with Kaine, he asked what Kerewa was doing.

"He sent Khai and Kailan out to get me, but I managed to escape!"

The terrified Kiwi reported. "They also said for me to never come back and for us to stay our side of our territory or else!"

As Kaine moved north, he realised he had completely misjudged Kehi's son. Kerewa was as strong, if not stronger than his father and he was also much more astute! Kaine had gained some more territory, but they were now completely isolated from the rest of the Island, a situation Kaine hadn't intended to be in.

As they approached Koha's old territory, they had expected to deal with quarrelling Kiwis, but it was strangely empty and silent. When they returned to his own area, all Koha's Kiwis were gone from there too. No-one had seen where the Kiwis had gone to. They had been around at bedtime, but had vanished when they woke. Kaine now knew he was dealing with something much more powerful than he could imagine.

Several nights later, the owls brought some news from the north. Kerewa was being thanked as everyone had escaped, including those in Kaine's area. They were all safe in Kerewa's territory and would make sure that Kaine and his community would never set foot in it again.

When Oriel received word of the changes in the Buller and the Tasman, he wondered how Kehi and Koha would take the news of the attempted challenge to his authority and the takeover of some of Koha's territory. In the Buller, Kerewa was accepting the fact that he wanted to keep the leadership after all.

CHAPTER EIGHTEEN

THE WELCOME

Kuri was feeding contentedly with other family members. It would soon be sleep time, when Kerewa came to see her.

"Kuri, you have a visitor." He announced with a smile. Mystified, Kuri and her family followed him to meet a pale grey female. At first Kuri thought she was Kohana, but she could see this Kiwi had different eyes. Also, she had a large animal with her that Kuri hadn't seen before.

"Are you Kohana's mother?" Kuri asked.

"Yes, I'm Kalea." Kalea introduced herself. "Kohana mentioned that your great grandmother Kuri saved Keoni when Kailee died. I lived in his old tunnels with Kupe when we were at the lake." Kalea informed her. "I'm here to see if you would like to visit them with me."

"We would be travelling on that animal?" Kuri asked

"Yes, please meet Charlotte." Kalea introduced her. "She is a Chamois. Charlotte is a valued member of our community at Three Sisters Mountain. Charlotte has agreed to take us, if you would like to come."

"Hello Charlotte. I would love to come."

"Hello Kuri. I'm pleased to be taking you to Lake Kaniere. It is such a beautiful place to visit."

Kuri's granddaughter Kaimani watched wistfully as Kuri said her goodbyes.

"Can I come next time?" Kaimani asked.

Her mother Kai and Kalea looked at each other and nodded.

"Would you like to come with us?" Kalea offered.

Kaimani's shining eyes spoke for her.

As Charlotte set off, Kai was quietly happy that a member of the family was travelling with Kuri on this adventure. At his office at the Department of Conservation, Doug was looking at his computer screen with interest. The male Kiwi was home at Three Sisters Mountain already. The distance was too far for him to cover on foot, which meant he had hitched a ride. The question was, how? Doug looked at the GPS location of the female. She too had travelled a long distance, but she was heading south. It was time to look at the Punakaiki cameras to see if there were any clues. He was pleased to see a stoat had come and needed to be collected. It wasn't till near morning that the answer was captured by the camera. First a Chamois strolled past. Shortly afterwards a stag and hind came along too. The Chamois returned with the male Kiwi on its back, but there was no further sign of the deer in the area. When Doug collected the stoat, he checked the burrows. Only Kanoa and Koana were present.

Kohana was happy with their progress as Syd and Daphne took them on her planned route through the Paparoa range, following the Punakaiki River up to the hilltops, keeping well away from any roads and settlements. Koha and Kamora found it difficult to adjust to sleeping on the deer's back at first, but soon succumbed to sleep to visit their dream worlds. In coming days and nights they would cross the Grey River to head further south through the Brunner area to the Marsden District, crossing many streams as they went.

Kehi's family didn't know it, but they had company as they quietly foraged in the forest. Boris the Boar had roamed the area for many years, after escaping from his paddock and successfully evaded all attempts to capture him. As Kohana clambered around the base of a large tree, she was aware of a strange smell and could feel something looking at her. When she spotted the creature that was staring at her, Kohana recoiled in horror. From the books in the school library Kohana recognised it as a Boar, she knew she was in trouble!

Kohana gave a scream as she started running for her life! As she tore through the undergrowth with Boris in hot pursuit, Syd's loud roar was answered by the stag on the deer farm. Everyone in the Marsden valley heard them and knew that they had a second Stag in their area. As Kohana and Boris shot past him, Syd put his head down and rammed Boris with his antlers. Boris was much too big to toss, so Syd drove and pinned him to the nearest tree.

After Syd had announced his presence, some of the men in the community had sat up with the intention of popping out to hunt for a feed of venison; but they were stopped by the screams of Boris which rent the night air as he realised that both his freedom and his life was about to end. The hunters weren't prepared to take on a wounded Boar in the middle of the night, so settled back down to wait for dawn.

When Boris eventually lay still, Syd withdrew; however a couple of tines from his antlers remained with Boris. After that meeting, everyone agreed it was time to move on.

As they crossed the bridge at the Taramakau River, Koha and Kehi became nervous; whenever they came across roads they knew that Humans weren't far away. To their relief the roads stayed empty. Everyone was happy when they crossed the Arahura River to be told they were nearly at the lake. As the deer climbed the forested hillside towards the lake, they were spotted by Protea Pigeon, who promptly flew to tell Oriel.

Kohana saw the pigeon take one look at them before heading off in the direction of Mount Tahua. They would not be allowed to sneak in quietly! Very soon they were surrounded by birds, all chatting excitedly as they escorted them to the lake. At the junction, Daylight was lighting the peaks behind the lake, the deep waters were dark and still, before the morning breeze came to ruffle its surface.

As they dismounted from Syd and Daphne, Kotare rushed over to paddle in the water. Kohana could see she would have to give him swimming lessons! As Kotare splashed, a long dark shape came near to him. Kotare turned to get out. He wasn't at all sure this creature was friendly; when it spoke to him.

"Hello who are you? Are you here for a visit?"

Kotare turned back to face the creature. It seemed to have a smile on its face.

"I'm Kotare. Yes, I'm here with my family. My Mum Kohana and Dad Kehi are over there."

"Oh! They are here at last! Everyone has been waiting for them to come. I will see you later." With that the creature disappeared towards the depths of the lake.

As the family came to watch Kotare as he paddled, Kohana spotted three owls flying towards them. She recognised two of them. Orlando and Odessa were coming! Behind them the lake ducks were flying in too, and the Bat colony could be seen descending from Mount Tahua. The trees surrounding the junction were already filling with birds, all here to see the new Kingdom leader.

Koha Kamora Koa and Kiana looked around in wonder at all the birds that had gathered around them and could see the owls ducks and bats approaching from Hans Bay.

"It looks like your welcoming committee is coming." Kehi grinned at Kohana, remembering all the animals he met on his last visit. He turned to Koha and his family. "They are only some of the creatures you will meet while you are here."

Syd and Daphne were about to slip into the forest next to the junction when they were stopped by a family of Pukekos. Peony and Pene had been foraging with their children Pearl Pansy Painga and Pake, when they had seen Kohana and her family arrive.

"Hello. I'm Pake. What are your names?" Pake wanted to know. He had heard all about Stan the stag and Delphinia his hind who used to live here. He wasn't about to let these deer slink away!

"Hello Pake." They greeted him. "I am Daphne and this is Syd."

"What happened to your antlers Syd?" Pake asked after seeing some had been broken off.

"On our way here, a wild Boar chased Kohana, so I pinned it to a tree." Syd said modestly.

"Wow!" Pake's eyes were shining. "Listen, everyone." Pake called out loudly. "Syd has saved Kohana's life! He stopped a wild Boar that chased her."

"Yes, and I'm very grateful!" Kohana replied in the silence that followed Pake's words.

Syd and Daphne found themselves mobbed by birds, thanking them for saving Kohana.

"Welcome to the Kingdom!" Oriel said as he landed before Kohana, with Orlando and Odessa behind him. They were followed by Daisy and Davie duck and their now large family who quickly gathered around the family, asking them questions about their life back home. Boronia Bat led the colony to the surrounding trees, surveying the scene, untill Kotare came up to them.

"Hello, I'm Kotare." He called out to the bats. He knew what they were, as the local bat colony attended his school. "Where do you live?"

"Hello Kotare." Boronia replied. "We live in a cave on Mount Tahua. The school cave is there."

"Do you have Kiwis at your school?" Kotare wanted to know.

"Not anymore." Boronia replied sadly, but we do have lots of other animals for you to meet and play with there."

"What kind of animals?" Kotare wanted to know.

"You haven't met the Hedgehogs, Possums, Stoats, Weasels or Wekas yet."

Kotare brightened at this news. He had met Possums and Stoats at his school, but hadn't met Hedgehogs Weasels or Wekas yet.

As dawn came to the lake, Kohana and her family remounted Syd and Daphne, to be led to Conical Hill. It was safer for them to stay with Kaori and Keely. Kotare was excited to find he was sharing a tunnel with Kian and Koa while Kiana shared with Kana. Both Kehi and Koha were happy to have Kohana and Kamora to themselves again in burrows that were more snug than they were used to.

"We will have to make a few changes to this." Kohana commented after looking around.

Kehi looked at her with wide eyes.

"Yes." Kohana confirmed. "I have been too busy to think about it, but I will be delivering an egg very soon."

"That means we will be here till after it's hatched." Kehi commented happily. He liked this place already and was happy they would be staying for longer.

Syd and Daphne had been sent to the other side of Conical hill, with the warning that if any noisy aircraft flew overhead, they were to keep very still till it passed.

They were happy to find they were in a protected valley between this hill and a higher mountain. Apart from some birds and possums, they had the area all to themselves.

In the Ohikanui valley Kalea pointed out Three Sisters Mountain to Kuri and Kaimani.

"We aren't going to visit?" Kaimani asked.

"We will call in on the way back." Kalea promised.

Both Kuri and Kaimani were in awe when they visited the pancake rocks at Punakaiki. They were even happier to know that Keoni and his mate Kaimani had been here too. Kanoa and Koana were delighted to have Kalea Kuri and Kaimani stay for their sleep time. Kanoa looked at Kalea's legs and knew the humans hadn't visited Three Sisters community yet.

At DOC Doug reviewed the camera footage at Paparoa to find a chamois with three Kiwis on its back had come to visit. One of them was pale like the female they were tracking. Were they related? His office was still planning for their visit to the Three Sisters community. It was much more remote and harder to access than Paparoa.

Kaimani looked at the bands on both Kanoa and Koana's legs, wanting to know what they were for. When it was explained that they were identity bands that humans had put on them, Kaimani became alarmed but Kanoa reassured her that these humans were here to help Kiwis stay alive. This was helpful when a little later a dog came to the burrow with some humans to give them checks and put bands on.

"We all match now." Kanoa quipped with a cheeky smile.

"I have to say, I wasn't expecting to return home with these on." Kuri commented with amusement. This was going to be a bigger adventure than she had expected.

CHAPTER NINETEEN

MEETING KEONI

Kohana and Kehi slipped out of their burrow in the evening light. The last rays of golden sunlight shone on the tops of Mount Tahua and the Alps beyond. The twinkle of lights could be seen in the houses over in Hans Bay. Kian and Kana were already showing Koa Kotare and Kiana the best feeding spots on the hill.

After admiring the view, Kehi returned to their burrow and started digging. The sound of Kehi's digging brought Koha and Kamora out of their burrow too.

"Was it too cramped for you?" Koha asked Kohana with a grin. They had plans to expand their burrow too, depending on how long they were staying.

"We are going to be staying longer than we expected." Kohana replied happily. "I have an egg to deliver soon."

"That settles it then." Koha pronounced before joining Kehi in expanding his burrow.

Kaori and Keely and Ketara came out of their burrows to feverish activity from both Kehi and Koha in their burrows.

"We will be staying a while." Kohana explained with an understatement, but her radiant smile gave her secret away.

"I was there for your hatching, and I'm thrilled that you have come here for your little one's arrival too!" Keely said as she came to give Kohana a cuddle.

Daphne came to see whether Kohana needed them this evening.

"No. Have a good rest." Kohana advised her. "We are going to be here for about three months till our next chick is hatched. We will let you know when we need a ride." Daphne returned to give Syd her good news. They had already settled into their home from home.

The sound of bats overhead as they searched for their night feed made Kehi and Koha look up. The night community at Mount Tahua was on the move. Some hours later when school lessons were finished Oriel came, calling for Kohana.

"I'm here." Kohana replied. "You want to know when I'm coming over?"

"Yes." Oriel agreed with a smile. "We are organising a gathering at the school." He didn't tell her that Kona, Kedar, Keka and Kane were all going to be there for her to receive her amulet, the mantle of Leader.

"Will tomorrow night be suitable?" Kohana asked.

"It will be perfect." Oriel agreed. "There will be plenty of room for you to sleep in the cave, so you don't have to rush back."

On his way back to Hans Bay, Oriel made a visit to the Islands. He wanted to see how Orlando and Odessa were managing their owlettes, who were still in the nest. He also came to talk to Kupe. Ollie had told him of the presence of Kupe's spirit on the Island and his wish for visitors and to be kept informed of Kingdom affairs.

As Oriel landed on a tree branch, he could see that Odessa was busy giving the owlettes a feed. He noticed with some concern that one was smaller than the other two and wondered if it would survive. It wasn't unusual for a smaller owlette to be pushed out of the nest by the others so they could have his share of food. The smaller owlette was still too small to survive the drop to the forest floor, or find food for itself. In his thoughts, Oriel made a call to Kupe.

"I am here." Kupe said as he appeared next to Oriel. *"They are coming along well, aren't they?"* Kupe added seeing Oriel watching the young owlettes.

"Yes, though I just hope they don't tip out the smaller one before it can fend for itself." Oriel expressed his concern. *"I've come to tell you of our gathering in the new school cave tomorrow night. Kohana and her family from the Buller are here, so I will give her, her amulet. All the other leaders are arriving for it too."*

"I will make sure Keoni and I are there for it." Kupe promised.

"Where are they all staying?" Kupe wanted to know.

"They are over with Kaori and Keely at Sunny Bight. It looks like Kehi and Koha are settling for a long stay here. Both of them were making their burrows bigger when I visited this evening. I may be wrong, but I think Kohana may deliver an egg very soon."

"Good! Kupe was happy to receive this news. *"I will get to see my new granddaughter or son."*

"I must get back." Oriel said as he finished his visit. *"I can hear someone calling me. I will see you tomorrow."* With that he launched to make his way back to Mount Tahua.

After Oriel left, Kupe watched the owlettes in the nest. Oriel was right! The two bigger owlettes were pecking at the smaller one as it tried to feed and took its food away for themselves.

"It's a shame Ollie can't be there." Kupe thought; as his attention turned to the gathering tomorrow.

"What am I missing?" Ollie appeared next to Kupe on his branch.

"Oriel is having a gathering at the school tomorrow night, to give Kohana her amulet." Kupe smiled at Ollie.

"I will make sure I'm there." Ollie confirmed, though his attention was now focused on the three owlettes who were clamouring for the food that Odessa had just returned with. The larger owlette in the middle was pecking at the smaller owlette who stopped appealing for food to stare at Ollie and Kupe. The little owlette's widened eyes and bobbing head to focus on them, told Ollie that this little owlette could see them. That could only mean that this owlette was connected to the Spirit World! Souls from the Spirit World were not to interfere with the living, but Ollie could see that this little Owlette desperately needed his help!

"That little Owlette can see us! He needs my help! Ollie told Kupe.

"Are you sure?" Kupe was doubtful.

"I am very sure, and I know they will destroy him!"

Ollie flew over to the branch next to Odessa and spoke to her.

"Odessa, it is Ollie. What are the names of your children?"

Startled, Odessa looked around, but couldn't see him, then realised he was communicating to her through her thoughts.

"The little one is Orion, our daughter in the middle is Oriana and our other son is Orel."

"Odessa, Orion is connected to the spirit world! He needs to be protected from the other two or they will kill him!"

"How? We can't be here all the time."

"You need to take turns at being away from the nest, so that one of you is here. Also they need to take turns at being fed first, so that Orion gets a fair chance of feeding. I have just watched you feed them twice. Orion didn't get any. He won't last long if that continues. Call Orlando and arrange something between you."

Odessa noticed that Oriana was pecking at Orion's head quite severely, though Orion was completely ignoring her to look at something next to Odessa. She knew that Orion could see Ollie.

"Oriana! Stop pecking at Orion! You are supposed to help, not hurt each other!" The anger in her mother's voice stopped Oriana. She hadn't heard her use such a sharp tone to them before. "From now on, you will take turns to get your food first."

"We need more food than Orion. We should be fed first!" Orel complained.

"You need more food because you are taking his food as well as your own! This will change!" Odessa spoke severely.

"What is going to change?" Orlando spoke as he landed next to Odessa. He was surprised to hear her using an angry tone to the children.

"Orel and Oriana have been taking all of Orion's food. He won't last long if we allow it to continue. So, from now on, they are to take turns at feeding first!"

"That is fair." Orlando agreed.

"Not only that," Odessa continued. "These two will harm Orion if we don't supervise them. Can you see the peck marks on his head?" Orlando was silent when he saw the red marks where a beak had repeatedly hit the skin on Orion's head. "We will have to take turns to be here, untill Orion is big enough to look after himself."

Orlando nodded his agreement. He didn't trust himself to speak as he was feeling angry at Orion's plight.

Also," Odessa continued, "I've had a visit from Ollie. Orion needs to be protected. He is connected to the spirit world."

"All we hear is Orion, Orion, Orion! I want to kill you!" Orel burst out.

"No you won't!" Orlando couldn't contain his anger, and struck Orel hard. To everyone's horror, Orel overbalanced and fell out of the nest, to tumble down to the forest floor.

"I need to come with you!" Orion spoke as Orlando turned to follow Orel to the ground. Orlando offered a claw to Orion to step on, before lifting him to his shoulder. Orlando then spread his wings to glide down to his stricken son. Odessa quickly followed them.

"I'm sorry." Orlando began, as he bent over Orel's broken body.

"I'm not!" Orel spat back at him. "When I get to the spirit world, I'm going to find Ollie and destroy him!"

"No you won't" Orion said firmly. He pointed his claw at Orel. "I'm sending you to Nudoor!"

Orel's eyes showed surprise before his spirit left him.

"What is Nudoor?" Orlando asked.

"It is a place where his spirit is contained so he can't harm anyone. His body needs to be eaten. Can we give it to the eels?"

Odessa picked up Orel's limp body and flew to the water's edge, before splashing the water. An eel quickly came to see what Odessa wanted.

"Orel our son has died. We are giving him to you."

"You want him to be in the sanctuary?"

"No. He is to be eaten."

"You are sure?" Odessa nodded her assent, before picking Orel up with her beak and waded into the water to place Orel before the eel. Very gently, the eel closed its mouth around the body and consumed it.

"Thank you." Odessa said before both the owls and the eel turned to go their separate ways.

"Why did Orel have to be eaten?" Orlando wanted to know as they returned to the nest.

"So his body can't be revived with another soul like his."

Back at the nest, Oriana was silent and compliant. She was missing Orel already. She vowed that when she got a chance she would get her revenge! Orion was not fooled by Oriana's submissive behaviour. He knew he had an enemy in the nest with him.

Charlotte strode through the familiar forest as they came near Mount Tahua. They had come a long way today and they all were ready for a rest. Skirting around the properties that had been thick bushland when Kalea last left, Kalea guided Charlotte to the old school cave, showing her where to hide if humans came along. Kuri and Kaimani were fascinated to see the pongas lining the walls and roof, and would have liked to explore some more, but reluctantly followed Kalea back out again. In the nearby tree Freesia Fantail could hardly believe her eyes. Kalea was here on a chamois and she had some female Kiwis with her!

"Kalea! We didn't expect to see you. You are just in time for the ceremony!" Freesia informed Kalea as she flitted around her. Kalea Kuri and Kaimani looked at each other with startled eyes.

"Where is the ceremony?" Kalea wanted to know.

"It's in the school cave." Freesia informed her. "I will show you the easy way to reach it. I expect you are hungry. You can feed on the way." As Freesia showed them the winding path up the steep slopes; Kuri and Kaimani were delighted to find an easy meal in the slopes as they climbed and to see glimpses of the lake that Charlotte had talked about. At the cave, Kuri and Kaimani were amazed to see a large crowd of all sorts of animals were already there, including a colony of bats on the ceiling that had the best view in the house. They all seemed to know Kalea who was mobbed by animals wanting to greet her. Everyone returned to their places and all became quiet as an owl flew down into the cave. He was followed by a large family. Among them Kuri and Kaimani recognised Odessa and Orlando. Orlando had an Owlette on his shoulder. The owls gathered near a book. On the cover it had a large Kiwi claw.

When Kuri and Kaimani saw the animals gaze turn to look at the entrance, they too looked up to see Kohana Kotare and Kehi coming down the fern covered slope, followed by a number of Kiwis, including Koha Kamora Koa and Kiana. When Kohana saw her mother, Kuri and Kaimani waiting, she broke into a big smile and came to give her a hug.

"I'm glad you could make it." Kohana said to them.

Everyone was interested to see the owlette's eyes widen and suddenly start looking up around the cave. They couldn't see anything, but obviously he could! Only Kohana could see what Orion was seeing. Ollie Kupe and Keoni were here for the ceremony.

"Dad, Ollie's here!" Orion tried to say it quietly, but didn't succeed. "Who are the two Kiwis?"

"They are Kupe, my Father and Keoni the first Kingdom leader." Kohana informed him with a smile.

There were gasps and grins from the crowd as Ollie Kupe and Keoni allowed themselves to be seen by all. Kaimani gave Kuri a hug as she shed tears of joy. She hadn't expected to see Keoni's spirit.

"Welcome everyone to our little gathering." Oriel began. "A special welcome also, to Kohana and her family from the Buller; and our guests from the spirit world." He looked up at Ollie Kupe and Keoni. "Kohana, can you come forward please?"

Koa noticed for the first time, the book. It was the same book he had seen and been drawn to at Three Sister's Mountain! Koa was transfixed as two possums and a stoat came forward to carefully open the cover. Inside were five envelopes. One had twine hanging from the envelope. The contents of the envelope; a small piece of Pounamu jade attached to the twine was placed on the page.

"Kohana, are you prepared to wear the mantle of Leader of the Kiwi Kingdom?"

"I am."

"Orlando and Odessa, will you come forward?"

Percy and Petunia Possum carefully lifted the twine from the page and opened it out for Orlando and Odessa to grasp with their beaks. Kohana came to them and put her head forward while Orlando and Odessa slipped the Amulet over her neck.

"Kohana Kiwi, you now carry the mantle of leader of the Kiwi Kingdom. You are to wear this amulet at all time as long as you live. In times of extreme danger to you or the amulet, it is to be returned to the book."

"I Will."

Cheers rang out and echoed through the cave system as everyone crowded around to congratulate Kohana. Kalea looked up at Kupe who was beaming at her. She smiled back; then pointed with her claw at Keoni, indicating she wanted him to come to her.

"You are privileged!" a slightly jealous Kupe spoke to Keoni. "My Kalea wants to talk to you!"

As Keoni approached Kalea, she brought Kuri and Kaimani forward.

"Hello Keoni." Kalea smiled at him. "There is someone here I want you to meet. They have come from the northern Buller, the place their family went when your kingdom ended." She turned to Kuri. "This is Kuri, the great granddaughter of Kuri who saved your egg and looked after you when you were hatched; and this is Kaimani her granddaughter.

"I want to express my gratitude and give you my thanks." Keoni began. "I'm aware of how lucky I was that Kuri gave me a second chance at life." He then looked at Kaimani. "I am also very happy to see that my Kaimani is being remembered through your beautiful granddaughter."

Kaimani could see Kuri was too choked with emotion to speak, so she spoke for her.

"It is our privilege to meet you too. We didn't know till recently when

Kohana paid our community a visit that the Kingdom had been restored. We have now joined it in Kehi's community."

"Have you seen the burrows yet?" Keoni wanted to know.

"We will visit them tomorrow." Kalea advised him.

"We will see you then." Keoni promised, before returning to join Kupe.

"They are visiting the burrows tomorrow. You can talk to her there."

"Good." Kupe responded, giving Kalea another smile before they disappeared from view.

During the noise and activity of the gathering as animals met new friends, Koa was once again drawn to the book. As he leant over and gently touched it with his claw, he was stopped by Oriel's voice.

"It's nice to know the kingdom's future leader is ready and waiting to take on their role."

Koa turned around to face Oriel who looked into Koa's eyes with a searching gaze. After being satisfied at what he saw, Oriel gave Koa a smile.

"It is too early for you to read the book, but are you ready for some education for your role?"

"I am." Koa confirmed.

"Go and introduce yourself to the leaders of the other communities and tell them you are interested in knowing how their communities are going. They will want to know how yours is going too." Oriel added with a smile.

Kiana saw Koa with the Kiwi Kingdom Book and his conversation with Oriel, and realised that she was no longer competing with him for leadership at home. Her hopes were dashed however when she saw Oriel seek out Kehi and Koha to speak with them.

"Hello Kehi and Koha." Oriel began. "I hope you have enjoyed your tour so far?"

"We have." Kehi and Koha agreed. "On the way Kohana took us on an interesting tour of the pancake rocks. While we were visiting Kanoa, humans gave us all a check and gave us these bands to go home with and Syd the stag saved Kohana from a wild boar that chased her! We are pleased to have a break here and to see the latest member of our family to be hatched. We wouldn't have experienced any of this if we had stayed home"

"I have some news for you from home." Oriel began. "Kerewa Khai and Kailan's leadership is going very well." Oriel hastened to add, seeing a frown forming on Kehi's face. Members' of Koha's community that have joined them have settled to the Kingdom way of life well too. However, others that went to Kaine's territory didn't adjust very well and he came down to Kerewa, apparently with the motive of killing anyone who opposed him and taking all the territory.

What did happen is that Kaine was advised to sort Kiwis in his own territory and Kerewa would deal with any problems in his. When it became clear Kaine intended to take Koha's territory, Kerewa negotiated for them to have half each. It was made plain to Kaine and his supporters that they were not to return to Kerewa's territory again ever! Arrangements were made to rescue all Koha's community in Kaine's territory and all are now living peacefully in Kerewa's territory."

"Thank you Oriel." Kehi and Koha were thoughtful as they digested this news. "Kohana and I talked about handing over to the next generation before we left. It seems it is going better than we could have expected. It also means I am free to live wherever I want now."

"You won't go back to live?" Koha asked. He was wondering what he was going to do, now that he no longer had a community to lead.

"I will go back for a visit of course, but I don't want to be breathing down Kerewa's neck when he is managing so well. It will be nice to live as an ordinary Kiwi and not have to make decisions for everyone all the time."

"We can still do that back home." Koha said thoughtfully. "We would only give advice if they asked for it."

"That should work." Kehi agreed as they went to join the family.

Kiana realised that now she no longer had a leadership role to look forward to, she needed to think about making a future for herself. Kiana also knew that her father's words also applied to her. She could live wherever she wanted now. She just had to find the right partner to share her life with.

Kian and Kana Kiwi found Kiana by herself, looking very thoughtful and a little glum.

"You are looking far too serious! Is everything alright?" Kana asked her.

"I've just found out all the plans I had for my future will have to change." Kiana told them with a smile. "I'm just trying to work out what to do next."

"Let the future take care of itself." Kian advised her. "Your family is staying a while now, aren't they?" Kiana nodded. "Mum is taking us for a visit to Keona, who is our Nana and also to visit Dad's family in the Arthurs Pass. Why don't you come with us?"

"I would love to come."

When Koa met the leaders of the other communities, and discussed the differences between their communities and his, he was invited to come for a visit. It was arranged that when Kona and Kedar went home, Koa would go with them.

None of the leaders mentioned it, but they sensed that here was a future leader. It would be good for him to see the Kingdom before he commenced his duties.

Kotare was having a great time meeting the young animals from the Kaniere community. The Stoats, Weasels, Hedgehogs, Possums, Ducks, Tuis, and Fantails all had stories to tell of their life here. They promised to come and collect Kotare to show him their favourite places.

CHAPTER TWENTY

KEONI'S BURROW

Kohana woke up knowing that it would soon be time to deliver her egg. She looked round her in the school cave. The entire Kiwi family was sound asleep surrounding her. Sun was shining in through the hole where part of the ceiling had collapsed many years ago; leaving a convenient slope to climb out of. Pongee steps now made the slope easier to negotiate. Kohana gave Kehi a gentle nudge.

"I have to get back to the burrow." Kohana advised him quietly as he opened one eye. "I need to deliver my egg."

"I will come with you." Keely offered Kohana. She turned to Kehi. "Tell Kalea that we have taken Charlotte."

"I will come back early," Kehi murmured, "so you can get a feed."

Kohana followed Keely who headed towards another cave, which was much darker than this one. Kohana was glad she didn't have to climb up the steep slope to get out of the cave or clamber back down Tuhua's steep slopes.

"This way is quicker and easier." Keely explained. "When I was young, Holly Hedgehog and I found the way here after we were trapped by a rock fall in the old school cave."

"Was that after the earthquake?" Kohana asked. Kalea had told her how Keely had been rescued after an earthquake. "Is it safe in there now?" Kohana wanted to know.

"Yes." Keely reassured her. "The walls and ceiling have been lined with Pongees." We have had earthquakes since then and everything has stayed intact."

Once in the cave, Kohana could see there were some blue lights on the ceiling. Glow worms lived here! There were mossy rocks to walk over and she could also hear a stream and a waterfall!

"Gloria. Its Keely and Kohana here, Can you turn on your lights for us?"

The cave was bathed in light as the glow worms turned on all the lights along their tails. Kohana could see they had a stream to cross.

Keely quickly ran forward to collect some pieces of driftwood to lay them across the stream. Carefully they crossed, without getting wet, unlike the last time when Keely fell in and had to be rescued by Holly Hedgehog.

"Where does that waterfall go? Kohana wanted to know.

"Probably to more caves and then into the lake." Keely advised her. "No-one has tried to find out in case they get trapped. Thank you Gloria." Keely thanked the glow-worms as they reached a long dark slope on the other side of the cave. As the lights dimmed, they made their way down to the bottom where there was a small hole in the wall. Keely quickly made it big enough for them to squeeze through.

"Welcome to the old school cave." Keely said as she led the way in. Dim daylight could be seen at the other end. Charlotte Chamois had been laid down and relaxing in the school cave. She felt safer in here as no-one could surprise her. To her consternation, the sound of scratching then part of the wall at the back of the cave fell down. Charlotte stood up and was about to flee, when she saw two Kiwis come through. One of them looked like Kohana.

"Kohana, is that you?"

"Yes it is me." Kohana confirmed. She was glad she didn't have to go looking for her. "I have Keely with me. Can you give us a ride over to Conical Hill in Sunny Bight? I need to deliver my egg very soon and I want to get back to my burrow.

"Of course I will." Charlotte agreed, as she sat down again to let them climb onto her back.

Their ride over to Sunny Bight was much quicker than if they had walked. As they sped through the forest, barking could be heard from some of the properties they passed; for the dogs could hear and smell them as they went by. Once back at her burrow, Kohana sent Charlotte to the valley between Conical Hill and Mount Graham. She was delighted to learn that Syd and Daphne were there too.

In the coming hours, with Keely by her side, Kohana was able to concentrate on delivering her egg. She was relieved to find it was easier this time and settled over the egg for a well-earned sleep.

At the DOC office, Doug and Malcolm were puzzling over Kohana's movements. She was obviously staying at Lake Kaniere. They noted her visit to Mount Tahua with a ride back to Sunny Bight. Was there a community there they didn't know about? They looked at their records for Lake Kaniere. Some years ago there had been a family they had checked at Hans Bay which had disappeared. Had they moved to Sunny Bight? And was this female related to them? They pencilled Lake Kaniere in for a visit.

Kehi woke in the afternoon light, wondering how Kohana was progressing with her delivery. He went over to Kaori who was awake too. He had dozed since Keely had left with Kohana.

139

"I will head back to the burrow." Kehi informed Kaori. "I promised Kohana I would come back early so she can have a feed."

"I will come back too, once the others are awake."

Their efforts to be quiet didn't succeed as very shortly all the Kiwis were awake, wanting to know where Kohana and Keely were. Before Kehi left, he found Kaori was coming with him while everyone else was going with Kalea to see the family burrow. When Tania Tui saw the Kiwis emerge from the school, she came along to the burrow too to keep an eye out for any animals or humans that might come along.

Kalea was able to show Kuri and Kaimani the burrow that their great grandparents had lived in, before taking everyone to the burrow that had been Keoni and Kupe's home. These tunnels seem strange, Koha commented to Kamora. I feel like there should be a tunnel here.

"You are right." A voice said behind him. Koha turned around and Keoni's spirit was there. "There used to be a tunnel there, but I filled it in so my mother could rest undisturbed. At the time, there was a Kiwi who wanted to take over this burrow for him-self, so I created some new ones and made sure it stayed in our family."

As everyone was admiring the Kingdom sign, Kalea slipped out to the stream near the tunnel she used to share with Kupe.

"You are up early." Kupe's voice came as he materialised beside her.

"We all are." Kalea smiled back. "Kehi has gone back to Sunny Bight to see how Kohana is going with delivering her egg. Charlotte took her and Keely over this morning."

"How are you going in your new life?" Kupe wanted to know.

"I am content." Kalea was able to reassure him. "Koro my new partner is very caring."

"You have other children?"

"No. I was lucky to have Kamaka and Kohana. After Kamaka was rescued, he had an adventure down in Fiordland. He found his way up to our community and has a son of his own now. I have laid eggs, but the local stoats insist on taking eggs before they can be hatched. Kapali has been down to see Kanoa to see what is being done for his community. Hopefully we will get help too soon."

"I'm glad you are being well looked after. Take care on your way home." Kupe said in farewell.

On Conical Hill, Kohana was glad to see Kehi's frame darken the entrance. She was starving hungry after not eating the last day or two when there wasn't room for her to take food. Though it was still daylight, Kohana wasted no time in going in search of a feed.

For once she worked her way down the hill to the shore, where trees leaned out over the lake, their exposed roots reaching down the bank into the water. As Kohana stood admiring the view, a splash distracted her. It was Ernie Eel. "Hello Kohana. I was hoping to see you while you are here. I expect you will be moving on soon."

"No." Kohana answered with a smile." I have just delivered my egg, so we will be here for a few months at least for our chick to hatch, before we move on."

"I would like to meet Kehi's family too, before they leave." Ernie added. "Tell them to come down and splash the water and someone will fetch me."

"I will." Kohana promised, before returning to the burrow. Kehi would want to get out for his feed soon.

Ernie wasn't only interested in meeting the great granddaughter of Kuri who saved Keoni, but he wanted to meet Koa, the next Kingdom leader.

Stars filled the night sky as Kalea led the Kiwis along the shore at Sunny Bight. Kotare insisted on going into the water for a splash. It wasn't long before some Eels came to investigate what the noise was about. Ernie was with them.

"Hello Kotare." The Eel greeted him. "Are you having a good time here?"

"I am." The little Kiwi answered him. "I wish I could stay."

"Hello Kalea." Ernie called out. "Are you going to introduce us to your visitors?"

Kalea drew each member of Kehi's family and Kuri and Kaimani down to the water's edge to talk to the eels, a new experience for all of them. Kedar Kona Keka and Kane all came down to say hello to Ernie as well. After asking Koa how he was enjoying his stay, Ernie asked what his plans were. When informed he was visiting other communities. Ernie then told him to come and visit again on his way back. Koa then realised that Ernie knew what his future was going to be.

"Is Ernie the leader of the Eels?" Koa asked Kane.

"Yes." Kane replied. "You probably already know that Oriel Owl is the

Guardian of the Kiwi Kingdom. Ernie is the leader of the eels at this Lake. Elanor is the matriarch and leader of the guardians who protect the lake."

"What is their role in the Kingdom? Koa wanted to know. "I hadn't seen or heard of Eels being part of the kingdom anywhere else."

"Kupe told me that Keoni made friends with the eels in his kingdom. At the time, any animal that ventured in or on the lake was fair game to be eaten. Eels were a food source for the Maori tribe in the next valley, so in exchange for warning the eels of any danger from humans, they eels promised not to eat any animals from the kingdom that came to the lake."

Also, the original kingdom was this lake and the hills and mountains around it. When humans came and the Kiwis were forced to flee, Keoni's supporters spread out around the Island, taking the Kingdom values with them. Some communities survived through to the present day. Others had to be rescued when Kupe revived the kingdom."

The more Koa heard about the original kingdom, the more he wanted to learn, but how?

"If you want to know more, you will have to wait untill Oriel lets you read the Kingdom Book." Kane said, reading Koa's thoughts.

Doug and Malcolm were given a big surprise when they checked the Sunny Bight Burrows the next morning. Not only was Kohana and her family here, but Kehi was sitting on an egg. The other females they had tagged at Paparoa were here too. They were pleased to find Keely and her family were here, though there was no sign of her brother and her parents. Another two families not known to them were here too, but strangest of all they found four males sharing a burrow. One they identified as a Rowi from Okarito. The other Rowi was tagged and a tracker placed on him. There were two Roa Kiwis with them, who were given trackers as well. Doug took note that Kohana and some, if not all of these males were probably leaders of their communities. For Kohana and three of the males now wore similar Pounamu stones around their necks to the one he had seen on the male from Three Sisters Mountain.

"I wish you could talk to us." Doug commented. "I'm sure you have quite a tale to tell us if you could."

"I agree." Malcolm replied. Rowi and Roa don't normally mix, but these Kiwis obviously do. I think that there has been a meeting of some kind here. Just what it was about and why it was held here; we will never know."

That evening Oriel came to farewell all the travellers going their separate ways. Kalea Kuri and Kaimani were heading north. Kiana was joining Keely Kian and Kana to travel to the Arahura Valley and Arthurs Pass with Keka and Kane. Koa was with Kedar and Kona as they made their way south. Teeny Tahr was giving them a lift.

"I will see you when I come back." Koa promised Oriel as he prepared to leave.

In the coming weeks, Doug would find that the unknown Rowi was in fact a Tokoeka from Fiordland, and wondered how he had eluded them on their checks in the area. Cameras were employed on their next visit. They also found that a whole community had joined the Arthurs Pass Roa that had spread to the Arahura Valley. Where they had come from was another mystery. Among them was the female that they had tagged at Lake Kaniere years ago. She now had a new mate and family.

When Kalea brought Kuri and Kaimani to Three Sisters Mountain, she found a few changes. Doug and Malcolm had been for a visit. Koro and Kalea were able to compare leg bands and she also noticed animal traps had been left near all the burrows. She also noticed the cameras placed in different places, but soon learnt to ignore them.

When Koa returned, he had tales to tell of meeting Eli and the Eels in the Haast. (much to Kona's disgust) The eels were pleased to learn that Kawaka was home safe and now had his own family. Koa was pleased to meet the young Kiwis who were settling in well after spending their first year at Franz Joseph. From Okarito he brought back memories of the grace and beauty of the Herons and spoonbills as they flew in to the lagoon and the sunsets that set in the ocean beyond. Kedar too was happy that their young Kiwis were settling in well after spending their first year away. In the Arahura Valley Koa had a long chat with Keona about her life and Kupe's reign. In the valley Koa caught up with Kiana, who liked the area so much, she had decided to stay. Up in the mountains of Arthurs Pass, Koa could see both the beauty and the harshness of life here and was amazed that the community coped with the changing conditions there.

Kotare took home lifelong happy memories of his stay at the lake. Visits were made to Dorothy Falls and to the Islands to explore the forests there. After seeing the beautiful books that Emily had made in the school library, he asked if a copy could be made for the library in the Tasman.

"I will see what I can do." Oriel said, knowing that Amy her great granddaughter would have to be contacted.

Kapali was happy when Doug and Malcolm finally came to do their checks and to leave the traps and cameras. Regular visits to clear the stoats weasels and possums from the traps finally paid off at the next season, when every family produced chicks.

Happiness also came to Kohana and Kehi one wet and windy night. Peeping from the egg in the previous day had told them their new chick would be here soon. As the egg cracked then split open, their very damp daughter emerged, then laid down for a sleep, exhausted by her efforts.

"She will be Kelia." Kohana decided.

Before Kohana went home, she took Kotare and Koa for a climb to the top of Mount Tahua. As they came out of the forest to the open area at the top, she could feel Ollie's spirit here. Kohana spoke to him as they stood looking at the view. *"I have come to say goodbye."*

"Farewell". Ollie replied. *"It's a shame you never made it to the other communities."*

"Koa visited them for me." Kohana replied.

"He will make a good leader when the time comes." Ollie observed.

"Yes." Kohana agreed. *"I am already teaching him everything I know."*

KOA'S

KINGDOM

CHAPTER ONE

KOHANA'S GIFT

Kohana Kiwi was resting comfortably in her burrow with Kehi. Their son Kotare and daughter Kelia were still asleep in their tunnels. Many changes had come since their return to the Buller from Lake Kaniere. D.O.C. had been to check on everyone and to install cameras and traps.

A shadow came across the entrance. It was Kerewa. He had a worried look on his face. Quietly Kohana eased herself out of the burrow. Oren and Opal were sitting in a nearby tree.

"Our Kiwis in the north think we are in for trouble. They are starting to see Kiwi's from Kaine's side near the border."

"They haven't tried to cross it or communicate with them?"

"No. They want us to send some more Kiwis up there. If Kaine does attack, they will be overrun."

"We need to have a meeting." With that, Kohana raised her head and put out a call that woke everyone who wasn't already awake. As Kiwis came out of their burrows, they were sent to the meeting area.

Once everyone was seated, Kerewa, Kailan and Kohana stood out front as Kerewa addressed the crowd.

"Thank you all for coming." Kerewa began. "We have heard from our Kiwis in the north that Kiwis from Kaine's territory are appearing near the border. They haven't tried to cross it or communicate with our Kiwis yet, but our Kiwis want extra kiwis from our community up there in case trouble starts. Our Kiwis will be overrun if they are attacked. We want volunteers to go up there to help."

There was discussion from family groups before Kiwis started to stand up and come forward. Kohana noticed that every family had sent at least one or more of their members to help. Kehi, Koha Khai and Koa also joined them.

Someone made the comment. "Is anyone staying to protect us?"

Kehi turned to Kerewa and Kailan. "If we are defeated, take the remainder of the community to Three Sisters community."

"We will." Kailan replied for them both.

As families said goodbye, Kehi gave Kotare and Kelia a cuddle before nuzzling Kohana. "Hopefully we won't be too long."

Kohana nodded, her heart heavy with the knowledge that many wouldn't return. She didn't worry him with the knowledge that she knew that this community would again come under attack while they were away, something she would have to try to prepare for.

Once Kehi's contingent had disappeared towards the north, Oren owl put out a call, which was passed on through the forest before them.

Kohana looked around at the remaining Kiwi families with a smile. "You should all be proud of the contribution your families are making to ensure our area is safe again. We are going to miss our family members terribly, but the best we can do is carry on normally. School is still on this evening." With that she led everyone to the school for their session.

Kohana didn't sleep well the next day. It wasn't just the fact that Kehi was absent; she had another vivid dream which was still clear in her mind. The men who had come with guns and cause terror on their last visit were coming again. This time they were bringing a dog with them. Kohana knew she needed to tell Kerewa and Kailan about it.

That evening she went in search of Kerewa. "Do you know where Kailan is? I need to talk to you both." Kerewa looked at his stepmother with alarm, but her expression didn't give any hint of the news she was about to give them. "I will be waiting for you in the meeting area."

A passing Kiwi stopped and asked. "Is this meeting private or can the rest of us attend it too?"

"I was going to speak to you all about it later, so you can come."

It didn't take long for word to get around the community and for them all to gather on the slopes of the meeting area.

"How many of you remember the visit we had from the humans with guns?" Kohana asked.

"How can we forget?" someone asked.

"I don't know when they are coming, but I know they will be returning; and this time they will be bringing a dog with them!"

In the stunned silence Kohana continued. "We need to prepare for this by moving you all to safety – preferably tonight! The question is where? If we stay in this forest, the dog will trace our scent."

Kohana then looked towards the river. "How many of you can swim well?" There was silence to this suggestion.

"This means we need help to get you across the river."

Kohana turned to Oren and Opal. "Can you find Syd and Daphne for me? The community needs a ride across the river."

Oren and Opal and other members of the owl community flew off towards the Ohikanui River, where Syd and Daphne now live. After crossing the Buller River, they came to the entrance to the Ohikanui and started calling to them as they flew down the valley.

"Syd, Daphne, are you there?"

Syd heard their calls, and at first didn't take any notice, untill Daphne heard their names being mentioned.

"They are calling us!" Daphne exclaimed. "I wonder what is happening!"

Syd immediately let out a roar, which brought all the owls to a nearby tree.

"Hello Syd and Daphne." Opal called. "Kohana has sent us. The men with guns are going to return, with a dog. She needs help to move her community across the river. Can you help her?"

"Of course, we can." Syd offered, knowing it was going to be a long and cold night for them, with many trips to cross the river.

Both Syd and Daphne were relieved to find that only half the community was present and extra Kiwis were able to be carried each load in woven bags that were kept at the school.

"Where are Kehi and all the others?" Syd wanted to know.

'There is trouble brewing on our northern border." Kohana told him. They have gone to help our community up there."

While Kohana and the community were waiting for the Owls and Deer's return, she organised for all the other animals that could not fly away to move to the north and not come back untill the owls came to tell them it was safe to return. She also visited the school cave and told Giana and the glow worms to keep their lights out while the hunters were nearby.

"Take care and stay safe." Giana glow worm said in parting.

Kohana stayed untill she was sure everyone was safely across the river. She saw Kotare and his friends mount Daphne. Kelia wasn't with them!

"Kotare! Have you seen where Kelia is?"

A look of alarm and guilt came over his face. In his rush to be with his friends, he had forgotten to make sure Kelia was with him.

"I'm sorry Mum. I lost sight of her on our way here."

"I will go back and get her." Kohana could now hear gunfire in the far distance. "Take care of yourself over there."

Syd stepped out of the water to collect the last couple of Kiwis waiting with Kohana.

"Are you ready?" Syd asked Kohana, He too could hear the gunfire in the distance.

"No. I have to go back and find our daughter Kelia. We will head for the valley to the north if we have time before they come. Thank you for looking after my community." Kohana said finally, giving him a little smile before disappearing back towards the community tunnels.

Kerewa and the community were shocked and anxious when they learnt that Kohana was staying behind to look for Kelia.

"KELIA!" Kohana called out as loudly as she could as she made her way through the forest. She tried to ignore the fact that the gunfire was getting closer!

She went into the family burrow to search the tunnels and was relieved to find Kelia curled up at the far end of her tunnel.

"Mum!" Kelia cried with relief when she saw her familiar form at the entrance. "I lost Kotare, so I came back here."

"Good girl!" Kohana reassured her, but with the sound of heavy footsteps and a dog nearby, she realised it was too late to leave. "I need you to stay very still and quiet now. I love you." Were Kohana's last words before she turned to move into the main tunnel. Then she remembered the amulet still around her neck and swiftly slipped it off.

In the main tunnel a bright light blinded her eyes. Kohana felt and heard the approach of the dog as it came to attack. With a growl, she also rushed forward, slashing at the dog's face and stomach with her long sharp claws, ignoring the dog's bites untill it finally managed to get a grip on her neck. Her fight only ended when darkness overcome her. The dog managed to drag her outside only to collapse itself.

"S%2# what are we going to do with it? He won't want it in this condition."

"Yeah, He will have to find something else to make his cloak out of. It was a mistake to bring the dog. We will have to get rid of it too!" The sound of the gun echoed through the tunnels.

After checking all the other tunnels were empty, they headed off towards the river. Rocks were tied to Kohana and the dog before they were thrown into the water.

The Owls weren't the only silent witness to the scene. The next morning Doug checked the cameras at the Buller community. His smile at seeing Kohana coming and going from the burrow turned to anger when footage of the hunters came onto the screen.

"Cheryl! Have you got the number of the Westport Police?"

Cheryl dashed in to see what the problem was. After seeing the footage, there were tears in her eyes as she dialed the number.

After sending the footage through, the Westport police called back. "We know everyone involved. We will be able to throw the book at them! Can you show us the site where it happened? It would also help to get some forensics."

"Certainly." Doug replied with grim satisfaction.

As soon as it was safe to move, Oren flew to the Ohikanui River to give the sad news that Kohana had been taken.

"What about Kelia?" Kotare asked. He was beside himself with worry about her.

"We don't know." Oren advised him. "We saw her go into the burrow, but she hasn't come out yet."

Some hours passed before Kelia dared to move from her spot in the tunnel. She was very hungry, but wasn't sure of what she would find outside. At the entrance she spotted the amulet. With a little smile she put it over her head. As she ventured further into the main tunnel, she saw her mother's white feathers. Realising her mother wasn't coming back to her; she picked one up and took it back to her tunnel. She was happy her mother had left these things for her. Kelia clutched the amulet again for comfort, before making her way out of the burrow for a feed.

"Kelia!" Opal called out to her. "Are you alright?" Opal didn't like being on the ground, but made an exception in this case.

"I saw you go in, but not come out again." Kelia saw Opal look at the amulet around her neck.

"Mum left it in my tunnel for me." Kelia gave a little smile as she fondled it again.

"They will want to take it later..." Opal began, trying to explain that only the Kingdom leader was to wear it.

"No one will ever take it from me!" Kelia was adamant. "Mum is gone! She left it for me!" She stomped off, leaving Opal looking after her with sad eyes.

Kerewa and Kailan debated whether to send word to Kehi that Kohana was gone. They decided to delay the news for now. It wouldn't help their ability to fight knowing she was no longer here for them.

The news was swiftly sent to Three Sister's Community and to Oriel at Lake Kaniere, but Ollie knew before anyone. He was listening to the sounds of the night when Kohana appeared next to him. She had a dog with her.

"Hello Ollie. I didn't expect to join you quite so soon."

"Why have you come to the spirit world?"

"The hunters returned to our burrows. They had this dog with them. His name is Titan. I had to fight Titan to stop him from reaching Kelia. We both moved to the spirit world."

"Was anyone else taken?"

"No. I managed to get the community to safety in the Ohikanui valley before they came."

"Why did you stay?" Ollie was puzzled.

"Kelia was missing, so I went back for her after I found she had become separated from Kotare. By the time I found her, the hunters were there."

"Why didn't Kehi go back for her too?"

"He wasn't there. He is leading a group to help protect our northern border. Some of Kaine's kiwis have started to appear near it."

"Is Koa with them?"

"Yes." Kohana gave Ollie a little smile. "He may have to wait a little while before he wears the amulet. I remembered to remove it before I faced the dog. Kelia is wearing it now. It is giving her comfort."

"She will have to give it back."

"Of course! But it will take a little time till she finishes grieving."

Kohana looked down at the Islands in the lake.

"How are Odessa and Orlando managing their family?

151

Ollie gave a little sigh. "They have had a rough time of it." He went on to tell Kohana about how Oriana and Orel had abused Orion, who had to be protected because of his connection to the spirit world. Ollie also told her of the death of Orel after he threatened to kill Orlando and his threat to come after Ollie in the spirit world to kill him too."

Kohana became alarmed. "Can he do that?"

"Fortunately, Orion sent him to Nudoor, a place where spirits with ill intent are isolated. He can't harm anyone there."

Kohana gave a sigh of relief.

"I will see you again. I need to go north to see how the Kehi and his group manage the confrontation." She then disappeared from sight.

Ollie wondered at the presence of the dog at Kohana's side. Opposing spirits didn't normally stay together in the spirit world. It could only mean that she needed protection in the spirit world, if so, from whom?

CHAPTER TWO

CHANGE IN THE BULLER

The sun was high in the sky when Opal saw and heard humans approaching the community burrows. She quickly landed at the entrance of Kehi's burrow and gave an alarm call.

"Kelia's sleepy voice answered her. "What is it Opal?"

"Humans are coming! Quickly run to the school cave."

Kelia didn't need to be told twice. Even though the bright light hurt her eyes, she swiftly ran through the forest till she reached the cave, stumbling inside and hiding in the darkness at the back.

"Hello Kelia." Giana the glowworm greeted her. She also noticed Kelia was wearing the amulet her mother Kohana usually wore. "What brings you to us in your sleep time?"

"Opal told me to come here as humans were coming back!"

"Where is your Mother, Kelia? Is she okay?"

There was a small silence before the little Kiwi answered.

"I don't know where she is, but the humans brought a dog with them. I heard her have a fight with it. When I went out, she had left her amulet for me. Some of her feathers were there too. I just know she isn't coming back to us." Kelia clutched the amulet tightly as she spoke.

It was Giana's turn to be silent as she digested this news.

"I'm sorry your Mum has gone. You can stay as long as you like."

The owls watched with interest as the police and Doug surveyed the scene at the burrows. They recognised Doug from previous visits to check everyone. Doug checked all the burrows. "They are all gone. Hopefully they will come back." The police took photos of Kohana's feathers, before placing some in a plastic bag. They also took some samples of the blood in the burrow and outside.

"It looks like we have a trail here." The police officer advised Doug as he took samples. "Did the Kiwi have a tracking device on by any chance?"

"She did." Doug replied with a smile and fossicked in his bag for his tracking equipment. When he turned it on beeps could be heard from the direction of the river. "Let's hope she is still attached to it!"

153

At the river bank the beeps were traced to the water. The police looked at Doug with an enquiring look.

"Can you swim well?"

"I did my life savers certificate."

Doug's first dive was among big rocks lining the river floor. Luckily the water was clear, so he had a good view. Just before he had to surface for air, he spotted a Kiwi claw wedged under a rock. A dog was there too.

"I think I've found both the Kiwi and the dog."

"Bring them both up if you can."

A short while later, Kohana and the dog were returned to the bank. Both were sealed into plastic bags before the trek back.

"Cheers for that Doug." This evidence has made the case "watertight." The police thanked him. "We will be in touch for the court case."

Once Doug and the police had gone, Opal flew to the school cave where Kelia was dozing. "Kelia, it is safe to come back now."

"Are you sure?"

"Yes." Opal reassured her. "I recognised one of them. He has been here before to help the community."

That Evening, Oren flew to the Ohikanui River to give them the news that Kelia was safe and that the burrows had been visited by humans that had been before to check on the community. Also, Kohana and the dog had been found in the river and had been taken away.

"We haven't told Kelia that her mother has been taken away. She saw her mother's feathers in the burrow and knows she isn't coming back to her." Oren paused for a moment before continuing. "Kelia found Kohana's amulet in the burrow and is now wearing it." Kerewa raised his eyebrows at this news. "It is giving her comfort, so we haven't tried to take it from her. Opal did try to tell Kelia that she will have to give it back, but she is adamant that her mother left it for her. It may be a little while before the next leader gets to wear it."

Kerewa went to find Katana who had been supporting Kotare since the news came that his mother had gone and tried to reassure him that Kelia was safe.

"I have good news, Kotare." Kerewa smiled at him. "Kelia is safe and is waiting for us to come back. You both can stay with us in Our burrow untill you are ready for your own burrows."

"What about dad? Isn't he coming back?"

Internally, Kerewa gave a sigh, but didn't show it. It was difficult to tell a child that had just lost his mother that he might lose his father too.

"Of course, we expect him to come back and you will share with him again if you want to, but dad is going to a big battle where there will be fierce fighting. Sometimes they don't come back." Kerewa put a comforting claw on Kotare's shoulder. "We can only hope that dad will come back, but be prepared in case he doesn't."

Kotare turned to Kerewa for a cuddle. His life that had been so happy and carefree was rapidly changing. He was just glad that he had an older brother for support when he needed it. As Kotare waited for his turn to cross the river, he realised that he would have to take his role of caring for Kelia more seriously. She too would be suffering the loss of their mother. Then it struck him that she had been there when their mother had been taken and wondered how she was coping.

Kotare's question was soon answered. On reaching the other bank. He ran to the family burrow to find Kelia hunched over, clutching the amulet tightly. Kotare sat down and cuddled her tight. They stayed that way for some time, untill Katana came to the burrow.

"Is anyone ready for a feed yet?"

"Kelia finally stirred.

"I am feeling quite hungry now."

"Good!" Katana smiled. "We have a feed ready for you at our burrow. You can stay there with us if you like."

"I will just fetch something." Kelia said, before running into her tunnel to fetch the feather she had collected. Inserting the feather into the twisted twine holding the amulet in place, Kelia then returned.

"I'm ready now." Kelia announced.

When Kotare saw what Kelia had done, he looked for one too and picked it up in his bill before following Katana and Kelia outside.

After Kerewa and Katana had made sure that Kotare and Kelia were settled, they went out to check on the school and feed themselves. Everywhere they went, Kiwis came to ask them how long they were staying.

Kerewa went to see Kailan; Kiwis had been asking him the same question. It was obvious that the community was feeling unsafe here now, but where was the best place to move to. They agreed that moving to the south of the

Buller River was too inconvenient to help their community in the north, if and when they needed it. They would only move to Three Sisters Mountain if Kaine succeeded in his quest for more territory and took over theirs. They also agreed to look in valleys in the neighbourhood to the north to see if there was a suitable site for the community to move to.

"I think we need to have a look at the map of this area before we go looking." Kerewa suggested. "We need to consider both access and security before we look at places for our burrows that won't get too wet."

At the school cave Kerewa and Kailan spent some time looking at the local maps, but they didn't give enough detail of the hills and valleys around them.

"We will have to go and have a look" Kerewa finally declared. "Perhaps if we follow this river." (Kerewa indicated a river which ran from the north. It flowed into the Buller not far from the Ohikanui)

"It sounds like a plan." Kailan smiled. We will go before daylight comes."

After having a good feed and letting their families know of their plans, Kerewa and Kailan set off. Oren Owl also was coming along on their adventure.

After skirting the headland, they lived on, Kerewa and Kailan came across the river they wanted to explore. They noticed that it was in flood.

"We should have a look at how high the water levels can be," Kailan mentioned with some unease. It was easy to be carried away and drown when flash floods occur. As they looked for telltale signs of water marks on tree trunks, they were alarmed to see that water marks were well above where they were standing and quickly scrambled above the water mark, just in time as the water level quickly rose and covered the ground where they had just been standing.

Steadily they walked upstream, the pre-dawn light making it easier to see tracks and trails running through the forest. They were glad of the thick canopy above that sheltered them from the harsh daylight as morning came and the day birds became active. Oren didn't appreciate the attention he received from the birds and hoped they would have a rest soon.

Heavy showers of rain set in during the morning, making the tracks boggy and they were getting wet and uncomfortable. Just when they were thinking of making some shelter, they reached the area they were seeking, flatter land at a fork in the river. Oren was happy to seek a dry spot in a tree to have a doze while Kerewa and Kailan explored the local area. Oren was disturbed by the noise of Kerewa and Kailan as they made a temporary burrow at the base of his tree.

"Is it any good?" Oren enquired.

"It isn't half as good as the area we already have." Kerewa's tone was full of disappointment. "We will just have to be well prepared if human hunters come back again."

Before they settled to sleep, Kailan became very pensive. "Kerewa, we have made a great team together. Have you considered that we may have to separate should the Kingdom win this battle? Someone will have to lead the north.

"I have." Kerewa answered with a sigh. "I know it will probably be me, as our family led the area for many years. I was trying not to think about it untill I got the call." Kailan nodded sympathetically, but also felt very glad that he wasn't expected to go to an area he had no knowledge of.

When they returned to the community that night, there was a big crowd waiting for news of their expedition.

"We know you are all unsettled after the recent visit by human hunters, but we haven't found anything as good as the area we have here." Kerewa informed them. "We will just have to organise ourselves to find a place of safety if and when they come again."

CHAPTER THREE

BATTLE FOR THE NORTH

As Kehi trekked north, he wondered what Kohana and the children were doing now. He was missing them already. He was also glad he had plenty of support for what he knew would be a big battle ahead. Kerewa had told him of his dealings with Kaine, and knew that Kaine couldn't be trusted. Kehi knew that Kaine was preparing for an attempt to take over Kerewa and Kailan's territory. There was no other reason for Kaine's Kiwis to be gathering near the border.

As Kehi and his group travelled, they also shared ideas on tactics to both defend their territory and to attack when Kaine's Kiwis encroached on their side. As they came near, Kehi sent word ahead with an owl that had been accompanying them, of their arrival.

"Are we glad to see you!" exclaimed the local Kiwi, who had come to meet them. "Nice to see you back Koha and Koa. Where is Kerewa?"

Koha smiled. "Kerewa is the co-leader of our community now, with Kailan. They are doing a great job of it too. Who is the leader here now?"

"We don't have a leader as such; everything is discussed and agreed to."

Koha and Kehi looked at each other and gave a little sigh. This campaign was going to be more difficult than they thought, but the alternative of letting Kaine take over this area wasn't worth considering.

"How many Kiwis do you have here and where are they all?" Kehi asked. "Just as importantly, how many of Kaine's Kiwis have gathered at the border?"

"Who's in charge?" the Kiwi wanted to know. "You or Koha?"

"We both are." Kehi replied.

"Where is everyone?" Kehi asked again. He had a feeling that time was short. The sooner that they were organised, the better!

"They are all waiting." was the reply.

"Hello." Koha greeted the local Kiwis. He noticed that only half of their numbers were here. "Is anyone doing regular patrols or have areas of the border to defend?"

His question was met with silence and some shaking of heads.

"How many of you are able and ready to fight?"

There was a small silence before someone piped up "We all are."

"I'm glad to hear it." Koha's tone was uncompromising. "Anyone not helping will be sent over to Kaine's side!" Seeing the incredulous looks on the local kiwis' faces, he added. "We are here to help you – not do it all for you. By, the way, we will not be taking any prisoners. They are to be eliminated."

"We will put one of our group with one of yours and give you an area to patrol. You will stay in that area to patrol eat and sleep. If you need help or to tell us anything, call out to the local owls" – Koha looked up with a smile to a large group of owls now gathered in surrounding trees. "They will pass your message to us.

"How long will we be doing this?" a local Kiwi asked.

"Till we know this territory is safe." Kehi replied.

The Kiwis were quickly organised and sent to their areas, with an owl also allocated to their area. It came as a shock to some local kiwis that Kaine's Kiwis were already in their territory. The first of their many battles began.

While Koa was moving to the territory he was patrolling, Kohana appeared next to him. His partner who was next to him didn't appear to see her. Koa knew immediately he was seeing her spirit.

"What happened?" Koa asked her in his thoughts.

"The hunters returned with a dog. After a fight it took me. Everyone else is safe. Kelia has my amulet. It is bringing her comfort. I will be watching over you." Kohana then disappeared. Koa realised his time to be Kiwi Kingdom leader had come – if he could survive the coming battle here.

When Koa and his partner arrived at their territory, they set out on their first patrol. Koa was shocked to hear his partner's attitude.

"I don't know we are bothering doing this! Why can't we take prisoners? The other side has been taking them!

"Is that what you've been told?" Koa asked him. The Kiwi nodded.

"Then you have been fooled! All of your Kiwis that they have taken are already dead. I know that you can't trust a word they say."

"How would you know that? You haven't been here." The Kiwi challenged Koa.

"Kaine came down to our community after Koha left and some of your community was causing him trouble. He left us in no doubt what he was going to do to every one of you who were on his territory! We agreed to a border with Kaine and made it clear that no-one from his community was to cross it. We have no doubt that he intends to kill all of you then come down and do the same to our community. We have to make a stand, so we are doing it here."

During this conversation, their owl Oliver started to call the other owls to come. He could see other Kiwis approaching and sensed trouble was starting here!

"You can fight them on your own!" the Kiwi retorted. "I don't see the point in fighting for a lost cause."

"You are just going to let them kill you, and us?" Koa's anger was rising.

"I don't care about you. I'm out of here!"

"You will have to fight me first!"

The Kiwi put up a halfhearted fight, but was easily subdued. As Koa turned to walk away, a voice stopped him.

"What did you kill him for?"

When Koa turned around, he was confronted by a number of Kiwis he didn't recognise. In front was their leader. This obviously was Kaine and he was in trouble!

Koa drew himself up and looked the leader in the eye.

"He was a coward! He refused to fight and was going to run away."

"Have you no compassion?" Kaine asked.

"You are asking me to have compassion, when you are being ruthless with all of our community yourself?" Koa countered as he put his claw up to defend himself as he knew Kaine would attack him at any second.

When Koa put his claw up, the owls immediately launched from the surrounding trees to attack Kaine and his followers. They weren't used to having their heads swiped by razor sharp claws from above and cowered in fear low to the ground.

"GO BACK!" Koa ordered Kaine and his followers. "GO BACK TO YOUR SIDE AND STAY THERE!"

Kaine had no choice, but to lead his followers back to his side of the border, followed closely by the owls.

When Oliver returned, Koa thanked him.

"Thank you for saving me. I owe you my life."

"We are happy to defend the leader of the Kiwi Kingdom." Oliver replied with a faint smile.

"That isn't common knowledge yet." Koa replied with astonishment. "How did you know?"

"News travels fast in our world." Oliver replied. "Every Owl in the kingdom now knows we have a new leader."

Just then there was a rustle from a nearby bush. "Who is there?" Koa called, immediately on guard.

"It's just me." called his friend Kerwin. "We heard you shouting, so I came to see what was up. Is it true that you are the Kingdom leader now?" Kerwin added with excitement.

"Yes, it is." Koa confirmed with a smile. "I have just learnt about it myself." Then Koa remembered something. "You mustn't spread the news just yet. Kehi may not know that Kohana has gone. He will be devastated when he finds out. Anyway, it's too early to celebrate. I have to survive this first."

Kerwin reluctantly agreed. "You're right of course. Where is your partner?"

"He is over there." Koa indicated the still body. "I wasn't expecting to have to kill one of ours!"

Koa nodded at Kerwin's incredulous eyes.

"He wasn't interested in defending or fighting for his territory, he just wanted to run away."

It was Kerwin's turn to be disgusted. "I hope there aren't any more like him we have to defend. You're on your own here now, just call us if you need help."

"I will do thanks. I'm lucky I have Oliver here too. I wouldn't be here without him."

After Kerwin left, Koa went to look for Oliver. Together they went in search of a feed. Koa did another patrol of his area, with Oliver shadowing him. Kiwis from the Tasman side saw them and left him alone. After their previous encounter with his owls, they weren't in a hurry for another one. As daylight approached, they went in search of a suitable tree for Oliver to sleep in and Koa made a temporary burrow under it.

"Don't hesitate to call me if you see or hear anything suspicious." Koa advised Oliver.

"I will." Oliver agreed.

Kaine was puzzled. The local group of Kiwis had remained dysfunctional since Koha had left. His Kiwis had been making forays into Kerewa's territory with little knowledge and hardly any resistance when they encountered them. It was easy to drag them back to his side and eliminate them.

All of a sudden there were more Kiwis along the border and these were organised and able to defend themselves. Who was in charge of this defense? They had to be eliminated before he could continue his plan to take over the area.

Koa was patrolling his territory when Oliver received a call from owls near Kehi and Koha's area. "Koa! A large number of Kiwis from the north are heading towards Kehi and Koha."

"Thanks Oliver. The future of the north is about to be decided. Can you get all the owls to tell Kiwis patrolling the border to head for Kehi and Koha's area?"

As Oliver put out the call, Koa starting to run towards Kehi and Koha's area. Kiwis that saw him running immediately knew something was up and joined him. Koa knew that the outcome of the coming battle meant that he would either be the leader of a kingdom that had expanded to include the Tasman, or that he and everyone on his side would have to flee for their lives.

Kaine's answer came that night when he and his supporters visited the area where Koha had his community. Koha was there, waiting for him. He seemed to be alone, except for a single owl sitting in the tree above him.

"What brings you here, Kaine?" Koha asked in a mild tone.

"So, you've come home." Kaine replied, not answering Koha's question.

Koha noticed Kaine's supporters were coming around both sides to surround him. Koha quickly looked up towards his owl. It stretched out his wings and gave a call.

Kaine and his supporters immediately found that they were surrounded by Kehi and his supporters. The battle to control both the Buller and the Tasman then raged. As Kaine and Koha fought, Kehi had to fight his way to help Koha who appeared to be coming second best in his battle with Kaine. Kehi completely ignored all the wounds he received as he slashed his way through to his friend. With an almighty blow to the neck, Kaine finally fell. On seeing their leader down, Kaine's supporters tried to run away, but were stopped by Koa and his supporters.

Koa and the other supporters had arrived as the battle was raging. "We will wait." Koa advised them. "If our side wins, we will stop Kaine's supporters from leaving. If Kaine's side wins, be prepared to run for your lives to the south!"

Kehi slumped at Koha's side and give him a smile. "We did it." He knew he wouldn't make it back to the Buller. "Tell Kohana I will see her in the spirit world."

Koa had seen his father's condition and came running over to hear his final words. "She already knows, dad. She is waiting for you." Kehi gave Koa an amazed look before his spirit left his body.

"What do you mean?" Koha demanded, giving Koa an incredulous look. "How do you know Kohana is in the spirit world?"

"As I was moving to my area to patrol, Kohana's spirit came to me."

"Why didn't you tell us?" Koha asked in a disappointed tone?

"I did consider it." Koa replied, "But I thought it best to wait till we knew the outcome of this battle. Kehi wouldn't have been in any condition to help you if he had known."

Koha knew the wisdom of Koa's words, remembering his conversation with Kehi's friend Khai, who told him how badly Kehi had taken the loss of Kiyo when she was killed by Kura and her supporters. Even now, Koha missed his daughter and at this moment he wasn't that sure that he would get back to the Buller either.

"You are right of course. You are going to make a good leader."

"Granddad;" Koa reminded him gently. "I am the leader now."

"So you are." Koha acknowledged him with a grin. "You have some sorting to do with this part of your kingdom"

"I certainly do!" It was Koa's turn to grin back at Koha, though neither of them realised how much Kiwi Kingdom values would have to be sacrificed to ensure the safety of this new area of his kingdom.

Koa then turned to address all of the Kiwis present.

"You are now in the Kiwi Kingdom. I will send for all of the Kiwis in the Tasman area and any remaining in the northern Buller to attend a meeting for your future. While we are waiting for them, Kiwis from the northern Buller are to sit here." Koa indicated an area on the bank behind him. "Kiwis from the Tasman are to sit here." Koa indicated a separate area on the bank.

"Shouldn't we all be sitting together now we are all under the same ruler?" someone called out. There were loud murmurings to this question.

"You will not have the right to sit together untill we know what your intentions are." Silence fell upon the crowd to Koa's measured response as they realised they were dealing with a power much stronger than they were.

In a short time, Kiwis in both the North Buller and the Tasman were visited by Owls and told that they were to attend a meeting to discuss the future of the area. While they were waiting, Koa organised half of his supporters to guard the Kiwis on the bank, with the other half sent out to find food for everyone.

Kerwin came up to Koa as everyone went to their allotted tasks.

"Koa, have you given any thought yet as to whom you will make the leader of the north? It will need to be someone you trust."

Koa looked at his friend with a smile.

"Are you volunteering?"

"I am. This area is my home and I know most of the territory over there too." Kerwin added with a twinkle of his eye at the thought of the risks he took to explore hostile territory.

"So that's where you went!" Koa exclaimed, remembering his friend's frequent absences. "Thanks, Kerwin. It's yours. I will give you the guidelines on managing it before you start."

As Kerwin moved away, Koa gave a small sigh of relief. He had been dreading the prospect of having to send for Kerewa to come and lead here. Now Koa could leave him with Kailan, where he knew Kerewa wanted to stay.

"Oliver." Koa turned to his owl. Can you send word down to the Buller that the Tasman is now part of the Kiwi Kingdom and that Kerwin is to be the leader of this area? He didn't add the news of Kehi's passing or that Koha was seriously injured, just yet.

Kerewa and Kailan were both relieved and puzzled by this news. *Had the northern Kiwis given in so easily?*

"There is no indication of how everyone is." Kerewa spoke with concern. "I think the situation up there is more volatile than Koa is letting on. I just hope he is coping with it well."

Kailan nodded. "He will tell us when he is ready."

"Hello Kehi." Kohana gave him a gentle smile as he joined her on her vigil over the scene below. "You can be proud of Koa. He has done well in this confrontation."

"Yes. The Kingdom will do well in his care. How long have you been...?" he paused unable to say the words they both knew he meant.

"After you left, the hunters came back with this dog. His name is Titan. I had to fight Titan to protect Kelia. Both Titan and I were unable to survive our injuries so we moved to the spirit world. We have become good friends to each other now."

Kohana then looked behind her with a smile. When Kehi looked, he found Kiyo was waiting for him. Kohana and Titan then disappeared from view.

CHAPTER FOUR

NEW THREAT IN THE NORTH

Koa looked at the large crowd in front of him, as they waited to hear what was being planned for their future. He noticed that as soon as the Tasman Kiwis had arrived, Kerwin went to sit amongst them. Kerwin was sitting next to a young female, who appeared very happy to see him again, much to the interest of everyone around them. Koa realised Kerwin had found his mate in the Tasman, but untill now couldn't pursue their relationship.

The surrounding Kiwis were also asking Kerwin many questions, looking at Koa as they did so. Koa knew they were trying to judge what sort of leader he was and what change he was bringing to them.

Koa also looked at his grandfather, Koha who gave him an encouraging smile. Koha was looking a little better after his wounds had been washed and he had fed. With time and care, he would make it back to his mate Kamora.

"Thank you everyone, for coming." Silence settled over the crowd as Koa's loud, clear and authoritive voice rang out. "If you haven't already heard, Kaine's attempt to take over Kerewa and Kailan's territory has failed." There were many murmurings and some wails as some females realised that their family members weren't returning to them. "There has been loss of life on both sides. I give my sympathy to those who have lost someone in their family."

"As from now, all of the territory that Kaine held is now part of the Kiwi Kingdom." A female voice then challenged him. "You will never rule us!"

Everyone looked at the dark female who had stood up and was advancing towards him, a young kiwi at her side.

"You have killed Kura, and now Kaine. We have many more members of our family to avenge them!"

As Koa comprehended the meaning of her words – that his kingdom would never be completely safe while Kura and Kaine's family lived, he noticed that the female had pushed the young kiwi forward. The kiwi was now running towards him with intent, followed by the female. She didn't notice the owls, led by Oliver sweep down from behind to pounce on her and pin her to the ground. As the young kiwi approached and lunged at him, Koa quickly stepped to the side, and with a quick swipe the young kiwi was left motionless on the floor.

"So, you will kill our children as well!" The female's voice was full of venom.

"Of course!" Koa's steely gaze showed everyone present that here was a leader that was as capable of being ruthless as she was. "How many of their children did you allow to live?" Koa pointed to the surviving northern Buller kiwis as he spoke. "We all know that you have killed every one of them that you found."

The female waited in sullen silence for the blow that Koa knew he had to make. Afterwards the owls returned to the trees as Koa addressed the crowd.

"Stand up all members of Kura and Kaine's family, and also any who won't accept the Kiwi Kingdom."

"What are you planning to do with us?" one asked as they stood up. "We don't all have her attitude."

Koa understood the Kiwi's concern that the female had put their lives at risk, but he took the time to give them all a searching look before he answered.

"Sit down those who are prepared to live in the Kiwi Kingdom." Koa said finally. All but a few sat down again; the others remained standing with defiant looks on their faces. Koa ordered those still standing to sit separate to everyone else, with a close guard on them.

"There are a few rules to live under in my Kingdom." Koa addressed the Tasman Kiwis.

"You will live as you have been, but you are to respect all animals and Kiwis you meet and you also are not to injure or kill animals and Kiwis you meet. A school will be set up in your area for you and other animals to attend and learn to get on with each other. You may only defend or kill if an animal attacks you or any of your family members. It is normal Kingdom policy to expel those who won't live by Kingdom rules. But I am warning you all now;" Koa added sternly, "If anyone from this community breaks the rules, you will be eliminated. Kerwin is to be the leader of your community."

"Why have you chosen Kerwin to lead us?" someone asked.

"I need someone I can trust to lead you." Koa replied. "I was going to send a member of my family here, but Kerwin volunteered. Given that this area is his home and he already knows your area well, I agreed." Koa noticed quite a few smiles to this news.

"What about us?" a northern Buller Kiwi called out.

"You have shown everyone that you are unable to govern or defend yourselves, so you will have to choose whether to live in Kerwin's community or come down to Kerewa and Kailan's community."

"And if we won't?"

Koa recognised the question was a challenge to his authority.

"You will be expelled to the Alps." Koa advised them, before adding. If you cause trouble from there, you will be dealt with."

"In the same way she has been?"

"Yes. You need to decide now, where you are going to live."

Koa quietly was pleased to see that the northern Buller Kiwis split up. Some went to sit with Kerwin's group, and most of the others went to sit with Koa's group. Only a few kept separate to begin their new life in the Alps. Koa looked at Oliver, who understood that those in the Alps were to be supervised.

Before Kerwin prepared to leave with his group, he came over to Koa.

"Are you happy to lead them without us being near?"

"I am." Kerwin smiled. "I can always send word if I need to. My community seems to be accepting me already."

"Good! Tell me if there are any changes that concern you and let me know when you have found a suitable place for your school and I will send some books up for you. We will be in this area untill Koha is fit to travel. Kerewa and Kailan will always help if you need it."

Kerwin nodded. He had much to do in his new role, but was looking forward to the challenge. It was nice to know he had help if and when he needed it.

As the northern Buller Kiwis prepared to leave for their life in the Alps, one came over to Koa.

"Are they to come with us too?" He referred to the Kiwis from the Tasman who had been under guard.

"No. You will have an escort to your new area." Koa indicated the Owls who were watching and waiting in the trees.

The northern Buller Kiwis then realised their plans to cause mischief in the Kiwi Kingdom communities was going to be prevented and that a lonely future now awaited them. They began their trek with stony faces.

Koa watched them go with some anxiety. He knew they would cause trouble if they could.

Koa turned around to deal with the remaining Kiwis from the Tasman, who he knew couldn't be allowed to be free, but found they were missing.

"Where are they?" Koa asked; panic rising within him at the thought that they had been freed.

"They've been sorted." Koha reassured him. "You have had enough to deal with."

Koa gave a sigh of relief. "Thanks Granddad. You need to rest now too. We need to get you strong so you can go home."

"Yes." Koha agreed. "The Buller is home now. I'm looking forward to getting back to Kamora."

As Koa and his group relaxed after the rigours of the night, little did he know of the coming threat to the Kingdom at Lake Kaniere.

CHAPTER FIVE

THE VISIT

Morning sunlight was filtering through the trees on the Island at Lake Kaniere as Orion rested on a branch of the nesting tree with his father Orlando. His sister Oriana slept nearby with their mother Odessa. They stopped using the nesting hollow to sleep, ever since the day Orion woke from a dream where he was being chased; to find Oriana was also awake and looking at him with intent. As Orion moved to swiftly leave the hollow, he felt the floor behind him start to give way, but in his haste to leave, didn't give it much thought.

"What's wrong Orion?" Orlando's tone was sharp as he heard and saw Orion swiftly emerge from the nesting hollow with a stricken look on his face.

"Nothing." Orion lied. "It's getting cramped in there now. It's time I learnt to sit out on the branches as you do." He added with a smile.

"But you can't fly yet!" His father reminded him, not fooled by Orion's excuse. Something had obviously happened to make Orion feel unsafe in the same space as his sister.

"I know." Orion replied, "It won't be long though." As he proceeded to preen of his feathers and test his wings.

"Come over here and rest by me." Orlando ordered him. Odessa had been resting on the other side of the hollow, swiftly came to sit on the other side of Orion. Realising that her chances to get her revenge for the death of their brother Orel, were disappearing, Oriana slowly emerged from the hollow with a little smile on her face.

"You are right, Orion. It is getting too cramped in there." Oriana declared as she took her place on the other side of her mother.

Orion enjoyed this new life out on the branches, seeing all the birds he had only heard before and the insects crawling on both the branches and foliage of the tree. Even the rain when it came, was welcomed to wash his feathers.

Oriana remained quiet and compliant, impatient for the day when she could fly and be independent of the constant presence and scrutiny of their parents. Her wish for revenge remained strong.

Meanwhile, there was consternation in the spirit world, when it was learnt that an owlette had been sent to Nudoor by a living owl. Only the leaders of the spirit world were given the power to send an animal's spirit there.

Who was this owl who had the power while he was still alive and why had he sent such a young owl into complete isolation? The last time, many centuries ago this had happened, the Spirit world was in danger. Owen, Oban and Oleus were sent to pay this owl a visit!

Oleus was secretly delighted to be sent on this mission. He had been waiting for Odessa and Orlando's owlettes to arrive, for he intended to use two of them in his plans to control both the living and spirit world. He was disappointed that one had been sent to Nudoor, but was comforted by the attitude of the other, who wanted revenge. He would use that hate to his advantage.

As the family rested in the morning light, Orion became aware that they were being watched. Usually it was just one of the day birds that lived on the Island with them. After checking out who it was, he would go straight back to sleep again. Today however was different. There were not one, but three adult Owls sitting in the next tree and they were studying him! As Orion bobbed his head about to focus his eyes on them better, he also knew instinctively that these owls were from the spirit world!

Orion's movements woke Orlando. He had a quick scan around them to find nothing amiss, but it was obvious that Orion could see something that he couldn't!

"What can you see?" Orlando asked him quietly. There was no point in waking the others unless they needed to.

"You can't see them?" Orion asked, equally quietly. "There are three adult owls sitting on the branch opposite us, in the next tree. They are watching us. I think they may be from the spirit world."

As Orion looked back at the owls, he could see they were looking directly into his eyes, to see what kind of soul he had.

"You don't recognize any of them?"

"No."

Although he couldn't see them, Orlando half turned and came closer to protect him from the scrutiny his son was under.

Meanwhile, Oriana had also woken and was looking around her; for she could also feel that something was here, even though she couldn't see it. She hoped that Orel's spirit had come back. She could see that both Orlando and Orion were awake too and were looking at the tree next to them.

"Can you see what it is?" Oriana asked. Her voice woke Odessa from her dream in the spirit world.

Orion suddenly turned and ran for the shelter of the nesting hole, Orlando followed him, trying to watch the other tree at the same time.

"What is happening?" Odessa called in alarm.

"Some owls from the spirit world are here. Something has scared Orion.

"Is that you Orel?" Oriana called out. No response came to her call.

"OLLIE!" Odessa screamed out. "OLLIE HELP US!" Then she remembered she needed to call him in her thoughts.

Orion rushed into the hollow, to shelter at the back. To his and Orlando's horror the floor gave way and with a squawk and a flutter of his wings Orion disappeared from view down into centre of the tree. Orion found his wings pinned close to his body and head as he tumbled and bumped his way downwards. After what seemed a long fall, he found himself in a large light filled space where he landed on a bed of ferns and sphagnum moss that Kupe Kiwi's friends had made on their visits to him. For a few seconds Orion lay there winded, not able to breathe or speak. He could hear his father calling him, but was unable to answer. A voice next to him then spoke. Orion looked around. It was Kupe Kiwi smiling at him.

"Hello Orion. Are you okay? I didn't realise I could receive visitors from up there." Kupe looked up at the dark space where Orion had come from.

Orion then gave a gasp then panted as he was able to breathe again.

"I think I'm alright." Orion was finally able to say, as he tested his wings and his claws. He was feeling sore and had lots of ruffled feathers. Looking up into the dark space above, he knew how lucky he was to be alive.

"Can you get Ollie?" Orion asked. "Some owls from the spirit world are in the next tree watching us. One of them intends to kill us all, and control the spirit world."

"Are you sure about this?" Kupe asked in alarm.

"Yes." Orion confirmed. "I could see it in his eyes when I looked into them."

Meanwhile, up in the hollow, Orlando was frantically peering into the dark space where Orion fell and was calling to him frantically. After calling to Ollie, Odessa came to the hollow to see what was happening. She gasped to see it was empty and a gaping hole had appeared in the floor of the nesting hollow.

"He isn't down there, is he?" Odessa asked tearfully. Realising that Orion may be dead or trapped in the bottom of the tree.

"I'm afraid he is." Orlando replied as he turned to comfort her. "He hasn't answered my calls since he fell."

The owls from the spirit world watched with interest and now concern, the family's reaction to their visit. They could see that this young owl was able to see them when he detected their presence. Owen and Oban were relieved to see a rare maturity, with no malice in this young owl's soul when they looked into his eyes, but they became concerned at his reaction when he looked into Oleus's eyes. What had he seen that made this young owl flee for safety? Owen and Oban looked at their companion and were disturbed to see his focus on the young owl's sister, who was now sitting alone on her branch. She didn't appear to be concerned at the fate of her brother, but was concentrating on looking in Oleus's direction. *Was she under his control?*

Both Owen and Oban realised that danger to both the living and spirit world was sitting next to them! *What role did Oleus have for this young female in his plans?*

After seeing the young owl, they now knew was called Orion disappear into the tree, they were now worried that something drastic had happened to the young owl before they could talk to him!

Oleus was pleased to see this young owl was afraid of him. Even though the little owl had powers most owls don't have, he should be easy to control and eliminate. After Orion ran from his gaze, Oleus concentrated his focus and energy on Oriana. He could see she could feel his presence, even though she mistook it for her lost brother. He would have pleasure in reuniting them when he took control. Oleus would have liked to reveal himself to her, but now was not the time.

Ollie Owl was resting happily in his spot; on Mount Tahua, when a distant voice calling his name disturbed him. As he opened his eyes, Odessa's plea came clearly into his thoughts.

Ollie please help us! Orion has seen some owls from the spirit world in the next tree. They gave him a fright that sent him to shelter in the nesting hollow. Now he has fallen into the tree! Why are they here, and what do they want from us?

Ollie appeared on the branch next to the nesting hole where Both Orlando and Odessa were now frantically calling down the hole in the nesting hollow.

"Hello Odessa. I heard your call. Where are these owls you were talking about?"

As Ollie spoke, there were calls and the arrival of owls from the forest surrounding Hans Bay, who had heard Odessa's scream for Ollie and had come to see what had happened for her to need him.

Owen and Oban looked at each other ruefully; this wasn't going to be a discreet visit after all. They would have to reveal themselves to everyone. Realising this too, Oleus was happy that he would be revealed to the young female after all.

Odessa and Orlando looked around. With Ollie was Oriel, their families, and all the Hans Bay owls that were looking at them with concern.

"They are in the tree next to us." Orlando replied and looked at the branch that Orion had indicated. Ollie looked at the branch and was surprised to see his father Owen, and two others sitting with him. His father was smiling at him.

Ollie was puzzled as to why their presence would scare Orion, when a call came from Kupe Kiwi.

Ollie, can you come here? It is urgent!

I will be with you shortly.

"Hello Dad, what brings you here?" Ollie said loudly for the benefit of everyone present. At that, Owen, Oban and Oleus revealed themselves to everyone, to gasps and smiles from everyone in the crowd, who had not expected to see Owen again.

Oleus smiled as he looked around inclusively at everyone, giving a special smile to Oriana as he looked ever so briefly into her eyes. That contact was enough. She was now in his control.

She gave the briefest of smiles back with her eyes.

Oriana knew immediately, that this owl was in control of her destiny. She settled down quietly to wait for her future to begin.

"We had heard that young Orion could see animals from the spirit world, so we came to pay him a visit." Owen explained.

"We didn't expect him to be afraid and run away from us. Is he okay?" Oban asked.

"We don't know." Odessa answered tearfully. "Odion has fallen into a hole in the tree trunk. We haven't heard from him since! He may be dead, or stuck in there if he is still alive." Odessa's voice was bleak, that she had probably lost her second child.

"Don't despair just yet" Ollie reassured her. "There is a big space at the bottom of this tree, with an entrance. I will go down and see if Orion is there." With that Ollie disappeared from view.

Owen was sorry Ollie didn't invite him to come too, but realised that if he came, the other two would have to come as well. Owen had seen the contact between Oleus and Oriana and knew she was now under his control. They had to be extra careful now to keep Orion away from Oleus!

Down in the space under the trunk, Ollie was very relieved to find Kupe and next to him was Orion, looking very ruffled, but otherwise unhurt. Orion was giving himself a good preen to straighten his feathers.

"Hello Kupe, Hello Orion." Ollie smiled at them. "You haven't been hurt from your fall?" Ollie asked.

"No. I was lucky I landed on the moss. I was trying to run from owls from the spirit world." Orion said in anguish. When Orion told Ollie of what he had seen in Oleus's eyes, he felt both fear and anger.

When Ollie returned to the waiting crowd, there was a hush as they waited for his news. Ollie turned first to Orlando and Odessa.

"I have good news for you." Ollie smiled. "Orion survived the fall." He is shaken, but is otherwise okay. He will have to stay down on the ground untill he has learnt to fly. Kupe Kiwi is with him. Kupe is going to show Orion how to find food untill he is independent."

"We will go down and give him food as well." Orlando stated with much relief.

"We will come over and check on him too." Oriel offered.

Ollie then turned to Owen and the owls from the spirit world. "Orion isn't ready for your visit just yet. You will have to return later when he has recovered."

"Of course," Owen responded with some disappointment. "Goodbye for now." He said in farewell before they disappeared from view.

Ollie turned to Oriel and whispered quietly, "Orion needs to be protected night and day. Also, everyone in the Kiwi Kingdom needs to be on their guard from those among the living and the spirit world who will destroy us.

"Who?"

Oleus in the spirit world. Oriana is already under his control."

"I will warn Koa and the other leaders."

Oriel spoke to Orlando and Odessa. "I will see you tonight." He then turned to the owls in his community. "I will see you all back at the school cave." Before turning to lead them back to Mount Tahua.

Orion had finally settled back to sleep after visits from his parents, relieved to see he was alright and promising to return that night, when a rustle at the entrance told him that they were no longer alone. Ophira his aunty came in with a smile.

"I have come to keep you company."

From then on, someone from the Hans Bay community remained with Orion at all times.

When Ollie returned to his spot on top of Mount Tahua, he wasn't surprised to find Owen was waiting for him.

"Where are the others?"

"Oban is keeping him busy."

Owen's eyes became bleak when Ollie informed him of what Orion had seen and why he had sent Orel to Nudoor.

"We have to stop them! The question is, how?" Owen said finally.

"Everyone in the Kingdom is being warned and Orion is being protected." Ollie informed him. "You need to warn everyone in the spirit world as well. How many friends does Oleus have in the spirit world? We will have to be careful of them as well."

"I am thinking of Oleus and Oriana's souls." Owen said finally. "Nudoor is the only safe place for them, but they can't be placed with anyone else, or together or with Orel."

Ollie noticed with sadness, that Oriana's life was already forfeit after being drawn into Oleus's scheme. As a moth is attracted to a flame, her attraction to him was going to be fatal. Ollie now knew why Kohana and Titan were together. What force was at work to protect her? Ollie then realised that he needed to contact Keoni and Kohana to warn them of the new danger to them.

In the Buller Kerewa and Kailan finally received the news that Kerewa had been dreading, that Kehi wasn't coming home and that Koa and Koha's return was being delayed untill Koha was well enough to travel. Kerewa in turn had to forward the news of a new danger to the Kingdom from the south. A young female owl called Oriana was under the influence of an evil spirit called Oleus.

CHAPTER SIX

ORIANA AND ORION'S NEW LIVES

As news spread of the new danger in the Kingdom, Oriana had no idea of the turmoil she was causing. Any day now she would be able to fly to her destiny, for all of her heavy downy feathers were gone. She knew that her vow to kill Orion was going to be hard now that he was on the ground and had a guard. She noticed with envy that he was already practicing flying among the lower branches of trees and catching food for himself.

Oriana stretched her wings. At last her feathers were much lighter. Her parents were away looking for their feed. They had promised to come and escort her on her first flight and search for food. She could feel eyes on her, and hoped it was Oleus, here to see her progress. She knew he would reveal him-self to her again when he was ready. She was excited to know what plans he had for her.

Down on the forest floor, Orion also had shed the last of his downy feathers and his Aunty Owena was showing him how to make short flights up through the branches to the top of the tree so he could make his first flight off the Island and join the rest of the community in the lakeside forest. They had reached the top when Orion suddenly ducked back under the cover of the foliage. Owena couldn't see anything around them, but swiftly followed him.

"What is it?" Owena whispered, seeing Orion was shaking in fear.

"He's here!" Orion whispered back. "Oleus is here!"

Orion looked down at the open branches below him and hoped They couldn't be seen from below. He shuffled himself along the branch, closer to the trunk so his profile was reduced. Owena came next to Orion and shielded him with her wing, pretending to preen her feathers.

Oriana felt movement on the branch and knew he was here! She turned her head and there Oleus stood. She gave him a beaming smile, but he didn't return it.

"Are you ready?" Oleus asked with an impassive face.

"I am." Oriana answered with an equally impassive face.

"Do you know where your brother is?" Oleus asked.

"He was still on the floor feeding when I last saw him."

"Good. Follow me."

Oleus swooped down between the branches. Oriana took a deep breath and followed him, scrapping some of the branches on the way. Eventually he landed on a low branch. Oriana had found it difficult to keep up with him and was panting hard when she landed next to him. Oleus frowned when he saw the state Oriana was in.

"How much flying have you been doing?" Oleus's tone was stern.

Upset and anger was rising within Oriana, but she managed not to show it.

"It was my first flight." Oriana chose not to look at him.

"I will return when you have had more practice.

When you see your brother, eliminate him." With that instruction Oleus disappeared from view.

When she got her breath back, Oriana took stock of her surroundings with mixed emotions. Elated from taking her first flight without injuring herself, Oriana was now tired and very hungry. She had no idea where her tree was and her flight feathers were in a complete mess! Worst of all Oriana realised, she was being used, but felt powerless to do anything about it.

Oriana started to preen when she spotted movement below her among the ferns. She allowed instinct to take over and immediately swooped on the luckless mouse. Oriana took her time to consume it as she sat on the forest floor. She could feel eyes on her again. This time she knew that it wasn't Oleus, and wondered idly why they didn't show themselves.

Sitting high in the branches, Owena and Orion silently witnessed the interaction between Oleus and Oriana. Orion almost felt sorry for his sister, but knew the next meeting between them would be a fight to the death.

When Oriana had finished preening her feathers, she slowly made her way through the forest, seeing if she could recognise her sleeping tree. When she heard her parents calling her, Oriana answered them with much relief, happy that they hadn't abandoned her in the way that Oleus had.

When Odessa and Orlando returned to the nesting tree, their hearts sank to find the branch empty. They both knew Oriana had been enticed away and wondered if she would ever return to their lives.

"I will call her anyway, just in case she still wants us." Odessa advised Orlando.

"How was your first flight?" Odessa asked when they found her. They didn't mention Oleus, but knew she had been with him.

"I need lots of practice." Oriana replied. On seeing the mouse that Orlando held, "Is that mouse for me? I'm starving!"

"You will have to catch the next one yourself." Orlando said with a smile after handing it over.

"I have caught one for myself." Oriana replied with pride, "but I'm still hungry."

They noticed with some concern that Oriana was quite disheveled, despite her attempts to preen all of her feathers and wondered where Oleus had taken her. Once Oriana had finished her mouse, she asked, "Can I join you on your next flight?

"Of Course!" Odessa smiled with relief. "Though, it will help your flying if your feathers are a little smoother."

"Do I look that bad?" Oriana immediately started to preen again

"It looks like you've been dragged through lots of bushes!" Orlando was blunt.

Once Oriana had flown out of sight, Owena led Orion out to the top branch again.

"Can you see if Oleus is still around?" Owena asked.

Orion took his time to scan the hilltops and sky around the lake.

"I think we are safe."

With that, Owena led Orion on a short flight across the water to the forest in Han's bay; where they received a big welcome. Word was sent to Oriel who greeted Orion with a big beam on his face. "Have you fed yet?"

"I have."

"Are you ready for your education?"

Orion nodded. Oriel led him to the school cave where new friends and a whole new world were introduced to him. Oriel decided that for safety, Orion was to sleep in the school cave with the bats during the day. Oriel showed Orion a little alcove out of sight of anyone that came into the cave where he could sleep in safety.

Oriana relished the flights she took with her parents during the following nights, with lessons on how to negotiate thick forest and also how to fly long distances without tiring too quickly – a skill she would need in coming weeks.

The night finally came when it was time to leave her Island home. Orlando and Odessa had warned Oriana that there wasn't enough food on the island to remain there forever.

As Oriana followed her parents from the Island, she noticed that they led her to the southern end of the lake, well away from the bay where they normally flew to. For several nights Orlando and Odessa stayed with her, making sure she was able to feed and was comfortable in the trees during sleep time. She also noticed they insisted on sleeping in a different tree each day – a strategy she realised would save her later when she was alone. During this time Oriana felt she was still being watched, but tried to ignore it.

The evening finally came when Oriana was left alone.

"It is time for us to start a new family, and for you to begin the life that you want too." Odessa spoke gently and with a smile.

Orlando and Odessa flew off towards the coast. They were heading for Lake Mahinapua where Orlando had grown up. They encouraged Oriana to head south where there were big forests and plenty of shelter and food to find. They had just flown out of sight when a large male owl appeared and sat next to her.

"You are Oriana, aren't you?"

Oriana stared at the owl, not knowing what to expect next. It didn't seem to be hostile, but it wasn't friendly either. She gave a little nod.

"You aren't welcome in this area. Move away from here."

Oriana didn't need to be told twice. Launching herself off the branch and using the strong slow wing beats her parents had taught her, to cover the distance she knew she needed to cover. To Oriana's distress the owl put out a call, which was answered by an owl in the forest in front of her. Oriana then realised that she was being tracked and landed in a big tree with plenty of foliage to hide in. She was now hungry, so very quietly flew under the canopy to find a feed. Afterwards Oriana looked around for a tree to settle in for the morning. There wasn't anything suitable here; it was time to move on.

As Oriana flew, trying to ignore the calls being put out to communities before her, she became aware that she wasn't alone. Oleus had found her! Her heart sank. Oriana now knew why she wasn't wanted in the communities, but how could she get rid of him? She needed to feed again. Ignoring Oleus's presence, she landed in a tree before scouring the floor for food.

"Why have you left the lake?" Oleus asked. "Did you do it?"

Oriana took the time to catch and consume her meal before answering him.

"I'm not welcome there anymore; in fact, I'm not welcome anywhere! Did you hear the owls calling to tell other communities that I was coming?" Oriana couldn't help letting her anger show.

"Did you do it?"

"Did I kill Orion? No, I didn't! I think he left the Island before I did. I have no idea where he is."

"Go back and find him!"

"I will be killed!"

"Look at me!" The command in Oleus's voice couldn't be ignored.

Slowly Oriana turned to look at Oleus, knowing she was lost.

"Go back and kill him!"

"I will." Oriana's reply was submissive.

Looking into her eyes, Oleus was satisfied with what he saw. He then disappeared from view.

Oriana sat there for some time, lost in her revere untill she realised she was surrounded by Owls. All of them had seen and heard her exchange with Oleus.

"Where are you going now?"

"I'm going to look for a tree to sleep in for the day."

"You aren't going back?"

"He didn't say when I had to go back."

"Where are you going to go?"

"My parents told me there is plenty of shelter and food in the south."

"We won't send you back. If you really want to avoid him, then keep below the canopy. Your journey will be slower, but it will be harder for him to find you."

"Thank you."

With that, Oriana set off again, this time keeping under the tree tops. After a short distance she could feel Oleus's presence nearby, so she found a tree with dense foliage and hid among the canopy untill his presence faded away.

In the spirit world, Oleus was angry! He had waited nearby to make sure Oriana obeyed him, but found she had snuck away. Obviously, her will was stronger than he had thought. When he found her again, he would make her suffer a little before escorting her back to the lake. She wouldn't give him the slip a second time! In the meantime, he would have to go looking for the spirits of the Kiwi Kingdom leaders that he knew had settled near the lake.

CHAPTER SEVEN

KOTARE'S MISSION

Titan was relaxing outside an old Kiwi burrow near the summit of Conical Hill. The sun was low over the Tasman Sea, promising to produce another golden sunset. Kohana had chosen the burrow as their space as the opening was completely concealed with ferns and it was warm and dry when it was raining. Even though they were now spirits, neither of them liked getting wet.

There were views to both Lake Kaniere and the Tasman Sea from here. She liked knowing that Keoni and Kupe Kiwi and also Ollie Owl were only across the lake. Kohana was visiting old haunts –First the burrow that Kehi had made bigger for the hatching of Kelia. She smiled at the memory of her first visit to this lake. Kohana slipped into the burrow that was Keely and Kaori's home. They and their children were still asleep. Kohana was about to slip out again when she froze. She could hear Titan growling and snarling – she hadn't heard him make that noise since their fight that sent them to the spirit world. She looked at Keely and Kaori. They remained at peace. Kohana was thankful they couldn't hear the noise Titan was making. *Who or what was it that was upsetting Titan?*

Kohana heard the sound of an animal landing and knew before it spoke that here was the one that she had seen in her visions – the one that wanted to destroy everyone from the Kiwi Kingdom in both the living and spirit world. Ollie had also warned her of him!

"Dog! Why are you growling at me? What makes you think I am a threat to you?" There was a pause. Then, "Why aren't you with other dogs in the spirit world?"

"This is my territory!" Titan replied with a growl. "Stay off it! I'm not sharing it with any other dog! Titan then proceeded to bark and growl at Oleus untill he moved on.

Oleus remembered that a dog had paired with a Kiwi. This one was very protective of his territory. He would remember to check the territory of this dog in future. Oleus started to make his way across the lake. As he did so, Kohana put out a call in her thoughts.

Keoni! Kupe! Ollie and Orion! Take shelter! Oleus is coming to Han's Bay.

Orion was out early for a feed. On hearing Kohana's call, he immediately flew back to the Bat cave and sheltered in his alcove. The Bats were waking up and preparing to leave for their night flights. Usually Orion was starting his evening search with them, so when he shot back into his corner, they knew something was up.

"Who's coming?" Orion was asked.

"Oleus is, from the spirit world."

"Is there anything we can do?"

"No. Just carry on as you normally do."

The bats weren't happy to leave Orion completely alone when such a danger was near. They arranged to leave some behind to protect him if needed.

From his position on top of Mount Tahua, Ollie had already spotted Oleus coming and hid under a nearby bush.

Keoni had been resting in his old burrow and was about to set off for his regular roam in the forest, when Kohana called. He decided to stay in, just in case.

Kupe was out of his burrow under the tree and roaming the island forest when Kohana's call came. He was too far from the burrow to get back and knew that Oleus would spot him if he kept moving around, so found some dense ferns and kept his head down.

Oleus came to the Island and gave it a thorough sweep. He knew that Kupe had a hidey hole under the tree where Orlando and Odessa had had their chicks. He checked there but it was empty. There was no sign of Orion either, so Oriana was right, that he was already off the Island.

Oleus knew Ollie liked the top of Mount Tahua, having enjoyed the view from there himself.

"Are you there Ollie?" Oleus called as he swept over the top of Mount Tahua, but his call remained unanswered. Ollie was either elsewhere or was choosing not to answer. It then struck Oleus that it was strange that everyone was missing – were they avoiding him? Oleus then remembered that Oriana had flown south after being made unwelcome here and realised that his plans had been exposed! There was only one animal that could know – that was Orion! With renewed determination Oleus started a slow sweep of Mount Tahua and Hans Bay. Orion had to be found and eliminated!

As Oleus was searching, Kotare had taken Kelia out with his friends in the forest looking for a feed. Suddenly, in front of them appeared his spirit friends who had escaped from the cave with him. Kotare's friends scrambled behind the nearest tree in fright while Kelia clung to Kotare in fear; not knowing what these creatures were.

"You can come out." Kotare called to his friends. "They are friends of mine from when I fell in the cave."

Slowly Kotare's friends came out from behind the trees and looked in awe at all the creatures; some of them towered above them with long legs and large claws, bigger than their own.

"Hello" Kotare greeted them with a grin. "What brings you here?"

"We need your help Kotare." Manu the Moa spoke with urgency. "Your family at Lake Kaniere is in danger. You are the only living animal we know who can tell them!" After explaining about Oleus from the spirit world and Oriana in the living world, Manu urged Kotare to go with him.

"Kelia will be coming with me. I am caring for her." Manu nodded his agreement. Kotare turned to his friends. "Can you tell Kerewa and Kailan for us?"

"We will."

Manu knelt down for Kotare and Kelia to climb on his back. They found climbing onto a spirit animal very different to a living one. Manu's feathers were so light Kotare was worried he would slip through them. Once settled they didn't need to be told twice to "hang on tight", which they did – to his neck.

Kotare's friends watched in awe as Manu lead his spirit friends up above the tree tops where they disappeared from view. They then looked at each other glumly as they knew the reaction they would get when they told Kerewa their news.

"I don't suppose they won't believe us when we tell them!"

"They will, when I tell them. I will come with you."

The young Kiwis looked up at the tree where the voice came from. For once they were relieved that Opal was watching.

Kerewa and Katana were out for a feed when Opal landed in the tree above them, Kotare's friends were approaching. Neither Kotare nor Kelia were with them.

"They have something to tell you." Opal called down to Kerewa. "I saw it as well."

When Kerewa heard the incredible tale that animals from the spirit world had taken Kotare and Kelia to Lake Kaniere, to warn Kaori and his family of the danger they were in, he knew he had to act.

"How soon can you get word down to Oriel and Kane? Kaori's family will have to move to Arahura Valley untill it is safe again.

Opal immediately put out a call, which was answered by owls on the south side of the Buller River.

In the spirit world the sound of the Moas and their friends running made everyone who heard them look up. Running was only permitted in an emergency! To their amazement there were living creatures with them. This was unheard of in their world. The rule of not interfering with the living was being broken. They decided to follow in case their help was needed too.

Kotare and Kelia would forever remember their journey to Lake Kaniere with the forest canopy, homes and towns passing swiftly below, the number of animals that joined them on their journey increasing as they went.

As Manu approached Lake Kaniere he slowed and found a spot on the slopes of Conical Hill to land and let Kotare and Kelia get off.

"Do you know where your families' burrows are?" Manu asked.

"I do. Thank you for bringing us. Come on Kelia."

As Kotare started making their way towards Kaori and Keely's burrow Manu turned to the crowd surrounding him.

"Guard this hill! Oleus is nearby. He must be prevented from harming anyone either in the living or spirit world. We have to beware of a living owl called Oriana too for she is under his control."

Kohana was still sheltering on Conical Hill with Titan when he gave a growl. She looked at what he was growling at and was amazed to see a giant Moa leading a large number of spirit animals to her hill. What was more amazing, he had Kotare and Kelia on his back!

"Quiet Titan! They are friends."

"Are you sure?"

"They have my children with them. Let's see why they are here."

Titan quietly followed Kohana as she followed the children up the hill.

Keilana was out with Keely and Kana for a feed when she spotted Kotare and Kelia making their way towards their burrows.

"Kotare! Kelia! What are you doing here?" Keilana called out as she made her way over to them. Keely and Kana also rushed over to them as well. Keely looked around. The children seemed to be completely alone. Something drastic must have happened to bring them all this way by themselves.

"How did you get here?" Keely wanted to know. "Have you walked all the way?"

"No." Kelia said shyly. "Our friends from the spirit world brought us." She looked around her with a big smile. Keely could see that Kelia was able to see something that she couldn't.

"Does your father know you're here?" Keely asked with some alarm.

"Dad died in the battle for the north." Kotare advised her. "We live with Kerewa now. My friends will tell him we are here."

"What about your mother?" Keely noticed the amulet around Kelia's neck for the first time. Kelia saw Keely looking at her amulet and clutched it tightly.

"Mum left it for me when the dog took her."

Kelia could feel someone behind her. She turned around to see Kohana and the dog were there.

"Mum?" Kelia asked, looking at the dog with alarm.

Kohana revealed herself and the dog.

"Yes darling, it is me and this is Titan. We are good friends now. We live here now. We are really interested to know why your spirit friends have brought you here."

Kotare then spoke up. "They came for me. I had Kelia with me, so I insisted she come too." He turned to Keely. They brought us here to tell you that you are in danger here." Kotare then told her about Oleus and Oriana. "You need to leave here untill it is safe to return."

Keely looked at Kohana, who nodded. "Oleus has been here. I know he will return."

"You aren't safe here either." Keely spoke to Kohana with concern.

"I have Titan." Kohana replied with a smile.

Keely put out an urgent call to Kaori who had gone with Kian down to the water's edge to see Ernie. As they were chatting, Kaori heard Keely's call and frowned.

"Something's up. I will have to see what Keely wants."

"I will stay nearby in case you need me."

"Thanks Ernie."

Kaori answered Keely's call and rushed up the hill, with Kian close behind.

Ketara had also heard Keely's urgent call and had come running too.

"We are in danger here. We have to leave." Keely greeted Kaori when he arrived on the scene to find Kotare and Kelia were here. "Animals from the spirit world brought them to tell us."

"Where are they now?" Kaori asked, his heart sinking at the thought of leaving here.

"They are here with us." Kelia replied with a smile.

"It's hard to believe in something you can't see!" Kaori spoke with frustration.

"We are all here! You will be killed if you stay." A booming voice from behind Kaori spoke.

Slowly Kaori turned around to see a pair of pale and very large clawed feet. His gaze travelled up a pair of very long legs to a thatch of white feathers covering the animal's body. A large pair of eyes above a sharp beak peered down at him.

"This is Manu the Moa." Kotare introduced him.

"But you are all...." Kaori broke off, not able to say the word dead.

"...In the spirit world." Manu finished for him. "Oleus is nearby. There is little time before he returns here."

"Kaori looked at Keely with stricken eyes. "I must let Ernie know what is happening before we leave." He then went tearing off down the hill.

Keely's words of "Be careful!" weren't heard as Kaori crashed his way through the trees and ferns on the steep slopes. Ernie heard Kaori's descent and wondered what happened to cause his hurry. Suddenly Kaori tripped on a rock and was sent flying head first into a tree. In the silence following Kaori's fall, Ernie knew he would never talk to his friend again. One of the Moas Moana had followed Kaori's flight down the hill went over to his still body and could see Kaori's spirit had left it.

"He has crashed into a tree! His spirit has left him!" Moana called out to Manu. Kohana looked around – she could see Kaori's spirit making its way across the lake towards the Islands.

Ernie then called to Moana. "Moa, I'm Ernie. Can you bring Kaori's body to me? I will make sure it is safe in our sanctuary."

Moana looked at Ernie. "You aren't going to eat it?"

"No. His friend Kupe is already safe there. We will make sure nothing ever interferes with it."

Keely shook her head with disbelief and grief that within minutes their life here was at an end and her soul mate was gone too. When she heard that Ernie wanted Kaori's body, she agreed with a wan smile. Kaori had never wanted to leave the lake, and now he had his wish. It was a comfort that he now was to rest with Kupe. Very gently Moana lifted Kaori's body and brought it to the water's edge. Ernie saw her approach and slapped the water with his tail. The lake eels quickly converged to join Ernie.

"Kaori is to join Kupe and Keanu in our sanctuary."

Moana gently lowered Kaori into the water where several eels came together to swim underneath him so he lay on their backs. The remaining eels formed a circle around them. With Ernie in the lead, they swiftly made their way out to the centre of the lake where Kaori was taken down to their sanctuary.

Keely was checking whether everyone was present and ready for their journey when a call came from one of the Moas.

"An owl is coming from the other side of the lake. I think it is Oleus!"

"Quick! Hide in your burrows." Manu ordered the Kiwis. "We will make sure he doesn't come in them." He looked at Kohana. "You need to go with them." Kohana didn't argue and led the scramble to hide in the burrows.

Oleus had no luck with finding Orion on the slopes of Mount Tahua. He had found the Bats' cave but some of them were still flying around in there, so didn't try to enter it. There was no sign of him in the forests of Hans Bay. Maybe he had left the lake area. When Oleus reached Conical Hill, he was struck by the number of spirit animals that occupied the slopes. He had no chance of checking the Kiwi burrows with them there. He also wondered where the dog was that was hostile to him.

"What brings you all here?" Oleus asked one of the Moas. They hadn't bothered with this area before.

"We like a change." Manu replied coolly. "What brings you here?"

"I was looking for someone."

"They aren't here now."

Manu waited some time after Oleus disappeared from view before softly calling to Keely. "You can come out now." When Keely and her family emerged, Kohana and Titan stayed inside the entrance. While they were inside, Kotare and Kelia had a final cuddle with Kohana they had been deprived of when she had been taken.

"We will escort you to your new home." Manu informed Keely.

"Thank you."

During that long night the family made their way through Sunny bight then across the hill to the Arahura valley where they made their way upstream. By now owls from Hans Bay were also shadowing them. When Oriel had received the news that Kotare and Kelia had come to warn Kaori and Keely, he had immediately flown across to the burrows to find them empty. He immediately called the owls at Hans Bay to search for them.

"Where are you going?" Oriel asked Keely when he caught up with them. He was concerned to see Kaori wasn't with them.

"We are going to join the group in the Arahura valley for now."

"I will let Keka know you are coming."

Oriel saw the sorrow in Keely's face and knew something had happened to prevent Kaori from being with them.

"Where is Kaori? Is he still at the lake?"

"He is resting peacefully with Kupe now."

"Did Oleus attack him?" Anger was building within Oriel.

"No. He was running to see Ernie, but tripped and crashed into a tree. It was an accident.

"Take care of yourself."

Keely nodded. She was feeling numb, not sure what she would do without him. Daylight was starting to form in the east when the family was met by Keka, Keona and Keio. Kotare looked around. Manu and the spirit animals were still with them.

"Can you take us home?" Kotare asked.

"We can." Manu smiled.

Kian and Kana were disappointed that Kotare and Kelia weren't staying with them, but were satisfied with the promise that they would return. Kerewa and Katana were in their burrow and wondering what Kotare and Kelia were doing when they appeared in the entrance.

"They are safe." Kotare said to Kerewa's enquiring look.

CHAPTER EIGHT

A NEW BEGINNING

Kaori looked down with amazement at his body which was lying still on the ground. He then realised that he was now in the spirit world. Kaori watched as a Moa came over to look at his body and then tell everyone his spirit had left it. Something was now drawing him to the Islands, so he let the force guide him across the lake.

Kaori was near the Islands when he felt something above. He looked up. It was an owl from the Spirit world. Kaori had always got on well with the owls at Lake Kaniere, but instinctively he knew this one was different and went on the offensive.

"What are you hovering over me for?" Kaori demanded. "I am far too big to be your meal! – Kaori put up his claw and motioned towards the owl that he was prepared to attack if necessary. "Go and find a mouse to annoy!"

At first Oleus thought Kaori might be the female from Conical Hill, but he quickly realised this Kiwi didn't have a dog with it and from its voice this one was a male.

"What is your name Bird, and where are you going?" Oleus demanded.

"My name is my business! – What is yours?" Kaori countered. I am going to the Islands. What business is it of yours, where I go?

"Do you know Kupe Kiwi?" the owl was thoughtful.

"Of course, I know him! – everyone around here does."

"Let me know if you see him!" Oleus demanded. Kaori raised his eyebrows and carried on his way. He had no intention of telling this Creature anything! He would have to find out who he was.

As he continued on towards Sunny Bight, Oleus was thinking the same thing about Kaori – he wasn't used to being challenged. He had a feeling this Kiwi was going to be trouble for him.

Kaori glided in towards the trees on the island where he knew Kupe had come with his mates years ago during the storm. Kupe had told him about the cubby he had made to shelter in with his friends. He would try to find it!

Oriana woke and looked around her. She had made her journey to the southern wilderness where no roads go. The only tracks were those made by deer. She noticed there were no Kiwis to be seen. Perhaps it was too wet for them here? One thing there was plenty of – mice for her to eat. She pounced on one to begin her meal. Oriana had matured to an adult now and consumed several mice each time she ate. As she ate, Oriana was aware that she was being watched. She looked in the direction she could feel their gaze. A male Owl, Ocene was watching her. Oriana swooped on another mouse. Instead of swallowing it, she held it in her claw.

"Do you want one?" Oriana offered it to him.

Ocene came over to sit next to Oriana.

"Are you Oriana?" Ocene asked.

Oriana's heart sank. Every time this question was asked, she was asked to move away. She liked it here and didn't want to move just yet. Should she lie? Just as quickly she rejected the idea and resigned herself to moving on again.

Ocene saw the conflicting emotions flicker across her face before Oriana answered with a guarded response.

"I am. Why?"

"I had heard about you." Ocene sat next to Oriana in a companionable silence. Oriana offered him the mouse again.

"I've already eaten." Ocene rejected her offer. "How long are you staying?"

"For as long as I'm allowed to." Oriana dared to hope she wouldn't have to move on again. "I like it here."

"Where is the spirit owl you are with?"

Oriana couldn't help showing fear in her face, before she controlled it to answer. "I'm hoping I won't see it again." They both knew that her hope would be in vain. Ocene could see that this female needed to be protected.

"You can stay with us for as long as you like, but I will arrange for someone to either be with you or be watching you at all times."

"Thank you!" The relief was plain in Oriana's face. She finally had found a new home and acceptance in a community who would protect her.

Kaori took his time as he combed the forest on the Island. He could see why Kupe had wanted to come. The canopy above created a thick roof. Kaori reveled in his exploration of the moss and ferns on the floor.

Kaori had looked at the bases of all the big trees, but couldn't see any obvious openings, and realised that Kupe's cubby was now hidden.

Kaori prepared to wade across to explore the Island next to it and wished that Kupe was here with him to enjoy it.

"But I am here." Kupe's voice spoke behind him. "Where are you heading?"

Kaori turned around with both sadness and joy to see his old friend standing there. He could see that his feelings were reflected in Kupe's face.

"I was going to explore the next Island." Kaori began. I couldn't find your cubby."

Kupe saw rain clouds gathering to the west. "That Island can wait. Come back to my cubby. We have much to catch up on."

When seeing the thick ferns which covered the entrance to the cubby, Kaori now understood why he missed it and was happy to follow Kupe into the large space under the tree roots. He was even happier to find a large bed of moss to relax on.

"You can thank Sam stoat and Percy Possum for that." Kupe smiled as Kaori made a beeline for the moss. "What happened to send you to the spirit world?" Kupe wanted to know.

"Kotare and Kelia from the Buller came with some spirit animals to warn us that we had to move as it isn't safe for us to be at the lake, with Oleus and Oriana under his control. I ran down to tell Ernie we were going. I stumbled and went head first into a tree." Kaori sighed as he finished.

"You never wanted to leave the lake." Kupe reflected.

"No," Kaori agreed, "but I didn't want to leave Keely either."

Kaori was glum at the prospect of the long wait before he was reunited with Keely again – if she did reunite with him again! It occurred to him she might find another mate before she came to the spirit world.

You haven't seen Oleus by any chance on the way here?" Kupe's words broke into Kaori's thoughts.

"I believe I did!" Kaori's indignation was plain. "This aggressive owl came and hovered over me. I told it I was too big to be its meal and to go and annoy a mouse! – and it did!"

Kupe's laugh rang in the hollow they sheltered in. Rain could be heard outside, but it didn't matter. They slipped back into the easy companionship they had shared during their living years. When daylight came and they settled for a rest, Kupe was happy his friend was here, for his years in the spirit world had been very lonely. He had much to teach his friend, for life in the spirit world was very different to that in the living world.

Learning to call and talk to spirits with his thoughts instead to talking; making your-self seen or invisible to others; and the ability to move quickly to other places were all things Kaori learnt to master with Kupe's help.

In the Arahura Valley Keely was grieving. She had looked forward to moving to the Arahura valley, but with Kaori gone, the nights were long as she went through her usual routine of feeding, though it was now with her children. Keely was gratefully they stayed close and kept her company. Both Kian and Kana were old enough to be completely independent, but they both knew their mother needed their support in her new life. They too were grieving for their father. They weren't risking the loss of their mother too.

Oleus was becoming more frustrated. His visits to Lake Kaniere were getting nowhere. The animals he sought kept well out of sight. Only one boldly strode about and ignored him on his visits to the Island. Oleus still hadn't learnt what his name was either. Other animals either didn't know him or refused to tell Oleus his name. On one occasion Oleus had come down on the Kiwi to teach him who was boss here. To Oleus's consternation the Kiwi turned and struck at him with such force, that if he had connected, Oleus's life in the spirit world would have ended.

Oleus had spoken to Owen and Oban about the aggressive new Kiwi spirit on the Island, but didn't get any sympathy from them.

"We heard about that." Oban answered Oleus's complaint. "He wasn't doing anything to you, so why did you try to attack him?"

"Animals are allowed to defend themselves." Owen added "If someone is being aggressive towards them."

Oleus decided it was time to make another effort to try to find Oriana.

In Fiordland Oriana had met a young male Ojen who was interested in her. At first, she avoided him untill one evening Ojen managed to confront Oriana and speak to her. "Why are you avoiding me?"

Oriana sighed. "I know you want me for your mate, but it won't work." Oriana's voice was full of sadness and regret. "I know that Oleus from the spirit world will find me sooner or later. It wouldn't be fair to leave you with a family to care for on your own. I can't stand the thought that Oleus could find and try to control our children as he has done to me."

"How do you know you would be leaving?" Ojen asked with concern.

"When I left home, Oleus found me and tried to force me to return there, to kill my brother. I pretended to obey him, but escaped and came down here. I know he won't let me escape a second time."

"Why does he want you to kill your brother?" Ojen was shocked.

"Orion is connected to the spirit world. He can see spirits." Oriana paused for a second. "I know that when we meet again, we will fight – and I will die."

Oriana's last words chilled Ojen to the bone. He now understood that he had to be strong for both of them.

"We haven't a moment to lose then, if our time together is to be short." Oriana looked at Ojen in shock as he came close to cuddle her. She found it hard to believe he still wanted her after knowing what lay ahead of them.

The whole community was sent to find a suitable nesting hollow.

One was eventually found - well hidden by foliage. When their family came – four little owlettes, Oriana stayed out of sight in the hollow with the children. Community members helped to feed them all.

The owlettes were well grown and soon due to leave the nest when Oriana felt she could not be cooped up in there any longer.

"I need to come out." Oriana told Ojen. Her tone wouldn't allow any Argument.

Ojen nodded, but was suddenly afraid. He knew their time together was almost over. He wanted to go with Oriana – to help and protect her, but knew the owlettes needed him more. They were her legacy for him.

Oriana had already prepared her children for her departure.

"I will have to leave soon." Oriana had told them. "I want you to learn well from your father and look after him too. Most of important of all, you are to care for each other."

CHAPTER NINE

GOING HOME

"Are you ready?" Koa looked at his grandfather Koha, who at last had a twinkle back in his eye and a spring in his step. Koha was impatient to get back to his mate Kamora. Koa didn't have anyone to go back to – just yet, but knew it would soon be time to choose a mate. He decided it was time for a visit to his Kingdom.

"I'm nearly ready." Koha answered. He looked around at his old territory for the last time. Koa joined him as Koha went over to the mound where his old friend Kehi lay and said a silent goodbye before rejoining the group heading to the Buller. "Let's go."

Koa gave a smile to all the Kiwis who had come here with them to rescue the kingdom. They were now anxious to return to their families. His smile also encompassed the local Kiwis who had chosen to live in the Buller with them. He also gave a smile to his friend Kerwin, who had come to see them before they made their trek south. Kerwin's leadership of the Tasman had been accepted better than anyone had hoped. His firm but fair attitude to disputes had won over anyone who had doubts about his ability to lead, and the establishment of a school had opened a new world to the Tasman Kiwis, including mixing with other animals.

As Kerwin disappeared into the northern forest, his owl leading the way, Oliver and his mate Ogene also led the way south for Koa and the Buller Kiwis.

During the long trip south Koa had time to think of what he needed to do next. Kona's son Kelan was now in charge of the Tokoeka community in Fiordland and Kahill was also in charge of the Rowi community in Okarito. A visit was needed to make sure all was well with them. He also needed to visit his sister Kiana in the Arahura Valley, to make sure she was still happy there, and also call in to Arthurs Pass to see how Kane's son Koen was managing in his new leadership role. His biggest concern though, was the news of trouble at Lake Kaniere, with the arrival of Oleus Owl, an evil spirit who had control of Oriana, one of Odessa and Orlando's children. Koa felt confident dealing with issues in the living world, but to help when the problem came from the spirit world that he had no knowledge of, left Koa perplexed.

A meeting with Oriana would be needed if she was still there and agreeable to meet him. He had no idea of what she looked like. If she was under the control of an evil spirit, what havoc was she creating among the living? There was also the issue of what Oleus was intending to do. What was he planning? Were his plans just for the living world, or was it for the spirit world too?

Koa spent many hours on the trek south mulling over what was happening and what to do about it. Koha saw the preoccupied look on his grandson's face and knew he was grappling with something he needed help with.

"What is the problem?" Koha eventually asked; when it became clear Koa wasn't going to ask for advice.

Koa looked at Koha with troubled eyes. "What do you know of the spirit world?"

"Only that we go there when we die. Why?"

When Koa told him of the problem, Koha could only shake his head. "I've no idea what to do about it either." Koha viewed his grandson with sympathy. "You will be heading south when we get back."

Yes. I will see if Syd and Daphne will take me."

Oriana reveled in being out of the nesting hole at long last. She had treasured the time she had spent with her children, but she knew she had to leave them before they left the nest. It would be too easy for Oleus to find them if she stayed. She had arranged with Ojen to come out during the day when it was more likely that Oleus was resting as well. She sat with other owls as she rested, so he could not attack her as easily when he found her, as she knew he would. Ojen took turns with owls in the community to sit with the owlettes while he came out to feed and to sit with Oriana.

One evening Oriana was searching for a feed when she felt Oleus's presence nearby. She swiftly returned to the branch she shared with the other owls, her head swiveling to catch sight of him.

"He's here!" was all Oriana had time to say before Oleus appeared immediately in front of her, with his claw stretched out to rake her chest. As Oriana drew back to avoid his claw, she felt his claw pierce her feathers and skin. She tried to fight back by raising her claw to his chest, but he seemed to melt away from her touch.

"Come with me!" Oleus demanded with a growl, hovering just out of reach.

"Goodbye and thank you." Oriana bade farewell to her friends with bleak eyes as she launched herself off the branch to head north, with Oleus following close behind. She didn't dare look back, or she would have seen a bereft Ojen who had joined the owls on her branch and was being comforted. Oriana tried to ignore the soreness of her chest as she flew; knowing that Oleus had weakened her and wondered if she would make it back to the lake. She took some satisfaction in the knowledge that whatever Oleus had planned for her, he now wouldn't succeed.

Oriana also tried to ignore the owl calls that were being made, warning communities ahead of them that she and the spirit owl were returning. Oleus heard them too. He realised too late that he should have kept himself invisible to both the living and spirit worlds. Oleus looked around, but was relieved he was unable to see anyone from the spirit world nearby. Little did he know that he was being tracked and watched at all times. Word was already being sent ahead in the spirit world that he had injured Oriana and was forcing her to return.

"I need to feed." Oriana called out when she needed a break, immediately diving under the canopy of the forest to search for food; giving Oleus had no choice but to follow her.

"You will eat when I tell you." Oleus tried to assert his control over her.

"You want me to die before I find Orion?" Oriana asked with indifference. "You have already weakened me."

"You aren't going to die! You are going to kill him!" Oleus retorted. He looked at the increasing red mark on her chest and realised that he had made a mistake in asserting his control over her by injuring her. He would not admit to himself that Oriana was right – that she might die before she returned to the lake.

"Go and get your feed." Oleus ordered her. "Don't try to escape as I will be staying with you."

When the news came to the spirit world leaders, of the return of Oriana with Oleus to Lake Kaniere, they knew it was time to act. Animals from the spirit world from near and far converged on the lake to witness the coming event, for they knew drama was coming to their world.

Owls in the living world that saw Oriana and Oleus pass, didn't try to hinder her path. They saw the injury to her chest and knew that she would not win any fight. Some of them chose to follow, to see what Oleus had planned for her.

Koa and his followers were approaching the Buller community when Kohana and Titan appeared beside him.

"Don't rush to go south." Kohana advised him. "There is no time for you to get there and influence the future." She then looked to the north east. "You have trouble coming from the North East." Kohana then disappeared as swiftly as she came.

Koha looked at the conflicted look on Koa's face. "What's up?"

"Kohana's just been! I won't be going south after all. "We have trouble coming from the North East!" Koa looked at Koha with grim determination, leaving Koha in no doubt what Koa had to do.

"We will come with you." Koha offered.

"Not this time." Koa rejected Koha's offer. "I have Oliver and Ogene to help. You need to set up defences around this community."

Oliver's heart sank when he heard this news. He had promised Ogene they would nest when they reached to the Buller. Oren and Opal had joined them and saw Oliver's dismay.

"You will need to rest, now Oliver. I will to go with Koa."

"Thank you, Oren." Oliver's relief was plain.

Koa wasn't happy that his owl wouldn't be coming with him on his journey, but accepted that Oliver needed to rest and have time with his mate too. Koa was happier when he learnt that Oren and Opal were coming with him.

There was rejoicing at the Buller community on the return of Koa and his followers. The North Buller Kiwis were surprised at the welcome they received, with burrows already prepared for them and forays to feeding spots, the meeting place and the school. They were reassured by those from their community who had come before them. They were very happy and settled in this community. It wasn't long before the North Buller arrivals were participating in all the activities that were offered in the school classes.

Koa had several nights rest, catching up with Kerewa and Kailan's news and filling them in with the campaign in the north. They were relieved to hear that Kerwin had been accepted in the Tasman and was managing it well. A collection of books was organised to send up to him. Syd and Daphne agreed to take them. They knew they were safe from humans on this trip.

At Lake Mahinapua, Orlando and Odessa were both happy and busy with their new family. Orlando's parents Odin and Ocena had helped them to find a suitable tree to nest in and were delighted to have young owlettes to fuss over. The young owls were now out on the branches and taking short flights under supervision.

"I expect it will be time to think of taking them over to the school, once they are flying properly." Ocena mentioned to Odessa one night as they watched the owlettes efforts to fly.

Odessa looked over towards Lake Kaniere with fear and sadness in her eyes.

"There isn't any rush."

Ocena picked up on Odessa's fear straight away.

"What is it?"

Odessa paused before answering.

"There will be a confrontation soon at the lake, between Orion and Oriana. I know that one, or maybe both will die."

Ocena looked at Odessa with silent sympathy. Odessa and Orlando had endured a great deal while bringing up their first brood, and now it seemed they were to lose them.

"We are glad you came to us to bring up this family."

"So are we." Odessa was able to smile. She missed her family at Lake Kaniere, but knew that her children were safe here; well away from all the dramas occurring there.

Odessa had been shocked to learn in a vision, the ending of Kohana's life by a dog. She was even more surprised another vision showed her Kohana and the dog's spirits together at Conical Hill, far away from the young family she had left behind. Odessa had a feeling that Kohana and the dog would be involved in the coming confrontation between Oriana and Orion and could only wonder how.

CHAPTER TEN

PLOT FOR POWER

As the Northern Buller Kiwis made their way east, each Kiwi was shadowed by an owl. If an owl needed to feed or have a rest, another would take its place. When it came time to sleep, the Kiwis chose to make a burrow together – it was the only time they had together where the owls couldn't see them or listen to what they were saying.

The owls could hear the murmurs of Kiwi talking from their perches in surrounding trees, but were reluctant to go down on the ground next to the entrance to listen, in case they were attacked.

The Kiwis didn't know it, but Kohana and Titan were watching them too.

"What are we going to do, with these owls shadowing us all the time?" Kakama Kiwi asked.

Kirwee Kiwi nodded grimly. "Hopefully they will leave us alone once we get to the mountains. We will pretend to settle in an area for a little while before we make our move."

"Will we take Kerwin's area?" Kakama asked.

"No. That wouldn't be wise just yet." Kirwee Kiwi replied. "Koa and his group are still around to help defend them. Kerewa and Kailan won't be expecting anyone to be coming from the East. "

"We need to vary the direction we walk too." Kakama suggested. If we keep heading straight to the mountains, the owls will notice."

"That's a good idea!" Kirwee replied with a smile.

Kirwee and Kakama's ruse to confuse the owls worked for some time. Their meandering trail weaved sometimes to the south then to the north; but always in a south easterly direction. When the Kiwis reached the Buller River, they were half way to their target. They had already skirted some mountain ranges, which had raised the owl's suspicions of where they were heading.

"We will rest here till the owls relax or leave us alone." Kirwee decided when they settled for their sleep.

"What if they don't?" Kakama asked with some anxiety.

"Then we will disappear!" Kirwee replied with a calculating smile. "When the owls are asleep, we will make our move." By the time they wake we will be far away and they won't know what direction we have gone."

"We are going to live here." Kirwee announced to the owls when they woke from their sleep and proceeded to feed and explore the local area. The Owls remained vigilant, keeping the kiwis in sight at all times. After a week of close surveillance, Kirwee had lost patience. "We will leave tomorrow."

The sun was high in the morning sky when the kiwis silently sneaked out of their burrow to creep away from the trees where the owls were sleeping. To Kirwee's horror, a passing Tui made an alarm call as it watched them sneaking among the undergrowth. He quickly sprung behind a tree, to some ferns, hoping he was out of sight. Kakama and Kerua stood still for several minutes, knowing that any movement would be detected and bring the owls over to check what was there. As the minutes passed by, there was silence and no movement from the trees above. Quietly Kakama and Kerua started to move forward. Kirwee was about to join them when the owls silently descended from behind to pounce on Kakama and Kerua. After a brief struggle, Kirwee and Kerua's lifeless bodies were left on the forest floor.

"We need to find the other one." Kirwee heard an owl say as they returned to the trees. Kirwee knew he couldn't move for some time with the owls now on alert, so he closed his eyes and dozed. Noise and movement in nearby bushes brought Kirwee back to full alertness again. It was a pair of Wekas who passed him to forage under the trees where the owls were perched. Kirwee took advantage of the Wekas presence to sneak away from the area. The changed light from the sunlight among the trees told Kirwee that it was late afternoon and that he needed to feed well then hide during the night while the owls were active. It was the only way he was going to stay alive and get to the Buller community.

Kirwee knew his plans had to change, now that Kakama and Kerua were gone. It was going to be much harder to take over the community by himself without anyone to help him. He knew that some of his friends had gone to Kerewa and Kailan's community. Perhaps if he could make contact with them, he might be able to persuade them to join him and overthrow the current leaders.

When Koa left the Buller Community, he made sure that someone was guarding the north east area at all times.

"Just make sure that everyone on guard is someone you can trust." Koa advised Kerewa and Kailan before he left.

"You don't trust any of the Kiwis you brought back with you?"

"They haven't proved their commitment to this community yet."

Kerewa and Kailan agreed with the wisdom of Koa's words. They couldn't take it for granted that the newest members of the community could be trusted with the community's security.

Kerewa and Kailan were to find that Koa had been right to be cautious with the new arrivals.

When the new arrivals found out that the north east area was being guarded, they guessed that their friends who had been sent to the Alps were causing trouble and were probably heading for this community.

"What will we do if they arrive here?" the question was asked by one who was enjoying their new life here and knew that the arrival of the outcasts would bring trouble for them. He realised that they would have to choose – between the community that had welcomed them or their old friends who had refused to change in their old community.

"We will help them of course! Whose side are you on?"

"I'm not on any side." He replied carefully. "I just don't want to return to the chaos we were living in back home. I'm enjoying it here. Aren't you?"

There was a silence before the answer came. "Sure we are, but our first responsibility is to our friends from back home! Don't forget it!"

When they asked if they could help with the northwest security, they were told to ask Khai as he was in charge of organising it.

"That's nice of you to offer to help the community" Khai said with a quizzical smile when they approached him; "given that you haven't been with us for long."

"We would just like to do our bit to help, now we are part of the community." was the smooth reply.

"That's kind of you." Khai twinkled back at him. "We always appreciate those who come and help in the community." Khai appeared to give their request a little thought. "Well," he said finally. "We have enough Kiwis to cover at the moment. I will let you know when we need you."

The North Buller Kiwis had to be content that they would be called upon when needed.

When Khai saw Kerewa and Kailan later that night, he gave a little sigh.

"What's up Dad?" Kailan was instantly alert to his father's pensive mood.

"The new arrivals came to offer their help with the patrols of the North West area this evening." Khai paused before continuing. "I had this feeling that they are here to help themselves, not us!"

"What did you say?"

"I thanked them of course, and then I told them that we have enough Kiwis for now and I will let them know when we need them."

"They were satisfied with that?"

"They seemed to be."

"It seems," Kerewa said slowly "that if the outcasts do reach here, we can expect a rebellion. I'm wishing I had sent someone with Koa."

"I think we are better off with everyone here." Khai replied with a bleak look, remembering the trouble they had with Kura who had tried to take over Kehi's community. "It's much harder to contain trouble when it's within."

Kerewa knew the truth of Khai's words as he also remembered the trouble his parents Kehi and Kiyo had during Kura's time in their community.

Kerewa now understood the fear that drove them to send his older brother Koro to Three Sisters Mountain and to send Kiyo to her parents Koha and Kamora to hatch and care for him along with his brother Koa and sister Kiana.

Kerewa then voiced the fear that was rising in his mind.

"Our families aren't safe here now."

"None of us are safe here now!" Khai's troubled reply shocked Kailan, who till now didn't realise the trouble their community was facing.

"Should we send them to the Alps too?" Kailan queried.

"Given that they haven't actually done anything to harm the community, we don't have a good reason to remove them." Kerewa discounted Kailan's suggestion. "Besides, it may be better to keep them here so we can monitor them better."

"Have we got enough of our own in the community to watch and defend against those that are here" Kailan asked. "And," he added, "What about Kerwin's community? Shouldn't we be warning him to beware and deal with any troublemakers up there?"

While they were talking, Kerewa became aware of Oliver who had followed them in case he was needed to send messages.

"Oliver," Kerewa spoke to him quietly. "Send word to Kerwin. If he has any trouble with his new community members, he is to deal with them as he sees fit. Expelling them is not an option!"

Oliver immediately flew off to call to neighbouring owls in
the north.

"Kehi would be proud of you." Khai expressed his admiration at Kerewa's
decisiveness. "Now we have to organise ourselves so we stay safe here."

In the Tasman Kerwin received Kerewa's message with both relief and
concern. He was relieved that he now had a solution to concerns some of
his community had come to him with, that the North Buller Kiwis weren't
fitting in well despite their efforts to welcome them and the community
didn't feel safe with them there any longer. Kerwin had been intending to
expel the North Buller Kiwis, but Kerewa's message meant that there was
only one solution left!

Kerwin was also concerned. It could only mean that the Buller community
was having the same problems with the North Buller Kiwis and they had
no intention of expelling them. There was no word from Koa in the
message. Was he having to deal with the kiwis that were expelled? Did they
have anything to do with this? A resolute Kerwin went off to see
community members he could trust.

As Koa set off, he asked Oren to call ahead and find out the present location
of the expelled Kiwis. The news that eventually came back was a challenge
for him. He now had only one Kiwi left to find, but the remaining Kiwi was
heading towards the Buller community, and had disappeared!

The Kiwi's disappearance could only mean one thing – it was sheltering at
night and travelling during the day while the owls were sleeping. – He
would have to do the same!

Koa conferred with Oren and Opal. They agreed to travel for the first half
of the night, feeding as they went, then would have a sleep untill the
beginning of daylight then continue on till the sun was overhead before
resting again. After a couple of days, they had adjusted to their upside-
down life of sleeping at night and moving during the day. They also put
calls ahead for owls to look out for a Kiwi that was moving down river
during the day.

Koa's strategy was rewarded when word came back that one had been
sighted moving steadily in their direction, though he was still some
distance away. Oren flew off to find where the Kiwi was and to follow him
untill he rested. He would then put out a call to let them know where the
Kiwi was.

Kirwee looked out of his temporary burrow. He could hear an owl calling.
He had a look at the owl, but it wasn't one that he recognised. It didn't

seem to be taking any notice of him when he came out to look. Satisfied that it was probably a local owl, Kirwee returned to his burrow to sleep.

Kirwee could not, however ignore the Kiwi who stepped out from the neighbouring tree to confront him when he emerged the next morning. He knew immediately who it was! Kirwee barely had time to register that Koa the leader of the Kiwi Kingdom was here when they engaged in a battle; that they both knew would be to the death. Oren and Opal watched anxiously the furious movements on the floor below them as Koa and Kirwee locked together with a flurry of blows at each other, neither giving way till finally Koa could feel Kirwee starting to tire and took advantage to take the fight, and his life from him.

Koa sat exhausted for some time, looking at his vanquished foe, knowing that this probably wasn't the last battle he would have to wage to keep his kingdom safe and wondered whether the other Northern Buller Kiwis were adjusting to their lives in their communities. He did not know it yet, but similar battles were going on at both the Tasman and Buller Communities.

Fights began among the Northern Buller Kiwis as they chose whether to support the outcasts, or the communities they now lived in. Kerwin had already organised his community to eliminate those who were causing trouble. Kerewa and Kailan swiftly did the same. Khai received the news that the outcasts were no longer a threat with much relief. They only had to deal with the malcontented amongst them.

Koa's journey back to the community took much longer than the one to find the outcasts. Kirwee had inflicted many injuries on Koa in his bid for both power and his life. Although Koa found a stream to wash his wounds, some took a long time to heal and would trouble him later in his life. Koa needed frequent stops to rest and feed, taking extra nights to rest if he didn't feel up to the journey.

Kerewa and Kailan were beginning to wonder what was keeping Koa from returning when Oren and Opal appeared.

"Where's Koa?" Kerewa asked with concern, seeing that Koa wasn't with them

"Koa's coming." Opal replied with anxious eyes as she looked behind them. "He was severely injured in the battle with Kirwee, so it has taken him much longer to get back again. Kerewa was shocked at the sight of his younger brother when he limped in. The fleet footed youth was gone to be replaced by one who had aged in years and would take some time to recover to anything near his former self. Koa did however, have a grin of triumph on his face as he greeted his brother.

"How has it been here?" Koa asked. He noticed the community seemed to be much quieter than the one he left. Kailan and Kerewa exchanged glances before giving him a grin back.

"The only Kiwis left are those who want to be here." Kailan answered for them. He paused before adding. "They've been removed from Kerwin's territory too."

"They've been expelled?" Koa asked, dreading more trouble in their communities in the future.

"No." Kailan replied quietly and firmly. "They have been eliminated."

Koa nodded his acceptance of their actions. He also had to accept that the Kiwi Kingdom rules that he was supposed to uphold would have resulted in the loss of both the Buller and Tasman communities - something he could not accept.

CHAPTER ELEVEN

CONFRONTATION

When the Spirit World leaders learnt that Oleus was forcing Oriana to return to Lake Kaniere, they came to await their return. To their consternation, they could see that the forest at Hans Bay and the hillside at Mount Tahua were crowded with animals from the spirit world, all waiting to see the fate of Oleus and Oriana.

When the order "Hide yourselves' from view at once!" was announced, the forest and mountain instantly became a sea of green. Those animals not yet able to make themselves' invisible quickly ducked for cover.

As Oriana slowly made her way up the lake, she had to force herself to stay in the air. She decided to have a break at the Islands as she knew she wouldn't make it any further.

"Where are you going?" Oleus called in anger as he saw she was steering away from Mount Tahua. He could also see she was getting slower as she flew.

"I'm taking a break on the Islands before I search for Orion."

As they approached the Islands, Both Oriana and Oleus could see some spirit animals standing under the trees. Kohana's large white form glowed like a beacon. Next to her was Kupe. On his other side, stood Kaori and Keoni.

Oleus decided to show Oriana what she needed to do to Orion, and flew ahead of her to attack. He knew that the unnamed Kiwi would protect Kupe and Keoni, so he went straight for Kohana.

Kohana stood unflinching as she saw Oleus come rushing towards her, with his claws outstretched.

Suddenly there was movement behind her as Titan silently rushed in. In a single bound Titan met Oleus in the air, holding him in his paws and Oleus's head in his mouth. They then disappeared from view.

Oriana saw the dog take Oleus and wondered where they had gone as she finally landed, completely exhausted on a nearby tree.

Kohana waited untill Oriana had her breath back before she spoke to her.

"Oriana, you are free now. We can see that Oleus has injured you. Oleus is being sent to a place where he will not be able to harm you or anyone else again. Once you have recovered, you can go back home to your family."

"No." Oriana replied. Although she was relieved that she was now free of Oleus, the need to be with Orel was strong within her. Oriana knew she couldn't kill Orion, but if he killed her, she would be able to be in the spirit world where she could find Orel. "I still have to see Orion before I go home."

"As you wish." Kohana replied. "Orion will meet you over on the cleared slope at Han's Bay. The Kiwis then disappeared from view.

Oriana knew she should feed to gain some strength before she moved on, but decided there wasn't much point if she was going to be in the spirit world soon. She was relieved that she didn't have to search Mount Tahua to find Orion. Oriana saw an Owl glide down the slopes of Mount Tahua and knew it was Orion. Oriana ignored the pain and weakness she was feeling as she made her way over the water to meet him.

As Orion glided down the slopes of Tahua, he was grateful, that at last the days and nights of hiding were now to end and he now had the chance to live a normal life. During his lessons at the school, Orion had met a female, Odette. They knew they would be together one day. It was a matter of waiting for the right time. He had heard that Oriana had been injured, but didn't take it for granted that he would win any fight between them. Although Orion could not see all the spirit world creatures waiting on the hillsides, he could feel they were there. As Orion flew in to land, he could see Oriel was waiting for him. With Oriel was Koen, the leader of the Arthurs pass community and Keka from the Arahura valley. As Orion landed, Oriel turned to the surrounding trees and gave a little nod. All of the Lake Kaniere community emerged to come forward to sit nearby. He could see Odette was amongst them and gave her a special smile.

As Oriana came in to land, she saw the Kiwis waiting with Orion and animals emerge from the surrounding bushland. Their meeting clearly wasn't going to be a private one. Oriana tried to land as close to Orion as she could but found that Oriel placed himself between them.

"Hello Oriana. Can you stand there please?" Oriel indicated a tree stump a little further away from Orion. "We have another matter to attend to before we deal with your relationship with Orion."

As Orion looked at his sister, he had to stop himself from rushing over to cuddle the clearly exhausted and badly injured creature that now stood awaiting her fate. Oriana could feel his look of pity and hated it! She steeled herself to be strong a little longer. A feeling of anger came over her – the anger that wanted him dead, from so long ago when they were young and their parents favoured him over her and Orel and made them share food equally. She was concentrating so much on the injustice of it all; Oriana had to bring her attention back to the present. She saw some spirit owls appear in the centre of the clearing. A couple of them Oriana recognised from the visit when she first met Oleus. The others were new to her. One then stepped forward to speak. His voice carried to the mountain top, so everyone could hear him.

"Everyone who has come here for this meeting may now reveal yourselves."

Oriana looked around her. The four spirit Kiwis from the Island were now next to her. The dog was next to them and was holding Oleus in a grip he could not escape from. Completely surrounding them on the whole side of the mountain was a sea of spirit animals, all here to witness the event.

"Oleus Owl," the Owl thundered. "You have been found guilty of attempting to overthrow the natural order of both the spirit and living worlds in order to gain control of them for yourself. You attempted to destroy spirit animals who were leaders. You also interfered with and have injured living animals in order to control them."

"You are now sentenced to infinity in Nudoor. There will be no contact with any animal you had influence over. Any attempts to influence anyone will be crushed!"

Oriana felt rather than heard something overhead. It was a giant white eagle! – It was bigger than any she had ever seen. As it glided in, there was a collective gasp from the hillside. It was a Haast Eagle. Most of the animals on the hillside hadn't seen one before either.

The Eagle landed beside Titan then scooped Oleus up in one of his giant claws before flying off with him. There was a small silence before the owl continued.

"Oriana Owl, you were given the opportunity to return home to have a normal life with your family. Why do you still want to see your brother who you vowed to kill?"

Oriana could feel her life begin to flow from her body. This was her last chance to avenge Orel! Oriana took a step towards Orion; her eyes were full of both hate and regret.

"I can no longer kill you, but I want you to kill me, so I can be with Orel!"

As Orion shook his head, Oriana lunged forward to try to strike him. Orion had known she would try to attack him and was ready for her swipe when it came. Orion quickly stepped aside and grabbed her claw to push her away. Oriana was so weak; she fell onto her back.

The Spirit World leader came over to look into Oriana's eyes. He could see that her spirit was about to leave her.

"Oriana Owl, you are still under the influence of Oleus! Your spirit will also be sent to Nudoor for Infinity. Any attempt to communicate with Oleus or Orel will be crushed!"

As the leader of the Spirit World stepped back another shadow came over the crowd. Another Haast Eagle was here!

Oriana listened impassively to the sentence she was given then closed her eyes as her world went black. She quickly opened them again as she felt herself being lifted up. She was looking into the eye of the eagle! *But I'm not dead yet!* Oriana's mind was protesting. Oriana turned her head to look below. She could see her body lying on the ground, with the Owls and Kiwi's surrounding it. Oriana then accepted that she was now in the spirit world.

As Oriana was being carried, she could hear Orel calling her!

"Oriana! I know you are here! Where are you?"

Oriana opened her beak to answer him, but the Eagle tightened its grip around her throat with one of his claws. She remembered the words of the spirit world leader and remained silent. She needed to be able to communicate!

At Han's Bay, Orion spoke to the spirit world leader.

"Her Body needs to be eaten, so no evil spirit can use it to come back to the world of the living."

"You did this with Orel?"

"Yes. It was given to the lake eels to eat."

The leader turned to Titan. "Can you take Oriana's body to the shore?" Titan obediently came to pick Oriana's body gently in his mouth.

The spirit world leader then announced "I believe this situation has been resolved. Everyone can go home."

"Not quite!" Kohana stepped forward. "This isn't over yet."

The leader looked at Kohana with alarm. What further danger did she know about?

"Oriana has children. She has left something for them. We won't know what it is till they come to look for it."

"They are being monitored at all times?"

"They are."

"Inform both Oriel and Ollie when they come."

With that, the leader of the Spirit World disappeared from view. All of the other spirit world creatures left too, except for Kohana and Titan who lead the Lake Kaniere community to the water's edge, where he gently laid Oriana on the ground.

Orion splashed the water with his claw, which brought Ernie to the shore.

"Hello! What brings you all here?"

Orion stepped forward.

"Hello Ernie. Oriana Owl has died. Her body needs to be eaten."

"Just like Orel's was?"

"Yes."

By now other eels had joined Ernie. Ernie wriggled out to grab Oriana before returning to the water where her body was consumed.

"Thank you." Orion called to them, before leading the community back to Mount Tahua.

Down at Fiordland Ojen suddenly shivered. He knew his mate was now gone. He had to try to live the rest of his life without her.   At Lake Mahinapua, Odessa looked over towards Lake Kaniere with tears in her eyes. "Oriana's gone to the spirit world."

"What about Orion?" Orlando asked as he cuddled her.

"He is still with us."

Odessa wasn't sure of the meaning of the visions she was seeing. First, she could see Oriana's spirit being carried away by an enormous white eagle, with Orion taking her body to the lake shore to give to the eels. Then she saw some young owls come to visit. One of them was like Oriana.

"Oriana has children. They are coming to see me."

CHAPTER TWELVE

ODELIA AND OGDEN'S VISIT

Ojen Owl was proud of his four owlettes who now were sitting out on the branches of the nesting tree. Members of the community continued to help to feed them. Most of their downy feathers were now gone and it wouldn't be long before they began their first flights and learnt to feed themselves.

Odelia, one of the owlettes looked at the filtered moonlight shining through the trees and wondered aloud what their mother was doing now.

"She is watching over you from the spirit world." Ojen replied.

"I want to visit the place Mum grew up in." Odelia persisted. "Can we go there?"

Ojen looked at his daughter, who was looking more like Oriana by the day and sighed inwardly. He had hoped to keep his children safe by encouraging them to live their lives here. He just hoped that Oleus was no longer a threat to anyone.

"We will see when you are older." Ojen wasn't going to make any promises. "You have to learn to fly well and feed yourself before you go anywhere."

At Lake Kaniere, Kaori was looking very thoughtful but didn't mention what was on his mind.

In the end Kupe couldn't stand the suspense any more.

"What are you thinking about Kaori?"

Kaori looked back at Kupe with a grin. "I'm trying to work out the mystery!"

"What are you talking about?"

"Don't you remember what Kohana said? Oriana has left something for her children here."

"She didn't go over to Han's Bay at all, did she?"

It was Kupe's turn to look thoughtful. "No, she didn't. Odessa and Orlando took her straight down to the southern end of the lake when she was able to fly."

"That means, whatever Oriana has left them, is on this Island!"

Kaori now had Kupe's full attention.

"She didn't get an education, so whatever she left, must belong to her."

"Feathers!" Kaori exclaimed. That's the only thing she could leave them without harming herself."

"You're right. We will have to organise a search!"

Kupe put out a call to Kohana, Keoni and Ollie in his thoughts.

"Can you all come to the Island? We need help to search for feathers – any that are here, just in case they belong to either Orel or Oriana!"

Ollie made a quick visit to Oriel on his way. Oriel quickly called all the owls in the area to come to the Island, including Orion and Odette. When Oriel explained what was needed, the whole Island became a hive of activity as the owls searched through the trees before joining the Kiwis to comb the floor.

Ollie was surprised at how many feathers they all found, which formed a pile beneath the tree. The nesting hole had been completely cleared of the downy feathers by Ollie. He was the only owl light enough to stand in there and not fall down into the middle of the trunk as Orion had done.

Feathers were also found in branches and on the floor from when both Oriana and Orion were learning to fly.

"What are we going to do with them all?" Kaori wanted to know.

"We will have to bury them," Kohana decided "but where is the best place to hide them, where they will never be found?"

"What about in the cubby under the tree?" Kupe suggested. "The entrance is hidden to anyone that doesn't know it is there. We can move the bed of moss that's there and bury them under it."

After examining the bed of moss and having it moved, Kohana agreed that this was the best place to keep them. Oriel and Orion quickly dug a hole deep enough to contain all of the feathers they had found. It was only when all the feathers were safely buried and the bed of moss back in place that everyone could relax.

Kaori was still feeling anxious that Oriana's children would find a feather that they had missed!

"What do we do if they manage to find one?"

"We will be accompanying the children and watching them closely." Oriel reassured him. "If they find any, we will take the feather off them."

"What if they want something to remember their mother by?"

"We will have to point out that it isn't practical to take a feather all the way back to their home."

The day came when Odelia was ready to leave. Ogden had offered to go with her, which gave Ojen some peace of mind. If Oleus was still around, Odelia had some protection. Ojen nuzzled them before they set off.

"Take care of each other, and make sure you come home safely."

"We will." Ogden promised him.

As Odelia and Ogden flew north, they enjoyed all the new places they visited and meeting new communities on the way. They had no idea that news of their movements were already being sent ahead of them. Eyebrows were raised when they revealed that Oriana was their mother. No-one had known that she had a family. When asked why they were making the journey, no-one could argue with their reasonable reply that they were visiting the place where their mother grew up and to visit their family there.

As Odelia approached Lake Kaniere, excitement mounted within her. "We are nearly there!" she called to Ogden. He smiled back, relieved that their journey was nearly over. He hadn't realised just how far their mother had travelled to live in their community. He was missing his father and two brothers back home already. Ogden wasn't able to think of home for long. Two owls were coming to meet them.

"That's them!" Orion called to Oriel, who had recognised Oriana's daughter as well.

Ogden led Odelia to a nearby treetop where Oriel and Orion joined them.

"Welcome to the Kiwi Kingdom." Oriel smiled to them both. He couldn't detect any malice in the young owls' faces. Orion smiled too, but knew that Oriana would try to contact them. He would have to be extra vigilant while they were here. Orion was relieved to see Ollie was flying in from his spot on Mount Tahua and that Kohana and Titan were also making their way across to them from Sunny Bight.

"We will take you to Han's Bay." Oriel advised them. "The family and community are waiting to meet you."

"Is that where Mum grew up?" Odelia asked, feeling impatient to get to the place where her mother had been.

"It is near there." Oriel replied sensing Odelia's impatience. "Don't worry, you will have plenty of time to see and explore the place where she was hatched and lived."

Odelia realised she had to be patient, that all would be revealed to her in its own time. Both Odelia and Ogden were amazed when they visited the school cave. Neither of them had been in a cave before, or meet different animals that quickly made friends with them.

"Did Mum come to this school?" Ogden wanted to know. He wanted to stay to attend the lessons here too.

"No, she didn't." Oriel said gently. "As soon as Oriana was able to fly, she flew south." Ogden felt that Oriel was holding something back. It was confirmed when Oriel added; "You should visit your grandmother Odessa over at Lake Mahinapua while you are here."

"We will." Ogden replied with some determination.

Afterwards some of the young owls took them into the forest to search for food before bringing them back to the tree where Oriel and his family slept during the day. From there, Odelia could see the Islands. She could feel that was where she needed to be and knew the Islands were where her mother had grown up.

Odelia woke early that evening. She would have loved to just fly off on her own to explore the Islands, but contented herself with preening untill the other family members woke.

Oriel could see the expectation on Odelia's face and knew that he couldn't delay the visit to the Island any longer.

Oriel put out a call to Ollie in his thoughts.

"Are you awake Ollie? We are taking Odelia and Ogden to the Island."

"I'm here!" Ollie replied. He was sitting next to Oriel.

"We are here too!" Kohana also replied from beneath the tree.

"Are you both ready for your visit to the Island?" Oriel asked with a smile.

"We are." Ogden smiled back.

Odelia and Ogden followed Oriel and the family to the Island next to the bay. Orion and Odette had come with them too. Odelia was surprised at how close the trees were packed in together and wondered how Oriana Orel and Orion managed to learn to fly here.

Orion read Odelia's thoughts. "You are wondering how we flew in here?

216

Odelia nodded and waited for Orion to explain how they learnt to fly in this crowded forest.

Orion paused a little before he spoke. There were memories he had to suppress so he didn't betray his feelings of the torment he had to endure while in the nest.

"Orel fell from the nest and went to the spirit world before he could learn to fly." Orion began. "I too fell from the nest before I could fly, but I survived."

"You had to live on the floor?" Odelia was amazed to hear his story.

Orion nodded before continuing. "Mum and Dad helped to feed me and my aunties came over to be with me and showed me how to fly with little flights from branches near the floor. Your mother did her first flight from the branches where our nest was. She became a little disheveled as she went through the branches." Orion paused as he remembered the battered figure that Oleus had forced to fly through the trees; "but she survived it and returned to the branch where she had been perching."

"Come and see the tree where we lived." Orion then led the way to the branch where he had perched after leaving the nest. As they came in to perch, Odelia could hear her mother's voice!

"Find my feather and swallow it."

Odelia looked around and couldn't see her. She realised that her father was right after all – her mother was watching over her from the spirit world!

"This is where she sat?" Odelia examined the branch. There weren't any feathers caught on here.

"It was." Oriel answered for Orion who was suddenly looking anxious. Orion was anxious because he had heard Oriana's call too and was now on guard.

"Is that the nest I can see in the trunk?" Odelia asked. "Can I look at it?"

"You can, but don't go inside."

"Why not?" Odelia couldn't hide her disappointment.

"It isn't safe." Orion replied in a calm tone. "The floor has become weak, so if you fall in, you will be trapped inside the tree;" Orion paused "forever."

Odelia carefully walked along the branch to the trunk. Placing her claws carefully into the tree bark near the entrance of the nest, she put her head inside. She was surprised at how large it was, but also how large the break in the floor was. There was evidence it had given way! Disappointment came when she saw there weren't any feathers in here either.

"Can we look through the forest while we are here?" Odelia asked as she brought her head out of the nest hole.

"Of course." Orion was relieved that she seemed satisfied with her look at the old nest. He turned to move away and show her the way down to the floor.

As Odelia pulled her claw out of the bark in the trunk, she felt something soft come with it. It was a small feather! Quickly she slipped it into her beak and swallowed it.

Ollie saw the movement and knew what she had done. "Orion! Odelia has swallowed a feather!"

Orion swiftly turned round to Odelia. He didn't know whether to be angry or afraid. "What have you done?' he demanded in a stern tone.

"I haven't done anything!" Odelia tried to bluster, but she went still as she could hear her mother call her again.

"Who can you see?" Oriana called? "Is it me?"

Odelia now could see a vision. It was of a female owl. She was at this nest with three little owlettes inside. She recognised her mother and Orion among the owlettes. The other one must be Orel.

"It is your mother." Odelia spoke slowly. She is at this nest to feed you all."

"Her power is now your power." Go to her...." Oriana's voice was cut in mid-sentence.

Orion inwardly heaved a sigh of relief. It was his mother's feather that Odelia had found. No harm had been done.

"You are not to touch any more feathers!" Orion remained stern. "I might have to kill you!"

"Are you serious?" Odelia couldn't believe what she was hearing.

"Yes!"

Orion looked around. "Where is Ogden?"

"He is exploring the floor with Odette. She knows what to do."

Orion immediately was anxious again.

"We need to catch up with them."

In the forest, Ogden was enjoying his time with his aunt, seeing both familiar and new ferns and mosses that covered the tree trunks that soared above them. He could see the lake between the trees and wandered over to the tiny patch of sand for a better look at the big mountain on the other side of the lake.

At the water's edge, he spotted an owl's feather half buried in the sand. With a smile Ogden picked it up and turned around to show it to Odette.

"Look what I've found! I wonder who it belongs to."

As Ogden spoke, Orel's cruel vengeful face appeared in front of him.

"Eat it!" Orel commanded him.

But Orel's face frightened him so much that Ogden dropped it and ran over to Odette and buried himself into her body. She wrapped her wings around him till he stopped shaking.

While Odette was comforting him, Kohana and Titan came forward to collect the feather and disappeared with it from view. When Oriel Orion and Odelia came on the scene, Odette was still comforting Ogden. Orion immediately feared the worst – that Ogden had eaten a feather too!

"It's alright Ogden, he can't harm you anymore."

"Are you sure? Who was that?" Everyone present, including Odelia was struck by the horror and fear on Ogden's face.

"That was your mother's other brother, Orel. He is in a special place where he can't harm anyone."

"Ogden found a feather by the water," Odette explained to Orion, "but Orel frightened him so much he dropped it. Kohana has made sure it is safe."

Orion gave a visible sigh of relief.

"If you see any more feathers while you are here, just show them to us, but don't touch them yourselves."

Ogden knew he would never forget that cruel face. "Why is he like that?"

Orion looked at Oriel, who nodded. They needed to know what happened to both their mother and Uncle.

"Both your Uncle Orel and your mother were under the spell of an evil owl called Oleus from the spirit world."

"But Mum wasn't like that with us!" Odelia protested.

"No, but she encouraged you to come here to look for feathers." Orion paused. "She was hoping you would find her or Orel's feathers, so you would become like them."

Odelia didn't want to believe it, but she remembered her mother's words when she had consumed the feather, and knew Orion's words to be true.

"Where are Mum and Oleus now?"

Orion felt sorry for Odelia. Her image of her loving mother was being shattered.

"They too are now in a safe place where they can't harm anyone."

"It's hard for you right now." Odette came and stood next to Odelia, "But just think of all the good things your mother did with you and try to teach them to your own children."

On their return to Mount Tahua, Ogden went to join in the night class that Oriel was teaching. Odelia was still too unsettled to take part. She stayed outside in the family tree, listening to the sounds of the night as she tried to come to terms with the feelings of shock that Orion had been prepared to kill her and the loss and betrayal she was feeling towards her mother. She remembered that Oriana had been sent south by her parents, Odessa and Orlando. Odelia needed to know why; and what was the power that Odessa had that Odelia now possessed? Her mission now, was to meet Odessa.

CHAPTER THIRTEEN

MEETING WITH ODESSA

Ogden didn't want to leave when it came time to move on to Lake Mahinapua. He now knew that when he went home to Fiordland, that he would take all the knowledge he could, to start a school there. Ogden had already spoken to Oriel, who had told him to come back to see him before he returned home.

Odessa was feeling ambivalent at the coming visit from Oriana's children. She was happy that Oriana had managed to have a normal life in the time she had lived in the south – a life that produced children. She was however wondering what the purpose of their visit was. Had any of the evil spirit that had possessed Oriana and Orel been transferred to them? Odessa decided she needed to act.

"Ocena" Odessa called, when she landed in a nearby tree. "Can you and Odin take the children over to the community at Han's Bay?"

"What's happening?" Ocena was concerned.

"I know that Oriana's children are on their way here. I want to make sure our children remain safe. I'm not sure what to expect while they are here." Ocena nodded and went off to collect Odin and the children.

As Odelia and Ogden made their way across the forest to Mahinapua, they saw a family with young owls making their way slowly the other way. Odelia wondered if she would ever feel able to enjoy family life like these ones were.

Although Lake Mahinapua wasn't as big as Lake Kaniere, the thick forest was a good shelter for many owls. Ogden and Odelia could hear some calls and wondered which ones were Odessa and Orlando.

They didn't have to wait long. The biggest owl they had ever seen came to land on the branch next to them. Odessa had sent Orlando to make sure Odin and Ocena and the family had left safely and to keep an eye out for the arrival of Oriana's children.

"Are you Orlando?" Oriana asked, remembering the vision she had when she swallowed the feather. "I am Odelia and this is Ogden. We are Oriana's children." They both were aware of the penetrating stare they received before he smiled.

"Odessa is expecting you." Orlando then turned to lead the way to Odessa.

"Hello. Did you enjoy your visit to Lake Kaniere?" Odessa asked when Orlando brought Odelia and Ogden to the branch where she was waiting.

"We did." Ogden answered for them. He turned to Orlando asking if he had been to the school there. Orlando grinned at Odessa. "Yes, it was how we met." While Ogden was chatting to Orlando, Odelia turned to Odessa with troubled eyes. "I found our visit confronting. The mother I thought I knew was very different to the one that Orion revealed to me. I have lots of questions to ask you about my mother and her brothers." Odessa nodded. She had expected it.

Orion told us that Mum and Orel had been under the spell of Oleus owl from the spirit world. What did you do when you found it was happening?"

Odessa thought for a moment, a vision of Oriana and Orel pecking and pushing Orion out of the way when she brought food, came into her mind. "I think they were under Oleus's spell right from when they were born. It was only when Ollie from the spirit world came and told us that Orion was connected to the spirit world and needed to be protected, that we knew there was a problem. They would have killed Orion if we hadn't protected him. It meant making Oriana and Orel share the food we brought equally and one of us was at the nest at all times."

Odelia didn't mention it, but she could see the visions that Odessa was having as she thought back on the life they had while bringing up her mother and her brothers.

"How did Orel and Oriana take it when they had to share?" Odelia asked gently.

Orel didn't take it very well. There was a confrontation where Orel threatened to kill his father. Orlando struck him with his wing which sent Orel out of the nest to the ground. Orel died of his injuries in the fall, but threatened to find Ollie in the spirit world and kill him too. Orion sent his spirit to Nudoor."

"What is Nudoor?"

"It is a special place where evil spirits are sent, so they can't harm anyone."

"How did Oriana take it when Orel was taken?" Odelia wanted to know. She could feel the hate her mother had for her brother.

"She was very quiet, but I know they didn't get on. Orion came running out of the nest one morning and refused to go back in. He made some excuse about it being time to sit outside."

Odessa paused as she thought of the visit from the spirit world leaders. "One day leaders from the spirit world came to see the living owl that had sent one to Nudoor. Only spirit world leaders can do that. Oleus frightened him so much that he ran to shelter in the nesting hole, and fell in."

Odelia gasped at her grandmother. "I remember that Hole! We saw it when we visited the Island where you grew up. There is a way out of the tree at the bottom otherwise Orion wouldn't be here now."

"Yes." Odessa agreed. "We organised for family members from Hans Bay to be with Orion and help him feed and fly while we looked after Oriana. When it was time for them to leave the Island, Orion was taken to Han's Bay while we took Oriana to the southern end of the lake and made sure she could take care of herself."

Odessa then smiled. It's nice to know that Oriana found a place where she could have a normal life and have a family."

"I'm not sure it was that normal." Ogden entered the conversation. Our nest was well hidden among the foliage and Mum sat in the nest with us four, the whole time after we were hatched. Other members of the community helped to feed us. We were nearly ready to leave the nest when Mum left. Apparently Oleus found her and made her come back to the lake. We never saw her again." Ogden added sadly.

"You still miss her." Odessa was sympathetic.

"Of course." Odelia replied matter of factly. "She was a lovely caring mother to us, so I am finding it difficult to accept that she tried to make us like her and Orel."

"What happened?" Odessa asked. She had a feeling that they would now find out the reason for this visit. Odelia sighed before she continued.

"After Mum left, I had this feeling I had to go to the place where Mum had grown up. She had left one of her feathers there for me."

Ogden piped in. "Dad wasn't keen on her coming so I came too."

"Your siblings didn't want to come too?"

"Yes, but Dad wouldn't let them come."

"When we reached the lake, I knew that the feather she had left for me was on the Island."

"Did you go over on your own?" Odessa was feeling alarmed at what was coming next.

"No. Oriel, Orion and Odette came with us."

Odessa waited patiently for Odelia to continue, even though her body was telling her to flee.

"I found a feather at the nest." Odelia continued. I felt compelled to swallow it and did." She saw the alarm on her grandmother's face. "It was your feather, Nan, not Mum's." Odelia smiled at her. "I am so glad it was, because she spoke to me and I could tell she hoped that it was her that I could see, but it was you, tending to them all."

Odessa's sigh of relief was short lived.

"It didn't end there though." Ogden cut in. "I was having a nice time exploring the floor with Odette, when I found a feather by the shore." Ogden still had a look of shock on his face as he remembered it. "I picked it up to show it to Odette and this.... Ogden paused "this terrible face appeared and demanded I eat it! I dropped it and ran to Odette! By the time the others came, the feather had been taken away."

"Who took it?" Odessa wanted to know.

"I think Odette said that Kohana had taken it."

"Who is Kohana?" Odelia wanted to know.

"She is in the spirit world now, but she was the leader of the Kiwi Kingdom. I was her guardian when I was younger, though that is another story."

"I would like to hear it one day." Odelia said shyly, feeling the wisdom that her grandmother had.

"When we caught up with Ogden and Odette, Orion made it clear we weren't to touch any more feathers – he had already threatened to kill me if I swallowed another one! Orion explained to us then about the evil spirit that had possessed Mum and Orel and that they had gone to a special place where they can't harm anyone."

The vision of the enormous eagle carrying Oriana away came back to Odessa.

"It's taking her to Nudoor, isn't it?" Odelia asked Odessa.

Odessa looked at her granddaughter. Odelia could see her visions!

"You can see it too!"

"Yes!" Odelia replied. That's where Orion gets his vision of spirit world animals from – you are connected to the spirit world too!"

While Odessa was digesting this knowledge, Odelia started to bob her head, trying to focus on something in the distance. Orlando saw her movements and tried to pick up what Odelia was looking at.

"What can you see Odelia?" Orlando asked. His tone was sharp.

"I can see some spirit animals." Odelia replied, not taking her eyes off the objections she could see. "They are coming this way."

"Can you tell me what they look like?" Odessa's voice was calm.

"One is a bird; they live on the ground at home, only they are brown. It has a large round body, a smaller head, very long beak and two long legs."

"Has the other one got a large body and head and has four legs?"

"Yes."

Odessa smiled. "The bird is Kohana and the other creature is Titan, the dog that killed her."

"What?" Odelia exclaimed. "Why are they together in the spirit world?"

"He was put with Kohana to protect her. They are good friends now."

"Can you see them yet?" Odelia asked Odessa. "They are by that big tree." Odelia pointed to where she could see the pair as they approached.

Odessa concentrated her eyes on the area that Odelia had shown her. She couldn't see anything. Then Odelia put her claw gently on Odessa's. Odessa blinked as a cloudy lens appeared to lift from her eyes.

"I can see them now." Odessa spoke with wonder. "I can see all the others as well! I had no idea they were here."

In the forest all around them were spirit animals of all kinds.

"They live beside us." Odelia replied. "It is just that we can't normally see them, unless they reveal themselves to us."

As Kohana and Titan approached the tree where Orlando and Odessa and their grandchildren were waiting, she could see that both Kohana and Odelia were looking at them with smiles. They both could see her! Kohana had been sent to see whether Odelia's consumption of Odessa's feather had any effect on her.

It was evident that changes had come to both of them, but who had influenced who? A quick glance at their faces soon told her what she needed to know. Odelia's calm face contrasted with Odessa's expression of wonder. Kohana now had to find out just how extensive Odelia's powers were and how safe the living and spirit world was, now that she had them.

"Hello Kohana. Hello Titan!" Odessa greeted them as they joined the family on the tree branches. Titan's tail wagged in response to her greeting.

"Hello Kohana and Titan" Odelia also greeted them. Titan went over to Odelia and looked directly into her eyes. When she put a claw out for him to sniff, he licked it and sat down beside her. This action by Titan both surprised and reassured Kohana, for he had never done that before to anyone. Whatever power and purpose she had was benign.

"You must have had a great deal to catch up on, with your grandparents." Kohana spoke with interest, knowing that this was the first time they had met.

"Yes we have." Odessa spoke for them both. I have learnt a few things as well."

Kohana noticed that Odelia was looking troubled. "What is it?" she asked her quietly.

"Neither the spirit or living world is safe! I'm not sure what to deal with first."

"We will help you! Just tell us what the problem is." Kohana tried to remain calm as she realised the power that Odelia now had. "We will start with the living world. What is the problem you can see here?"

The feathers on the Island that are hidden; they have to be destroyed or my brothers will try to come and find them. Also I will have to go home and get any that she left in the nest."

Kohana thought for a moment. "I will tell Kupe and Kaori to collect them and give them to the eels to eat. I will come with you to collect the ones from your family nest."

"Who are Kupe and Kaori?"

Kohana smiled. "Kupe is my father and Kaori is an old friend of his. They live on the Island now they are in the spirit world. I will tell them to arrange another sweep of the Island in case any more are missed."

"Good." Odelia smiled her acceptance of Kohana's plan.

"Before we go, what is the problem in the spirit world?"

"How do you normally communicate in the spirit world?" Odelia wanted to know.

"In our thoughts; Why?"

I thought so. Oleus Orel and Oriana are communicating and are planning to escape! Watching them isn't enough. They have to be restrained and contained!"

"Are you sure about this?" Kohana couldn't hide her shock at this news.

Odelia nodded. Suddenly she started looking around before concentrating on a point near the Alps.

"Who are you calling to?" Kohana could hear her calling "Hirone"

"I am calling to one of the eagles." Odelia replied in a matter of fact tone. "They are the guards of Nudoor." before continuing to call. As Odelia called, a massive white pair of wings passed overhead to land in the tree next to them.

"Hirone." Odelia commanded him. "Oleus Orel and Oriana are planning an escape! From now on Oleus Orel and Oriana are to face the wall only. Gather as many eagles as you can to make sure that they comply. I will call you again when I have organised a means to contain them."

Hirone flew off towards the Alps, calling as he went.

"What do you have in mind to contain them?" Kohana asked.

Odelia looked at a spider spinning its silken web and smiled. "Spiders' webs - Lots of them! I will search for them tomorrow."

Odelia then changed the subject. "Are you able to tell Kupe about the feathers?"

Kohana nodded and spoke to Ollie in her thoughts.

"Ollie can you hear me?"

"I can."

"Odelia says the feathers are still a danger. Can you organise Kupe and Kaori to dig them up and give them to the eels to eat. Also can Oriel and the community do a sweep of the Island to make sure there aren't any more left there? If we don't get them all, Odelia's brothers will come looking for them."

"Is that all?"

"No. The spirit world still isn't safe from Oleus, Orel and Oriana."

"they are planning to escape, so Odelia has arranged for Hirone the eagle to bring in more eagles to supervise them before she can arrange for them

227

to be contained. I am going with her to the family nest to make sure that none of Oriana's feathers are left in there."

"Thank you."

Kohana turned to Odessa Orlando and Ogden. "We will be back as soon as we can."

Titan knew they were on the move and moved back to his usual position at her side.

"Once we leave, we will be invisible to everyone in both the living and spirit world. Speak to me in your thoughts only, while we are on this mission – and keep your wings in."

Kohana grabbed Odelia's claw as she nodded and they disappeared from view.

There was a small silence after Kohana and Odelia departed. Orlando broke it by speaking to both Odessa and Ogden.

"Are you hungry?"

"I'm starving!" Ogden replied.

"So am I." also from Odessa.

As Orlando and Odessa showed Ogden where the best feeding spots were, Odelia and Kohana had reached Fiordland and Odelia was guiding Kohana and Titan to the tree where the nest was hidden. Seeing familiar faces and members of her family was hard as she could not reveal that she was among them and had to concentrate on the task she was here for.

At the nest Odelia and Kohana silently worked to clear the feathers from the space, giving them to Titan to take to the river where eels had gathered to feed. Odelia was relieved when it was time to return home. She had a final look at her father as he sat alone looking into the night. He hadn't found another partner yet and was still missing his life with Oriana. He could feel someone watching him and hoped it was Oriana watching over him.

Kohana chose not to stay when she brought Odelia back to Mahinapua. "I need to get back to Lake Kaniere to make sure that all the feathers are dealt with there. I will see you tomorrow."

"Thank you." Odelia gave Kohana her gratitude. "We will look forward to seeing you again then."

"What sort of spiders' webs do you want?" Kohana asked before she left.

"I want the thick spiders' nurseries. They need to be intact."

In Nudoor, the directive to face the wall had been met with resistance. Oleus Orel and Oriana only complied after they had been surrounded by Haast Eagles. They were given the choice to comply or be destroyed. The owls also now found there was no let up from their guards' scrutiny. They were now guarded at all times.

When Hirone lead his eagles to Odelia the next morning, there was a long line of Owls waiting. Each owl held a branch, with a spider nursery sitting on top. While Oleus Orel and Oriana were sleeping, the branches were quietly placed behind each owl. A small opening facing the owl was made in each spider nursery. When Oleus Orel and Oriana woke, they found they were now bound in a world of white from which there was no escape.

CHAPTER FOURTEEN

KOA'S QUEST

At last Koa was ready for his visit to his kingdom. He was also ready to look for his mate. He had no idea where he would find her or where they would set up their burrow. He decided to let fate look after itself. Kerewa was sad his younger brother was leaving. He had no idea if or when he would see him again.

Oren and Opal were also with him on this trip. Oliver was still busy with his family, so Oren took advantage of the trip to see places that Orlando and Odessa had been to, and also pay them the visit that Orlando had invited them to when they returned home.

Syd the stag and Daphne his hind had returned from their trip to the Tasman and were happy to take him down the Ohikanui valley to the Three Sister's community. Koa loved the wildness of the valley as Syd and Daphne took him on a leisurely stroll among thick forested hills as they followed the river towards its southern source. Koa was acutely aware of the journey that Kohana had made along the same river to bring the Kiwi Kingdom to the north.

Odion Owl flew to find Kapali Kiwi, the leader at Three Sisters Mountain community. "You have a visitor! He is coming up the hill from the Ohikanui side."

Kapali swiftly ran to see who his visitor was. There had been no warning that anyone was coming. To his surprise and delight, Koa was climbing up to meet him. He seemed to be alone.

"You came all the way from the Buller on your own?"

"No." Koa smiled. "Syd and Daphne brought me to the bottom of the hill. How is your community going now that DOC is monitoring and setting traps?"

Kapali beamed as he replied. "It has made all the difference here. All families are producing young chicks each season now and most of them are surviving."

Koa enjoyed his stay at Three Sisters Mountain. He viewed how the School was run, noticing that each community had adapted the lessons to suit their community's needs.

Before Koa left, Kapali came to him with his son Kuaka.

"I am handing over the leadership of our community to Kuaka."

"Are you ready for this role and to uphold the laws of the Kiwi Kingdom?"

"I am." Kuaka replied with a grin.

Koa held out his claw for the amulet that Kapali was wearing and slipped it over Kuaka's neck.

"I look forward to working with you Kuaka. You do of course have your father to consult for any issues, but let me know as well."

Charlotte the Chamois gave Koa a lift to Kanoa at the Paparoa community. He was delighted to find Kanoa and Koana were fussing over the latest member of their family.

"You have a name for him?"

Kanoa grinned. "He will be Kamoku."

"He is like your father?"

Kanoa nodded. "If I didn't know better, I would say he has come back to us!"

Koa was happy that Charmaine Chamois was available to take him on the next leg of his journey. It would have taken him some months to walk. Oren and Opal were impressed with the mountains that surrounded them as they made their way up the Taramakau River to Arthur's pass. For Koa, it was a return to a place that had challenged him on his last visit when it had been snowing. Koa was also interested in how Koen was managing the leadership role. Conditions in the alpine area could be very extreme.

"All is well here." Koen was able to confirm." Our community numbers are stable and we have the Arahura Valley to retreat to if conditions get too bad up here."

Koa was out feeding one night when he saw a large female feeding on her own. She gave him an encouraging smile before moving on with her feed.

Koa quickly followed to catch up with her. "I'm Koa. I see you are on your own. Where is your mate?"

"I'm Kewena. My mate died when he was hit by a car as he crossed the road. She looked with sadness at the small ribbon of tarmac visible in the valley below.

"You have children?" Koa asked.

"We had laid an egg, but I wasn't able to look after it on my own, so it failed." Her voice was full of regret.

"No-one came to help you?" Koa's sadness matched her own.

Kewena shook her head. "They were all busy with hatching their own."

"Are you here to live?" Kewena asked hopefully.

"I'm here for a visit." Koa replied. He noticed her disappointment at his words, "But I will be returning for you." Koa had decided to be bold. "Unless of course; you would like to come with me?" He asked with a quizzical smile.

"Where are you going, and how long will you be away?" Kewena was fascinated by the proposal she had just received.

"I'm the leader of the Kiwi Kingdom." Koa explained, so I am visiting the communities in the Kingdom to check that all is well. I have been to half of them and will be visiting the Arahura Valley next before heading south to our other communities."

"What about family time?" Kewena asked. She could not see him supporting her in raising a family when he was on the move.

"If you come with me, we will do what my parents did. – When it is time to deliver and hatch our chick, we will have an extended stay at the community where we happen to be in; till it is big enough to travel with us."

Kewena gave Koa a beaming smile. "When do we leave?" Her life of grief and loneliness had just become one of excitement and adventure!

At the Arahura Valley Koa was happy to catch up with his sister Kiana. She now had a mate and was waiting for the arrival of their first chick. Keka and Keio were also thriving in their life in this valley which was much milder and quieter than the one they left near Okarito. DOC was monitoring here too and had left traps, which helped the survival rate of their chicks.

Koa saw one of the cameras and gave it a little smile as he passed. Little did he know that Doug had been wondering whether a new leader would emerge after the death of Kohana. Doug knew that Koa was from the Buller community, and had watched with interest as he had visited Three Sisters Mountain Community, followed by his visit to the Paparoa community and now he was at the Arthur's pass and Arahura. It was time to pay a visit.

When Doug and Malcolm disturbed Koa and Kewena's sleep the next morning, they were delighted to find that Koa had a female from the Arthur's pass community with him. A quick check on their health was followed by some tracking devices which were attached to their legs.

"It looks like he's been in the wars." Malcolm commented on the old wound scars that Koa now carried.

"What is this?" Kewena asked Koa with alarm, the big devices that she and Koa were now wearing.

"Don't worry about it." Koa tried to reassure her. "Mum and Dad had them too. They let the humans know where we are and make sure that we are well."

Kewena made friends with Keona and Keely during their time at Arahura. It helped Keely a great deal that here was someone else that had the recent experience of losing their life partner too.

When it was time to move on to Lake Kaniere; Koen came with them. He had caught Koa up with the developments involving Odessa and Orlando's children and the meeting where Oriana had been sent to Nudoor in the spirit world. Now the kingdom was being visited by some of Oriana's children. They had caused some consternation by seeking some of Oriana's feathers. Although Odelia had consumed Odessa's feather instead of her mother's, now Oriana's daughter had powers which no living creature had ever had before. She needed counseling on how and when to use them.

When Oriel flew into the school cave one evening, Koen was there, with Koa and a female that was obviously Koa's mate. Oriel was both surprised and delighted that Koa had found a mate and had brought her with him. "Have you decided where you are staying while you are here?"

"We have already organised ourselves and made a burrow under one of the nearby trees." Koa grinned back at him.

This pleased Oriel even more. The last time Kiwis had made burrows on the mountain was back in Keoni's reign when they were hiding from visiting Maori raiders.

"Koen has told me about the visit from Oriana's children. I would like to meet them. Where are they now?"

"Odelia and Ogden are over at Lake Mahinapua with Odessa and Orlando. Before they came, Odessa sent Orlando's parents Odin and Ocena here with her children to make sure they stayed safe. They will be here later when lessons start." Oriel paused. "Did you know that Odessa has power now that she didn't have before?"

Koa shook his head. "What kind of power does she have now?"

"She is completely connected to the spirit world, as Orion is."

Koa was wondering how and where he could meet Odelia without compromising the safety of Odessa's children, when Oriel broke into his thoughts.

"We are having a meeting here tomorrow evening, for everyone to meet you again. Odessa and Orlando are bringing Odelia and Ogden over for it."

"You knew we were coming?"

"Of course! You should know by now that not much happens around here without me hearing about it." He gave Koa a grin. "Ernie wants to see you as well."

"Who is Ernie?" Kewena wanted to know.

It was Koa's turn to smile. "There are many creatures in this community that you haven't mixed with before. Ernie is one of them." I will take you to meet him after the classes."

Kewena had been surprised by the bats that lived in the cave, who had called out to Koa when he climbed down into the space. She was fascinated later when a procession of different animals came into the cave. Ducks, Hedgehogs, Pigeons, Possums, Pukekos Owls stoats' weasels and Wekas all came and sat quietly on the woven flax mats on the floor for the lesson. Kewena wondered why there were no Kiwis in this community. Afterwards Koa took Kewena down the mountain side to the lake, feeding as they went.

Kewena had seen glimpses of the lake through the trees, but the size of it amazed her when she stood on the shore and saw how big it was. She was baffled when Koa leant down and started to splash the water with his claw outstretched. Kewena was startled when a dark head broke the surface of the water and swam up to them.

"Hello Koa! Who is this you have brought with you?"

Koa grinned at Kewena before introducing them.

"Kewena, this is Ernie. He is the leader of the Lake eels. Ernie please meet Kewena my mate. She is from Arthur's Pass community."

"Are you going to be living there when you have finished your travels?"

Koa looked at Kewena. They hadn't got round to discussing where they would live when they settled, so he left it to her to reply.

"I would have loved to live here." Kewena began, "But we will probably settle in the Arahura valley."

"If you ever change your mind, we would love you to bring Kiwis back here to live again." With that Ernie slipped back into the dark depths of the lake.

"Do you feel up for a climb?" Koa asked Kewena with a grin.

Kewena looked around her. She looked up at the mountain they had just come down. The top was hidden in the darkness.

"Do you mean to the top?" Koa nodded. "There is a track that humans have made that goes to the top. We are quite safe from meeting anyone at this time of day."

Koa led Kewena to the track and let her take the lead. She was grateful that he let her lead and climb at her own pace, for the track seemed quite steep in places.

Ollie Owl was enjoying the view from the top of Mount Tahua. Twinkling lights were visible from both sides of the lake. He heard footsteps coming and immediately hid, even though he knew he couldn't be seen by living creatures. To his surprise it was Koa, and he had a female with him! Koa brought Kewena to the spot that Ollie had just vacated.

"Do you think it was worth the climb?"

Kewena looked at the shapes of the mountains around them, the shape of the lake below and the twinkling lights by the shoreline. "I do!" she replied. "I would like to stay and see it in the daylight."

"We can do that." Koa agreed. "It's going to be a few hours before daylight comes, shall we have a feed while we are up here?" Kewena was quite hungry after the long climb, so didn't need any persuading to start a search. Koa let her lead the way as they moved off.

"Ollie, can you hear me?"

"Yes! I'm right beside you."

Koa had a quick glance around. Ollie was remaining invisible.

"I see you have a mate. Do you have children yet?"

"She is Kewena. Not yet, but we will do. Have you heard about the meeting tomorrow evening in the cave for us to meet everyone again?"

"No."

"Can you tell Keoni, Kupe and Kohana?" Koa paused. *"Odessa and Orlando is bringing Oriana's children Odelia and Ogden over from Lake Mahinapua."*

"Is she?" Ollie was startled by this news. He knew that Odessa had sent her children over to Lake Kaniere to protect them during their visit.

"Also, can you arrange for the leaders of the spirit world to be at the meeting too?"

"Yes, though they will want to know why."

"Odelia now has power that no living creature has had before - she has control of the eagles that guard Nudoor! I think it would be appropriate that she be required to give a pledge to both the living and spirit world that she won't use her powers to harm."

"I will see to it! I will see you tomorrow."

Koa felt Kewena rub against him. "What are you thinking about?" Koa smiled at her and rubbed her back.

"It is going to be a big evening tomorrow. I will formally give my pledge as leader of the Kingdom." Koa paused. "Have you seen animals from the spirit world before?"

Kewena looked at Koa wide-eyed. "You mean animals that have died?"

"Yes." Koa confirmed. "We don't normally see them, but on special occasions like this they join in too. Most of them have been leaders of this community."

"Where will we be heading after this?" Kewena wanted to know. She was feeling the early signs of new life within her.

"We will hitch a ride and go to Fiordland first. It is the furthest community south from here. Then we will visit our Okarito community on the way back. By the way, the Kiwis down there are different to us."

"How different?"

"They have long brown hair. They are a different species to us."

"Did your parents have any of their chicks down there?"

"No, but I do know of a couple of mothers who travelled down there as we are doing; and everything was fine." Koa looked at Kewena with a little smile. "When is ours due?"

"In a moon or two."

CHAPTER FIFTEEN

THE MEETING

Kewena had never seen such a gathering in her life. The cave was filling rapidly with animals, all were chattering to each other. Some she had seen the night before at the classes. The bats above were chattering loudly as well. They had left the cave at this time the evening before, but they had no intention of missing this. Then a large family of owls flew in, led by Oriel. A hush came over the cave as they took their places. Kewena hadn't noticed it before, but a large book was sitting out in front. It had a large claw mark on the cover.

Koa was standing next to Orion Owl who was smiling at something he could see above the crowd.

"Are they all here?" Koa asked Orion.

"They are." Orion confirmed. "I wonder who invited the spirit leaders."

"I did."

Orion looked at Koa with surprise.

"I'm not the only one who will be expected to take a pledge this evening."

Orion knew immediately what Koa was intending to do, and gave him a big smile.

"Thank you everyone for coming." Oriel began. "We especially welcome back to our community Koa our Kingdom leader. We welcome Odelia and Ogden from Fiordland and also Odessa and Orlando and their family. Lastly we welcome our guests from the spirit world."

At Oriel's words, all of the spirit animals from their community revealed themselves. With them were the spirit world leaders, who gave everyone a smile.

Odelia could see all the spirit animals when they came in. She guessed that the Kiwis were previous leaders. She wondered about all of the owls. Had they all been part of the community as well? Odelia couldn't explain why, but she suddenly felt nervous! There was no indication in the expressions of the visitors' faces that she had anything to worry about.

"We are here this evening," Oriel continued "to not only welcome Koa back to our community, but to initiate him into his role as leader. Please come forward Koa."

Pinky and Peaches Possum also came forward to open the book that was sitting in front of Oriel. From a pocket inside the cover a piece of twine was hanging. Oriel grabbed it with his claw and pulled out an amulet and laid it on the page. Koa could see it was very similar to the one that Kelia now wore.

"Koa Kiwi, you have been chosen as leader of the Kiwi Kingdom. Are you ready for this role?"

"I am."

"Do you Koa promise to uphold the laws of the Kiwi Kingdom?"

"I do."

"Do you Koa promise to serve and protect all the animals of the Kiwi Kingdom?"

"I do."

"Do you Koa promise to promote a kingdom where all animals live in harmony with each other?"

"I do."

"By the power invested in me, Oriel Owl, Koa Kiwi, you are now leader of the Kiwi Kingdom."

Oriel nodded to Pinky and Peaches Possum. They came forward together to lift the twine from the book then came to Koa who leaned forward as they lifted it over his head.

"Koa Kiwi you now carry the mantle of leader of the Kiwi Kingdom. You are to wear this amulet at all times as long as you live. In times of extreme danger to you or the amulet, it is to be returned to the book."

"I will."

There was cheering and clapping in the cave once this was done. When it began to subside Koa held up his claw, so silence once again descended on the cave.

"Thank you all for coming to welcome me to your community and I hope that I will serve you well in my role. Some of you will be aware that some of our guests here tonight are the leaders of the spirit world. Can you please come forward here with me?"

Pinky and Peaches quickly moved the book out of the way, while the leaders came to stand with Oriel and Koa.

"Most of you present are aware that Orion was born with a special gift - the gift to see and communicate with the spirit world." Koa gave Odessa and Odelia a reassuring smile. During Odelia and Ogden's visit, both Odessa and Odelia have also received the same gift. This gift comes with great responsibility to both the living and spirit worlds; to use the powers that you have for the benefit of our worlds and that it will not be misused. Will you both come forward please?"

Odelia fluffed up her feathers in indignation.

"Orion should be taking this as well, given that he threatened to kill me!"

The spirit leader looked at Orion with a raised eyebrow.

With a smile Orion stepped forward. Odelia had no choice but to follow. Odessa stepped forward with her.

"Do you Odessa, Odelia and Orion pledge to use the power given to you to protect the living and Spirit worlds from those who mean to harm us?"

"I do." Odessa answered

"I do." Odelia replied, following Odessa's lead.

"I do." Orion declared loud and firm.

Afterwards the leader came and laid his claw on each of their heads. Odelia realised that he was making a connection between himself and each of them. From now on he would know what they were thinking, seeing and doing.

CHAPTER SIXTEEN

SOUTHERN REUNIONS

When it was time to say goodbye, Kewena didn't want to leave. She had met so many new friends here, and promised to come back again. Koen had already gone home the previous night.

The sun was still setting as Koa and Kewena rose that evening for a feed. When they returned to the cave, Teeny Tahr was waiting for them. He was on his way home to Fiordland. Kewena looked at Teeny with wide eyes. She had seen them in the distance, but had never been this close to one before.

"We are having a ride on this animal?" Kewena asked Koa doubtfully.

Koa smiled and nodded. "Meet Teeny."

"Hello Teeny. Do you give animals a lift often?" Kewena asked nervously.

"Not that often, though I gave Koa and the Kiwi leaders a lift last time he visited the south."

"You've been down there before?" Kewena was relieved.

"I have and I loved it. I'm looking forward to showing you all the special places I've been to and introduce you to the friends I've made down there too." Koa looked up at Teeny. "Can you kneel for us to get on?"

As Teeny obeyed, Kewena was also relieved that they didn't have to climb far to reach his back. She didn't need to be told to hang on tight as Teeny stood up again. Oriel was there to see them off.

"Have a good trip, and thank you." Oriel called as they made their way towards the Alps. Kewena would always remember this journey through dense forests and high mountain passes, which sometimes had snow under foot and views that seemed to go on forever. When it was wet, they would take shelter in the forests till the rain had passed. The night finally came when Teeny said goodbye. They were down in Fiordland.

"Have we far to go to reach the community you are visiting?"

"Not far. We will have a feed before we go and find them."

As they steadily moved through the forest floor, Kewena noticed it was much damper underfoot here and everything was covered in mosses and ferns of all kinds. Kewena was pulling out a worm when a large pair of feet planted themselves in front of her.

"You're a long way from home, aren't you?"

Kewena looked up. It was one of the brown Kiwis that Koa had told her about. He was looking at her with smiling quizzical eyes. Kewena grabbed the worm with her foot and offered it to the Kiwi. She was obviously in its territory. The least she could do was make a peace offering.

The Kiwi solemnly accepted the worm and swallowed it.

"I see you have met Kelan already!" Koa's voice came from behind her. "Kewena is my mate."

"You've made it back again! I thought you would be too busy!" Kelan the Rowi leader commented when he spotted his old friend behind her. He also spotted the amulet. "So it's official you have the leadership now."

"I do. I'm pleased to come down here for a break."

Kelan looked at his friend. He had changed a great deal since his last visit. He had aged in years and had scars from fighting.

"You're welcome to stay as long as you like."

"Thanks, though Kewena will be delivering her egg sometime before the next moon."

Kelan couldn't help showing his delight. "We don't mind if the next kingdom leader is hatched in our territory."

Before Koa and Kewena settled the next morning, he took her to the river below the waterfall and started to throw stones into the pool at the base of the falls.

"There are eels here?" Kewena remembered the eel she met at Lake Kaniere.

"There are." Koa replied. Just then an eel's head broke the surface of the water, so Koa started to splash in the water, which brought the eel straight over to them.

"Hello Eli! How are you all?"

"We are all well. Are you ready for a ride?"

"Not this time. I have my mate Kewena with me."

"Would you like a ride along the river Kewena?" Eli offered.

"Thank you for the offer, Eli, but I am carrying a chick, so it is best that I don't." She didn't mention that she had tested the water and it was far too cold for her to be in it!

Oren and Opal also enjoyed their time here too. It was wonderful to catch up with Orlando and Odessa at Lake Kaniere, though she had been preoccupied with the presence of Oriana's children. Opal could see that Odessa wanted to have a talk, but this wasn't the time. "We will call in to see you on our way back." Opal promised. "Hopefully things will be quieter for you then."

Oren and Opal were out feeding one night when they were met by a local owl who wanted to know who they were and what they were doing here.

"We are Oren and Opal from the Buller community, many nights flight from here. The Kiwi Kingdom leader, Koa Kiwi brought us here on his visit. We have just been to Lake Kaniere. We should be heading that way on the way home."

The name Lake Kaniere made the owl's ears prick up. "I know one of our Owl's Ojen would like to meet you. I will be back shortly."

Ocene also came when Ojen met with Oren and Opal.

"Hello, you are a long way from home!" Ocene greeted them. "I hope you are enjoying your stay here."

"We are." Oren replied. "It is nice and quiet here."

"You have been at Lake Kaniere?" Ojen interjected. He was anxious for news of his children. "Did you see Ogden and Odelia there?"

"We certainly did!" Opal replied. They arrived for the ceremony with their grandparents Odessa and Orlando.

This news gave Ojen some relief. Oriana had never mentioned her parents, but the children had obviously found them and were accepted by them.

"What was the ceremony?" Ocene asked with interest.

"Koa Kiwi was formally made leader of the Kiwi Kingdom. The local owl community are the guardians of the kingdom. They were there to witness it along with all the other animals in the community."

Ocene and Ojen digested this news with interest. They didn't have any contact with other animals in their area at all.

"If Koa Kiwi is visiting the Kiwi community here, are they going to be in the Kiwi Kingdom too? How do the animals at Lake Kaniere get together?" Ocene wanted to know.

"They have a cave where the local Owl leader holds classes for all the animals to get to know each other and learn things they don't learn at home.

We have established a school at our community in the Buller. I know the new leader north of us in the Tasman has started one too. There is a school south of us at Three Sisters Mountain, and there is one at Arthurs Pass in the Alps."

"I wonder why we haven't had one here." Ocene was puzzled.

"I believe that the local leader wasn't keen on it," Oren advised him, "but you have a new Kiwi leader here now. He might be more interested in starting one."

"Can you ask him?" Ocene asked tentatively.

"Certainly I will." Oren agreed. "Why don't you come with us?"

Koa and Kelan were having a chat when Koa heard Oren calling him.

"I'm here Oren! What's up?" Koa called back to him.

Oren and Opal landed on a nearby branch. They had a local Owl with them.

"This is Ocene the leader of the local Owl community. He has heard about the Kiwi Kingdom and wonders if the Kiwi community is interested in starting a school for the animals here."

Koa grinned at Kelan. Kelan had been too scared to suggest starting one while his father was alive. But that wasn't an issue now.

"Hello Ocene. I'm Kelan the local Kiwi Leader, and yes, I'm interested in starting a school for all the local animals. We need to find a suitable cave in this area to hold it in and someone will need to attend the school at Lake Kaniere to learn how to set it up."

"I will arrange to send some books down when that's done." Koa added to the conversation.

"How do I find you?" Ocene asked Kelan.

"This area is my patch. Just call me!"

Koa and Kewena were feeding when they heard the movement of large hooves behind them. They quickly hid behind a tree to find the animal had stopped. Koa peered around to find him-self looking into the face of a female deer. Koa remembered that deer at the lake hills had come down to Fiordland. Was this one of them?

"Hello, I'm Koa."

"Hello, "I'm Delphinia."

"Did you used to live at Lake Kaniere?"

Delphinia smiled. "I did. I would love to visit it again someday."

"We will need a lift back there some time. Can you take us?"

"I would love to!"

Koa looked up at Oren and Opal sitting in the tree above them.

"I will send Oren to find you when we are ready to leave."

"I will look forward to it."

Delphinia was happy. Stan the stag that had been the leader of the herd had recently gone to the spirit world. The hinds were now free to choose where they went – untill another stag came to lead them again.

Koa and Kewena were snuggled up in their burrow, but water was dripping in from the rain pouring down outside. Kewena was fed up with feeling damp. She was also feeling anxious whether their egg would survive these conditions. She had been talking to the local females who accepted that some of their eggs would fail because it was too damp. Kewena knew it wouldn't be long before she would have to lay her egg. It was time to act!

"How soon can we go back?" Kewena asked in a tone that couldn't be ignored.

Koa looked at her determined expression.

"As soon as the rain clears I will organise it."

Kahill the Rowi Kiwi was foraging near his burrow when the sound of hooves made him look up.

"Kahill! Are you there?" a familiar voice called out.

"I'm here." Kahill called back.

Kahill grinned as a deer hind he recognised from long ago appeared in front of him. On her back were Koa and a female. She was ready to have her egg anytime too! Kahill swiftly thought of a suitable place for her. His father Kedar's old burrow might be suitable with some changes, he knew Koa would make.

"Hello Delphinia! Kahill greeted her. It's lovely to see you Koa. I see you may be with us for an extended stay." Kahill smiled at Kewena.

"This is Kewena." Koa introduced her. "We've just been down to visit Kelan, but it was too wet to stay to deliver and hatch our chick there, so we are on our way back."

"Do you have a dry burrow for us to use?" Kewena cut in. She could no longer feed and knew that she would have to make this place "home" till their chick was able to travel.

"We do. Come to my burrow. My mate Kiori will look after you while Koa and I make your burrow suitable for you."

Koa turned to Delphinia and Oren and Opal.

"We are going to be here for some time now – till our chick is hatched and able to travel. You all can have a good rest."

Leaving Kewena with Kiori, Koa and Kahill did some furious digging to make Kedar's old burrow long and big enough for their needs. Koa fetched some ferns to line it before heading back for Kewena.

Kewena's inspection of her new home brought a smile to her face. Koa and Kahill gave an inward sigh of relief. Kiori sent them both off to have a feed. This egg wasn't going to wait any longer to be laid. When they returned, Kewena was sitting on her egg, and was sleeping. Kiori was watching over her. The trip here from Fiordland and the effort to produce the egg had exhausted her.

"I will let her rest for a couple of hours, before I take over so she can feed." Kiori agreed to stay to watch over Kewena while Koa and Kahill sneaked off to feed and catch up with each other.

Kewena enjoyed her time at Okarito. Kiori had taken her under her wing and had become a good friend.

One evening Kewena slipped out to have a quick feed before she took over the incubation of the egg. Neither Koa nor Kewena had slept much during the day as they could hear the beeps of the chick in the egg. They could also hear tapping which meant their chick would soon be here.

Kewena had just left when Koa heard a big crack. He quickly got up off the egg to find it split open. There amongst the broken shell was their very wet and bedraggled son. After lifting his head to take a look at his father, the exhausted chick flopped back down again to sleep.

When Kewena returned, Koa was standing with a big grin on his face. At his feet was a partially dry chick, still asleep in the shell.

"Do we remove the shell when he wakes up?" Koa asked.

"No. We let him absorb the yolk that is in there." He will move out of it when he is ready."

"What will we call him?"

Kewena looked at Koa with a little smile. "What was your father's name?"

He looked at his son. "Welcome to your life Kehi."

At Lake Kaniere Odelia was having flashes of a vision she didn't yet understand. What she did know was that the Living and spirit worlds weren't safe. The fight for control of the spirit and living worlds was just beginning.

ODELIA'S

CHALLENGE

CHAPTER ONE

THE DELIVERY

Amy heard familiar scratching at the front door of her bach at Hans Bay. She fetched her map book and the slate she now had to communicate with the animals that came to her door.

She smiled to see Oriel Owl and Peaches Possum standing before her.

"Hello." Amy greeted them. She held up the map book. "You want some more books?"

Amy laid the slate down in front of Peaches who snatched the chalk to write "more books" before passing it back to her.

Amy then laid the map book on the floor in front of them.

"Where are they going to this time?" Amy asked with both interest and excitement. Oriel had shown her where other schools had established and now another one was being started. Oriel looked at the map intently, moving his claw down the coast before pointing his claw at an area in remote Fiordland.

"It is wet there." Amy wrote on the slate. Oriel looked at the words and nodded.

Amy went to her cupboard which held her roll of plastic contact and a glass of water and brought them back. She covered the map book with the contact then poured a little water over the book. Oriel and Peaches looked with amazement as the water ran off and the book stayed dry.

Oriel pulled the slate towards him with his claw to write "good"

Amy knew this was much further than their usual delivery, and reached for the slate.

"How will books get to Fiordland?"

Oriel looked at the words before writing "Deer or Tahr"

Amy then made an offer. "we take books to Fiordland in our car" She also showed Oriel the road where the books would travel.

"yes Ogden will come."

Ogden was excited as he followed Oriel down Mount Tahua to the bach where Amy and Terry lived. Ogden was going to miss all the friends he had made while here. His visit here had been a big adventure for him.

Now he was going to have another one to go home. Ogden had made sure he had fed well before this journey as he didn't know whether he would feed again before he reached home. Being in a car with humans was a new experience he wasn't sure about, but it would take him home much quicker than he could fly.

Amy had asked Oriel to bring Ogden down the previous evening to show them how he would travel in the car. On the ground was a big wire frame with an opening that he could get in or out of which Amy called a cage. Amy put some layers of paper inside on the bottom with a log laid across the middle then covered the top and sides with materials she called towels, telling them that this was to help Ogden have a rest during the daytime. She took the towels off and asked Ogden to try hoping in then out of the cage. The cage seemed strange. The bars were very much thinner than any branch he had ever sat on, but were much tougher when he tried them with his beak. As he hopped up onto the opening, Ogden nearly fell into the cage, but after some balancing was able to sit there. He then jumped inside and was surprised at how noisy and slippery the paper was when he landed on it, but he found it was warm and appreciated the branch Amy had put in for him to sit on. Amy encouraged Ogden to come out before she placed the towels on the sides and top before telling him to try getting in again. Ogden sat in the opening and now found it was a completely different space – darker and much cosier. Yes, he could have a sleep in here. Lastly, with the towels still in place, Amy called Ogden out to have a sit on top of the cage. This is where Ogden would sit when he wasn't resting.

Daylight was still some hours away as they landed on the bach roof. The outside light was on and they could see Amy and Terry packing some crates into the boot of the car. Oriel gave a small hoot to let Amy know they were here. She looked around and smiled and patted the top of the open door to the back seat. Oriel led Ogden to sit on the top of the door. Ogden peered into the car. On the middle of the back seat the cage was strapped in place with the towels over it. He could see the opening to get into or out of it. Amy went to the other side of the car and encouraged Ogden to come and sit on top of the cage. Ogden looked at Oriel. It was time to say goodbye.

"Have a good trip. They will take good care of you. I have let your community know that you are coming, so they will be looking out for you."

"I will be back some day."

Ogden took a deep breath and took the plunge to enter the car and landed on the seat next to the cage. The feel and smell in here was strange too. "Come up here." Amy encouraged Ogden to the top of the cage. He tried spreading his wings to fly, but it was too cramped, so he went over to the opening and found he could climb up the side. Once Ogden was up on top,

Amy reached into a box and pulled out a dead mouse and laid it at Ogden's feet. Even though Ogden had eaten, he could still find room for one of these! It was cold when he picked it up, but that didn't matter. Oriel was right. They were going to look after him well on this trip. Ogden looked round while he was savouring this treat. Oriel had gone and Amy was shutting the back doors before coming round to sit in the front seat.

How noisy human cars are! Ogden thought as the car doors were closed. He saw the outside light turn off before Terry's form emerged from the darkness to sit in the other front seat. Ogden was given a fright when the motor sprang to life, but was relieved when it reduced to a quieter hum. Lights came on outside the car and on dials on the front dashboard. Ogden could only guess at the meaning of the numbers in the dials. Ogden clung on tight as the car began to move gently out of the driveway onto the road. He was amazed at how quickly the car moved in the surrounding forest and gasped as an owl swooped down low in front of the car. Luckily the car missed the owl. Ogden then vowed he would never swoop anywhere near a human car and would teach other owls not to do it either.

Amy was offering Ogden another mouse, but he looked away. He didn't need it and there was too much of interest for him to see outside. The mouse was returned to the chilli bin. Amy and Terry talked quietly as they continued their journey. Ogden found himself relaxing his grip, only tightening when the car manoeuvred tight corners.

As the car travelled south, outside the darkness gradually lifted, giving Ogden a clear view of all the surrounding forests and the Alps beyond. He recognised the shapes of some of the mountains from his flight up to the lake. When the sun rose over the Alps Ogden closed his eyes and realised how tired he was. It was time to try the cage for a nap. Carefully Ogden moved over to the edge and let himself down the side, which was much harder than climbing up! Amy looked round with a smile to see Ogden letting himself into the cage. Inside, Ogden sat on the log and faced away from the opening. It was a smoother ride down here and dark enough to be able to rest. With a happy sigh Ogden closed his eyes.

Ogden opened them again when he realised the car had stopped and the motor was silent. It was still daylight outside, but the sun was now in the opposite direction. Ogden put his head out of the cage opening to see Amy looking at him. She smiled and showed Ogden a page from the map book that he now recognised as the South Island. Amy tapped a point on the map then swept her finger down the line that Ogden now knew was a road. He could see they weren't there yet. Ogden smacked his beak. He suddenly was quite hungry! Amy pulled out the mouse she had offered Ogden earlier. This was quickly consumed along with another two. Terry was using a long tube outside the car. Ogden could hear the sound of liquid being pumped in behind him. He didn't like the smell of the fumes that came into the car! Luckily they didn't linger for long.

As the light became dimmer, Ogden could see the sun was low in the sky. Ogden came out of his cage to sit on top again. He was recognising familiar hills and mountains now. He was nearly home! Then he saw Ocene sitting in the top of a nearby tree. Ogden flapped his wings and let out an almighty call that nearly deafened both Amy and Terry.

"I think we are there!" Terry murmured with a grin to Amy as he slowed the car to find a safe spot to pull over. Ocene hadn't heard Ogden's call because of the noise of the motor, but he did see the movement of wings in the back of the car. Ocene came down to a nearby branch for a closer look at the car which had stopped. Yes! Ogden was in there. Ocene put out a call to tell Teeny Tahr and Kelan Kiwi to come. Amy got out and opened the back door for Ogden, who wasted no time in jumping down from the cage to exit the car, to join Ocene on the tree branch.

"Welcome home." Ocene greeted Ogden before calling out again. This time Kelan's voice answered him in the distance. Amy and Terry looked at each other. They now recognised the call of a male Kiwi. As the Kiwi calls came closer, Amy and Terry could also hear the hooves of a larger animal, which stopped when it came close to the road.

"I doubt they will come onto the road." Amy guessed. "I think we should get the books out and take them in to them." Amy then wrote on the slate for Ogden. "We will bring the books" and held the slate up for him to see.

"They are bringing the books." Ogden said to Ocene who relayed this to Kelan. Amy and Terry followed Ogden and Ocene into the forest with the crate of books. Amy was holding a woven harness which had two bags attached to it. Teeny wasn't sure about the humans when they approached, but he recognised the harness that Amy held. He had worn one to carry the animals when they went up to Arthur's Pass for the snow trips. Teeny, his massive body now reached Terry's shoulder; immediately sat down for the harness to be put on, much to Terry and Amy's relief. Carefully they brought it over and placed it gently on his back. They then proceeded to fill the bags with the books they had brought. When they stepped back away from Teeny, Kelan immediately came forward and jumped onto Teeny's back. They had a long way to walk home and he preferred a ride instead of fighting his way through the thick forest. On feeling Kelan's extra weight on his back, Teeny immediately stood up and turned to make his way back to Fiordland where he felt safer. Amy and Terry looked at Ogden and Ocene who sat on a nearby branch while the transfer was made.

"Goodbye" Ogden hooted to Amy before they accompanied Kelan and Teeny back home.

CHAPTER TWO

DIANELLA AND DIANTHIA'S RETURN

There had been rejoicing at Lake Kaniere when Delphinia had returned with Koa and Kewena and their new chick, Kehi. They were back in the burrow near the school cave, with Kehi joining the classes too. Kewena knew she could return to the Kiwi community in the Arahura valley any time, but she was enjoying the friendships she had formed here. Delphinia was happy to be back in familiar territory on Mount Tahua and just wished Dianella and Dianthia were here to share it with her. She knew that Dianella had been left on the farm when Dianthia escaped and wondered whether she was still producing young now. Delphinia had tried to persuade Dianthia to come with her on her trip back to the lake, but she wasn't interested. Dianthia was settled now in Fiordland and had no wish to risk her life on a trip back to a place she had been taken from.

Dianthia didn't know it but she would soon be wishing that she had joined Delphinia on her trip north, as her remote Fiordland home was no longer the safe haven she had come to. Dianthia was grazing quietly in a forested valley with Dulcie Dorothea and Dehlia when a familiar smell made her look up with alarm. Humans were here! Then the rapid approach of heavy footsteps could be heard. Dianthia swiftly sprung behind the nearest large tree just in time as the sound of rifle shots cracked through the trees. The sound of her friends attempting to flee along with alarm calls from birds in the surrounding trees also filled the air. Luckily for Dianthia, the hunters were concentrating on her friend Dorothea now lying wounded on the ground and missed her form pressed close to the tree trunk. Once they had passed her, Dianthia quickly scampered off in the opposite direction. The sound of a single gunshot rang in Dianthia's ears as she ran for her life, knowing that she wouldn't see Dorothea again.

Dianthia ran for several kilometres before she allowed herself to slow down, all the while listening for the sound of humans behind her. The rustle in bushes near her, made Dianthia shy away nervously. She was about to start running again when a deep voice spoke to her.

Dianthia! What is the matter? Have the hunters been shooting at you?

Dianthia looked around. Amongst the bushes was Teeny Tahr. He was completely changed from the young tahr she knew when she lived at Lake Kaniere. Only his twinkly eyes were the same. She nodded miserably. Teeny had seen Stan the Stag with his herd, including Delphinia and Dianthia. Now she was alone and needed to be protected.

"Was anyone taken?" Teeny asked with concern.

"Dorothea was taken. I don't know about Dulcie and Dehlia."

"What about Stan and Delphinia?"

"Stan is in the spirit world now. Delphinia met Koa the current Kiwi Kingdom leader while he and his mate Kewena were here. She took them up to Okarito for their egg to be delivered. I think she is taking them back to Lake Kaniere when their chick is hatched." As Dianthia spoke more shots could be heard in the distance.

"Where are you heading now?" Teeny wanted to know. He was feeling uneasy at being here now too.

"I think I will head up to Lake Kaniere to join Delphinia. Nowhere is really safe to be any more."

Teeny nodded his agreement. "I will come with you."

Leading the way, Teeny showed Dianthia his favourite route, through thick forests to the Alps. She didn't mind the steep slopes or the snow as they traversed high mountain passes – always at night when humans weren't around. The night finally came when they reached a familiar swing bridge at the Hokitika Gorge.

"We are at the Gorge!" Dianthia spoke with delight. She now knew she was nearly home.

It was early morning, the sun not yet up. Delphinia was grazing on the Alps side of Mount Tahua when she spotted two familiar figures making their way across the Styx River! Swiftly she strode down the mountainside, trying not to slip in her haste.

"Dianthia!" Delphinia called out in delight and relief that she wasn't alone any more. "It's lovely to see you too, Teeny. How long are you staying?"

"I will be with you for a while. My home in Fiordland isn't as safe as it used to be."

On the deer farm Dianella was being separated from her daughter. She had named her Daisy. The field they were in was covered with them. All the other females thought she was strange for giving her children names. They didn't have names, so they didn't see why their children should have one either.

Dianella knew that she would be put with the stag again soon. While she continued to have young, she was safe. She sometimes wondered where Delphinia and Dianthia were now. She had watched with envy as Dianthia had made her escape and taken the other hinds in the field with her. Fred the farmer had been angry when he saw the empty field and the hole in the fence and had spent a great deal of time fixing the bank beneath the fence and put in some plants to stabilise the bank. Just to make sure, he now had an electric fence on that bank, so there was no hope of getting out that way.

Dianella was given a shock the day that Fred came round to check her and all the hinds that had been mated with the stag. She and several others were put in the field near the house. This was the place deer were placed before they were sent away. Dianella knew her time here – and her life was nearly over.

When the truck came the next morning, a feeling of fear came over Dianella. She wanted to escape, but didn't know how. All the other females were obedient as they were led to the truck, but Dianella had other ideas, and ran wildly around the paddock, and kicked out when approached too closely.

"What's wrong with this one?" the truck driver asked. "Why is she so skittish?"

Fred sighed. "This one is too intelligent for her own good. She is the last of the wild ones that I brought to the farm. She knows what's coming. Hang on a minute; I will just get something from inside."

When Fred returned he had a rifle under his arm.

Dianella knew immediately what he was carrying. *Was he going to kill her right here, in front of everyone?* As he moved across the field towards Dianella Fred put the rifle up to his shoulder ready to aim. Trembling, Dianella stood her ground untill Fred cocked the rifle. She knew that he wasn't bluffing. Reluctantly Dianella slowly started to walk towards the truck, keeping an eye on Fred as he followed her, all the way to the truck. The other hinds were shocked to see that Fred was pointing a long stick at Dianella as she walked into the truck.

After the door slammed shut, the other hinds were asking Dianella questions.

"What Happened? Why was he pointing that stick at you to get you in?"

Dianella just shook her head and remained silent. They would find out soon enough. She wasn't going to scare them with the knowledge of what lay ahead. She noticed they all were tied to the side of the truck, but they didn't do it with her – perhaps they were frightened of being kicked! This thought gave Dianella some satisfaction. Dianella had to brace herself against the side of the truck as it rocked and rolled over the bumpy driveway out of the farm. Out on the main road Dianella relaxed a little as the truck picked up speed. She had no idea how long they had been travelling when there was a screech of brakes, and a loud bang before the truck lurched to turn onto its side then slid along the road. Dianella braced herself when the bang came, but found she was thrown onto her side. She was thankful that she wasn't tied up as the others were, and now struggling to breath. Next thing Dianella knew she was tumbling out of the truck – the door had burst open.

For a couple of minutes Dianella sat there stunned at the shock of being in an accident. Then cars began to stop and people were getting out. Dianella realised that she had to move if she wanted to be free again. It took a couple of tries, but Dianella managed to get onto her feet. Shakily she forced her legs to move. She was feeling battered and bruised but nothing was broken. Dianella looked around. She could hear the ocean on one side. She knew freedom lay in the other direction. Slowly but steadily she made her way across the road and into the nearly bushland.

Dianella wanted to lie down somewhere and rest to recover, but she also knew her life depended on keeping on the move as sooner or later someone would come looking for her. Sure enough, a few hours later a helicopter came to the scene of the crash and started to check the bushland where she had fled to. By now Dianella had crossed the Arahura River and Mount Tahua lay in front of her. Dianella was relieved to reach a certain cliff face which was covered with ferns and bushes. She poked her head in among the ferns. *Yes! It was still here!* Quietly she pushed through the ferns to the dark space, lined with bungees. In the old school cave Dianella finally felt safe to lie down to have a deep dreamless sleep.

Outside Foxglove Fantail was beside herself with excitement and went looking for Freesia and Frangipani. When Dianella finally began to rouse back to consciousness, she was no longer alone. Teeny Tahr along with Delphinia and Dianthia, and all the community were gathered around her. They had been concerned to find her nonresponsive to their calls. Her body was covered in bruises and grazes. While they were waiting in their vigil, they could hear a helicopter outside flying over Mount Tahua. They were relieved when it eventually flew away.

"Dianella! At last you are awake." Oriel exclaimed. "Welcome home."

"Thank you." Dianella replied. She looked at Delphinia and Dianthia. "Where is Stan?"

"He has gone to the spirit world."

"I was being sent there too, but the truck that took me off the farm was in an accident. I managed to escape."

Fred was disappointed as the helicopter pilot dropped him back at the farm. They searched both the accident site and a check of Mount Tahua where Dianella had been captured. The use of thermal imaging had revealed nothing. He could only wonder where she was now.

CHAPTER THREE

THE NESTING TREE

"Are you here or in the Spirit World?" The question brought Odelia swiftly back to the present. She smiled at the concerned face peering at her. She had met Osborne at the classes at the school cave on Mount Tahua. Odelia had tried to ignore him when he showed interest in her, but he had persisted since she had been left alone.

Odelia had been surprised at how much she missed Ogden's company since he had returned to Fiordland. Despite her intentions not to get involved with anyone, Odelia now had a mate of her own. She also now understood how her mother Oriana felt when she met Ojen. Keeping her family safe was more important than ever.

"I'm here." Odelia replied. "I'm trying to think of a suitable place to have our family. Shall we have a look at the Islands?"

"You want to use the same tree that your mother was raised in?" Osborne asked with concern. He knew of all the problems that Odessa and Orlando had there.

"No. That tree isn't suitable. I'm thinking of the other Island. It is bigger and has more trees to choose from."

"You don't want to be near family?"

"It is best if we have our own tree."

Odessa and Orlando were staying at Lake Kaniere now their children were attending the school. Odelia had been invited to join Oriel's and Orlando's families in their trees, but had chosen to sleep in her own tree. She didn't mention it, but it was safer for everyone if she was separate.

Even though Oleus Owl's spirit was now bound, Odelia now knew he was as much a danger to her now as he had been to her mother. She just had to work out how. Odelia accepted the supervision the leader of the spirit world now had over her. She was comforted that he seemed to be a benign force. The knowledge Odelia was being observed at all times by something else she could not see unnerved her. She wasn't sure yet whether it was here to protect or waiting for an opportunity to destroy her.

Dusk was settling over the lake hills as Odelia led Osborne on their flight to the Islands. As she passed the Island where her mother was hatched, she felt something drawing her to the tree, but firmly ignored it and pressed on to the next Island. Below her Kupe and Kaori's spirits were fossicking under the trees. Kohana and Titan were with them too.

"What brings you over to the Islands?" Kohana called to Odelia in her thoughts.

"We are looking for a nesting tree."

"Let me know if you find one."

"I will. I still don't think Odessa's tree is completely safe."

"Why?"

"As I passed, I could feel I was being drawn to it."

"I will check it for you."

As Odelia and Osborne checked all the old trees, on the other Island, Kupe and Kaori joined Kohana in searching every part of the tree. As Kohana reached the nesting hole Titan gave a loud growl and pushed Kohana out of the way, snarling and trying to bite the force he knew was there.

"Show yourself!" Kohana ordered the spirit she now knew had been hiding in the space. To her horror, Titan yelped then whimpered as he was sent flying. After the spirit struck him, leaving a big welt on Titan's body Titan then felt himself being lifted with force and flung out of the way.

Odelia heard the commotion from the next island and knew trouble had returned to the Lake, confirming her fears that it was dangerous for her to nest near anyone else in the community. Osborne saw Odelia look over to the next island and frown.

"What is it?"

Odelia sighed. "As I passed the nesting tree that Mum and her brothers were brought up in, I could feel I was being drawn to it, but ignored it. I asked Kohana to check the tree as I thought it still wasn't safe. I've just heard Titan barking before he was injured and I also heard Kohana call the spirit to show itself. I know it was waiting for me."

Odelia looked at Osborne with determination. "It is more important than ever now, that we find a place here to nest. It is too dangerous for me to be near anyone else in the community. Come on, we have a lot of trees to check."

With renewed vigour, Odelia flew from tree to tree, checking for any hollows they could use. Osborne had intended to check separate trees, but now it was apparent that Odelia was in danger, he had no intention of letting her out of his sight!

"What about this one?" Osborne suggested.

He had spotted a tree where the top of the tree trunk formed a hollow with the branches and foliage protecting the hollow from above. They were protected from weather from all directions by the neighbouring canopy.

Odelia smiled. "That will suit us fine."

As they searched the island forest for a feed, Odelia communicated with Kohana.

"Are you both alright?"

At Odelia's side, Kohana replied. "We will be. Titan was shaken by the rough treatment. We are trying to work out what sort of spirit could treat him like it did."

"I think it was a bird." Odelia was thoughtful as she looked at the welt on Titan's body.

Kohana took another look at the mark. "I believe you are right. I will be staying close to you from now on."

"Thank you, but make sure you aren't putting yourself in danger to protect me."

"We won't be alone."

Kohana stayed silent after that, leaving Odelia to her thoughts which were racing!

Oleus had control of birds! What sort were they?

Then Odelia gasped. The vision she had been having, now was clear. The Haast Eagles were being attacked!

"What are you seeing?" Osborne could see she was in the spirit world.

"The Haast Eagles that guard Nudoor are being attacked by Harriers!"

Osborne remembered the enormous size of the Haast Eagles that came to claim Oleus and Oriana. "Can't they look after themselves?"

"Not when they are outnumbered! I must contact Hirone."

"Hirone, can you hear me?" Odelia called in her thoughts.

"What is it?" Hirone's voice boomed in her head.

"You and all the Haast Eagles are in danger from Harriers. Oleus has control of them."

"A Harrier is no match for us."

"They are when you are outnumbered! I have seen it! Try to make sure none of you are ever alone for they attack while they are hidden. One tried to lure me to within its reach while it was hidden. You all need to be hidden too."

Silence met Odelia's words. Hirone didn't tell Odelia was that her vision had already occurred. One of the Haast Eagles had already been destroyed. They didn't know till now how it had happened.

"You are being protected?"

"Yes."

"It was a Harrier that attacked Titan?" Kohana spoke.

"That claw mark tells me it was. Everyone in both the living and spirit worlds need to be on guard."

"I will let both Ollie and Oriel know."

Odelia looked around her. The wind was stronger and the tree branches were starting thrash about. "We are going to have a storm. We may be safer on lower branches."

Osborne didn't argue, and followed Odelia to a spot which was protected from both the wind and the rain when the deluge came.

Once the storm had passed, Odelia returned to their nest site to see how it had fared. They were surprised to find a large branch from a neighbouring tree had come down over their tree, squashing the branches and foliage down close to the hollow which had stayed dry. Odelia and Osborne looked at the now private space and smiled at each other.

"Perfect!" Odelia declared.

CHAPTER FOUR

KOTARE & KELIA'S JOURNEY – THE FLOOD

Kelia Kiwi was feeding quietly before the class in the cave was due to start, when she heard rapid footsteps. She moved to step out of the way only to be confronted by Kahine. Kerewa and Katana's son was younger than her, but he had already made it clear he intended to be leader when he was old enough. Kelia looked around for Kotare for support, but he was out of sight.

"How long are you staying here?" Kahine asked in a tone that told Kelia she was no longer welcome here.

"This area is our home." Kelia tried to defend her right to be here.

"Not for much longer!" Kahine's tone was final. "When I become leader, you will be moved on if you are still here then."

"What is wrong with you?" Kelia asked in frustration. "We aren't intending to challenge you for leadership, so we aren't a threat to you."

"I don't believe you!" Kahine looked at the amulet Kelia still wore. "You still are wearing the leader's mantle. You should have given it back by now."

Kelia clutched the amulet tightly. "Mum left this for me when she was killed. It is the only thing I have from her. No one is taking this from me, including you!" Kelia then stomped off, stopping any further conversation.

During the school lesson Kelia's mind was elsewhere. She was glad Kotare and his friends had come. She needed to talk to him before sleep time. Since their parents had died, they had shared a tunnel in Kerewa and Katana's burrow, but Kahine's attitude made that impossible now.

"We need to talk." Kelia quickly spoke to Kotare as the lesson ended. Kotare looked at the set look on her face and knew something had happened. He quietly followed her to their parents' old burrow. His friends waited outside.

"This is where we need to sleep from now on." Kotare was alarmed at this announcement. He hadn't been happy to stay at the place where their mother had been killed. "We aren't welcome in this community anymore."

"Did Kerewa say that?" Kotare was shocked.

"No, but Kahine did. He also made it clear we need to move to another community soon. If we are still here when he becomes leader, he will move us on."

"Why?"

"He thinks we are a threat to his leadership, even though I told him we have no intention of challenging him for it."

Kotare looked at his friends with sadness. He had hoped to live his life here with them when they were old enough to have families of their own. He tried to smile at Kelia as he made his suggestion.

"It looks like it is time for another of our adventures." Kelia smiled too, as she remembered the last one. Only this time their journey would be to find a new home.

"Have you fed yet?" Kotare asked.

Kelia nodded. "I did, before class."

"Are you up for a swim across the river, or do you want to go the long way round?"

"I don't mind a swim." Kelia decided. The sooner they left this area to happier she would be.

When they come out of the burrow, Kotare shocked his friends with his news.

"Kahine has made it clear we aren't welcome here any longer. He will make us leave when he becomes leader so we are leaving now to find a new home." Kotare informed them. We will visit my cousins in Arthurs pass and live there or at Lake Kaniere."

"I want to come with you." Kewa spoke up, realising that he wouldn't see Kotare again.

"We want to come too." Keka and Kerei spoke up.

Instead of slipping away quietly as they had hoped; their families had to be found and be told of their plans and goodbyes said.

"What brought this on?" Kerewa asked with puzzlement at their sudden decision to leave. There had been no indication of their wish to move on.

Kotare managed a smile. "I've been thinking for a while that it's time for the visit we promised Kian and Kana when we left them and I want to see Lake Kaniere again."

"So you're planning to come back?"

"Of course, though we may have families then." Kotare kept the smile on his face.

"Alright then, have a good trip; but we will miss you."

"Thank you for looking after us." Kelia added as she gave Katana a hug.

Both Kotare and Kelia were grateful that Kahine was absent when they said their goodbyes, so they didn't have to pretend to say goodbye to him.

Khai and Kailan also came to say goodbye to them.

"Have a good time down there. We will keep in touch." Kailan said in parting. Kotare could see the sympathy in Kailan's eyes and knew that he was aware of why they were leaving.

"Thanks. We will look forward to it."

When Kelia and Kotare and his friends came to the river, Syd and Daphne were waiting to take them across. Oliver had been sent to fetch them to ensure everyone crossed safely. Kotare and Kelia could swim, but his friends had yet to learn. They would have had to walk the long way round to the swing bridge to cross the river. Kelia was happy she didn't have to get wet just yet.

Kerewa Khai and Kailan watched Syd and Daphne cross the river and disappear into the Ohikanui Valley. They turned to find Kahine watching behind them.

"They didn't say goodbye." Kahine complained in an injured tone.

"You knew they were leaving." Khai replied quietly and moved on before Kahine could reply.

"Why didn't you tell us they were going?" Kerewa could be heard demanding in an angry tone as Khai and Kailan walked swiftly away. He realised with Khai's words that Kotare and Kelia would not be coming back and that Kahine was responsible for their decision to leave.

Once in the Ohikanui valley, Kotare insisted on getting off and walking. He wanted to explore the place that he had travelled through when he was little. – He chose not to think of his stay there when their mother was taken. Besides, there was no hurry to reach their new home where new responsibilities awaited them.

Kotare heard a flutter in the tree above them. He looked up to find Oliver and Ogene were here to make sure they stayed safe during their journey. Syd and Daphne were also happy that the Kiwis had chosen to walk during this stage of their journey. They would have a leisurely stroll through their home before the proper journey began.

When sleep time was due in the morning, the making of a temporary burrow was a joint effort at the base of a tree that was also suitable for Oliver and Ogene to rest in as well. Oliver and Ogene were enjoying this trip. There was plenty of time to find their own food while keeping an eye on the Kiwis.

When Kotare woke that evening he could hear water running nearby. He looked around to find Kelia and his friends still sleeping next to him. He then remembered they were now on a journey to their new life. Kotare looked out at the river. There was a section here that was shallow and sheltered; ideal for learning to swim! When Kewa Keka and Kerei woke, Kotare and Kelia were already outside waiting for them by the water.

"Come on." Kelia urged them with a smile as she plunged into the water. "It's time for your first swim." Kewa Keka and Kerei looked at each other with some trepidation and amazement as they slowly came forward. This trip was going to be an adventure in more ways than they had expected. After some instruction, they plunged in and after getting used to the shock of being in cold water, they found they were enjoying themselves. Their voices and squeals and splashes woke Oliver and Ogene who went off to search for their feed. Syd and Daphne had already walked further up the valley and were preparing to rest for the night while the Kiwis were making their way towards them.

During the coming evenings, the Kiwis began their night with either a paddle or a swim if the area was safe for one, untill one afternoon Kotare woke with a start, the sound of water was different. He looked around to the sound – the water was a raging torrent, very close to their burrow and rising rapidly.

"Wake up! Wake up!" Kotare yelled at Kelia and his friends. "We have to get out of here NOW!"

Shocked, Kelia and his friends followed Kotare out to higher ground as water started to fill the burrow they had just left. As they climbed, Kotare started to look for tide marks on the steep bank. When he spotted them, he was shocked at how high the river could rise.

"We have to go up there." Kotare pointed to trees another 10 metres up the bank. "We won't be safe untill we are up there."

Oliver and Ogene were still in the tree above the burrow, woke to Kotare's voice and then saw them climbing the hill.

"What's happening?" Oliver called.

"The river is in flood. Come up to safer ground."

Oliver was shocked to look down to see the base of the tree where the burrow had been, was now well under water. They could now feel the power of the water rushing against the trunk. Quickly Oliver led Ogene up the bank to trees above the still climbing Kiwis. Oliver looked up the valley. Dark clouds were approaching from that direction.

"It's going to rain here soon as well." Oliver warned them.

When Kotare was confident they were safe, they chose a tree to shelter under – there was no point in travelling in pouring rain if they didn't have to. The Kiwis and Owls then set out for a feed before the rain set in. Oliver and Ogene took extra mice back to the tree with them to save flying in the rain later. Kotare was wondering whether Syd and Daphne were safe when the sound of their footsteps could be heard approaching.

"We are here!" Kotare called out to them.

"That's a relief!" Daphne called when she saw him. "We were worried that you might have got caught in the flood. We will stay nearby from now on."

For two days the rain fell on the valley. The Kiwis taking turns to slip out for a feed, which didn't take long as the rain had brought the worms close to the surface. Kotare noticed that by the time the rain had passed, the water level was up near the tide mark he had seen earlier.

As the deer led the kiwis up the valley, there were many obstacles for them to pass. Many fallen trees logs and foliage now littered the banks where the flood had been. They also had to skirt a slip where the waterlogged ground had given way, sending part of the hillside down to the river; it's usually clear waters now muddy brown. There was to be no more swimming is these waters on this journey.

CHAPTER FIVE

PAPAROA RANGE

One evening Syd came to Kotare. "We are near Three Sisters Community. Are you going to visit them?"

"I don't know if or when I will be back this way again, so yes, we will visit them."

"We will be nearby when you are ready to move on. Just send Oliver down to find us."

As the Kiwis made their way up the mountain; Oliver and Ogene flew ahead to find Odion and Oana.

"What brings you here?" Oana called with astonishment. There had been no word that they were coming.

Oliver smiled. "We are accompanying Kelia and Kotare and his friends. They are on their way to their new life in the south."

"I will let Kuaka know."

When the Kiwis finally made it up to the community, a warm welcome was waiting for them. Food and fresh burrows had been prepared, and a visit of the school cave was organised too. Kelia was interested in books she hadn't seen at their school cave.

"What's happening up there?" Kuaka asked; when he had a moment with Kotare alone. He knew that these Kiwis hadn't left their community without good reason.

"I told Kerewa that we are visiting Kian and Kana at Arahura valley and also Lake Kaniere. He expects us to return, but we won't be. His son Kahine has made it clear we aren't welcome there any longer. My friends decided to come with me when I told them we were leaving."

"Why is Kahine against you being there?"

"He has decided we are a threat to his leadership when he gets it. He said he would force us out when he is leader if we hadn't left before."

Kuaka was silent for a few moments as he digested this news. He came and gave Kotare a cuddle. He and Kelia had already been through so much with the loss of their parents.

"Have a good trip to the other communities, but remember there is a home here for you all if you would like to come back."

"Thank you. I will certainly think about it."

The Kiwis enjoyed themselves so much, when it was time to move on they were sorry to leave. Oliver flew ahead to find Syd and Daphne as they made their way down the mountain.

"By the way, there is a home for us here, if we want to come back." Kotare told Kelia and his friends.

"That's good to know." Kerei commented. He had seen a female he was interested in and she showed signs of being interested in him too.

"Can you take us to Punakaiki?" Kotare asked Syd when they met up with them. Soft predawn light was spreading over the hills. Beyond them the Tasman Sea was shrouded in darkness.

"Of course." Syd agreed as he and Daphne sat down to let the Kiwis onto their backs. Kewa, Keka and Kerei were nervous and held on tight as Syd stood up again. The last time the Kiwis had been on their backs, they had sat in woven baskets. Riding bareback was a new experience for them. Kotare and Kelia rode on Daphne. Oliver and Ogene came to join them once the Kiwis were settled.

Kewa Keka and Kerei tried to stay awake as they journeyed through the Paparoa Range towards Punakaiki, but the rocking motion soon sent them to sleep. It was evening when the Kiwis woke. Syd was no longer walking and was grazing quietly with Daphne as he waited for the Kiwis to wake. Oliver and Ogene were already sitting in a nearby tree and Kotare and Kelia were also down on the ground, searching for their first meal of the night.

"Where are we now?" Keka asked as he noticed the changed landscape. Dense bushes and Nikau Palms hugged the hillside. Keka sniffed the air, which was filled with a different smell to any he was used to.

"Welcome to Punakaiki. We are on the coast here. You can smell the sea spray." Kotare replied as Syd let the Kiwis off his back. "Once you've had a feed, I will take you for a walk."

As Kotare led the Kiwis down the hillside the sound of crashing water became louder. When they came to a road Kotare stopped and listened intently for several minutes before leading them over the other side and into the bushes. They were about to enter a smaller path when a voice spoke behind them.

"You've picked a good time to visit. The Blowholes are going well tonight."

They turned around to find a Weka looking at them with a quizzical smile.

Kotare returned the Weka's smile with a grin. "That's good. This is their first visit."

"Allow me to escort you." The Weka Offered. "There are still a few humans around this evening. If I suddenly dart into the bushes, you go in too."

Kotare was nervous at this news, but wasn't surprised. The paths here had been created by humans. He just hoped they didn't run into any. Kotare kept Kelia and his friends some distance behind the Weka as he cautiously walked along the path through the bushland. When the Weka darted into the bushes on the side of the path, they did the same. Soon the sound of footsteps and human voices came. They had seen the Weka and stopped to watch him move quickly out of sight. They then proceeded past the Kiwis without noticing them. A few minutes passed before the Weka came back.

"I will just go ahead and see if any more humans are here. They have usually gone home by now."

They waited patiently for the Weka to return. Kewa was alarmed that the ground under their feet shook when the sound of waves were crashing. *What sort of place is this?"*

"It's all clear!" the Weka came back with a grin.

Kotare led the Kiwis out of the bushes and down the path into the open, to a place that would stay in the Kiwis' memories forever. All around them were strange rocks that were stacked on top of each other in thin slabs, in all shapes and sizes.

"These are called Pancake rocks by humans." Kotare explained to Kelia. "They look like pancakes they like to eat."

Kelia didn't know whether to be frightened or amazed at this place, which trembled under her feet as the waves crashed into the rocks beneath them. Suddenly there was a whooshing sound and they were sprayed with water as a wave was forced up through the nearby blowhole. Kelia shrieked as she was soaked with the water which had a strange taste. Kewa Keka and Kerei also gasped as they were soaked as well. They stood well back when the next one came, marvelling at the spectacle of the water spray over the rocks. As the others watched the blowhole display, Kotare recognised a rock that he had stood on with his parents when he was little. He remembered his mother saying that he would return.

"I'm here at the rocks Mum." Kotare spoke in his thoughts.

Kohana heard his words and smiled.

Kotare knew that he would return here again, just as he felt compelled to visit Lake Kaniere too.

Kanoa and Kamoku were feeding when a rustle in the bushes made them look up. Before them stood two Kiwis that Kanoa instantly recognised. Three others were new to him.

"Kotare! Kelia! What brings you here?"

"We are on our way to Arahura and the Lake. I thought we would see how you are while we were passing." Kotare introduced his friends. "Kewa Keka and Kerei are coming with us."

"You walked all this way?"

"No. Syd and Daphne have brought us. They are resting."

Another rustle in the bushes brought Koana to join the meeting.

"Has everyone fed? It is going to rain soon. Come to our burrow." Without waiting for an answer, Koana led the way to the burrow - expecting everyone to comply, which they did.

During the next few hours several squalls came through while they sheltered in the burrow and told Kanoa of their adventures on their way. Kanoa was a little jealous that he couldn't just go and join them on their journey.

Koana was happy for some female company for a change and asked about Kelia's life in the Buller. She knew that Kotare and Kelia had lost both their parents and wondered how they managed on their own till now. Kelia read her thoughts and smiled.

"We've been lucky that Kerewa and Katana took us into their burrow after Mum and dad went to the spirit world, but it's time for us to make a new life for ourselves now."

Koana frowned at this news. Neither Kotare nor Kelia were fully adult yet. Even though young Kiwis were fully independent at their age, most young Kiwis kept contact with their family unless they were forced away.

"They sent you away?"

"No." Kelia replied quietly. "Their son Kahine did."

Kelia could see a fierce look in Koana's eyes – she was ready to do battle!

"It's alright," Kelia hastened to add. "A home is waiting for us at Three Sisters Mountain if we want."

The fierce look left Koana's eyes. "I'm glad to hear it. If you settle at Three Sisters, do come down and visit." Koana didn't mention it, but she committed Kahine's name to her memory – just in case he ever visited. She would make him sorry he had treated his family members so shabbily!

With promises to come back and visit again, Kotare led the way back to Syd and Daphne. Everything was very wet from the previous rain and the newly damp ground was full of treats for them to feed on. Oliver and Ogene were happily sheltering in the tree above the deer. They had sensed the rain was coming and made sure they had extra food to snack on while the rain came through.

CHAPTER SIX

LAKE KANIERE

Oriel Owl was taking his class in the school cave at Mount Tahua when the sound of footsteps coming down the stairs made him look up. To his delight Kotare was leading Kelia and three other kiwis down to him. He had heard from Kuaka and Kanoa to expect them, but didn't know when.

"We will restart class tomorrow." Oriel told the students, who instead of scampering away, stayed to meet the new arrivals. The Kiwis were soon surrounded by animals. Kotare and Kelia were questioned on what they had been doing since they last were here – Kelia had been hatched here on her last visit and was looking forward to exploring places that Kotare had visited. Kewa Keka and Kerei were fielding questions on their life in the Buller and the school they went to up there. Outside Syd and Daphne and Oliver and Ogene were happy that they were free during the time the Kiwis were here.

Oliver and Ogene could hear other owls nearby and knew that they would meet the locals shortly. Before Oliver could lead Ogene on a hunt for their next meal, a pair of owls landed on the branch next to them. Word had already been sent to Orion that a Stag and hind with a pair of owls were coming with Kotare and Kelia and several other Kiwis.

"I'm Orion and she is Odette. Welcome to Lake Kaniere. I see you have brought Kotare and Kelia back to us. Who are the other Kiwis with them?"

"We are Oliver and Ogene." The Kiwis are Kewa, Keka and Kerei. They are friends of Kotare's. They are looking to start a new life too."

"Do you think they will settle here?" Orion was immediately interested.

"I'm not sure. They have been offered a home at Three Sisters Mountain and they will be visiting the Arahura Valley to see Kian and Kana as well."

"Odette will show you where the best feeding places are, and you are welcome to shelter in the family tree while you are here. I will look for Koa Kiwi and his family and let them know that their visitors are here."

Koa already knew that Kotare was here. Syd and Daphne were making their way to the eastern side of Mount Tahua, when a voice at their feet made them stop.

"Syd! Daphne! I had heard that Kotare and Kelia were coming. Did you bring them?"

Syd looked down at Koa's familiar form and smiled.

"Yes we have. We have brought a few of Kotare's friends as well."

"I will go and meet them. Are you going to the other side of Tuhua?"

"Yes. It is quieter and safer there."

"You will meet three hinds that are living there. They were brought up here, but have been away for some time. They will have quite a story to tell you of their lives."

"There is no stag to protect them?"

"No. He went to the spirit world."

Delphinia Dianthia and Dianella were browsing happily when the familiar sound of deer hooves came towards them. Wondering who it might be – they didn't know of any other deer still in the area, Delphinia walked towards the sound, to find a Stag and hind coming towards her.

"Dianthia, Dianella, we have company."

When Koa Kewena and Kehi went to sleep the next morning, their burrow was much more snug than usual with an extra five kiwis to find space for. Kotare was full of plans to show Kelia and his friends' places he loved from his last visit.

When Kotare emerged from the burrow the next evening, everyone else was still sleeping. He had plans to visit Ernie. He took a couple of steps to find familiar white claws and long white legs stretching into the foliage above him

"Manu?" Kotare spoke quietly.

"Hello Kotare." Manu spoke just as quietly. "We are here to protect you."

"What are you protecting us from?"

"Spirit Harriers. Both the Spirit and living world is in danger from them. They attack when they are hidden."

"Are they anything to do with the evil spirit that came to Sunny Bight?"

"Yes. He controls them."

"Where is this spirit?"

"He is bound in Nudoor in the spirit world, but he is able to control spirit Harriers. We know he is using them to try to get free again.

"What is he bound with? Kotare wanted to know.

"Spiders' webs. Why?"

"How big is Nudoor?"

"Very big" Manu was silent for a few seconds as he followed Kotare's line of questions. "Are you suggesting we cover Nudoor with spiders' webs?"

Kotare nodded. "You say the Harriers are hidden, but you will be able to see if they disturb the webs." While Manu digested this idea Kotare made another suggestion.

It's nice to see you Manu, but shouldn't you and your friends be hidden as well, in case you too are attacked?"

Manu looked at this young Kiwi who was wise beyond his years.

"You are right. No-one is safe on view anywhere while this threat is here." Manu immediately disappeared from view.

Down at the water's edge, Kotare revelled in having a paddle before taking the plunge for a swim. He hadn't realised that he had made so much noise till a familiar grey black form rubbed against him.

"Welcome back Kotare." Ernie Eel grinned at him. "Are you on your own?"

"Hello Ernie. I have brought Kelia and some of my friends with me."

"I would like to meet them later."

"You will. They like to swim too."

When Kotare returned to the burrow it was empty. Koa and Kewena were showing Kelia and his friends where the best feeding spots were. When Kotare joined them, they wanted to know where he had been, after see how wet Kotare was.

"I've been for a swim and caught up with Ernie." Kotare grinned at them. "You will meet him later."

"Wake us up next time!" Kewa complained. "He was missing the swims they had in the Ohikanui River before the flood came through.

Kotare took Kelia and his friends for their first lesson at this school cave, where they made new friends and delighted in reading both new and familiar books.

The following evening, plans were being made. A trip to Dorothy Falls was being organised. Oriel sent the Possums and Hedgehogs down to check on the boat. When word came back that it was fine, Oriel announced to the class that they were going on a nature trip to Dorothy Falls. Kotare and Kelia were immediately excited. Kotare was happy he would show his friends one of his favourite places from his last visit. Kelia was also happy to see the place where Kotare had so much fun. She had been too young to see it last time. Kotare's friends were wide-eyed at the large body of water they could glimpse in the darkness as the moon briefly shone between the clouds.

"Can you see the bottom?" Keka wanted to know.

"No. It is far too deep for that." Oriel replied as he organised everyone into their seats on the boat. Oriel looked at the sky. There were plenty of clouds about to hide the moon (and them) from any humans that may be up. He couldn't detect any rain or strong winds that might cause trouble on this trip.

Neither Kelia nor Kotare's friends had been in a boat before, another new experience for them. As they made their way down the lake, Kotare felt nervous, but couldn't understand why. Then he remembered that his spirit friends were here, so he ignored the strange feelings he was having and settled back to enjoy the ride.

Once they reached the stream leading to the falls, the boat was stowed before they started their nature lesson.

"As we walk up to the falls," Oriel began, "I want you to see how many different plants you can name."

As the students looked at, felt and smelt the different bushes and trees they came across there were many calls naming what they thought the plant was.

As the Kiwis were looking at a bush, a voice quietly spoke to Kotare. "Your plan is working."

Kerei also heard the voice and turned around to see who was there, but couldn't see anyone.

"What plan, Kotare? Who is talking to you?"

Kotare smiled. "Do you remember the spirit animals that came to bring Kelia and me here to warn family to move?" Kelia and his friends nodded. "Well, they are here now. You can't see them because I told them to stay invisible."

"Are they here to take you away again?"

"No. This time they are here to protect us."

Before any more questions could be asked, Oriel was calling them. "Kiwis keep up!

Kotare swiftly moved on to lead them to the other animals who were now paddling in the stream near the falls. The moon was out again, shining its silvery light on the falls as it cascaded down among the ferns and bushes lining the shear banks on each side.

All too soon, it was time to return to the boat. As they made their way back up the lake; Kotare's feelings returned again; only stronger this time. Kotare looked around nervously. He knew something was coming, but he didn't know what or where from.

"What is it Kotare?" Oriel had already noticed that the wind was stronger now. He hoped it wasn't bringing a change in weather before they got back to shore. He could also see that Kotare was looking alarmed at something he couldn't see.

"Can we go to the Island?" Kotare asked. "We need to shelter."

"Good Idea." Oriel agreed.

As the boat turned to head towards the Island, there was the sound of a clash of bodies, the scream of a large bird that Kotare knew to be a spirit Harrier and the roar from the Moa as it fought to stop the Harrier from reaching the boat. There was much splashing and thrashing of the water before it became calm again.

"What was that?" Oriel asked Kotare with alarm, on seeing the stony expression on his face.

"That was Manu the Moa protecting us from a Spirit Harrier. Oleus in the spirit world has control of them. We need to hide in Kupe's cubby. I know that more of them will be coming."

CHAPTER SEVEN

THE ISLANDS

Odelia and Osborne looked at their two little owlettes with delight. The extra care they had taken to find a suitable site and make it safe had paid off. They had arranged to have one of them at the nest at all times, being careful that no animal saw them come or go and to conceal the entrance. Sometimes they would feel a large bird land on the large branch above the nest. There was no sound, which made Odelia suspect a spirit Harrier was here, looking for her. The owlettes were taught very early to be silent when there was activity near the nest.

They both knew the day would come when their owlettes would leave the nest and they had to prepare them the best they could, to be strong enough for the flight to the forest across the bay. Each night the owlettes took turns to stretch and flap their wings, ready for when the heavy down on their wings and body was replaced with flight feathers.

From time to time Ollie would come down from his perch on top of Mount Tahua to the Island, being careful to remain hidden, to watch how Odelia and Osborne were raising their family. He was impressed at how cautious they were when near the nest and how careful they were to conceal the entrance. Even he only managed to get a glimpse of the owlettes within. Reporting back to Oriel on how they were progressing.

One night Ollie was observing the nest. Osborne had just come back with a feed for the owlettes, so he knew that Odelia would be out soon. A large pale shadow glided over the islands. To his horror it came to land on top of the log that lay over the nest. It was a spirit Harrier! Kohana had told him of the danger from the Harriers, now that Oleus had control of them and that she and Titan were staying close to Odelia and her family. The Harrier stayed for several minutes, looking around carefully and listening intently, before moving on to the next Island and the forest surrounding the lake. Ollie was relieved that Odelia waited untill the spirit Harrier had long gone before she emerged from the nest.

One evening, Odelia noticed that more spirit animals had come to the lake on Mount Tahua and wondered what had brought them here.

"Do you know anything about the spirit animals being here?" Odelia quietly asked Kohana.

"No, but I will find out for you." As Kohana spoke, the animals disappeared from view.

"Something must be coming, if they are hidden." Kohana commented. "I will warn the others."

The next night, Osborne was out feeding when he saw the community boat sailing up the lake. It had some young Kiwis on board with the Oriel and the animals from the school. He recognised one of them as Kotare, Kohana's son.

"Kohana, do you know your son is here?" Osborne called as he reached the nest.

Kohana immediately came to look. "Kelia is here as well. I will have to find out what brought them here." Kohana then had a thought. "You can tell Odelia that we have an explanation for the spirit animals that are here. They are here with Kotare and Kelia."

Odelia had just returned to the nest after feeding and with food for the Owlettes when the boat returned. Kohana was shocked to see the flurry in the water beyond the boat and knew that a Harrier was here and it had tried to attack the boat! Who was it trying to kill? Was it Oriel, or was it after Kotare and Kelia? If so why?

Kohana saw the boat head towards the Islands and knew that more Harriers were coming!

"Odelia! Osborne!" Kohana called urgently. "Don't come out till I tell you it is safe. More Harriers are coming!"

"Thanks for telling us." Osborne called back.

Kohana then put out a call to Orion Ollie Keoni Kupe and Kaori. *Make sure you take shelter or stay hidden! A spirit Harrier has tried to attack the boat with Oriel and the school animals. They are coming to the Island for shelter. I know more Harriers are coming.*

Ollie called back. *Are Odelia and Osborne safe?*

Yes.

Once the animals had quickly vacated the boat and it was hauled ashore, Kupe and Kaori appeared to escort them swiftly to their cubby at the base of the tree. Once inside, Oriel started a head count. Before he could finish, Kupe called "hush!"

As silence settled on the space, Oriel listened intently, but he couldn't hear anything. It was obvious though that both Kupe and Kaori could hear movement outside. Both of them faced towards the Harriers as they searched the forest outside. At one point both standing in front of the opening, ready to attack if a Harrier found its way in beyond the thick growth of ferns covering the entrance.

When Kupe and Kaori relaxed a little, they knew they were out of immediate danger.

"I will see if any are still around." Kupe advised Oriel before disappearing from view.

When Kupe returned, he had bad news. Some of them are clustered in the trees around the boat. They know you are here somewhere and are waiting for you to come back to the boat." Kupe looked at Kaori. "We may have to evacuate them while hidden."

Kaori nodded. "It's the only way. How are we going to do it and where will we take them?"

Kupe thought for a moment before he spoke. "Everyone, I want you to form a line and hold each other's paw or claw."

Once that was done Kupe asked Kaori to hang onto the claw of the nearest animal, which happened to be Kelia.

"Now hide yourself Kaori." Instantly Kaori and all the animals disappeared from view.

"It works!" Kupe smiled. "You can reappear now Kaori." When Kaori reappeared, all the animals appeared with him.

Kupe then walked to the other end of the line and put his claw on the claw of Hovea Hedgehog. "Is everyone holding each other firmly?" Kupe asked. When a chorus of "Yes" came from all the animals, he continued. "When Kaori and I hide, you will be hidden too, so that nothing, including the spirit Harriers will see you. It is important you stay silent while we are hidden. We are going to take you to the school cave. Are you ready Kaori?"

"I am."

"Hide."

With that command, Kupe and Kaori and all the animals disappeared to begin a journey the animals would marvel at and remember all of their lives. Swiftly Kupe lead the line of animals through the opening to the forest and into the air where they weaved through the trees to the canopy before bursting out into the open. Kupe's speed increased as they flew over the bay to the forest on Mount Tahua before coming to the opening of the school cave where Kupe lead the group down the slope to land on the cave floor.

"You can release each other's paws and claws now."

As Kupe and Kaori released their hold on the animals, everyone reappeared in view.

"Thank you for saving us." Oriel began.

277

"While this danger is here, I think everyone should go home and stay out of sight."

As Kupe was speaking, he saw Koa start to lead Kewena and Kehi down the stairs.

"Stop Koa!" Kupe called out to him. "It isn't safe here! Quickly run home and hide till we tell you it is safe."

Shocked, Koa turned and swiftly led his family back to his burrow. They had just entered it when a shadow came over the entrance, which was well hidden among ferns. A spirit Harrier was here.

In the cave Kupe had sensed the Harrier was near.

"Everyone hold each other's paws and claws. We need to be hidden again. A Harrier is coming. Just follow what I do."

Some Bats were in the cave when Kupe appeared with the animals. When they heard a spirit Harrier was coming, they quickly dropped onto the shoulders of the animals as they joined together again.

On the neighbouring Island, Odelia and her family were also in immediate danger. Harriers were also clustered in the trees around the nest. One of them had realised that the arrangement was a nest. If no-one came out soon, they would rip it open and look.

Kohana looked at Titan. *We have to get Odelia and her family out while hidden.*

Odelia, Kohana called her in her thoughts. *Harriers are sitting outside your nest. I need to get you all out.*

Get Osborne and the children out before me!

I will send Titan in first. The children are to sit on his back and hang on tight. I will then come in and get you both.

It was a squeeze in the nesting space when Titan appeared amongst them. Quickly Odelia placed the owlettes on Titan's back. As soon as they were in place, Titan disappeared from view. Kohana then came into the space. She was about to grab Odelia and Osborne when the branches of the nest started to rip apart. They could see the Harriers eyes on them. As the Harrier's claw reached in to grab Odelia, Kohana grabbed Odelia's and Osborne's claws to disappear.

Kohana quickly found that a there were no safe places at this lake.

The Harriers were searching everywhere that the owls and Kiwis were known to live. With Titan at Odelia's side, Kohana turned and swiftly led the family towards Lake Mahinapua.

When Orion heard the call from Kohana, he immediately put out a call to all the owls in the area.

"Oleus is sending his spirit Harriers here. We need to either hide or leave."

Several females immediately crowded round him with concern. "What about our owlettes in the nest? We can't leave them."

"Put them on your shoulders and fly with them."

"How long have we got?"

"Not long. They are already on the Islands. They will be here soon."

Orion went back to Odette who was now anxious after hearing his call.

"We are taking you all for a ride." Orion told his four owlettes, before picking up the smaller two and placing one on each of Odette's shoulders. The larger two were quickly placed on Orion's shoulder before he led the way towards the west.

"Where are we going?" Odele asked. She had two owlettes on her shoulder and was lucky another female was carrying her other two owlettes. She was wondering where her mate Oriel and the school children were and hoped they were safe.

"We are going to Hokitika." Orion advised her, as he headed for the twinkling lights of the town in the distance.

"Will there be enough trees for us all there, and won't we be in other owls' territory?"

"We won't be in any owls' trees. There is a big building there on the edge of the town at the racing track. It will have plenty of room for us all. There should be plenty of food there at the track for us as well."

"Why are we going to a building which humans' use? Won't the humans chase us away?"

"The humans won't know we are there. They only use it in summer time. We are going there because the spirit Harriers won't be expecting us to shelter in a place that humans have made."

As Kohana approached the forest at Mahinapua, she could see that some of the Owls were flying towards them in a panic, giving out alarm calls as they flew. Kohana immediately landed in the nearest tree. She released Odelia and Osborne, so they were visible to the Owls.

"Find out what the problem is. We may have to head north if the Harriers are here."

"What is the problem and where are you heading?" Osborne called to the approaching owls.

"Something we can't see is killing owls at our Lake. We are going over to the other one." The owl looked towards Lake Kaniere.

"No! You can't go there!" Osborne exclaimed. We have just come from there. It is Harriers from the spirit world that are killing owls. You need to come north. Tell families to bring their children. If necessary put them on your shoulders."

The Owl immediately put out the call to other owls before following Odelia and Osborne north.

Orion, where are you? Is everyone safe? Kohana called him in her thoughts as she and Titan accompanied Odelia and Osborne on their flight north.

We are safe. I am leading the community to the race course at Hokitika.

I am bringing Odelia and her family. Also the owl community at Mahinapua are coming as well.

Are they being attacked too?

Yes.

The only ones missing are Oriel and the schoolchildren.

I saw them go to the island where Kupe and Kaori are. They will look after them.

At the school, Kupe sensed that the Harrier had entered the cave. He immediately led everyone out. Over the treetops on the slopes of Mount Tahua they flew towards the Arahura Valley then followed the river to the east. There was only one place they all would be safe. When Kupe detected Kiwis in the forest below, he brought the animals down to the ground. Kupe released Hovea Hedgehog and Kaori released Kelia Kiwi so that everyone was now visible. Kupe spoke to Oriel before they left them.

"Oriel, if you call out someone will come. Some of the local Kiwi community are here. We are going back for Koa and his family."

In Koa's burrow, he was cuddling Kewena and Kehi. He realised that they were now trapped here. They had no idea if or when it would be safe to go outside to feed.

To his relief, Kupe and Kaori's spirits appeared in the burrow with them.

"Oriel and the children are safe at the Arahura community. We are taking you there too. We all will be invisible while we are travelling."

"Is anyone there? It's Oriel and the children from the school." Oriel called out at the top of his voice.

Immediately they were surrounded by Kiwis who were astonished to find Oriel Owl and all the children from the Lake Kaniere school in their midst and with them were Kohana's children Kotare and Kelia with other young kiwis.

"Is anyone else coming?"

"Kupe and Kaori are bringing Koa and his family."

"What's going on?" came a voice in the bushes. It was Keka.

"Keka," Oriel's relief was plain. "The community at Lake Kaniere is being attacked by Spirit Harriers. The Harriers are under the control of Oleus. They are trying to kill all living animals there. You haven't had anyone killed here?"

Keka shook his head. "How did you get here?" He was immediately worried the Harriers had followed them here.

"Kupe and Kaori brought us. We were hidden, so the Harriers couldn't see us."

As they were talking, there was another call nearby. It was Koa.

"They've just brought Koa and his family." Oriel explained.

"Stay here while I fetch them." Keka instructed him.

Kewena was very relieved to see Kelia and Kotare and his friends among the animals gathered around Oriel when they joined them. Keka wasted no time in leading everyone to the community burrows, where all the children were given a place to sleep and someone to show them feeding spots. Koa quickly made a burrow near Keka's for his family. Kelia shared a burrow with Kana while Kotare and his friends shared with Kian.

Koa went to Oriel who was standing at the base of a nearby tree, looking very troubled. Above him the bats had found a spot in the dense canopy to shelter.

"I know you usually sleep in trees, Oriel, but you are welcome to stay in the burrow with us till the danger is over." Koa offered him.

Oriel nodded and followed Koa into his burrow. Oriel didn't usually like dark enclosed places, but now for the first time since the boat was attacked, he felt safe. So many thoughts and questions were going through his head, with no answers to any of them.

"We are just going for a feed. We won't be long." Koa informed him, but Oriel was already lost in a world of his own.

A local owl saw the arrival of Oriel and the children and how troubled he was when Koa led him into his burrow.

"Something drastic has happened at the lake! Oriel is here with the school animals and he is sheltering in a Kiwi burrow!"

Very soon a crowd of Owls were gathered in the tree above the spot where Koa had made his burrow.

Koa saw them as he came back to the burrow. "You are waiting for Oriel?"

"What happened to him? Why is he sheltering in your burrow? And, has he fed tonight?"

"He took the students on a trip on the lake in the community boat when it was attacked by Harrier's from the spirit world. Luckily some other spirit animals protected the boat and they were brought here. My family had to be rescued from the Harriers as well. Oriel is sheltering with me because it is a safe place for him right now. I'm sure he will welcome any food you can bring him untill he feels able to find his own."

A rat was immediately dropped at Koa's feet. "Thank you. I will give it to him."

"Why are spirit-Harriers attacking living animals?

"Have you heard of the spirit Owl called Oleus who was sent to Nudoor?"

"Yes. Why?"

"He now has control of Harriers in the spirit world. I haven't found out yet why they are attacking living animals. It would be a good idea for you to be careful from now on where you fly and when. Make sure you aren't exposed in the sky for too long."

"Thank you for the warning. We will let all the communities know. We will also be back later with some more food for Oriel."

With that, the owl put out a call which was answered by another in the distance.

Near the school cave at Lake Kaniere, parents were anxiously starting to gather. There was no sign of Oriel or the children after their school trip. They had heard the owls calling, but now there was complete silence. They went to Koa's burrow, but there was no sign of him and his family either! Where was everyone?

As Orion led the community of owls towards Hokitika, an owl from the bushland at Kaniere saw the crowd and came to join them.

"What has happened for you to leave your area, and where are you going?"

"Spirit Harriers are attacking animals including owls at the lake, so we are moving to the town race course till it is safe."

"I will let them know you are coming."

As Orion approached the grandstand at the race course, several owls were waiting for them on the roof cap. They watched in silence at the tired owls, many with young owlettes on their shoulders landed next to them.

"What trees do you want to use while you are here?"

"We won't be using trees." Orion answered them. "We are going to use this building. The spirit Harriers won't be expecting us to shelter in a building that humans have made."

With that, Orion led his community down to the seating area. Facing to the north and enclosed on three sides with a high sloping roof above, the terraced seats rose high towards the back, with plenty of room and privacy from hostile eyes for everyone. Orion encouraged everyone to occupy the area up the back which was also protected from any wind and rain that may come from the northern direction.

Orion, where are you? Kohana called him in her thoughts. *We are approaching the town.*

I will come to meet you.

"I am just going to meet the Mahinapua community who will be joining us." Orion announced to the crowd who were busy choosing their spaces to roost in for their families.

The local owls, who had been watching with interest the visiting owls settle in, were startled to hear this latest news.

"Yes." Orion confirmed. "The Lake Mahinapua community have been attacked as well." He then flew up onto the roof to spot where the Mahinapua owls were before flying out to join them.

CHAPTER EIGHT

ODELIA'S CHALLENGE

Odelia was searching the bushland surrounding the race course for a feed for the children, along with several other owls when she sensed a spirit Harrier was coming. Letting out an alarm call for all the owls in the stand to hear; Odelia then ducked low in the bushes and kept very still. The other owls nearby did the same.

In the Grand stand, everyone ducked low and silence reigned. The Harrier landed on the roof and sat there for several minutes, scanning the area around him. He knew that the Owls from Mahinapua had come this way, but there was no sign of them. Perhaps they had gone further north. After satisfying himself that they weren't here, he moved on.

While Odelia was hiding, a field mouse came to sit next to her, grooming itself before moving into thick bushes nearby. Odelia knew that any movement would be detected, so had to be patient and remember where it had gone to. When she was sure the spirit Harrier had gone, Odelia reached forward with her claw into the space where the mouse had gone. Although she missed that mouse, she did flush out some others, who were quickly caught.

"Is it safe now?" a quiet call came from nearby.

"Yes. You can carry on hunting."

The owls in the stand were relieved to see Odelia flying normally as she returned to her family with their feed. They then resumed their normal routine.

As their owlettes consumed their feed, Odelia sat quietly and appeared calm, but internally she was becoming angry. Why wasn't anything being done about the Harriers that were now causing chaos in the living world. Odelia already knew the answer in her mind. Oleus was controlling them. It was time to stop him, but how?

Odelia brought a vision of the spirit leader into her mind. *"Why aren't you doing something?"*

"What do you expect me to do?" The spirit world leader's voice came loud in her head.

"You know that Oleus is controlling the spirit Harriers? They are killing all living owls and animals that they can find. Spirit world animals aren't safe from them either. Oleus has to be stopped."

"How do you expect me to stop him?"

"Neither the spirit or living world will be safe till Oleus is eliminated."

"Whoever eliminates a spirit animal will also be eliminated."

"So you won't do it?"

"No."

Odelia deliberately made her mind blank for some time after this conversation as she prepared herself for what lay ahead. Finally she took a deep breath and looked around her. Osborne was looking at Odelia with concern. He had seen she was in the spirit world and wondered what was to happen next.

"I have to talk to Odessa for a minute. I won't be long."

When Odessa saw Odelia approach, the serious expression on Odelia's face told her that something was up.

"If anything happens to me, will you help Osborne to bring up our children?"

Odessa looked at Odelia with alarm. "Of course I would, but what have you seen?"

"Nothing yet, but I have to go to Nudoor."

Kohana are you here

Yes.

"Why are you going there?" Odessa shook her head.

"The only way to stop Oleus and the Harriers taking over both the spirit and living world; is to eliminate him. I am the only being that is prepared to do it."

"What about the Harriers? They will kill you before you get there."

"I will get Kohana to take me. While we are travelling we will be hidden. I will probably be killed afterwards, but it has to be done if our community is to survive."

"How do you know you will be killed?"

"The spirit world leader told me that whoever eliminates a spirit world animal will also be eliminated."

"Be very careful and try to come back to us!" Odessa spoke with both pride and sadness that her granddaughter was embarking on such a dangerous mission to save the world they knew.

As Odelia returned to Osborne, she called to Hirone in her thoughts.

Hirone can you hear me?

Yes.

How many Harriers have you eliminated?

Several of them. Why?

How many of your Eagles have you lost?

Only one, thanks to you.

I am coming. It is time to end the chaos and loss of life Oleus is creating here.

They are attacking the living world?

Yes. The spirit world leader won't do anything to stop them or Oleus.

Odelia was calm and had a smile on her face as she joined Osborne. "I've just been to let Odessa know that I am going to Nudoor. Don't be upset." Odelia quickly added as she saw the stricken look come over Osborne's face. "If anything happens to me, she will help you with the children."

"Do you have to go?" Osborne knew Odelia might not return to him.

"Yes. Oleus will not stop the Harriers from hunting us untill we are dead. He has to be dealt with."

"Come here." Osborne brought the owlettes with him to give Odelia a cuddle, not knowing if or when they would have another one.

Without looking back, Odelia launched herself to fly to a nearby tree. Once on the branch, she felt Kohana's claw on hers and knew that she was now hidden.

"Do you know where Nudoor is?" Kohana asked.

"It is in the Alps. I will know it when I see it."

The Alps were cloaked in heavy cloud as they approached them, making it necessary to check the tops of many peaks. Then Odelia saw it – a range with sheer rock walls, its peaks obscured from sight. She pointed to it with her claw.

Kohana took Odelia above the clouds. The only peak visible was Mount Cook further to the south. Back down below the cloud base, they approached the range slowly and carefully. Once they reached the rocky walls, they rose inch by inch as the grey cloud swirled about them. They came to a rocky platform. A white stoat was lying relaxed in sleep. To a normal living animal's eye the scene was normal, but both Kohana and Odelia could see all of the spider's webs cast as a net over the whole area, the threads glistening in the moisture from the cloud surrounding it.

Hirone, I am here. Odelia informed him of her presence.

I detected something was near. When you find what you seek, I will have to be with you or the eagles will kill you. Where are you now?

I am by the Stoat.

You are hidden. Who is hiding you?

Kohana then spoke. *It is Kohana and Titan.*

As they moved along the mountain top, they passed various animals. Some were sleeping, others were awake. Those who had accepted their fate were lying relaxed. Others were pacing restlessly as they contemplated ways to escape. Then they came to one that was facing away from them. Not only was the area covered in spiders' webs, but the animal also was completely covered in a cocoon of web.

I have found one of them.

That is the young male Orel. From now on Odelia you will need to be visible, but I will be visible with you. Kohana and Titan you may leave her now.

As Kohana removed her claw from Odelia's, Odelia had to put her wings out to stop herself from falling as she now was alone and visible to the many eyes she knew could see her. She could also feel the huge wings of Hirone hovering above her, watching her every move.

Swiftly Odelia moved forward to land on the web net. Swiping it away she then landed on Orel's back. Odelia could feel two pairs of eyes very close to hers but ignored them as she slashed vigorously at the cocoon.

"What is your intention owl?" One of the Haast Eagles challenged her.

"He has to be destroyed. The spirit and living world will not be safe while his spirit exists."

"How do you know this?"

"Orel is my uncle. He is under the control of Oleus."

"We can do it for you."

"It is best that I do it. Whatever creature destroys a spirit can expect to be destroyed. I have to deal with both Oriana and Oleus as well."

As Odelia exposed Orel's head, his face swung around in triumph.

"Release me!" Orel demanded.

Odelia's answer was to make a final slash. Beneath her claw the body disappeared and the cocoon collapsed to a little pile on the ground.

Odelia turned around to Hirone.

"Where is Oriana?"

Hirone put out a claw for Odelia to land on. He proceeded with her to the other side of the mountain. They were now accompanied by the two other eagles. When Odelia exposed Oriana's head, she turned her head around to see Odelia looking at her.

"You have come to release me after all." A look of triumph came onto her face. It turned to shock as Odelia's claw pierced her head. When the cocoon that Oriana occupied lay in a little pile on the floor, Odelia felt both pain and regret at what she had just done.

"I have sent you to Orel as you wished."

As Odelia turned around to Hirone, she had a feeling that time was running out.

"They are coming aren't they?"

"Oleus is calling all the Harriers." Hirone replied as he put out his claw.

As Hirone carried her towards the area where they could hear an owl calling; Hirone also put out a call to all the Eagles who formed a barrier around him. Oleus now knew that Orel and Oriana were beyond his control.

As Hirone and Odelia approached the platform where Oleus was still cocooned, Harriers were already arriving and engaged the Eagles who were protecting Hirone and Odelia. Odelia had to concentrate all of her attention on the cocoon in front of her; ignoring the screams and clashes of bodies around her. Flying off Hirone's claw so he could join the fight, Odelia hacked through the webs to the cocoon, to be confronted by three Eagles.

"Join the fight!" Odelia ordered them before flying onto Oleus's back.

289

Odelia only partially uncovered the cocoon to exposed Oleus's head while he was screaming for his Harriers to come, which only stopped when her claw pierced his head.

"You reign is over." Odelia told Oleus as his cocoon collapsed beneath her.

Odelia immediately turned around and put her claw out toward all of the battling Eagles and Harriers in front of her. She then called out in a voice so loud that every creature in the spirit world heard her.

"SPIRIT WORLD HARRIERS STOP! YOU WILL LISTEN AND OBEY!"

Immediately all activity above her was suspended as she continued.

"OLEUS NO LONGER CONTROLS YOU. I AM NOW YOUR MISTRESS! ALL HARRIERS ARE TO RETURN TO THE SPIRIT WORLD AREA WHERE YOU CAME FROM TO RESUME YOUR NORMAL ACTIVITIES."

The Harriers meekly turned away to return to the areas they had been called from.

"Thank you for your help." Odelia's thanks encompassed all of the Eagles who had fought in the battle. "You may resume your normal activities too." She then spoke to Hirone. "I have a family to go back to. Let me know if there are any more problems you need help with."

Kohana, where are you?"

"I'm here!" Kohana and Titan were right next to her. *"We couldn't help you, but we weren't going anywhere!"*

"I'm ready to go home."

"Thank you." Hirone replied before Odelia disappeared from view.

Two Eagles approached Hirone as Odelia left. "Shouldn't she have protection?"

"You are prepared to be her Guardians in both the living and spirit worlds?"

"We are."

"Make sure you are hidden at all times."

The Eagles had just disappeared from view when the leader of the spirit world arrived with Owen and Oban. They looked at the broken web and the little pile of web from the cocoon on the ground, knowing that Oleus had been destroyed. The spirit world leader confronted Hirone.

"Did Odelia do this?"

"Yes."

"What about Orel and Oriana?"

"They have been destroyed too."

"Where is she?"

"She has gone back to the living world."

"Why did you let her go? You know she has to be destroyed."

"Oleus and the animals he controlled destroyed animals in both the living and spirit worlds. They were not destroyed. Odelia has just stopped the destruction and sent the animals Oleus controlled back to normal lives. Odelia deserves a normal life in both the living and spirit world too."

"So, it is up to me to destroy her."

As the leader spoke the words Hirone flashed a look to the eagle behind him. The eagle stepped forward to strike the leader, ending his existence. Hirone turned to speak to Owen and Oban.

"Let me know when you have chosen your new leader."

Owen nodded before leading Oban away.

Owen and Oban looked at each other as they flew. Whether the Eagles realised it or not; they now controlled the spirit world. Till now they had always complied with all instructions they had been given. Now they were dictating who lived – the role of the spirit world leader. There was also the question of what to do about Odelia. She not only controlled the Eagles of Nudoor, she now controlled the Harriers as well.

CHAPTER NINE

GOING HOME

Dawn was breaking as Odelia landed on the rail of the grandstand. Most of the owls were asleep, but Orion, ever alert to any noise nearby was instantly alert.

"We can go home tonight." Odelia spoke as she came over to him.

"Are you sure?"

"Yes. Oleus Orel and Oriana will not trouble anyone again and all of the Harriers have been sent back to their spirit world homes to live their normal lives."

"You did that all by yourself?"

"The Eagles helped me."

As Odelia made her way to Osborne, Oleander her daughter spotted her mother and called out with glee. "Mum's come back!" The joy that shone in Osborne's eyes as he watched the approach of his mate; was reflected in her own. At last they could lead a normal life without fear.

A couple of owls called when Odelia passed them, "Where have you been? Osborne has been miserable all night!"

"I've just been to put the world right." was Odelia's vague answer.

While Odelia was settling to a well-earned sleep with her family, Kohana was putting a call out to Ollie Keoni and Kupe.

Everyone can go home and live their normal lives. Oleus Orel and Oriana are no longer a danger. The Harriers are no longer a threat either. They have been sent back to their spirit world homes. The owl community will be returning tonight.

Keoni was happy he no longer had to be hidden as he patrolled his area. Ollie heard Kohana's call, but he was in a meeting of spirit owls, led by Owen and Oban.

"Koa are you there?" A quiet call came from outside his burrow. Koa wondered who was disturbing him during sleep time as he put his head out and squinted in the bright daylight. It was Kupe.

"I've come to tell you we will come to take everyone back to the lake tonight. The danger from Oleus and the harriers is over. Orion is bringing the community back from Hokitika tonight too."

"Oriel will be glad to hear it. He has been hiding in our burrow the whole time we have been here. I was getting worried about him. Kewena and I will be staying here now as well as Kelia and Kotare and his friends."

Kupe nodded. He didn't blame the Kiwis choosing to stay here with the Kiwi community. "We will see you tonight."

"Who was that?" Kewena wanted to know as Koa returned to her.

"It was Kupe. He told me the danger from Oleus and the Harriers is now over. He is coming back tonight to take Oriel and the children back to the lake."

At the mention of his name Oriel woke up. "What's happening?"

"It's safe to go back to the lake. Kupe is coming back tonight to collect you and the children. Orion is bringing the community back from Hokitika tonight as well."

"Good!" With a sigh of relief Oriel settled to the best sleep he had since coming here. He was missing Odele and his family and he no longer had to wrestle with the worry of who the Harriers were targeting in his community.

The twinkle of street lights pierced the dark sky, as Orion led the Kaniere community out of the grandstand at the race course. Odele was glad to be going home. She was missing Oriel and wondered how he was after the attack from the Harriers. Their owlettes seemed to be heavier than when she brought them here.

Odessa and Orlando led the Mahinapua community south to the Lake. They had enjoyed their stay at Kaniere, but had decided their home would be at Mahinapua. The children were able to make the trip to Kaniere for their lessons at the school now independently.

The local owls saw the exodus and came to see what was happening.

"The danger is over. We are all going home." Orlando informed them.

"We will tell everyone. Safe travels."

At Arahura Valley, goodbyes were being said as Oriel and the children gathered together for their trip home.

Manu are you there? Kotare spoke in his thoughts.

We are here. But it was Moana Moa who spoke to him

Where is Manu? Did something happen to him while we were in the boat?"

There was a small silence before Moana replied. *Manu defeated the Harrier, but he was badly injured. We don't know whether his spirit will survive.*

It was Kotare's turn for silence as he realised the sacrifice the Moa made for him.

I hope his spirit recovers. I have some good news for you. Oleus and the Harriers are no longer a threat. The Harriers have been sent back to their spirit world homes. Kelia and I are staying here for now while we decide where we are going to live.

Where is Oleus now?

Oleus Orel and Oriana were destroyed by Odelia.

Where is she now?

She went home to her family.

Oriel managed to keep his feelings to himself, but he was still feeling vulnerable while out in the open. It was going to take some time for him to be comfortable out in the trees. He wondered if Odele would mind sleeping in the school cave while he learnt to adjust to being in the open again.

"Are you ready?" Kupe asked as he stood holding Hovea Hedgehog's paw. Midway down the line Oriel checked that everyone was holding one another. Kaori was at the other end.

"We are ready." Oriel confirmed.

As Kupe and Kaori whisked them up above the treetops to glide above the river, Oriel panicked and tried to let go. Fortunately Kaori had warned the animals either side of him that Oriel wasn't well and that they were to hold him extra tight if he tried to let go.

"Oriel it's alright! Remember you are safe now."

"I know I'm safe, but I don't feel it!"

Kupe and Kaori looked at each other. Kaori nodded.

"Everyone, keep holding paws and claws and close your eyes till we tell you to open them." Kupe instructed them.

When Kupe told them to open their eyes again, they were in the school cave.

"Thank you!" Oriel spoke with relief. "Children, you can go home to your parents. You will have tomorrow night off as well."

Oriel didn't realise it, but he was having a mental breakdown. It would be some time before he was well enough to take lessons at the school or undertake his duties as Kingdom guardian.

When Orion led the community to Hans Bay, there was no sign of Oriel in the family tree, but he could see some of the animals who went with him on the boat trip. Realising Oriel was at the school, he left Odette at the nest with their owlettes, promising to be back soon.

Orion was shocked at the state of Oriel when he saw him and realised he was having a crisis. The attack from the Harriers had a worse effect than anyone realised. His duties would have to be shared out while he recovered.

Kupe; how was Oriel at the Arahura Valley?

He hid in Koa's burrow for the entire time. The local owls were bringing food for him. He doesn't feel safe out in the open.

Orion immediately flew to Odele to tell her his news. She agreed that their home would be in the cave for the time being. Orion then helped her to take the owlettes to the school cave. When the other owls saw what was happening, they followed him to the cave. On seeing Oriel's state, they quickly rallied around to find food for the family before they searched for their own.

Odele spent the rest of the night holding and comforting him. Their young owlettes sensed something was wrong, kept quiet instead of begging as they normally did, and waited to be fed, all the time watching with big anxious eyes as mum cuddled dad.

Odelia and Osborne decided to return to their old nest temporarily, while they found a new one at Hans Bay. The Harriers had made a mess in their bid to grab Odelia and Osborne. Neither of them were comfortable here now, even though the danger was over. Both Odelia and Osborne kept having thoughts of the Harriers reaching in for them.

Osborne was longer than usual while away for his feed. Odelia thought he was searching for a nesting spot, but came back with the grave news of Oriel.

"The family would like us to take over Oriel's nest while they are in the cave. They expect Oriel will be there for quite a while." Odelia nodded her agreement. She was relieved she didn't have to stay here any longer.

"We are taking you for another ride across the bay." Osborne advised their Owlettes. With that Odelia and Osborne lifted Oleander and Oregon onto their shoulders for the short flight to their new home. What Odelia was to learn, was that she now had an escort wherever she went. She could feel eyes on her, but thought they were the spirit animals she could see in the forest around her. It was only when Odelia flew into the school cave with some food for Oriel and Odele's owlettes that she realised that the eyes had come with her.

Who is there? Odelia spoke in her thoughts. *I can feel your eyes on me and why are you hidden?*

We have been appointed your guardians in both the living and spirit worlds. Hirone ordered us to stay hidden.

Thank you.

Odelia then realised that from now on she would also have to go in places where the Eagles could also follow or observe her.

CHAPTER TEN

DECISIONS

High in the Alps a large number of Owls had been summoned to a meeting led by Owen and Oban who stood out in front.

"Some of you may have already heard of the news that our spirit world leader has been destroyed by the Eagles of Nudoor. Oban and I can confirm that this is true as we witnessed it. Apart from advising you of the events which led to it, we now have the duty of appointing another leader."

Owen paused as alarm and mutterings among the crowd grew.

"Also," Owen continued in a louder tone to regain everyone's attention. "We need to discuss whether we need to take any further action regarding the female owl Odelia, who not only controls the Eagles of Nudoor but now also controls the Harriers as well. The issues of our leader's death and Odelia's control of the Harriers are connected.

When Oliver and Ogene returned from Hokitika with the owl community, they went looking for Kelia and Kotare and his friends. They were nowhere to be seen at the school cave where Oriel was too unwell to answer questions or in the forest when they searched it. They spotted the Hedgehogs and landed near them to find out where they were.

"Have you seen the Kiwis since the community returned?" Oliver asked.

"They all have stayed on in the Arahura Valley." Hovea Hedgehog told them. "They won't be coming back."

"Thanks Hovea." Oliver thanked her before leading Ogene to the other side of Mount Tahua to let Syd the stag and Daphne know.

Syd and Daphne were resting with Delphinia, Dianella, Dianthia and Teeny Tahr when they heard an owl calling for Syd. It was Oliver.

"We are here." Syd called back quietly. "Are the Kiwis ready to move on?"

"They are already at Arahura Valley." Oliver told him, before explaining all the events of the past few nights. "We will go to Arahura Valley to see what their plans are. We will be back."

"It looks like our little rest here is nearly over." Teeny was the first to speak after Oliver and Ogene left. He hadn't mentioned it, but the nights were getting cooler, meaning that his home in the south was now safer to travel to and stay in, now that hunting season was finished.

Syd looked at the three hinds. "You are welcome to join us when we head north. We never have to worry about humans or their noisy machines coming over us in our valley. There is plenty of food and shelter there for us all."

At the Arahura Valley, Kelia and Kotare were feeling restless too. This community was different to what they were used to. There was no school here and there weren't as many young Kiwis to mix with. Kotare knew there was a school up at Arthurs Pass, but also knew the conditions up there could be extreme in the winter months. Kotare was relieved when Oliver and Ogene landed in a nearby tree.

"Oliver! We are glad to see you. We are ready to go back to Three Sisters Mountain. Can you tell Syd and Daphne? We will come to the Lake and meet them there."

"We will let them know you are coming." Oliver and Ogene flew off towards Mount Tahua.

"Who were you talking to?" Kewa asked. He and Keka and Kerei were nearby. Keka had a female Kopara with him.

"That was Oliver and Ogene. The owls have returned to the lake as well. Kelia and I are going to return to Three Sisters Mountain. Are any of you going to come with us or are you staying here?"

"Where is Three Sisters Mountain?" Kopara wanted to know.

"It is a large mountain further up the coast from here." Kotare pointed to the Paparoa mountain range to the west. "We will be getting a ride there on Syd stag and Daphne." He saw her eyes widen at the thought of riding on deer and added "They gave us a ride here."

"We will be coming." Kewa and Kerei spoke.

Keka looked at Kopara. "I liked it up there. Why not come for a visit. If it is too awful for you we can come back again."

Kopara agreed to the visit. She wasn't sure about being so far from family and was happier knowing she could come back if she wanted.

"I will just tell my family I am going." Kopara spoke

"I will let Koa know we are moving on too." Kotare added. In the end they all walked together to let the community know they were moving on.

As they were saying their farewells, two young kiwis Korari and Kowhai approached them.

"Where are you going? Will you be coming back?"

"We are going to Three Sisters Mountain." Kotare informed them. "We have been offered a home there. We liked it there when we visited it on our way here." Kotare paused for a moment at the troubled looks on Korari and Kowhai's faces. "It will be some time before we return as we will be settling there."

"Can we come too?" Korari asked.

"Of course you can. You don't mind riding on a deer?" Kotare asked with a quizzical smile.

"You rode on one to come to the lake?" Korari asked in wonder.

"We did." Kotare grinned.

"If you can, then we can too." Korari grinned back.

"I will join you for the walk to the lake." Koa advised Kotare. "I want to see how Oriel is getting on."

Soft predawn light was spreading over the lake hills as Koa led the Kiwis into the school cave. Oliver and Ogene had gone to tell Syd that the Kiwis were here. Korari and Kowhai looked in wonder at the bats as they settled themselves on the ceiling; a few having a squabble at the space their neighbours were taking. They were also wide-eyed at the mats and books in the school area.

"This is a school." Kotare told Korari and Kowhai. "They have one at Three Sisters Mountain as well."

Koa went over to Oriel and his family. Although Oriel was now asleep, strain was visible on his face.

Odele smiled to see Koa here to see them.

"He's had a bad night." Odele spoke quietly. But, at least he is eating now."

Koa looked at the row of mice at their feet. "The community is looking after you?"

"They are." Odele smiled.

Kotare looked at his friends. "Anyone for a last swim before we leave?"

Their answer was to lead everyone down to the lake. Korari and Kowhai hadn't been in water before, so Kotare and Kelia showed them some strokes to practice in the shallows while Kewa Keka and Kerei splashed in deeper water.

A long dark shadow came darting in amongst Kewa and Keka who squealed in surprise then called out "Ernie!" when they saw who it was. Korari and Kowhai looked anxiously at the eel and were about to run when it approached them, but Kotare reassured them with a grin.

"Ernie is our friend. He won't hurt you."

"Hello Ernie. This is Korari and Kowhai. We are showing them how to swim. We will be heading off soon for Three Sisters Mountain."

"Hello Korari and Kowhai. I hope you return some day. Have a good trip Kotare and make sure you come back for a visit."

"We will." Kotare promised.

"Are you nearly ready to go?" Oliver called to Kotare from a nearby tree. "Syd and the hinds are coming."

Kotare was surprised but pleased to see that Delphinia Dianella and Dianthia were also coming when Syd and Daphne arrived to collect them. Kelia showed Korari how to get on Daphne and Kotare showed Kowhai how to mount Syd. Keka and Kopara mounted Delphinia while Kewa and Kerei rode Dianella and Dianthia. As the sunlight rose over the lake hills Syd leisurely strolled through the forest to the Arahura valley to cross the River and headed north.

As they set off, Kotare asked Kowhai how their family felt about Korari and her leaving them and the community.

"I don't think they will mind much at all." Kowhai replied matter of factly. "Our parents are with other partners now and have their families. Korari and I have been looking out for each other for a while now."

"Kelia and I have been doing the same." Kotare replied, understanding why these two Kiwis wanted to leave and make a fresh start. He then told her about how their father was lost in a war for territory and how their mother was taken by a dog that hunters brought with them to their burrows.

"That must have been scary!" Kowhai exclaimed. "What did you do?"

"We were lucky that we heard the guns coming in the distance, so most of us found a safe place before the hunters came (Kotare wasn't going to mention his mother could foretell the future), but Kelia became separated from the rest of us and went back to the burrow. Mum went looking for her. By the time she found Kelia in the burrow, the hunters were coming."

"Is that stone Kelia wears round her neck from her mother?"

"Yes. It brings her comfort."

Korari Kowhai and Kopara would forever remember their ride to their new home. Surprising themselves at how they enjoyed the rocking motion which sent them to sleep quicker than they thought possible. Kopara was also happy that she had two females for company on this trip and she already knew Kowhai from home. They happily settled into the new routine of riding during their sleep time in the day and stopping for their feeds at night while the deer rested.

"Are we stopping at Punakaiki?" Kewa wanted to know when they reached the Paparoa Range.

"We can do." Kotare grinned back at him.

At the meeting of the Owls in the Alps two decisions had been made. The first was that Oban was to be the next Spirit Leader. The second was that Odelia had to be dealt with. It was reassuring that she had sent the Harriers back to their spirit world homes, but it was not acceptable that she retained control of them. If she did not relinquish control of them, she would have to be destroyed.

CHAPTER ELEVEN

THE MEETING

Odelia was sitting at the nest with Oleander and Oregon while Osborne was away feeding.

"You need to leave here." The words were spoken by Haina, one of Odelia's guardians.

"What has happened?"

"The spirit owls have had a meeting. Oban is now the leader. Also it has been decided that if you don't relinquish control of the Harriers they will destroy you."

Odelia sighed. At this moment she understood how her mother felt when she was being pursued by Oleus and hounded by all the other owls wherever she went.

Odelia thought for a moment. *Leaving here isn't an option for me to take. It won't matter where I go, the Owls will find me sooner or later. I don't want the life my mother had, living in fear and hiding. The Harriers need to be controlled by someone or they will start to rampage again. I will hand control of the Harriers to Oban. It will be his responsibility if they misbehave.*

Is that your final word on the matter?

It is.

I will tell Hirone.

Haina?

Yes

While I am at the meeting will one of you stay with Osborne and the children? If necessary move them from here.

We will.

Odelia scanned the forest around her. She could see the spirit animals were acting normally. There was no sign of the owls yet. She wondered if they were already observing her. When Osborne returned, Odelia seemed to be extra alert.

"I'm expecting a visit from the leader of the spirit owls. They aren't happy that I have control of the Harriers."

"What are you going to do?"

Odelia smiled. "I will hand control of them to the spirit leader. She then looked at Osborne with sadness and regret. "The alternative is to be destroyed"

Osborne looked alarmed. "What if he can't or won't control them?"

"I will be guided by Hirone's wishes."

Odelia came back from her feed and to leave her donation of food at the school cave. Oriel was looking a little brighter, but still wasn't able to face the prospect of venturing out of the cave. Ollie was waiting for her. *Oban the spirit leader has sent me to bring you to a meeting.*

I will come. Where is it being held?

Over on the clearing behind the houses.

Odelia turned to Osborne. "Ollie is here to take me to the meeting." Odelia gave both Oleander and Oregon a hug before Osborne wrapped her in his wings. As Ollie waited for Odelia to say her goodbyes to her family, he realised she already knew about the meeting and was prepared for it. He wondered who had told her about it. This meeting was supposed to be secret.

"I was hoping we wouldn't have to go through this again!" Osborne spoke with both anger and grief that his mate's life was at risk again.

"Hopefully I won't be long."

As Odelia set off with Ollie, she set the pace. He noticed she stayed out in the open, not flying among trees as owls usually did. He also noticed that all of the spirit world animals spotted them and were watching their movements.

Spirit World Animals! Odelia called out loud enough for everyone in the area to hear her. *Please be a witness to the meeting I am attending with the Spirit World Leader.*

All the spirit world animals immediately began to follow Odelia and Ollie to the meeting. As Odelia came in to land, Ollie led her to a tree stump. Surrounding it were all of the spirit world owls who had attended the previous meeting.

The owls were alarmed that the area was immediately surrounded by spirit world animals.

"Who sent them here?" Oban asked with both annoyance and alarm.

"I did." Odelia replied. "I asked them to be witnesses to this meeting."

"You don't trust us?"

Odelia didn't reply to Oban's question, but gave him a stare that let everyone who saw it in no doubt that she didn't. Odelia could feel that an eagle was within touching distance of her, so she made herself relax a little, but remained alert for any sudden moves by any of the owls. She turned her head to give all of the owls a piercing look before turning her attention to Oban.

"You know why you are here?" Oban asked.

"I have an idea."

Oban stepped forward. "You have too much power over other animals. You are to relinquish your control of the Harriers."

"And if I don't?"

All of the owls took a step towards her.

"That won't be necessary!" Odelia's tone was sharp. "You can all step back again."

The owls remained where they were.

Odelia slowly lifted one of her claws and pointed it at Oban. The owls took another step towards her as she lifted it.

"Of course I relinquish my control of the Harriers." Odelia's words stopped the owls advance towards her. "However, the Harriers need to be controlled by someone; otherwise they will rampage to kill innocent animals again. I Odelia appoint you Oban the current spirit world leader the Master of the Harriers. It is now your responsibility to control them and to ensure they live by spirit world rules."

"But you can't.... I don't have...." Oban struggled with the implications of what Odelia had just done.

"I just have! And you WILL!" Odelia thundered at him. "What kind of leaders are you, to willingly put innocent animal lives at risk?" As she swept her eyes around the owls, she noticed some were moving in on her.

Odelia swiftly put her claw out to grab the eagle's claw next to her. To the astonishment of the crowd (and the fury of the owls) Odelia immediately disappeared from view.

Hirone!

I am here.

Do these owls control the land across the ocean?

No.

Can you take me and my family over there?

We will.

Osborne was astonished when Odelia appeared next to him on the nest. The anguished look on her face told him the meeting hadn't gone well.

"We are leaving. Quick, put Oregon on your shoulder." Osborne hastened to comply, while Odelia put Oleander on her shoulder. "We are ready." Odelia instructed Hirone.

The family felt a large pair of claws wrap around them before being lifted up into the air.

"Close your eyes" Hirone instructed them.

When Hirone told the family to open their eyes again, they were in a forest, but it was a completely different landscape to the one they had left.

Thank you, Hirone.

The guardians remain with you. I will only contact you if you are needed.

"Where are we?" Osborne asked as he took Oregon off his should to place him in the hollow of the tree trunk. As Odelia removed Oleander from her shoulder, she smiled.

"Welcome to Australia my love. The owls will never find us here. They don't control this area."

Back at the lake Oban was furious. "Search this land till you find Odelia! She is to be destroyed!"

While the other owls spread out to search for Odelia, Ollie made a call to Kohana.

Kohana, can you hear me?

I can

Is Odelia with you?

No. Why?

I took her to a meeting with the Spirit world leader. It didn't go well as she handed control of the Harriers to the Leader. She has made him the master of all the Harriers. Someone who was hidden has spirited her away. There is now a hunt on to find and destroy her.

I will let you know if I see her.

Kohana didn't mention it, but only one animal would have done this. - Hirone the leader of the Haast Eagles. She wondered where he took her to. She thought of Nudoor. No-one would think of looking for her there. She decided to take a look at Nudoor.

Some of the spirit animals immediately made their way over to the nesting tree where they knew Odelia and Osborne were staying with their family. They were just in time to see Odelia and Osborne put their Owlettes onto their shoulders before they disappeared from view again. Ollie followed the spirit animals to the nesting tree, but by the time he arrived Odelia's family had gone as well. He put out a call to Orion.

Orion

Yes

Odelia and her family have left the area. We don't know where they have gone. There is a search now to find and destroy her.

At Lake Mahinapua Odessa saw some spirit owls making a thorough search of the forest. When one came near and gave her a searching look, Odessa decided to speak to it.

What are you searching for Owl?

Have you seen Odelia and her family?

No. Why?

Someone is hiding her from the spirit leader. Odelia is to be found and destroyed.

Why?

She made the leader the responsible for all the Harriers.

After the owl moved on, Odessa made a call to Odelia.

Odelia, it is Odessa. Can you hear me? Where are you?

Odelia heard Odessa's call, but didn't answer in case one of the owls also heard her answer. It was better to just disappear completely.

CHAPTER TWELVE

NEW BEGINNINGS

When the deer stopped to rest in the hills near Kanoa's community, everyone was glad their journey was nearly over. Sleeping on a moving deer wasn't the same as a proper rest in the comfort of a burrow.

Kotare was given a shock when they approached Kanoa's burrow. A stoat was sniffing around the entrance. Kotare quickly chased it off. A quick peek inside showed the burrow was now abandoned. Kanoa had passed to the spirit world, his body still resting as if he was asleep.

"We can't leave Kanoa to the Stoats!" Kotare exclaimed. "Help me to cover him."

Quickly Korari Kewa Keka and Kerei helped to dig a large hole where Kanoa was laid to rest. A mound now covered the place where he lay. While Kotare and his friends were caring for Kanoa, Kelia wondered where Koana and their son Kamoku were. She put out a loud call in the hope she was still nearby.

"Koana; Are you there?"

In the distance, a faint call answered her. "I'm here! Who is it?"

"It's Kelia."

"I'm coming."

The sound of rapid footsteps heralded Koana's arrival. Kamoku was trailing behind her. The Koana who appeared before Kelia was completely different to the one Kelia had seen on her last visit. This Koana was haggard and worn. The happy and confident Koana was now gone with the loss of her soul mate. Kelia ran forward to give Koana a big hug.

"What's going on?" Koana asked with a frown, on hearing furious digging in her old burrow.

"When we arrived, a Stoat was hanging around the entrance to your burrow. Kotare and his friends are burying Kanoa so it can't touch him."

"Thank you." Koana's eyes had tears of gratitude. "I should have tried to do it, but..." Koana's voice broke off.

"Is anyone looking after you? If not, would you like to come with us?" Kelia offered.

"I would love to come with you." For the first time a little smile came to Koana's face. "This area has too many memories for me now."

When Kotare and his friends emerged from Kanoa and Koana's burrow, Koana and Kamoku were also waiting with Kelia and the females.

"Koana and Kamoku are coming with us." Kelia announced to them. Kotare nodded his agreement.

"Before we head back to the deer, we will go for a walk down to the rocks."

"What kind of rocks are they?" Kopara Korari and Kowhai wanted to know. None of them had heard of the pancake rocks before.

"It's a special place." Was all Kelia would say.

As they made their way in, it was well after dark, but the bright moonlight bathed the area in bright light. Kotare was grateful that this time they didn't have to worry about running into humans. There was no sign of the Weka that Kotare had made friends with last time, which disappointed him.

Tonight the ocean was showing her gentler side – the waves only smacked quietly against the rocks. The blowholes remained empty and silent. Kopara Korari and Kowhai wandered in silence among the rocks, marvelling at their shapes and the shadows they cast. Koana led Kamoku around the rocks, introducing him to the place she had last come to with Kanoa.

"You are right." Korari quietly spoke to Kelia when he found her on her own, looking out at the twinkling lights from the fishing boats off the coast. "This is a special place." Kelia looked at him and smiled. They hadn't spoken of it yet, but they both knew they would have a life together some day.

"Yes, we will be back."

Korari smiled. "I will look forward to that."

Kotare led Kowhai to the rocks where his parents had stood when he was little. He knew that here was the female he wanted to spend the rest of his life with, and he wasn't going to let any of the Three Sisters Mountain males get a look in.

"Kowhai, have you thought about what you want for your future yet?" Kotare asked. For once he was serious instead of his usual carefree self.

Kowhai looked at Kotare with a twinkle in her eyes. In truth she had set her heart on him when she first saw Kotare at Arahura and was devastated when she learnt he was leaving before she could get to know him. The chance of the ride here had taken care of that.

"I know exactly what I want." Kowhai then took a deep breath. "And I hope you will be sharing it with me." It was her turn to be serious.

A grin spread over Kotare's face as he realised she wanted him as well. They stayed cuddled together on the rock untill Kewa called out.

"Are you two going to stay and be a fixture on there?" Kewa was more than a little jealous that Keka and Kotare had found their mates. He knew that Kerei was already interested in a female at Three Sisters community and he hoped he would find one too. Little did he know of the competition among some of the females that were hoping for his return.

When Kotare led the Kiwis back to Syd and the deer, Oliver and Ogene were waiting in a nearby tree.

"Oliver, can you go ahead to Three Sister's community and let them know we have a few extra's coming with us, including Koana and Kamoku?"

Oliver and Ogene immediately set off. They too were happy their journey would soon be over.

They were ready to nest again. The only decision to be made was would they nest here or return to the Buller. They decided to ask Odion and Oana if there were any suitable trees nearby for them to nest in.

It was still early evening when Syd led the deer to the base of Three Sisters Mountain and sat down to let all the passengers off.

"Thank you so much." Kotare spoke quietly to Syd. "This journey would have been much more difficult without your help." Kotare then spoke to Delphinia Dianella and Dianthia. "I know you will have a much more peaceful life up here."

"You have been to the valley before?" Delphinia asked.

"I've been through there twice." Kotare grinned at her. "Mum and Dad brought me through when I was little and I came through again on my way down to the Lake. I loved it in there."

"Come and visit us sometime." Delphinia offered.

"I will bring Kowhai for a visit."

Kohana and Titan slowly circled Nudoor from above before alighting on a peak nearby. She thought that she hadn't been detected, but Hirone flew over and landed next to her.

Did you find what you were looking for?

You know I didn't. How do you know I am here?

Most animals can't detect others who are hidden, but I can feel when something is nearby. I remembered the feeling I received when you brought Odelia here and knew you had returned to look for her.

Where is she? I know you are hiding her.

All I can tell you is that she is safe. Hirone paused before adding *It is safer for her and you, if you don't know.*

They will find her sooner or later.

No they won't.

She has protection?

Of Course! They have pledged to protect her in both the living and spirit world wherever she is.

I thank you for that. Will she be coming back?

Hirone paused to think for a moment. *No. She isn't expecting to.* Hirone didn't tell Kohana that animals who witnessed the meeting were angry at the treatment Odelia had received and that whispers of a rebellion was now spreading in the spirit world – led by spirit world Harriers who had witnessed the meeting and Odelia's flight to safety. They wanted their Mistress back.

Kiwi Family Tree

<u>Roroa</u>

Kamoku & Kailee → Kamoku in Paparoa range
          ->Kaimi
          ->Keoni

Kamoku & (1) Keteri – Kanoa & Koana - Kamoku
      (2) Kalama

Kaimi & Kekona to Arthurs Pass → Kaori, Kalasia, Kalei

Kaori & Keely – Ketara, Kian, Kana
Kalasia & Kapali – Kuaka
Kalei & Karua – Kawaka

Keoni & Kaimani to Paparoa range →Keanu

Keanu (1) & Keona – Kupe, Keely, Keilana
Keio   (2) & Keona – Keon, Kailah

Kahika to Okarito → Keka

Kaipo to Three Sisters Mountain → Kapali & Kalasia - Kuaka

Kale & Kuri - Kaimani, Kaliyah. Kale & Kuri to North Buller → Kuri –
Kai - Kaimani

| Arthurs Pass - | Kanai & Kalama – Kekoa, Kalea |
| - | Kane – Koen |

| Lake Kaniere - | Kupe (1) & Kalea – Kamaka, Kohana |
| Three Sisters - | Koro (2) & Kalea |

North Buller -   Koha & Kamora – Kiyo (1) & Kehi – Koro, Kerewa,
                                                Koa, Kiana
Buller   -   Kohana (2) & Kehi – Kotare, Kelia

| - | Kerewa & Katana – Kahine |
| - | Koa & Kewena – Kehi |

<u>Rowi</u>

Kahui to Okarito → Kedar & Kerry – Kahill & Kiori,
                                  - Kohia

Kaga to Fiordland → Kona – Kelan

The Owl Family

Lake Kaniere

Odette   – Mother of Orion,
Orion,   - The first Guardian of the Kiwi Kingdom (Keoni's reign)
Olivia   - Orion's Sister
Ogilvie   - Orion's brother

Owen (guardian) & Odelia   – Ollie, Orchid
Ollie (guardian) & Odina   – Oriel, Odelle
Orchid & Oswin – Ophira, Owena, Odessa

Oriel (guardian) & Odele

Odessa & Orlando – Orion, Orel, Oriana

Odelia & Osborne – Oleander, Oregon

Lake Mahinapua

Oscar & Olivia   – Odin.
Odin & Ocena   – Orlando
Orion & Odette

Fiordland

Oriana & Ojen   - Ogden, Odelia
Ocene (leader)

Rapahoe Range

Ozzy & Orena

Three Sisters Mountain

Odion (leader) & Oana

Buller

Oren (leader) & Opal
Oliver & Ogene

About the Author

Rosemary Thomas was born in 1951 and lived in Hokitika on New Zealand's West Coast. Educated at Westland High School, Thomas moved to Perth Australia where she married and had two children. Thomas worked as a registered Nurse. In retirement, writing and making craft to raise funds for charity keep her busy.

Printed in Australia
AUHW010613230120
322784AU00001B/1

9 780648 740612